THE DRAGON'S BLADE

Christopher Mitchell is the author of the epic fantasy series The Magelands. He studied in Edinburgh before living for several years in the Middle East and Greece, where he taught English. He returned to study classics and Greek tragedy and lives in Fife, Scotland with his wife and their four children.

By Christopher Mitchell

THE MAGELANDS ORIGINS

Retreat of the Kell
The Trials of Daphne Holdfast
From the Ashes

THE MAGELANDS EPIC

The Queen's Executioner
The Severed City
Needs of the Empire
Sacrifice
Fragile Empire
Storm Mage
Soulwitch Rises
Renegade Gods

THE MAGELANDS ETERNAL SIEGE

The Mortal Blade
The Dragon's Blade
The Prince's Blade
Falls of Iron
Paths of Fire
Gates of Ruin

Brigdomin Books Ltd
First Edition, September 2020
ISBN 978-1-912879-43-4

For all the guys in my old team

ACKNOWLEDGEMENTS

I would like to thank the following for all their support during the writing of the Magelands Eternal Siege - my wife, Lisa Mitchell, who read every chapter as soon as it was drafted and kept me going in the right direction; my parents for their unstinting support; Vicky Williams for reading the books in their early stages; James Aitken for his encouragement; and Grant and Gordon of the Film Club for their support.

Thanks also to my Advance Reader team, for all your help during the last few weeks before publication.

DRAMATIS PERSONAE

The Royal Family – Gods and God-Children
　　God-King Malik, Co-Sovereign of the City; Ooste
　　God-Queen Amalia, Co-Sovereign of the City; Tara
　　Prince Montieth, Recluse; Dalrig

The Royal Family – Demigods
　　Aila, Fugitive
　　Naxor, Former Emissary of the Gods
　　Marcus, acclaimed Prince of Tara
　　Kano, Commander of the Bulwark
　　Amber, Elder Daughter of Prince Montieth
　　Jade, Younger Daughter of Prince Montieth
　　Ikara, Governor of the Circuit
　　Lydia, Governor of Port Sanders
　　Doria, Courtier to the God-King
　　Vana, Prisoner of Prince Marcus
　　Mona, Chancellor of Royal Academy, Ooste

The Mortals of the City
Rosers
　　Daniel Aurelian, Young Militia Officer
　　Emily Omertia, Young Noble of Tara
　　Lord Chamberlain, Advisor to the God-Queen
　　Nadhew, Taran Lawyer

Evaders
　　Nareen, Co-owner of Blind Poet
　　Dorvid, Co-owner of Blind Poet
　　Bekha, Rebel

Dalrigians
>Hellis, Grey Isle Captain

Reapers
>Talleta, Servant

Icewarders
>Yaizra, Convicted Thief

Blades
>Maddie Jackdaw, Young Private
>Rosie, Maddie's Younger Sister
>Tom, Maddie's Older Brother
>Hilde, Blade Captain
>Quill, Wolfpack Sergeant

Hammers
>Achan, Convicted Rebel
>Torphin, Conscripted into the Rats

The Outsiders
>Corthie Holdfast, Champion of the Bulwark
>Tanner, Wolfpack Soldier
>Buckler, Champion of the Bulwark
>Blackrose, Prisoner

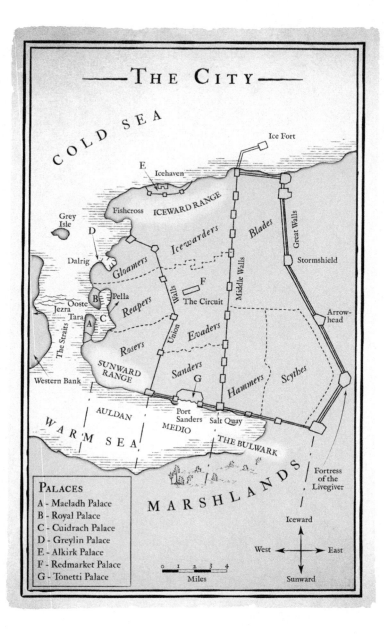

CHAPTER 1

HIDING OUT

The Circuit, Medio, The City – 6th Marcalis 3419

Bekha shook her head, her eyes on the news sheet. 'Lady Aila.'

Aila frowned. 'What?'

'Nothing,' said Bekha; 'I was just reading that there's been no sign of her for a month, when every Blade in the City is hunting her. It's like she's disappeared.'

Aila glanced away. She had been hiding in the Circuit as Stormfire since her cousin Naxor had rescued her from Pella; living with a band of dissidents who were all wanted by the authorities for one reason or another. She glanced at Bekha, whose boots were up on the table as she read the news sheet.

'I wonder if she's dead,' said the mortal. 'That would explain it.'

'Maybe she's just resourceful.'

Bekha snorted. 'Lady Aila wasn't the worst of them by any stretch of the imagination, but she's still a demigod and, deep down, they're all the same. Arrogant, spoiled, entitled. I'd bet this Aila wouldn't have the first idea of how to survive without all the comforts and wealth that have cushioned her life for so long.'

Aila narrowed her eyes. 'But she's been alive for nearly eight hundred years; she must have learned a thing or two.'

'You're the last person I thought would be defending them,' said Bekha, raising an eyebrow.

'I'm not defending *them*, I'm defending *her*,' Aila said. She rubbed her face. 'If she's standing up to Duke... I mean Prince Marcus, then she's fine by me.'

'A lot of Evaders would disagree with you; the prince has restored order in the Circuit, and we've not had a riot since he took over. The place is actually starting to recover.'

'Come on,' said Aila; 'he paid for the riots, and now that they've stopped, he's taking the credit for bringing peace back to Medio? He set the whole thing up, and now he looks like a hero?' She shook her head. 'It won't last. Once the ordinary folk in the City see that he's only interested in power and helping his Roser lackeys, they'll realise how good we used to have it with Khora in charge.'

Bekha stared at her. 'Khora? Stormfire, are you feeling alright? For years, I've heard you say nothing but bad things about her, and now you've decided that she was actually all right?'

Aila felt a tight knot form in her stomach, and she looked away. While she was using her powers to appear as Stormfire, she knew that Bekha wouldn't be able to see any tears if she cried, but she was determined to keep her composure.

'Well?' said Bekha.

'At least Khora never sent Blades into the rest of the City.'

'Most Evaders would rather have them in the streets than the Tarans. The best thing Marcus has done is to pull the Rosers out of the Circuit.'

'Yeah, but where has he put them? In the fortresses along the Union Walls. Why?'

Bekha shrugged. 'They needed to go somewhere.'

'But why the Union Walls? It's to keep the folk of Medio out of Auldan.'

'Now you're just being paranoid.'

'No, you're being naïve. Do you think the new Prince of Tara cares about the people of Medio? His government's made up of Rosers who think Evaders are barely human. I'd have never put you down as gullible, Bekha, but I guess I was wrong.'

Bekha frowned, and went back to reading the news sheet. Aila glanced at her for a moment then sighed, her eyes drifting over the damp walls of the cellar. She watched as a spider dangled from its web in the corner of the room, and wondered why her powers wouldn't allow her to appear as an animal. A massive scary spider or a roaring dragon might be a useful disguise to terrify people. It would also be handy to appear as a rock or a tree.

She shook her head. After a month of hiding in damp cellars amid abandoned slum housing, she was starting to fray around the edges. Unable to reveal who she really was, she had been given no opportunity to talk to anyone about Corthie, or about what had happened in Pella. Sometimes she felt as if it had all been a dream, and she often wished that were true.

The handsome champion that she had loved was being portrayed as the murderer of Princess Khora, and Lord Kano as the heroic warrior who had apprehended and executed Corthie for the horrific crime. The new authorities had produced evidence that appeared to show Khora conspiring to have him killed, and, thus, Corthie's motive had been revenge. The most frightening aspect of Marcus's re-writing of history was that so few people seemed to question it. It was neat, and simple. Apart from Aila and her brother Kano, only a handful of Blades that had been present at the time knew the truth. As Stormfire, Aila had forced herself to sit in silence whenever she heard someone repeat the official version of events, and the only way to do that had been to suppress the memories herself. Because of that, she had hardly wept, not for Corthie's death, nor for Khora's; as if she were in denial about everything that had happened or, as if it had happened to someone else.

'Do you want a drink?'

Aila glanced up. Bekha's news sheet was lying folded upon the table and the woman was looking at her.

'What?'

'A drink? Do you want one?'

'I don't know. Do I?'

Bekha shook her head. 'What's the matter? You've been in a mood for days.'

'I've been stuck in here for a month; no wonder I'm in a mood.'

'You're not stuck in here. As far as I know, the Blades aren't looking for you; you could get up and walk out any time you like.'

'Are you throwing me out?'

'Of course not; after everything you've done for us, you can stay as long as you like. But, if you don't tell us what, or who, is chasing you, there's nothing we can do to help.' She sighed and put her elbows on the table. 'Look, we like having you here, but you seem... different, Stormfire, so I can only think that something bad has happened to you.'

Aila nodded and tried to remain calm, but was squirming on the inside. Different? She thought she had been playing the role of Stormfire well, but over time her own personality had been coming to the surface in her less-guarded moments. She had never appeared as someone else for anything close to a month before, and the mental effort had exhausted her.

'I'm here for you,' said Bekha, 'if you ever want to talk about it.'

A young man barged into the room before Aila could respond. He rushed over to the table where they were sitting, panting. 'Blades are approaching.'

Bekha swung her boots off the table. 'From which direction?'

The young man stared at her. 'All of them.'

'Malik's ass. They've found us.'

Aila got to her feet. 'We need to get out of here.'

Bekha remained silent for a moment, then nodded. 'Go and get your things, then meet me at the gate by the canal.'

'They're coming that way too,' said the young man; 'there's no time.'

'Calm yourself,' said Bekha, rising.

They went through to the adjoining room and climbed the steps to the ground floor of the ruined warehouse where they had been staying.

A handful of other dissidents were by the top of the stairs, their expressions lined with anxiety. Twenty yards away, by a massive set of gates, another one of their number was standing, her face peering through the broken glass.

She turned. 'They're everywhere,' she cried; 'hundreds of them.'

Far off to the right, another gate was smashed in, its doors battered open, and soldiers started running through the entrance. The group of dissidents panicked, and began scattering. One shoved past Stormfire, nearly sending her flying back down the steps into the cellar.

'Bekha,' Aila said, grabbing her friend's arm, 'I can't get caught.'

'I don't intend to get caught either,' Bekha said, her eyes hardening. 'Follow me.'

She bolted away through the warehouse as cries came from the soldiers. Aila raced after her, hearing another entrance being smashed in, and the sound of glass shattering over the concrete floor. Bekha sped into a row of offices and workshops, a layer of dust and debris covering the ground. Ahead of them, a squad of Blades burst through the doors, and Bekha skidded to a halt, then turned left. Aila rushed after her, and they came into a derelict toilet block at the back of the warehouse.

'In here,' Bekha cried, gesturing to a dank storeroom. They hurried inside and Bekha closed the door. 'Where is it; where is it?' she said, pulling boxes and crates to the side.

'I can hear their footsteps,' said Aila by the door as she watched Bekha turn the room upside down.

She shoved a heavy crate to the side, revealing a wooden hatch cut into the wall by the floor, then turned to glance at Aila. She put a finger to her lips, then pulled the hatch open.

'We'll need to squeeze through,' she whispered, crouching down by the opening. 'Follow me.'

She clambered through the small entrance, and Aila watched as her legs disappeared into the darkness. She heard the footsteps get closer and dived over to the corner of the room, climbing through the hatch. It was too narrow to turn in, so she eased the hatch door shut with her foot, plunging the tunnel into darkness.

'Don't stop,' she heard Bekha whisper from the darkness in front of her.

Aila nodded, and began to crawl.

The next two hours were spent in utter darkness, as Bekha and Aila scrambled along a series of narrow drainage and sewage tunnels. For a while they could hear the sounds of pursuit, but they had faded slowly into the distance the further they had crawled. Aila's clothes were wet, and stank, and her self-healing was continually patching up the abrasions on her hands and knees from the rough, concrete surface. As she was beginning to wonder if Bekha knew where they were going, she heard a loud splash ahead of her.

Aila paused, her hands feeling the ground in front of her in the darkness.

'Watch out for the drop,' said Bekha, her voice coming from below. 'Wait a minute; I can get us some light.'

Aila heard the noise of someone wading through water, then a harsh creaking of metal. A grey light spilled into the tunnel and Aila squinted. The floor ended a yard ahead of where Aila was crouching, and below were concrete walls and a pool of water. Bekha was standing next to a grille in the wall, through which the dull light of evening was filtering. Aila crawled forward, then lowered herself; dropping the last few feet into the pool.

'Where are we?'

Bekha peered out of the grille. 'A canal by Ironbridge Fleshmarket. There's a pavement right over our heads.'

Aila gazed down. 'So this is rainwater I'm standing in?'

'Yeah.'

'Praise Malik.'

Bekha climbed up onto a ledge above the water line, then sat down. She looked exhausted, and had cuts and scratches on her face and arms.

She glanced at Aila. 'They knew we were there.'

Aila pulled herself up onto the ledge, dripping water from her clothes.

'They surrounded us in minutes,' Bekha went on, as Aila sat next to her. 'How could they have known? We've been so careful. And all those soldiers, just for us? Completely over the top.' She glanced at the tunnel entrance above them. 'And they might still be looking for us.'

Aila lowered her eyes; she had been dreading this conversation, but the time had come. If they were going to survive, Bekha would need to know the truth.

'They probably are,' she said; 'looking for us, I mean.'

Bekha turned to her. 'Why would they be? We've been inactive for months, and had nothing to do with the riots.'

'They're after me.'

'You?' Bekha raised an eyebrow. 'But I've already told you a hundred times, your name isn't on any wanted list.'

'It is, you know; it's right at the top.'

'I, uh... what?'

'Prepare yourself.'

'For what?'

'For this.' Aila dropped her powers, and showed herself as she really was.

Bekha's mouth opened, and she scrambled backwards, her hands flailing at the wall.

'Don't scream,' said Aila. 'This is who I really am.'

'But... but... you're a demigod!'

'Yes. Hi.' She waved.

'Lady Aila?'

'Yes.' Aila blinked, then her eyes started to well as a wave of relief swept over her. The constant burden of having to use her powers, and the effort of concealing who she was, had been lifted. She put a hand to her face as a tear slid down her cheek. Not now, she told herself.

'Lady Aila?'

'I think we've established that.'

'But, where's the real Stormfire?'

'I've been her all along. I can take the appearance of anyone I choose.'

'You mean you've been lying to me for years? All this time, whenever I spoke to you, you were lying?'

Aila nodded. 'There were things I could get away with as Stormfire that Lady Aila would never have been able to do. I did good things as Stormfire.'

'You're a liar.'

'Yeah. A good one; had you fooled.'

'You used your demigod powers on me; I feel used. I don't even know who you are.'

'I'm Stormfire.'

'No, it was all an act.'

'An act that we're going to have to use if we want to get out of this alive. That's the only reason I'm telling you; do you understand? I can look like anyone.'

Bekha shook her head. 'A normal person would at least apologise, but no; that's not the demigod way. I'm just another little mortal to you, here and gone in a minute or two; someone to use.'

Aila drew her knees up to her chest and rested her chin on them, her arms hugging her legs. Bekha was right. Stormfire was an act, a mask that she could slip on and off whenever she chose, whereas to Bekha she had been a real person, someone she had trusted; someone she had liked. Aila's jaded conscious began to stir. Bekha had lost a friend. She thought of Corthie and took a breath, suppressing her feelings, and pushing him from her mind. Not yet.

'I'm sorry.'

Bekha frowned. 'I don't believe you; you're just trying to say whatever you think will get me to cooperate.'

'I've been thinking it through, trying to see it from a mortal point of view, which, I admit, I hadn't been doing, and I am sorry. I still count you as a friend, to me you're still the same person.'

'Of course I am; I'm not a two-faced liar.'

Aila looked away; the venom in Bekha's eyes too much to bear.

'Maybe you could look at it from my point of view. Imagine never dying, but being trapped. I wanted to help the people of the Circuit, but I spent two centuries of imprisonment after the Civil War, and if I was caught doing it again, they might have thrown away the key. The only way I could do good was by using my powers, and I'm sorry that you hate me for it, but I would do it again. Do you remember those children we freed from the gangs a few years ago? Should we have left them where they were, to save you from getting hurt?'

Bekha said nothing.

'There was another reason I had to tell you,' Aila went on, 'which would explain how they found us. My sister Vana can sense the location of other demigods; she can home in on their self-healing powers.'

'So we've been in danger all this time?'

'To be honest, I thought being down in that cellar might hide me from her. She was in Ooste, last I knew, working in the Royal Palace for Khora, but I'm guessing Marcus summoned her to Tara, and forced her to search the City for me. The good news is that searching tires her out. She's fine if you're in the next room, but looking through the Circuit would have taxed her, and it'll be a day or so before she'll be able to do it again. That's the bad news; I'm going to have to keep moving from now on. I can't risk staying in the same place again. If I do, they'll catch me.'

Bekha glanced at her. 'What will they do to you, if they catch you? Will they kill you?'

'No. Worse. I can handle dying; right now, I'm not even sure what to live for.'

'What's worse than dying?'

'If Prince Michael had survived the Civil War,' Aila said, 'then his plan was to pair me with Marcus. He wanted the demigods to breed a new generation of gods, and had a whole scheme worked out. The new Prince of Tara wants to revive his father's plan.'

'Marcus wants you?'

'He wants me to bear his children. I'd rather die.'

'But isn't your brother Marcus's Adjutant? Wouldn't he protect you?'

'Kano's lost to me; he's not my brother any more, not after what he did to Khora.'

'What? I thought he tried to defend her against that renegade champion?'

Aila's anger rose. 'No. Marcus is spreading lies. What you heard happened is not true. Kano murdered Khora; Corthie was trying to protect the princess, and me, when he was killed. I was there, Bekha, I saw it all.' Tears welled in her eyes, and Aila gave up trying to suppress them. She felt as if a dam was bursting, but didn't care. Her breath became ragged as wracked sobs were ripped from her chest. Corthie. She stopped trying to block his image from her mind, not caring what Bekha thought as she dissolved into tears.

She had lost everything, and the City had become a prison. Compared to having to endure a life on the run, death seemed almost preferable.

A hand was placed on her shoulder. 'Does Marcus know it was Kano?'

'Of course he does!' she cried, her eyes streaming; 'they planned the whole thing, don't you see? They sent Corthie to kill Khora, knowing he wouldn't do it, and arrived in time to ensure he could be blamed for her death. And that "evidence" showing Khora was trying to kill him, it's all lies too, it was Marcus who was trying to kill Corthie.'

'This changes everything,' Bekha said. 'Marcus killed Khora? He's making out that he only took power because the princess had been murdered. We need to get the truth out there to the people.'

'And who would believe you? The only thing I want is vengeance; it's the only reason to stay alive. Vengeance for Khora, and vengeance for Corthie.'

'Did this Corthie mean something to you?'

For a second Aila hesitated, then she plunged in. She was already a weeping mess, and was tired of the lies. 'I loved him.'

'But he was mortal.'

'I know; I tried not to get involved. I knew it was stupid, but I couldn't help it.'

'Did he love you?'

'Yes.'

There was a long silence. Aila closed her eyes and wept, her head on her knees, almost oblivious to Bekha's presence, as every long-suppressed emotion came flooding out. The minutes blurred as the light from the canal outside began to fade into evening.

'How can I help?' said Bekha.

Aila took a breath. 'Have you got a hanky?'

She heard a rustle of clothes and a soft piece of fabric was placed into her hand. She wiped her face.

'I'm sorry about before,' Bekha went on; 'it was the shock. I loved Stormfire; idolised her a little bit, if I'm honest, and it felt like you'd tricked me.'

'I did trick you. You don't need to apologise; I get it.'

'I know over a dozen safe houses within the Circuit. We can start moving between them. One overnight stay in each, just like you said, so we can keep one step ahead of your sister Vana. At the same time we'll start to spread the truth. There's a printing press in one of the locations that I've used to make up pamphlets, we can post the truth at every junction. The people will rise up against Marcus if they know what really happened.'

Aila glanced at her. 'Why would you do this?'

'I remember the children we saved. Apart from Yendra and her daughters, you're maybe the only demigod who's ever cared about the mortals of the City. For all the help you've given us, I think we owe you a little in return.' She turned and peered out of the grille. 'It's getting dark; we should make a move soon.'

Aila nodded, but her spirits were deflated. She had thought that crying might have helped her in some way, but it had only made her feel more hopeless and miserable.

'What was he like?'

'What?'

Bekha attempted a smile. 'The champion?'

'Annoying,' Aila said; 'one of those guys who is irrepressibly good-natured and cheerful, no matter how bad things get. He told me every-thing would be fine, but it wasn't. He was also the only person who could see through my powers; he saw me, regardless of whose appearance I'd taken.'

'Did your brother kill him?'

'He's not my brother any more; I told you. But yes. Kano ordered the Blades to loose, and they did. Corthie took four bolts and went down. He'd charged them so that Khora and I could get away, but I blew it. I just stood there, staring at his body on the gravel, and the Blades grabbed us. His last thoughts would have been that his sacrifice had been in vain, because of me.'

'It wasn't in vain; you're still alive.'

'Only because my cousin Naxor rescued me.'

'Lord Naxor? Wanted posters of him are all over the Circuit, along-side yours. Can he change his appearance as well?'

'No. I guess if Vana is looking for me, then she'll also be looking for him.'

'Maybe we should look for him too.'

'There's no point. If Naxor doesn't want to be found, then he won't be. He has something, a secret device of some kind that he used to rescue me. I don't know how it works, but he can use it to hide. He might be out of Vana's range for all I know.'

'How far does her range extend?'

'I'm not sure. It covers the whole City, I think, so maybe twenty or thirty miles or so?'

Bekha gazed into the dark pool of water. 'And what are your feelings towards Lady Vana?'

'Are you saying we should kill her?'

'If she's the only demigod who can track you, then it's worth considering.'

'Marcus will have surrounded her with soldiers, not only to protect her, but to stop her from running away. But, she's my sister. We've never got on, but I don't want to see her dead.'

'Alright. Shall we make a move?'

'Where?'

Bekha glanced up and pointed. 'Through there.'

Aila squinted up into the gloom. Above them was a metal hatch leading to the road that ran over their heads.

'Do you have other vision powers?' said Bekha. 'Can you look outside to see if anyone's there?'

'Nope. Changing my appearance is all I've got.' She stood, wiped her face again, then placed the handkerchief into a pocket.

You see me as a road maintenance worker with a bag of tools over my shoulder.

'Woah!' cried Bekha. 'Could you warn me when you're going to do that?'

'Sure. How do I look?'

Bekha narrowed her eyes. 'Convincing.'

Aila stretched up with her arms, and her fingers grasped the handle of the hatch. 'You ready?'

'Yeah,' said Bekha, getting to her feet.

She pushed the hatch with her hands, and it lifted an inch. It was heavy, but she managed to get her fingers into the gap, and shoved it to the side. She pulled herself up, and poked her head through the hole. Outside, the street was deserted and quiet. Thick clouds hung in the sky, and a cold mist was drifting over the canal. She hauled herself through the hatch and onto the cobbles, then reached down with her arm, and helped Bekha clamber up to the surface of the road. Aila slid the hatch cover back into place, and it fell with a clang.

'Hey!' came a shout from the other side of the canal.

Aila glanced over, and saw a squad of heavily armed Blades approach.

'Stay calm,' she whispered to Bekha as the soldiers crossed a bridge over the waterway.

'You know the curfew rules,' said one of the Blades. 'You should be indoors by now.'

'Sorry, officer,' said Aila, bowing her head. 'I had an urgent repair job in the drainage tunnels, and it took a bit longer than I'd expected.'

The Blades glowered at them. 'And who's this?' said one, pointing at Bekha.

'My apprentice.'

'A little old for an apprentice, isn't she?'

Aila shrugged. 'I take what I can get, officers.'

One frowned. 'Let's see your permission-to-work slip.'

You see me holding up the correct document.

The Blades peered at the illusory piece of paper.

'Fine,' said the officer, 'but keep a better track of time on your next job. If we catch you out after sunset again, your ass will be in a cell before you can blink.'

'Understood, officers. Thank you.'

'On your way, then.'

Aila and Bekha bowed their heads, then turned and hurried away down the side of the canal. Bekha let out a deep breath of air as they turned a corner.

'I can't believe we got away with that.'

'My power does have its uses.'

Bekha frowned. 'So it seems.'

'You'd better get used to it,' Aila said as they turned into a dark alleyway, 'because this is our life now.'

CHAPTER 2
NO NAME

The Cold Sea – 6th Marcalis 3419

T
he Cold Sea – 6th Marcalis 3419
        The beams of the ship creaked in the darkness as the stern
rose and fell. Corthie tried to get comfortable, but the chains were
digging into his wrists and ankles, and the wooden deck was filthy and
damp. Through a door a few yards in front of him, other prisoners lay
crammed into the hold, but Corthie had been kept separate for the
entire voyage, including the time he had spent in hospital on a small isle
recovering from his wounds. Since leaving Pella, he had only seen a few
faces; a couple of Reaper guards, and a man who was always with them.

He sat up, abandoning any attempt to sleep. The cold was too
intense, and from the grey light seeping through the mesh of a hatch, he
guessed that it was morning. His stomach growled from hunger, and he
wondered if they would remember to feed him that day. The wounds
from the crossbow bolts had been slow to heal, and even after a month
he could still feel them. His ability to heal wasn't, as many imagined, a
mage or god power, and was diminished by any lack of food. At the
Great Walls of the City, he had been well-fed, and able to eat as much as
he had wanted; whereas he had shed weight on the low rations he had
been given as a prisoner.

Still, he was alive. He could put up with any amount of cold or discomfort; his long training at Gadena's camp on Lostwell had conditioned him to endure, and his frustration was more due to the direction the ship was taking, bearing him away from the City; away from Aila and Blackrose.

The door in the bulkhead opened, and the two Reaper guards walked in, their companion following them through the entrance, a thick, hooded cloak covering his features.

Corthie eyed them as a guard placed a bowl and mug onto the wooden beams. He reached out when the man's hand withdrew, and grasped the bowl.

The man gestured to the guards. 'Leave us.'

Corthie watched as the two soldiers left the room.

'Are you finally going to speak to me?' he said, picking up a chunk of hard bread.

The man turned to him. 'I didn't feel the need for any contact. I have a job to do, and I will do it.'

'What's your name?'

'That is of no relevance. The ship will be docking soon. You will be the last to leave, once all of the other prisoners have been taken ashore.'

'Are you going to help me escape?'

The man emitted a low laugh. 'No. Besides, there is nowhere to escape to. There are nothing but tar sands and ice fields for miles around; and even if you made it past them, the lands on the other side of the Straits from the City are infested with greenhides. The only way out of here is on a boat.'

'Tar sands?'

'Yes. You'll see. Once I've handed you over, the two guards and I will be going back to the City. My master wants you to stay alive, and the only way to do that in this Malik-forsaken place is to work hard and keep your head down. The regime here is strict and harsh, and I advise you to do as they say.'

'And then what? Is someone coming for me?'

'I'm afraid that's none of my concern.'

'Salvor must have told you something before we left.'

'Not about that; my master only said to make sure you were kept alive.'

'What's happening in the City?'

'I've been on this ship with you for the last ten days, how would I know?'

'But we stayed on an island while I was getting better; you must have learned something there.'

The man gazed at him, his eyes dark in the shadow of the hood. 'Everyone believes it was you who killed Princess Khora.'

Corthie snorted. 'I underestimated how much of an asshole Marcus was. Kano, I knew about, but I should have listened to... never mind.'

'And the aforementioned Marcus is now Prince of Tara.'

'And Salvor, is he alright?'

'My master remains in Cuidrach Palace as Governor of Pella.'

'So he swore allegiance then?'

'Evidently.'

'And the other demigods? Any news?'

'Most of them have taken the oath to the new prince, in front of the God-Queen herself. Of the God-King, there's been no word, so it's assumed he has acquiesced with the take-over. I think there are only two rebels: Lord Naxor and Lady Aila, but the local gossips of the Grey Isle knew nothing more than that.'

Corthie's heart jumped at the mention of Aila's name. The news might be half a month out of date, but he clung onto it. If he was going to get through whatever struggles were ahead, he needed something to hold on to, and there was nothing he wanted more than to be with Aila again. He treasured the image of her in his mind, of how she had looked in the rose garden the night they had met.

'Watch out for the other prisoners,' the man said, breaking Corthie out of his thoughts. 'If they discover who you are, and let's face it, with your height and build that probably won't take too long, they might target you. Khora wasn't universally popular, but she had her supporters, and I imagine you might face some opposition.'

Corthie shrugged. 'Bring it on.'

Low voices echoed through from the deck above, and the motion of the ship slowed.

'Why's it so dark?' Corthie said, gazing up at the grey light filtering through the hatch. 'I was promised winter sunshine. It is winter, isn't it?'

'Yes, it is, but we're so far iceward that the sun barely rises above the horizon here, which also explains the cold. This is as warm, and as light, as it gets here; but that's good news as far as the greenhides are concerned. They don't like it this far iceward, and raids are rare.' He glanced at Corthie and nodded. 'I've done my part. I've warned you, and told you what you needed to know. Remain here, I shall speak to the captain.'

'Wait,' said Corthie. 'I know you work for Lord Salvor, but you still haven't told me your name.'

The man turned and left the room without answering, leaving Corthie sitting on the damp deck.

A slow hour passed as the ship reached the side of a pier and docked. There were footsteps, and cries from the deck above, and then the prisoners in the main hold were removed in a painstaking operation that seemed to last forever as Corthie waited, impatient and alone. The prisoners were herded across gangways, and Corthie could see their shadows through the mesh of the hatch as they disembarked. He listened, and could hear muffled orders being barked out, as the main batch of fresh prisoners were reviewed and assigned to various labour camps or duties. The majority were being sent to the tar sands, but others were called out for work in the kitchens, laundry or maintenance workshops. After that, there was silence again for a while, and then the door in the bulkhead was opened.

Salvor's agent entered, along with the two Reaper guards and another man, who glanced at Corthie with curiosity.

'So this is him, eh?' he said. 'This is my secret passenger?'

'Yes, Captain,' said Salvor's man. 'I trust the extra... compensation you have received for your trouble guarantees your silence also?'

The captain grinned. 'Sure, sure; just as we agreed. There's no record of him ever being on board, but you ain't going to be able to hide him once he's set foot on land.'

'That's not your problem.'

'Indeed, it's not.'

Salvor's man nodded to the Reaper guards and they stepped forward. One was holding a hammer and a thick iron pin, and he knelt by Corthie's shackles and unfastened them from the wall with a few heavy blows.

Corthie stood, the chains clanking as he stretched his limbs. He pulled on a slim thread of battle-vision, enough to leave him feeling sharp and alert. The guards stepped back a pace, their crossbows levelled at him.

Salvor's agent nodded. 'Let's go.'

Corthie walked forward, the guards letting him pass between them as he left the small compartment where he had been sealed for ten days. The rest of the hold was empty, excepting the stench left by the over-crowded prisoners, and Corthie knew he could easily take down the four men with him, chains or no chains. But then what? He couldn't pilot an entire ship on his own, even if he had known everything there was to know about boats, but he barely knew how to row, never mind sail.

'Keep moving,' said the captain; 'right to those stairs at the end.'

Corthie glanced at him, and saw the fear in his eyes. 'I hope you were well paid,' he said, halting, 'but you owe me three dinners. Three days out of the ten on this ship, no food came to me. Where is it?'

The guards tensed as the captain and Salvor's agent exchanged a glance.

'Well? I'm not getting off this boat until you hand over what you owe me.'

The captain frowned. 'I don't owe you anything.'

Corthie folded his arms. 'I'm waiting.'

Salvor's man frowned, then nodded to the captain. 'Do it.'

'But, I don't have time; we need to get him...'

'Do it.'

The captain rubbed his forehead, then disappeared into a small compartment.

Corthie winked at one of the guards as they waited.

'This is no time for games,' said Salvor's agent.

'It's not a game; I'm hungry. If I have to do this... whatever it is, then I need to eat.'

The captain re-emerged, holding a half-loaf and a long strip of cured meat. He handed it over to Corthie, who wolfed it all down in under a minute, his stomach groaning with satisfaction.

Salvor's agent shook his head. 'Can we go now?'

Corthie nodded, and they began walking again. Corthie reached the steep set of stairs and climbed. The first thing he noticed was the smell, a sour, almost eye-watering stench of burning oil that filled his nostrils. It over-powered the odour from the hold until it became the only smell detectable. His head reached the level of the deck. The sky above was dark but clear of clouds, and many stars were shining, while a freezing wind buffeted his face. He reached the top and stood on the deck. He remained still for a moment, taking in everything around him.

The ship was docked by a long, wooden pier set within the breakwaters of a large harbour. Beyond the docks was a narrow, rocky promontory that was covered in a selection of ramshackle buildings, all of them silhouetted by the thick smoke and red flames rising from an enormous edifice on the edge of town. The smoke rose up above the promontory, forming a dark cloud covering it, while the flames provided the settlement's illumination.

'That's the refinery,' said Salvor's agent next to him.

Corthie nodded. 'And what's that, then?'

'It's where the tar is collected and divided into useful products; I'm sure you'll learn all about it. Now, turn your gaze in the other direction for one moment.'

They shifted on the deck, and Corthie took a look at the way they had come. The sea was dark and still, and littered with huge chunks of floating ice, many higher than the mast of the ship.

'We're close to the icefields,' said the agent. 'There is nothing but darkness and cold that way.'

'Which way is the City?'

'The other way. The ship turned in the night to enter the bay, and sailed sunward for a couple of hours.'

Corthie stared iceward. 'Has anyone ever crossed the icefields?'

The agent shook his head. 'There is no "crossing"; it's impossible. After another hundred miles or so, there is nothing but complete darkness and the low temperature would kill you in minutes. It's the same sunward. If one travels across the marshes opposite Port Sanders for a hundred miles, there is nothing but desert, and the sun and heat get stronger and stronger until life becomes impossible.'

'So everything lives on a narrow strip between the ice and the desert?'

'Yes. I assume this is different from... wherever you hail from?'

'Very.'

The captain joined them and gestured to the gangway. A few sailors paused from their work to watch as Corthie walked to the slim plank. Standing on the pier were a dozen people dressed in thick furs and cloaks, their faces protected from the bitter wind by scarves. Their eyes tracked him as he walked down from the ship, their hands resting on their weapons. The agent and guards followed him down to the pier, and Corthie swayed for a moment as his balance adjusted to the feeling of solid ground.

The agent spoke to the people gathered on the pier, and they set off again, striding down the wooden walkway amid the freezing wind. The two Reaper guards kept their crossbows pointed at Corthie's back as they left the pier. To their right, a boat was being loaded with large barrels stained black from tar and oil, while the workers were being watched by armed guards. They left the harbour front and entered a network of rough, makeshift tracks that glistened with frost. A small handful of the buildings were made of stone, and the agent led Corthie towards one of the largest.

They entered the building, passing more guards, and Corthie was taken to a small cell on the ground floor. The guards pushed him in and locked the barred entrance. The two Reapers that had accompanied him on the voyage began to relax, their faces lightening as the agent strode away.

'You heading back home, then, lads?' Corthie said to them as he stood by the bars.

One glanced away, but the other nodded. 'Yeah, praise Malik. The sooner we get out of this dump the better.'

'Don't speak to him,' said the other Reaper; 'you know our orders.'

'But we've delivered him, at last. The hard part will be not telling the wife where I've been for the last twenty days when we get back.'

Corthie smiled. 'Tell her the truth.'

'Yeah, right,' said the guard; 'I'm just going to tell her that we were escorting the most wanted criminal in the City, who everyone thinks was executed? If Marcus knew you were here, boy, you'd be dead.'

'But you know I'm innocent, eh? You know it wasn't me who killed Khora?'

The two guards glanced at each other. Before either could answer, the agent walked back into the room, with another man and more guards.

'Here he is, Governor,' said the agent; 'Corthie Holdfast.'

The man approached, staring at the champion. He shook his head. 'You're asking me to risk everything. I won't be able to keep this a secret for long. Sailors talk.'

'It'll be fine,' said Salvor's agent; 'no one will believe gossip, not after so many are convinced they saw him lie dead in the gardens of Cuidrach Palace. I trust the compensation is adequate?'

'And I'll receive the same again when I return to the City at the end of my term?'

'As long as he's still alive.'

The governor nodded. 'Tell your master that I shall do as he asks. I can't guarantee his survival; the tar sands are dangerous, but I won't throw his life away.'

They shook hands. The agent gave one last glance towards Corthie, then he and the two Reaper guards left the room. The governor waited until they had gone, then he turned to Corthie.

'You're mine now, lad.'

'And who are you?'

'I am Governor Dyzack, and as far as you're concerned I may as well be the god of this town. Do you realise how much I've been paid to keep you here? Even if I were to forego the other half of the payment, I would still be a very rich man. In other words, your death would be of very little concern to me. And if word does leak out, and Marcus sends soldiers to hunt you, then I'll not hesitate to separate your head from your body so they can take it home to show the new prince; do you understand?'

Corthie smiled at him. 'I've killed thousands of greenhides; do you think I'm frightened of you?' He lifted his hand. 'You say you're like a god; did you know that I crushed a god's skull with this hand? Come a little closer and I'll happily demonstrate.'

A couple of the governor's guards snorted.

'Well then,' said the governor, 'it looks like you'll need broken in first.' He nodded to the guards. 'Open the door and beat him. Don't kill him, but make sure he understands the consequences of threatening me.'

Corthie laughed and rubbed his hands together as the lead soldier unlocked the gate. The champion thrummed his battle-vision, taking in the size and shape of each of the eight approaching guards. They were in leather armour, and each was carrying a two foot stave. Three rushed him, their weapons high, and Corthie sprang forward to meet them. He buried his fist into the first guard's face as he ducked to avoid a blow. A stave smacked into his shoulder, and he ripped it out of the soldier's grasp and rammed the butt-end into the man's nose, breaking it. He wielded the stave himself, catching another guard on the chin as more blows rained down on him. He downed a fourth guard, doubling him over with a blow to his stomach, then a heavy swing caught the side of his head and he saw sparks in his eyes.

More guards had been called, and over a dozen crammed into the cell, surrounding him. Each time his fist connected with one of them they would fall back, slumped to the ground, but he was still weakened from the journey, and his battle-vision powers were sluggish. A fifth guard fell, then a sixth, before Corthie was driven to his knees, his hands raised as the thick staves landed on him from all sides. A hand came too close, and he grabbed it, crushing the man's fingers in his grasp until he heard him scream.

A stave battered off the back of his head and he fell, blood coming from the wounds on his face. The blows continued to strike him as he lay motionless on the ground.

'Enough,' said the governor.

Corthie's left eye had swollen shut, but he opened his right a crack, and saw seven guards being carried out of the cell. He smiled, then passed out.

He awoke outside, shivering in the freezing cold. The chains connecting his wrists had been removed, but shackles were connecting his left ankle to an iron post that had been driven into the frozen ground. The wind was howling, biting through his thin clothes and he glanced around, trying to get his bearings. To his right, he could see the harbour between the sides of the ramshackle buildings in the way, and the refinery was to his left, filling the dark sky with flames and thick, black smoke.

There was a wooden wall behind him, so he scrambled closer to shelter from the wind and noticed a man next to him, his ankle shackled to another post, and a bruise covering half of his face.

Corthie nodded to him. 'Did you need broken-in too?'

The man stared at him. He had a thick woollen cloak round him, and a fur-lined hat. 'I thought you were going to freeze to death.'

'A bit of cold doesn't bother me,' Corthie said. He touched his face, trying to gauge the extent of the damage. His left eye was still closed, and there was blood matted into his hair. He nodded. 'Nothing broken at least. Do they always beat up new arrivals?'

The man shook his head. 'Only the ones they think will be trouble.'

'I threatened to crush the governor's skull; does that count?'

'Yeah,' the man laughed. 'I'm Achan. Who are you?'

Corthie paused for a moment. Should he try to hide his identity? He remembered what the governor had said about Marcus sending soldiers if he found out he was still alive.

'I have people after me,' he said, 'and no offence, but I don't know you.'

'That's fair, I guess,' said Achan. 'Did you arrive this morning?'

'Aye.'

'I didn't see you get off the boat with the others.'

'No, I was kept separate from them. Wait, have you been out here all day?'

'Yeah. I was caught trying to smuggle a message onto a departing ship. This is what they do when the prison's full; they stick us out here in the cold.'

'Is everyone here prisoners; apart from the guards?'

'Most, though there are a few with debts who are here to earn gold. There are folk from all over the City in Tarstation, and every few weeks another boat-load is brought in to replace the ones who have died.'

'How do they die?'

'Some freeze to death in the icefields, others drown in the tarpits. A few are beaten to death by the guards every now and again, if they want to remind us who's in charge. Where are you from, no-name?'

'You mean what tribe do I belong to?'

Achan nodded.

'You go first.'

'Fine,' said Achan. 'I'm a Hammer.'

Corthie squinted. 'Really? I half-believed they were mythical. I saw the high walls around the territory of the Scythes and the Hammers, but this is the first time I've actually met one.'

Achan smiled. 'So, you're a Blade? Figures, from the size of you. Looks like we're enemies.'

'Why?'

'Are you completely clueless? It's the Blades who keep the Scythes and Hammers oppressed. We're slaves; those walls you saw are to keep us in, not to keep the greenhides or anyone else out. Have you any idea what goes on behind those walls? The misery, the cruelty?'

Corthie shook his head.

'This is exactly what's wrong with the City. The Hammers make half of the goods for Auldan and Medio, and no one has the first idea of the conditions we live under, and no one cares. Except Princess Yendra, if the stories are true. She was the only one who ever gave a rat's ass about us. The Evaders think they have it bad? Well, they should see how we live. At least they're free to walk the streets.'

'This has all been kept from me,' said Corthie. 'I didn't know any of this.'

Achan raised an eyebrow. 'Come on. The Blades have been doing this to us for a thousand years.'

'Aye, but I'm not really a Blade.'

'Show me your arm.'

Corthie lifted his left sleeve to reveal the Blade tattoo, and Achan leaned in closer to read the inked lettering.

'Wolfpack?' he frowned, then his eyes widened. 'Are you a champion?'

'Aye, but shush. Damn it, I wasn't going to tell anyone. Marcus and Kano would kill me if they knew I was still alive. Gadena always said my big mouth was likely to get me in trouble.'

Achan's eyes darkened. 'Marcus and Kano want you dead? Why?'

'They're trying to frame me for someone's murder.'

'And how do you feel about them, truthfully?'

Corthie shrugged. 'I hate them. Give me five minutes alone with either and I'd rip their heads off.'

Achan nodded. 'Alright, I'll keep your secret. Maybe we're not enemies after all. I got sent here because I kept causing problems for the Blades. I have a big mouth too.'

He silenced as a group of guards approached.

'On your feet, you two,' the officer said.

Corthie and Achan stood, and guards released their shackles from the iron posts, while others covered the prisoners with their crossbows.

They were led away from the harbour and into a network of rough tracks, where low, wooden shacks lay on either side. They stopped off at a store depot, and Corthie was issued with warm, though tattered and filthy clothing, then they were taken past a guard post and into one of the low shacks.

'Prisoner Achan,' said the officer; 'the governor has told me to inform you that you are being relocated to this accommodation block, as you have proved a disruptive presence. And you,' he said to Corthie, 'welcome to your new home. Work begins tomorrow.'

They were taken along a narrow passageway, where doors led off on either side. The officer checked a document, then opened one of the doors. Inside were three bunk beds, two of which were already occupied by four prisoners. Corthie and Achan entered, and the door was closed and locked behind them.

Four sets of eyes glowered at them from the shadows.

'Not that asshole Achan,' growled one. 'And who's the freak?'

Corthie rolled his shoulders. 'Shall we get this over with now, lads? Anyone who touches me or Achan will be eating their own teeth. All at once, or one at a time; come at me any way you want.'

One of the men gripped the side of the bunk bed and launched himself at Corthie. The champion smiled, dodged and slammed his fist into the man's mouth, dropping him to the floor. The others stared, but didn't move.

'Are we done?' Corthie said.

No one spoke.

'Excellent.' Corthie eyed the empty beds. 'I'm taking the bottom bunk.'

Achan glanced at up at him, his eyes wide. 'Sure, no-name. Anything you say.'

Corthie stepped over the unconscious prisoner and lay down onto the bed. He closed his eyes. The mattress stank, and had hard lumps that dug into his skin, but compared to the hold of the ship it felt like luxury.

'Who are you?' said one of the other prisoners.

Corthie didn't answer, his mind already drifting off into sleep.

CHAPTER 3
A LAST LESSON

T ara, Auldan, The City – 17th Marcalis 3419

'Not the face!' cried her grandmother as Emily dodged a blow from the wooden sword.

Emily lunged out at her sparring partner, and he parried, the two swords clacking together.

'In fact,' said her grandmother, 'that's enough for today. Your mother would kill me if you went home all bruised.'

'But I'm only just getting warmed up,' Emily said, keeping her sword raised, 'and it's my last lesson.'

Her sparring partner lowered his wooden blade and smiled. 'You've learned everything I have to teach, ma'am.'

'Yes,' said her grandmother, walking over from where she had been sitting by a table. 'One skipped lesson won't make any difference, not after six years of practice.'

Emily handed the sword to her sparring partner. 'I'm going to miss this.'

Her grandmother smiled. 'Daniel seems like an open-minded young man; I'm sure he wouldn't have any concerns if you wished to continue training.'

'He'd probably be alright with it; it's his mother I worry about.'

'You're not the only one, dear. You having second thoughts?'

'None. I'm marrying Daniel, and no one's going to stop me.' She held out her thumb and index finger an inch apart. 'I'm this close to being free, Grandma. An over-bearing mother-in-law I can put up with.'

Her grandmother nodded as the sparring instructor tidied away their training equipment. He picked up his large bag and slung it over his shoulder.

He bowed. 'It's been an honour and if, as Emily Aurelian, you require any more practice, I'd be happy to assist.'

Emily inclined her head. 'Thank you.'

'Yes, thank you,' said her grandmother.

The man bowed again and left the room.

Her grandmother nodded to a chair. 'Take a seat, girl.'

They walked over to a table by the wall of the large room and sat. Her grandmother poured warm water mixed with wine into two cups as Emily watched her. Her grandmother's face was relaxed, but her eyes showed the anxiety she was feeling on behalf of her only grandchild.

'Lady Aurelian has plans for you, I'm sure,' she said. 'Daniel's an only child like you, and his mother will be wanting to ensure that you do not take her place in her son's affections. At the same time, she'll want to know that you are utterly loyal to him; it's a narrow line upon which you will have to tread, dear.'

'And his father?'

'Lord Aurelian is rarely at the mansion, or so I believe. He spends his time managing the various properties owned by the family, leaving his wife as the authority within the household. Or, it was her authority that forced him from the house; either way, it's Lady Aurelian that you shall have to deal with. And then there's the matter of children. Have you and Daniel discussed it?'

Emily laughed. 'And when do you think I've had the chance to speak to him? I've seen him twice since you took me to their villa in the hills; once when I had to sneak downstairs when they visited, and once by accident on the quayside when the God-Queen was there.'

'How ridiculous,' said the grandmother as she shook her head. 'If it had been up to me, I would have had you both together for far long periods of time, so you could at least find out a few things about each other. You know, I made the same mistake with your mother; I didn't allow her to see your father before they got married. I was so keen to see my daughter find a husband, I neglected to allow her the chance to see if she liked him first. It pains me to see the same thing has happened with you and Daniel.'

'Danny's nothing like my father.'

'You're right, he's not. However, there may be other things about him that you don't like, but it'll be too late when you're all living under the same roof. This is not Pella, you can't just get divorced here because you don't like your husband. Regardless, Lady Aurelian will probably mention children to you; be prepared.'

'I will be, Grandma.'

'Good girl. Now, as I said, Daniel seems like a nice young man, but even nice young men can become lazy and useless husbands. Make sure he knows, right from the beginning, that you expect to be treated by him as your equal; if you allow him to walk over you at the start, then he will continue to do so. He is your ally, your partner; not your master. Respect him, but demand his respect in return. Good men do not fear clever, strong-willed women; they seek them out and hold them close. You have a future that is independent of his, so do not allow his dreams and desires to erase your own. I have watched over you since you were a baby, and have seen you blossom into a young woman with the potential to become anyone you want to be.'

Emily smiled.

'What's funny, dear?'

'I was remembering the way you acted at the villa when we met Danny.'

'Oh yes?'

'Yes. You were fawning over him like a schoolgirl.'

Her grandmother laughed. 'A practised act, my dear girl. Might I say that you played your role well that day, also; I've never seen you so wide-eyed and awestruck.'

'Did it work?'

'You tell me.'

Emily recalled the look in Daniel's eyes when she had gone to his room. 'I think so.'

'Good. Well, that's an end to your training. I hope I have been able to fill the gaps in your education over these last few years; your father has the oddest ideas about what girls should be taught, or not taught if I were to put it more correctly.'

'I'm grateful for all the lessons, Grandma.'

'But you enjoyed the ones that involved fighting the most, though, eh?'

Emily nodded. 'Yes, I'll not lie. I like the feel of a sword in my hand, and the self-defence classes were useful. I'll know what to do if I ever come across an Evader in a dark alley.'

Her grandmother said nothing for a moment, her mouth expressionless, but her eyes narrowing. Emily frowned, waiting for whatever was troubling her Grandma to come out.

'Your father's ideas,' she said eventually, 'do him no credit, and it pains me to hear his prejudice come from your lips.'

'But the Evaders are different, Grandma; you can't deny it. The Rosers, Gloamers and even the Reapers are basically all the same kind of people, which makes the Icewarders and Sanders our distant cousins; but the Evaders? They've never really belonged, have they? I know my father has some pretty crazy ideas about what we should do regarding this simple fact, but I don't share them. I have no desire to see them all die; I have no desire to see any harm come to them at all, but a little separation wouldn't hurt.'

Her grandmother shook her head. 'Let's not argue about it; you're young, and once your father's influence has worn off...'

'Please don't patronise me, Grandma, not on the last day of our lessons together.'

'All right. You probably should be thinking about returning home. To be honest, I'm surprised your mother let you visit me today.'

'I didn't tell her.'

'Why ever not, girl? On Amalia's grace, I despair. What did you tell her you were doing?'

'I snuck out of the house without telling them anything. I figured they wouldn't let me come here, and I didn't want to heighten their suspicions.'

'You have a brass neck, girl, and no mistake. Were you planning to waltz back into your home as if nothing's happened?'

'Something like that. What are they going to do? What can they do?'

'Go now, please.'

'But I haven't washed or changed.'

Her grandmother raised an eyebrow. 'You barely broke into a sweat today; we've spent most of the time talking. Go, now, and I'll see you later.'

'Fine,' said Emily, getting to her feet. She leaned over and kissed her Grandma on the cheek, then turned for the door. A Reaper servant was standing in the hallway, and she gathered Emily's hat, scarf and fur-lined cloak from the pegs by the front door.

'Ma'am,' she said, bowing.

Emily wrapped the scarf round her neck, then pulled the cloak over her shoulders, feeling the warmth of the fur against her skin. She strode to the door and the servant opened it for her, bowing. Emily stepped outside into the crisp winter morning and filled her lungs with the fresh, cold air. She placed the hat on her head, and smiled. A beautiful day, she thought. The sky was clear, and stretched from blue to pink to red above her head. She walked into the street, and pulled a pair of white leather gloves from a pocket. The temperature was bitterly cold, and in a few steps she had felt her fingers go almost numb. Her grandmother lived on a street lined with elegant townhouses on one side, and a park on the other, with grass, flowers and a grove of oak and beech trees.

She smiled to a young couple with a pram as she walked past the trees, and imagined doing the same thing with Daniel. Would he be the kind of man who would be interested in taking walks with the baby?

Would she enjoy it? She shuddered. Babies. She pushed the thought out of her mind. Plenty of time for that later. Much later.

She turned left at a junction and saw the heights where Maeladh Palace sat, its dark exterior shining in the sunlight. Along from it were the trees and rooftops of Princeps Row, where the Aurelian mansion was situated. She had climbed the steps and taken a good look at the place after meeting Daniel at the villa, to see what kind of life he had to offer her; but had been inside only once, when she had crept into his bedroom. Her heart raced at the memory. She had been terrified of being discovered by his mother, but it had been worth it for the look on Daniel's face when he had realised what she had done. Going to him that second time had been a gamble, but her own desire had played a part; it hadn't all been about getting him to commit. In hindsight it had worked out. As the only other time they had seen each other since had been at the harbour watching the God-Queen anoint Prince Marcus, she was glad that they had created another memory to share.

An avenue lined with silver birch opened to her right and she followed it. Grand townhouses and small villas lay on either side beyond the double row of trees, and pigeons were pecking the dirt by the twisting roots. She saw her house in the distance, and sighed. She was going to have to brazen it out; there was no time for a tearful apology or some other act of contrition.

Halfway along the avenue, she noticed a stall selling flowers. She walked over to it, and took a look at the various blooms on offer. Some of the stock was old, and the selection was small compared to the summer months.

'Can I help you, miss?' said a voice.

She lifted her head, and glanced at the smiling young man behind the counter. He was a Reaper by his dress and accent, but was handsome nevertheless.

'I'll take a bouquet. Wrap the stems, but don't bag it.'

'Certainly, miss.'

'Miss', she thought. Not for much longer. She pointed out the flowers she wanted, and watched as the man made up the bouquet for her, trimming the excess leaves and cutting the stems to the same length. He wrapped the bottom in green paper and she handed over some silver coins.

'Thank you, miss. You live round here?'

She smiled. 'For another few hours.'

He raised an eyebrow as she took the bouquet and turned for home. She held the flowers close to her chest; they would be a useful distraction, she thought. How could you be angry with someone who was carrying a bunch of flowers?

She walked up the short pathway and pulled on the bell of her front door. She had keys in her purse, but it was out of reach round her back and she waited for a moment before the door swung open.

The Reaper servant stared open-mouthed at her for a second, then stood aside to allow Emily to enter the Omertia home.

'Ma'am,' she whispered as she bowed, 'your mother is looking for you.'

Emily heard the sound of weeping coming from the sitting room to the left and she walked in. Several servants turned to stare. Her mother was in an armchair, tears streaming down her cheeks. She was oblivious to Emily's presence for a moment, but then she noticed the glances of the servants and turned.

Her mother's despair transformed to rage in an instant.

'Where have you been?' she cried, standing. 'Are you trying to ruin us?'

Her father hurried into the room, his expression twisted with anger. Emily almost flinched from him, but steadied herself, her fingers clutching onto the flower stems. He approached until his face was only inches from hers.

'Where were you, girl?'

'I was at Grandma's.'

'What? You sneaked out of the house to visit *her*?'

'I wanted to speak to her.'

'Look at the state of your mother,' he cried; 'you wicked child. After everything she's done for you, you would spoil the day she has been looking forward to for so long?' He raised his hand, his fist clenched. 'Ungrateful little witch.'

'No,' said Emily's mother, 'don't strike her. What would the Aurelians think if she goes to them covered in bruises?'

Her father spluttered. 'She must be punished.'

Her mother placed a restraining hand on her husband's arm. 'Not today. She knew we wouldn't be able to touch her, which is why she did it. It's her final act of rebellion.'

Her father pushed her hand away. 'This is your fault, woman. You spoiled this girl, and look how she's turned out; no respect, no humility. She mocks us and you say we should do nothing. At least after today I won't have to listen to her pathetic bleating; how I wish I could say the same about you.'

He lashed out, striking his wife across the face with his open palm. As she cried out, Emily pushed her way between them, an arm raised to shield her mother.

'No, father,' she said.

He glared at them for a moment, then turned and strode from the room, the servants scattering to get out of his way. Emily's mother sank into a chair, a hand on her face as she wept. Emily put an arm round her shoulder.

'Leave him, mother,' she whispered.

Her mother shoved her away. 'This is your fault. You knew how he'd react and yet you went ahead and did it anyway. He was right; you are spoiled, and ungrateful. We've given you the best of everything the City has to offer; you live like a princess, and yet, on this day of all days, you choose to spite me. Why do you hate me? Sometimes I wish you'd never been born.'

Emily stood, straightened her back and nodded. She placed the bouquet of flowers onto the side table.

'I'm going to get ready,' she said, then left her mother weeping in the armchair.

Four servants had been assigned to help her prepare. After washing, she sat still in her underclothes in front of the mirror on her dresser while her long blonde hair was swept up and styled above her shoulders, and her make-up was applied. The servants, of course, said nothing about the shouting or her mother's tears, but Emily knew they had all witnessed it.

Her cousin Abigail walked in while the finishing touches were being made to her lipstick. Emily kept her head still, watching Abigail from the corner of her eye. She had wanted one of her friends from school to be her bridesmaid, but her father had insisted it should be his brother's younger daughter instead.

'Hi, Emily,' she said, perching on the edge of a seat. 'Excited?'

Emily waited as a servant carefully removed the smudges from round her lips with a scrap of cloth.

'I saw your mother crying on the way in,' her cousin went on; 'you think she'd be happy on your big day.'

Emily pressed her lips together, then smiled. 'I think they're tears of joy. Your hair looks nice; who did it for you?'

'Mother hired a new Reaper girl. She's useless at pretty much everything else, but good with hair.' She plucked a bottle of wine from the bag she had carried in, then glanced at one of Emily's assistants. 'Open this and bring a couple of glasses.'

The servant took the bottle and bowed. 'Yes, ma'am.'

'I can't believe your father managed to book the palace as the location,' Abigail said.

'It's a reception hall within the palace grounds,' said Emily, 'not the actual palace.'

'Still, it'll send everyone wild with envy. And from there, you'll only be two minutes from the Aurelian mansion. How does it feel to be joining the elite?'

'We're Omertias, Abbie; we're already the elite.'

'Yeah, but the Aurelians? Come on. The last mortal princes of Tara? My mother's furious that she took Chamberlain's money. It could've been me, you know. Lady Aurelian approached my parents before they approached yours. It should've been me getting married at the palace today.'

Emily said nothing, keeping her face still as blusher was dusted over her cheeks. The servant returned with the open bottle of wine.

She set down two glasses. 'Should I pour, ma'am?'

Abigail narrowed her eyes. 'How else are we supposed to drink it?'

The servant bowed and filled the two glasses. Abigail picked one up and took a sip. 'Not having any?'

'Thanks,' said Emily, 'but I think I'll stay off the wine for now. I want to keep my head clear.'

'You'll regret it once all of the boring speeches start. I bet your father has a long one planned. And think about later tonight, when you get to the Aurelian mansion; you might need a couple of drinks for that.'

Emily smiled out of politeness.

'I wonder what Daniel is like,' said Abigail, her gaze drifting.

'Yes,' said Emily, noticing the jealous streak in her cousin's eyes; 'I wonder.'

'One day, you'll be Lady Aurelian.'

'One day.'

Abigail drank more wine. 'It's not fair. If my parents hadn't taken the bribe, it would've been me.'

'My parents took the Chamberlains' money, too, Abbie.'

'They did?'

'Yes, but after Daniel returned from the Circuit, my mother sent a letter to his mother, and... well, here I am.'

Abigail's eyes hardened. 'What? You mean that you went behind my family's back and stole him from me?'

'I did nothing of the kind, Abbie, and I'd rather you didn't say things like that; at least not today.'

'Has your mother no shame?'

Her make-up ready, Emily stood. She gazed at her reflection in the mirror, ignoring the sullen expression on her cousin's face. In a few hours' time, she would never have to put up with her cousin again. She told herself to be civil. Let anyone say whatever they wished; she was unreachable, she had moved beyond caring about what they thought any more. She noticed a couple of faded old bruises on her abdomen, but couldn't recall if they had come from an old sparring session or had been inflicted at the hands of her father. She didn't think Daniel would ever raise his hands to her, but if he did, he would be in for a surprise.

She smiled at one of her servants. 'Time for the dress.'

'Did you not hear me?' said Abigail. 'I asked you a question.'

'To save you embarrassment, I was pretending you hadn't said it.'

'Your mother went behind my mother's back; do you deny it?'

'You are aware that I had to actually meet Danny?'

'Oh, "Danny", is it? Like you know the first thing about him. I bet you just batted your eyelashes and showed him a bit of cleavage; do you think your looks make you better than the rest of us? They don't, they just make you look cheap.'

Emily took a breath, as her earlier resolve strained. She felt an urge to strike her cousin, and lowered her eyes. That was something her father would have done, not her. Emily may be her father's daughter, but she knew she had to break free, not just of his control, but of his influence.

One of her make-up servants caught her glance. 'You look beautiful, ma'am.'

Emily blinked. Had a Reaper servant just shown her more kindness than the rest of her family put together? 'Thank you,' she said, 'but if that's true, it was only with your assistance. What's your name?'

'Talleta, ma'am.'

For a moment Emily considered throwing Abigail out of her room and appointing Talleta her bridesmaid instead.

'Would you be my flower girl today?' she said. 'And afterwards, I would like you to come with me to the Aurelian mansion. I'm allowed to bring one servant; would you like the job?'

The Reaper girl blushed. 'I think your mother has already appointed Reina to that position, ma'am.'

'Well, it's not up to her; it's up to me. Reina's nice, but I'd prefer someone my own age.'

'It would be my honour, ma'am.'

Abigail snorted.

Emily ignored her as two other servants approached with the dress. Emily's eyes widened. She had seen drawings of it in the dressmaker's office, but it had been kept in storage since arriving at the house. It was stunning. The top half consisted of an ivory and cream bodice that would leave her shoulders bare, while hugging her waist and hips, while the long white skirt flared from the knees into a lace train. The tiny clasps on the back had been unhooked, and Emily stepped up onto a chair as the servants brought the dress closer. Talleta offered a hand and Emily took it, then stepped down into the dress. The servants pulled the bodice up and Emily breathed in as the clasps were re-fastened. It was a tight fit, but she smiled as she saw the results in the mirror. The servants all took a step back, and one of the older ones started to cry.

'You look like a vision, ma'am,' said Talleta.

'Yes, gorgeous,' said the older servant between sobs.

'Thank you.' Emily glanced at her cousin. 'It might be time you got into the bridesmaid dress.'

Abigail frowned. 'I've seen it. Why peach? Could you not have picked a colour that suited me? I'll have no chance with the boys in that thing.'

'This day might not be about you, Abbie.'

'So you're deliberately wanting me to appear foolish?'

Emily felt something snap inside her. 'Frankly, Abbie, I didn't even want you to be my bridesmaid at all; I was forced into asking you. If you don't want to do it, then kindly remove your ass from my chair and bugger off.'

There was a knock at the door as Abigail stared at her.

'Yes?'

'It's only me,' said her father, poking his head through the entrance. He caught sight of his daughter and walked in. 'Ah, you make me proud, girl. What a sight.'

He leaned over and kissed her on the cheek, smudging her make up while leaving the scent of brandy in Emily's nostrils. He swayed a little as he took a step back.

'Don't move, ma'am,' whispered Talleta as she picked up the blusher and a small brush.

'Is mother ready?' Emily said as the servant fixed her make up.

'Who knows?' he said. 'She's been in the bathroom so long I fear she may have drowned.' He laughed at his own joke while Emily smiled. Patience, she told herself. She glanced at Abigail, but her cousin looked away.

'Abbie's just about to get her dress on too,' Emily said. 'She thinks it looks amazing. Peach was a good choice of yours, father.'

'I'm glad you both like it,' he said. 'As soon as I saw the colour, I knew it would suit our little Abbie.'

Abigail smiled at him, then shot a glare of venom at Emily as soon as he looked away.

Emily laughed as her cousin got up and left the room.

'It's good to see you happy,' her father said, 'and I'm glad we can forget that nonsense earlier. It's all worked out for the best. You'll be an Aurelian soon, with one foot in the palace. Now that we have a prince again, may Amalia give him blessings, the time is ripe for a new era of Roser supremacy in the City. Like the Omertias, the Aurelians have always prided themselves on being of true Roser heritage. Three and a half thousand years, and not a scintilla of foreign blood.'

She hid her loathing and smiled. Just a few more hours to go.

'And you'll be a wife,' he went on, shaking his head. 'My little girl, some other man's wife. Remember to honour and obey him; a true wife ministers to her husband's needs, and always puts him first. Your role is to support him, and no one likes a nagging scold as a wife, so remember that too.'

'I'll try, papa.'

He smiled. 'You haven't called me that in a long time. I like it.' He glanced at the clock-window. 'It's almost noon; our carriage will be here shortly.' He gestured to the door. 'Shall we?'

Emily looked around her bedroom for the last time. It looked different from normal, as the wedding preparations had taken over, but it remained the place she had called home for her entire life; the room where she had felt safe, where she had retreated to whenever her father had hit her or her mother, and where she had lain each night planning her escape.

'Yes, papa,' she said. 'It's time to go.'

CHAPTER 4
CORPORAL JACKDAW

Arrowhead Fort, The Bulwark, The City – 17th Marcalis 3419

'Mum and dad miss you, you know,' Tom said. 'I wish you'd visit them.'

'I wish I had the time,' said Maddie, 'but I can barely spare the ten minutes to come out here and speak to you. Thanks for coming, though. How's life? Did dad make it through Sweetmist without getting that rash again? Malik's ass,' she said, glancing around, 'it's quiet out here; seems like Arrowhead's deserted.'

'Everyone's fine,' her brother said. 'Mum and dad are doing alright, apart from worrying about you.'

Maddie looked up as they walked through the castle's interior courtyard, to see if there was any sign of Buckler, but the red dragon's eyrie seemed empty.

'It would help,' he went on, 'if they knew what you were doing. They've never believed that nonsense about repairing walls.'

She frowned. She had been enjoying the distraction of being outside in the sunshine for a while, and didn't want to be reminded of her life in the lair.

'How's the little toerag?'

'Rosie's fine,' he said. 'She's finished building her own small ballista in the backyard, made from scrap parts she found on a dump by the side of Stormshield. She sends her love.'

'Yeah, right she does. And what about you? What winter schedule are you going to be on? I heard that the Fourth Battalion are on the outer walls this month.'

'They are, but my company's been seconded, along with a few others. We're not going to the walls this winter.'

'Eh? Don't tell me you're...? Are you going into the City?'

He nodded. 'Yeah. Peacekeeping duties in the Circuit.'

'So they're stripping the wall battalions? How are the rest of us supposed to keep the greenhides out?'

'Don't be melodramatic. It's just the reserves and a few extra companies. There will be plenty of Blades left to defend the walls, and remember, we'll all be back well before summer when the proper fighting season begins. And you'll have Buckler.'

Maddie lowered her eyes. 'But no Corthie.'

'I wondered when you'd bring him up. Surely you're not still pining after that traitor?'

'I love you, brother, but if you say that again I'll punch you in the face. I don't care what the news sheets say, I don't believe it.'

'And how would you know?'

'I know; I just know.'

'You seem to be taking this very personally. He was good at killing greenhides, and it did come as a bit of a shock, but who really knew him? He spends one season here, and then goes berserk during the Fog of Balian? Thank Malik Lord Kano was there.'

Maddie swung her fist, connecting with the side of her brother's jaw. His head went back and he cried out.

He stared at her, clutching his chin. 'You little...! In the name of the God-King, what was that for? Is there something wrong with you?'

She pointed a finger in his face. 'Never say that asshole's name to me again.'

'Who, Lord Kano?'

She clenched her fists.

'But why?' he said. 'What's he ever done to you?'

'I don't want to talk about it.'

'But...'

'Leave it.'

'With Marcus in Tara, he's the acting Commander of the Bulwark, Maddie. Did you say something to rile him? He has the power to send you to the Rats, or anywhere else he chooses.'

'Do I need to punch you again? If you don't change the subject I'm leaving.'

He shook his head at her. 'Fine, so we're not to talk about Corthie, or Lord you-know-who. Or your job. Is there anything else I'm not allowed to mention?'

'I thought this was supposed to be a family catch-up? Tell me something about mum or dad.'

'Mum's battalion have switched to making riot shields for the soldiers going to Medio; a big order came through. Uh, dad's job's the same, he's still training the raw recruits and Blade cadets. I've got another few days before my company goes to the Circuit, so I'll spend it with them and Rosie. It would be great if you could visit while I'm still in the Bulwark; I can't even remember the last time all five of us were in the same room together.'

'It was at the beginning of summer,' she said; 'six months ago. Look, I know what you're saying, and for once I agree. I'd love to pop back home for a day or two, but I can't; not right now. Pass on my love, even to the little toerag, and tell her not to kill anyone with her homemade catapult.'

'It's a ballista.'

'Whatever, Tom; I quit the arbalest course, remember? It's a thing that shoots things. And, good luck in the City; at least one of us is getting to see the sights.'

'From what I've heard about the Circuit, it doesn't sound like it'll be much fun.'

'Just don't get killed or anything stupid like that. You may be a twat, but you're still my brother.'

He smiled and leaned forward with his arms open.

'What are you doing?' she said. 'Are you trying to hug me? Eww.'

Her brother frowned. 'I just thought it might be a while before I see you again and... never mind.' His arms fell to his sides. 'You're an idiot.'

'Alright then,' she said, and embraced him awkwardly. They separated. 'Sorry, I'm not used to touching people; makes me feel a bit icky.'

He smiled. 'I won't ever try again, so don't worry. Take care, little sister.'

Maddie watched as he turned and strode across the castle forecourt towards the entrance gates. He was a good brother, she supposed, and it wasn't his fault he knew nothing of what had happened with Lord Kano. At least he had come to visit her in Arrowhead, and it had been nice to hear that her family were all doing fine. She had been surprised at how keen she had been to go home to see them all before Tom was transferred to Medio, so she supposed that she must miss them after all; or maybe it was because her life in Arrowhead had been so miserable over the previous month. She glanced over at the low entrance to the lair where she lived and worked, and decided that she still had a few minutes left. She turned and walked to the nearest steps that led to the battlements. As she climbed, she looked out over the fortress. It was a beautiful winter's day; cold but fresh, and she liked the way her breath hazed in front of her face when she exhaled. There was no wind, and she loosened her scarf as she neared the top. The battlements of the fortress's inner walls were almost deserted, and she gazed out at the view. The outer walls below her were also sparsely occupied, but the moat wall beyond that was guarded with the same numbers as usual. Packs of greenhides were roaming the area in front of the moat, and there were larger concentrations of them out of range of the artillery of the Great Wall. Occasionally a missile would fly out from over the defences and strike a group of greenhides if they got too close to the moat, but it was quiet in the main.

Her leg began to ache in the cold, and she leaned on the battlements to take some pressure off it. The damp conditions of Sweetmist hadn't helped with her healing, but she was nearly there, and her limp had gone. She glanced up at the sky, searching for Buckler, but there was no sign of him. He was probably sleeping in his lair, or being pampered by his dozen assistants. She smiled, imagining how different her life would be if she had been assigned the red dragon, rather than the black.

She made her way back down the stairs, pausing halfway to rest her leg and to drag out her break a little longer. The flutter of anxiety that her brother's visit had quelled began to return, that familiar feeling that had been present for a month, ever since Blackrose had been told the news about Corthie's execution. She reached the bottom of the steps and turned right, heading under the arched opening that led to the front door of the lair. She took her keys out and selected the correct one, then glanced around. She unlocked the door and slipped inside, closing it behind her and hanging her scarf up on a peg.

Captain Hilde appeared in the hallway by the kitchen door. 'Ah, it's you. That was a long ten minutes, girl.'

Maddie shook off her coat. 'My brother's a blabbermouth; I couldn't shut him up.'

Hilde smiled. 'A likely story. I'm warming some apple cider; do you want a mug?'

'Yes, please.'

Maddie watched as Hilde disappeared back into the kitchen, then hung her coat by the front door. She dreaded spending time with the captain, who was trying to pretend that everything was fine and back to normal. Maddie was forbidden from mentioning the arguments that had seen Blackrose threaten to kill Hilde, and the captain in return had promised to never speak ill of Corthie. Such were the rules of the truce that the captain had laid down, and Maddie had done her best, but her nerves were frayed from the effort to engage in small talk with her. She steeled herself; she was doing it for Blackrose; for Mela.

She walked into the kitchen as Hilde was filling two mugs with warm cider. She held out one for Maddie.

'Thanks.' She sniffed it, savouring the apple and the spices that Hilde had added.

'You can make the next batch,' said the captain. 'So, how's your family been keeping?'

'Alright. Tom's been posted to the Circuit and Rosie's built a trebuchet in the back yard.'

Hilde frowned. 'A what? Wait, did you say Tom's going to the Circuit?'

'Yeah; peacekeeping.'

'Hmm. Duke Marcus, I mean the prince, has certainly been emptying the barracks of any spare Blades. There are several thousand occupying Tara and Pella, as well as those who've been deployed to the Circuit. I wonder what his long-term plan is.'

'He was an asshole as a duke, and he'll probably continue to be an asshole as a prince.'

'How will it affect us, though? If the Blades aren't recalled by the start of summer, we could struggle. Anyway, your mother and father; are they well?'

'Yeah, they're fine, I guess.'

'I could cover you for a few days if you wanted to visit them.'

Maddie laughed before she could stop herself. 'What, and give you time to change the locks?'

Hilde's eyes narrowed, then her expression changed and she laughed. 'The maintenance crews in Arrowhead are never that quick. I'm serious though; two days, and I promise I won't do anything to the locks.'

Maddie nodded. Maybe she should take the captain up on her offer. Two days away from the lair, in a place where she could lose herself in the welcoming embrace of her family; even the inevitable squabbles and niggles seemed alluring to her.

'I'll think about it; thank you.'

'You're welcome. You're due a break, you've been working hard.'

Maddie nodded. 'Any change today?'

'None, but don't be down-hearted. Blackrose has gone for longer periods in the past without speaking. She needs time to sort herself out after the... excitement of last month. She'll come round; it might take a while, but she will.'

'She's not spoken for over a month before?'

'She didn't speak to anyone for almost a year when she first arrived in Arrowhead. That's what I'm seeing here, Maddie. Blackrose got herself into a state about the... champion, and it's like she's gone back to that time; non-communicative, sullen, not eating. I thought at the time that her swearing allegiance to the Blades would prove to be a passing phase, and so it proved. I can see how hard this has been on you. You allowed yourself to get carried away, and I certainly don't blame you for that, but now you can see what her true nature is. I don't mean this to sound cruel, Maddie, but Blackrose will never leave this lair, and you'll have to come to terms with that at some point.'

Maddie bit her tongue. The captain had remained ignorant about the flight that the black dragon had taken, and Maddie had seen no reason to enlighten her, knowing it would only serve to reignite the bitter arguments that had split them before. She lived from day to day wondering if Hilde would remove her from her position as she had so often threatened. Blackrose had ordered her not to, but in the state she was in, would the dragon even notice her absence?

'If you don't feel like going in today, I'll understand,' Hilde went on. 'The boiler needs loaded with coal and there's a supply of meat and milk due to arrive from the Scythe farms later this morning. You can handle all of that, and I can deal with the grumpy queen today.'

'No, I want to go in, especially if I'm going to go away for a break.'

Hilde smiled. 'That's fine. You go in today, then, and you can take a carriage this evening to Stormshield or Plaza Six, whichever is better for getting to your family. It goes without saying, of course, that you can't tell them anything. Remember your oath. I trust you didn't speak of it to your brother?'

'No, I kept quiet, like I'm supposed to. '

'Good girl. Now, before you go in, I have a surprise for you. Follow me.'

Hilde walked out of the kitchen and Maddie followed her to her office. The captain went to her desk and opened a drawer.

'I've written a letter to my superiors in the Fourteenth Support Battalion,' she said, holding out a folded note. 'They leave me to make these kind of decisions, so it should be a formality.'

'What kind of decisions?'

Hilde smiled. 'Decisions to do with my assistant. I've recommended you be promoted to corporal for all of your hard work. That's six months you've been here, longer by far than any of my previous assistants, and I think you deserve a little lift.'

She handed the note to Maddie and she read it.

'It'll mean a pay rise,' said the captain, 'and your disciplinary record will be wiped clean. I assume you'll want your pay, minus deductions, sent to your family as before?'

'How much extra is it?'

'Fifty sovereigns a month. Not a massive boost, I know, but it's your first steps. I can see you as a sergeant in another few years if you keep it up, though.'

A sergeant? Maddie wondered if Hilde had been drinking again. She seemed sober enough, so Maddie assumed that the captain had decided to appease her; offering her trinkets to stay and keep her mouth shut. Her natural reaction was to rebel; to tell the captain what she could do with her promotion, but she had harmed herself many times in the past by refusing to nod along with what she had been told to do. For the sake of Blackrose, Maddie buttoned up her pride.

'Thank you, Captain.'

'You seem a little surprised.'

'I honestly didn't think I'd ever get above the rank of private. My brother's going to be livid; he's served for three years without even a sniff of becoming a corporal. Can I tell them?'

Hilde grinned. 'Of course, as I said, it should be a formality, and you can start calling yourself a corporal right away.' She reached into the drawer again and withdrew a small fabric badge. 'Sew this onto your left shoulder.'

Maddie took it, her eyes scanning the corporal insignia.

'Congratulations,' said Hilde, holding out her hand.

She placed her hand in the captain's and they shook.

'We've had our fair share of bumps in the road, Maddie,' Hilde said, keeping a tight grip on her hand, 'but I think we're through the worst of it. Don't you agree?'

'Yes, Captain.'

'Excellent. Right, back to work. I'll get my overalls on and start loading the coal. I'll see you before you go, yes?'

'Yes.'

Hilde released her hand. Maddie stared at the badge for another moment, then slipped it onto her pocket. She smiled awkwardly, then turned and left the office.

A corporal; she was a corporal, she thought as she walked towards the entrance to the lair. Under normal circumstances, she would have been ecstatic, but instead she felt a little soiled, as if she had accepted a bribe to do something wrong. She would still flaunt it in Tom's face, though, and she imagined her parents' shock when they found out. Her disciplinary record being cleared was even bigger news, and shielded her a little from being sent to the Rats. Of course, what Hilde could grant, Hilde could remove, and she wondered when the captain would first deploy the threat of demotion to keep her in line.

And fifty extra sovereigns a month? Hardly great riches, but enough to start saving for her old age, if she made it that far.

She reached the gate and placed her hand on the smooth wood. She took a long breath, then opened the gate and stepped through. The reek hit her immediately, as it always did. The rank odour of uneaten meat from the many meals the dragon had ignored mixed with the usual animal smells, combining into a noxious taint that hung in the air. Both the black and the red gates were closed, as they had been for a month, as if nothing had happened. It was just the way Hilde wanted it.

Her heart broke a little more with every step she took towards the cavern where Blackrose was confined. The worst part had been the dragon's lack of resistance when the soldiers had come to re-attach her to the chains in the wall. She had just lain there, silent and unresponsive, and had allowed them to place her back into captivity without even a murmur of complaint, when she could have killed them all and flown away. Buckler had been angry; he was probably still angry, she thought, at the black dragon's change of heart, and she doubted he would ever listen to her again.

She opened the hatch in the black gate and stepped into the cavern.

'Hello,' she said. 'Good morning.'

Blackrose did not react. She was lying in the corner of the cavern where she always slept, her head on the ground and her eyes closed. Her wings still held some of the glossy sheen from when Maddie had rubbed gallons of ointment into them, but they were slowly deteriorating to their previous state with every day that passed in the cramped conditions of the cavern. The huge shackles were back on her rear right leg, and sores were visible where the steel met her black scales.

Maddie hauled away the previous day's feeding trough, trying to ignore the stench from the rotting meat and soured milk. At least it was winter, she thought; the flies of summer would have been unbearable. She dragged it over to the chute that led to a deep midden, and tipped the contents in, watching as the grey pieces of flesh slid down the dark opening.

'So, my brother visited today,' she said, as she filled a bucket with water. 'He asked me if I wanted to go and visit my family for a day or two, and the captain said it was alright, so I might go; I don't know. It would feel a bit weird, to be honest, being away from here, even just for a couple of days, but maybe I need a break. Hilde seems to think so.'

She poured the full bucket into the trough, washing away the clinging remnants of guts and blood, then dragged it away from the chute and towards the black gate. There was a tub of ointment sitting by the hatch and she picked it up.

'I'm going to put some of this on those sores,' she said as she walked up by the right flank of the dragon. 'We can't have your leg looking like that. Have you been scratching it? I don't remember seeing sores when you had the shackles on before.' She halted by the large limb and scooped out a handful of ointment from the tub. 'I hope this doesn't hurt,' she said as she began applying it to the sores. 'If it does, just let me know and I'll try to be more gentle. So, my folks are all doing fine. My little sister's a maniac, did I ever tell you? She's built her own artillery in the back yard of my parents' house, from spare parts, would you believe? You'd like her, I think. She's a bit like me, except more sarcastic, and she's very clever with her hands; she can fix just about anything. She's a pain in the ass, of course, and she can be a right cheeky toerag, but I guess I do actually miss her.' She stood back, her eyes scanning her work. 'There. Feel any better? That should help ease it a bit.'

She took the tub of ointment back to the hatch and set it on the ground. 'I'll mop next,' she said; 'see if we can get rid of that smell. You're probably used to it by now, but it makes my head hurt whenever I come in here.' She picked up the bucket and filled it with water again. 'Anyway, I've been thinking. It's all I've been doing, actually, since I can't talk to anyone about it, and you haven't spoken to me in a month.' She added some soap and dunked the mop into the bucket. 'So, Corthie,' she said; 'I've been trying to piece it all together, and I think I'm slowly getting there. The Quadrant thingie, that's important, right? You and Corthie needed it to get home. He was going to steal it, wasn't he, but something went wrong?'

She paused for a moment as she began to mop the cavern floor. What was she doing? The dragon hadn't even acknowledged her presence, let alone spoken to her. Still, talking was better than silence.

'It occurs to me,' she went on, 'that the Quadrant will still be in the City, somewhere. Maybe I could steal it for you? I know what you're thinking; if Corthie couldn't manage, then how would little old me be able to do it, but I can be pretty sneaky if I have to be. If you happened to know where it was, or who has it, then we can make a new plan. How about it?'

Blackrose remained silent and Maddie wondered if the dragon was asleep. Maybe she had gone into hibernation, like some animals did every winter, and Maddie's words hadn't even reached her.

'Everyone thinks that Corthie murdered Princess Khora,' she went on, persisting despite the sadness in her heart, 'but I know that's a load of donkey dung. He was trying to get the Quadrant, and they framed him for Khora's murder. That's the truth, I'm sure of it.'

'And what would you know of the truth?' growled a low voice.

Maddie jumped in fright, dropping the mop onto the floor. She turned. Blackrose's eyes were still closed. Had she imagined it?

'Did you just speak?'

One great eye began to open. 'I did. You are mistaken, girl, about many things.'

'Oh yeah? Like what?'

'Corthie, for one.'

'What do you mean?'

'He came here the day he was executed, do you remember?'

'Of course I do, I've thought about it a million times. I've gone over every word he said to me. He knew, or guessed, that he wasn't coming back.'

'I told him to kill Khora.'

'What?'

'He came to me, unsure of what he should do. He was worried that he wouldn't be able to go through with it, and I told him to kill Khora, so that nothing could interfere with our plan. Don't you see? This is all my fault. I sent him to his death, and my life is as good as over. I destroyed my own last hope.'

Maddie stared at her.

'Do you understand?' said Blackrose. 'There is nothing left for me but a slow death. I estimate that I can survive without food for a few months; my healing powers are strong, but that is the end that I have chosen, and there is nothing you or Hilde can do about it.'

'No. There's always hope. I can steal the Quadrant; just tell me where it is. I can do it; I'm your rider, and you told me your true name. I'm not giving up, Mela; I refuse to.' She paused, as tears came to her eyes. 'You're not going to die. I won't let you.'

'My dear Maddie, my mind is made up. There is only one thing more that I ask of you.'

'What?'

'I am frightened, girl. I don't fear death, but I do fear the slow path that leads there, and the pain and loss of dignity it will bring. It will be a difficult end, without honour, and I fear to go through it alone. Stay with me, girl, stay with me to the end. Every day I have listened to your voice as you have worked to clean up the mess of my life. It comforts me, girl; don't leave me; promise you won't leave me.'

Maddie rushed toward the dragon, and threw her arms round the creature's massive head, all thoughts of visiting her family abandoned amid her grief.

'I love you, Mela,' she said, as she closed her eyes. 'I'll never leave.'

CHAPTER 5

IN THE PITS

Tarstation, The Cold Sea – 2nd Monan 3419

The thick tar clung to his clothes and skin, seeping inside his gloves and boots as he waded in the pit. A wooden crane was dangling a hook overhead, and Corthie and the others attached the full barrel to it. An empty barrel was thrown down from the back of the nearby wagon as the full one was lifted clear, and the three prisoners in the pit began filling it, lowering the rim of the barrel under the level of the viscous tar so it could trickle in.

Achan spluttered as a gout of oil spattered over his face. The tar came up to their thighs, and the ground beneath was uneven. Occasionally, they would trip over the body of someone who had fallen in and drowned in the pit. Prisoners would go missing sometimes, but such was the impossibility of escape that everyone would nod when they heard the news, assuming that the tar had swallowed them up.

'Here,' said Yaizra, throwing a cloth to Achan.

Corthie held onto the barrel as Achan grabbed the cloth and rubbed his face. Yaizra had a skin of water strapped over her shoulders and she poured some into Achan's eyes as the man groaned. Corthie glanced at the wagon. It was the last of their shift, and they only had a few more barrels to go before they had to take the filled wagon back to the refinery. The sky was a dark grey, almost black towards iceward, despite it being early afternoon, and the cold wind froze everything it touched.

'That better?' said Yaizra. 'Can you see?'

'Get a move on,' cried one of the two guards by the wagon, their bodies and faces wrapped thickly against the cold.

'Come on in and give us a hand then,' Corthie said to them. 'That'll hurry things up.'

The guard snorted. Over the month he had been in Tarstation, Corthie's big mouth had got him in trouble more times than he could count, but the guards were starting to get used to him, and in recent days had been more likely to laugh or scowl than report him for another beating. Achan and Yaizra rejoined him by the barrel, and they hefted it up towards the hook. Achan's eyes were red and puffy, and his face was streaked with oil. He stumbled, his feet catching on the rough ground, and the heavy barrel slipped. Corthie tried to grab it, but his gloves were slick and the barrel fell, knocking Achan off his feet. He let out a yell, then disappeared under the tar; the barrel slowly sinking over the spot where he had been standing.

'Achan!' Yaizra cried, her eyes wide.

Corthie and the woman reached down with their arms into the thick mire. Corthie caught hold of the rim of the barrel and heaved it up out of the tar, his muscles straining. He lifted it clear and hung it from the hook.

'I feel him with my foot,' Yaizra yelled. 'Over here.'

Corthie waded over. He took a deep breath, then plunged his arms and head down into the tar, feeling the sucking weight and pressure around him. His long arms reached out and he felt with his fingers, touching rocks, and scattered boulders, then an arm. He inched his hand along until he found Achan's shoulder then hauled him up, Yaizra helping by grabbing onto him as he leaned over.

Corthie rose out of the tar, Achan held under one arm, dripping oil. Corthie felt a cloth smear across his face, then a splash of water over his eyes.

'Let go of him; I've got him,' said Yaizra.

Corthie opened his eyes and they stung in agony from the oil. He raised his hands to his face.

'Don't touch them,' Yaizra said, as she pulled Achan to the side of the pit. 'It'll only make 'em worse.'

The guards were staring, but neither of them were calling for more work as they watched Achan being dragged up onto the frozen ground next to the pit. Corthie followed Yaizra to the side of the pit, tar clinging to his hair. The woman was wiping Achan's face, then she leaned over him and breathed into his mouth while thumping his chest at the same time.

'What are you doing?' Corthie said, then he blinked as Achan spluttered back into life. 'Oh, that.'

The man vomited a black train of sick down his front as he gasped and panted on the icy ground.

Corthie glanced at Yaizra. 'You saved him. I thought he was finished.'

She smiled. 'You saved him too, Holdfast. Thank Malik for your weirdly long arms, eh?'

The two guards wandered over. 'The little weasel's alive, is he?'

Yaizra glared at them. 'He needs to see the camp doctor.'

'Yeah, right. How about you get back to work? You've got two barrels yet to fill.'

Corthie laughed. 'Quit being lazy and toss them down, then. We can't fill them if they're up on the wagon.'

The guards stared at him for a moment, then walked back to the wagon.

Yaizra glanced at him, a smirk on her lips. 'You tell 'em, Holdfast.'

'How is he?'

'He'll live.' She left Achan's side and rejoined Corthie in the middle of the tar pit. She was a strong-looking woman, and a few inches taller than Achan, but unlike him, she had left her thick coat on the wagon.

'You don't seem to mind the cold,' said Corthie.

'I'm from Icehaven. I was ten years old before I saw the sun for the first time.'

They stepped back as a barrel landed on the surface of the tar, splashing them with oil. They pushed it down, submerging the lip as it filled.

'There's no sun in Icehaven?'

'The Iceward Range is too high; it blocks it out. The entire town is in permanent shadow.'

Corthie grunted, and lifted the full barrel up as Yaizra guided it onto the crane's hook.

'Why would anyone build a town in such a stupid place?' he said as the crane arm was swung back over the wagon.

Yaizra squinted at him. 'And I thought you had some brains, Holdfast. It was built there because it's safe from the greenhides. It's cold and dark; just what they hate. If the rest of the City ever falls, Icehaven will be the last place standing, and we'll see who's stupid then.'

The last barrel splashed down in front of them.

Achan groaned from the side of the pit and sat up. His hair and face were plastered with tar, and he glanced around as if in a daze.

'Be more mindful next time, ya clumsy oaf,' Yaizra yelled at him as she and Corthie filled the last barrel.

They lifted it onto the hook, then waded back to the side of the pit. Corthie pulled himself up out of the tar and onto the icy, broken ground, then turned and helped Yaizra out. They each took an arm and lifted Achan to his feet, where he swayed and tottered.

'Stick him on the back of the wagon,' Yaizra said, as they carried Achan past the crane.

A prisoner was standing on the wagon's chassis, lowering the last barrel into position as the two guards watched. Corthie and Yaizra hoisted Achan up, and sat him on the back ledge, his feet dangling.

'Are we done?' said one of the guards. 'Let's go.'

The prisoner who was standing on the wagon dropped onto the driver's bench and pulled the reins. Ahead of the wagon, two large oxen began moving down the reinforced track that led between the tar pits to the refinery. The two guards climbed up to get a seat, while Corthie and

Yaizra trailed along behind on foot. Corthie glanced around, his eyes still stinging from the oil. All around them were dozens of pits similar to the one they had been in, and tracks snaked their way among them, linking the tar to the refinery. The glow from its flames was lightening the sky, and casting the vast icefields into shadows of deep-red. On his right lay the warmth and light of sunward; the direction he would need to take if he was going to make a run for it. Estimates of the width of the belt of ice ranged from fifty to five hundred miles, depending on whichever person he had asked; all that had united them was their belief that any prisoner who tried to cross it would die.

He glanced at Yaizra. She was new in the camp, and had been put into the same bunk room as Achan and Corthie, the prison not separating the men from the handful of women who had been sent to Tarstation. She had punched Corthie in the eye when he had said hello, and he had decided at that moment that he should try to make friends with her. Achan stuck close by him, benefitting from Corthie's protection, but he was the only friend Corthie had made in the camp. The other prisoners all seemed to loathe him or fear him, or a combination of both. In the twenty-six days since arriving in Tarstation, there had only been seven when Corthie had not been involved in some kind of fight; usually with the other prisoners, but there had been several run ins with the guards as well. His height and size made him a target.

Yaizra noticed him looking at her. 'Why you peering at me, Holdfast?'

'I'm wondering if I should take you with me when I escape.'

She laughed, a harsh sound that grated his ears. 'You're a funny big lump. Go on then, what's your plan? I could do with some entertainment.'

'I haven't got a plan. Personnel first; plan later.'

'Can you sail?'

'No.'

'Hmm. Can you fly?'

He laughed. 'Can you sail?'

'What, just because I'm from Icehaven, you automatically think I'm a seafarer, eh? Are you stereotyping me?'

'Are there boats in Icehaven?'

'Malik's crotch, you are clueless. It's the biggest port on the Cold Sea, bigger than Dalrig even. Don't they have schools in the land of the Blades?'

'Can I trust you to keep your mouth shut if I tell you something?'

'It depends. I'm grateful that you and Achan helped me when I first got here, but I'm a suspicious girl, and people have always got other motives. I've been wondering what yours is. You haven't told me what you got put in here for, and that makes me even more suspicious. You're bad at keeping secrets, I can tell. You hardly know me, and already you're bursting to tell me whatever it is; so, go on then. Tell me, and then you'll see if I can be trusted.'

'My only motive is to escape,' he said, 'and I'm looking for a small group that can work together. You, me and Achan.'

'That's not much of a secret. Everybody dreams of escaping this dump.'

'The secret is that I'm not a Blade.'

'Ooh. That's a bit more interesting.'

'When did you leave Icehaven?'

'Middle of Marcalis; about twenty days ago.'

'Did you hear about Duke Marcus's takeover?'

'Of course. I mean, I was in prison at the time, but I heard.' She glanced up. 'Why's the wagon stopped?'

Corthie looked up. Ten yards ahead of them on the icy track, the wagon had come to a halt. The sound of voices drifted over as they approached. Corthie reached the back of the wagon, and looked ahead. Blocking the track was a group of nine prisoners, their faces covered in scarves, and their hands grasping a range of weapons, from iron bars to pickaxes and shovels.

'Malik's ass,' whispered Yaizra. 'What do they want?'

'Me, probably.'

'You? I knew you'd made a couple of enemies, but this looks planned.'

'Get out of here.'

'Why?'

'Because those boys are going to put me in the hospital. I'll take out a few of them, don't worry about that, but there's no point in you getting beaten up as well.'

A voice rose up from the men on the track. 'We only want Corthie Holdfast. The rest of you should walk away.'

The two guards got up from the driver's bench, along with the prisoner who had been holding the reins. Corthie watched as the guards and the prisoner ran down the track, then he climbed up onto the wagon, stepping over Achan on the back ledge.

'You after me, boys?'

One of the group, a bear of a man, stepped forwards, hefting an iron bar. 'You need to pay for what you did. It's not right that you got away with it.'

'And what is it that you think I'm guilty of?'

'We're all Sanders,' the man said; 'you murdered our Princess.'

'I didn't murder Khora, Kano did. I know you won't believe me, but it's the truth. I was set up to take the blame. So, you can come at me, if you want. You know I'm handy in a fight, and you know I won't be the only one who'll end up in a hospital bed tonight.'

The bear man shook his head. 'You're not going to the hospital, lad. We're going to drop you to the bottom of a tar pit when we've finished with you.'

Corthie nodded. 'I wondered when it would come to this.' He powered his battle-vision, allowing it to surge through his body. 'Any time you're ready, boys.'

The bear man raised his hand, brandishing the iron bar. There was a loud clack, and the bear man stumbled, his eyes rolling up into his head, then he collapsed to the ground. The other men glanced around, but the land surrounding them was dark and quiet. There was another clack, and Corthie caught what had caused it; a stone flew through the air, and smacked into the forehead of another Sander, felling him with a grunt.

Corthie heaved a barrel up from the bed of the wagon and launched it through the air at the group of men. It crashed into them, knocking over three men and spilling its contents onto the rest. Corthie leapt from the driver's bench. He swept up the iron bar and charged into the group, swinging. With oil covering their faces, they stood no chance against his battle-vision, and in less than a minute every one of them was lying on the frozen ground.

He glanced into the deep shadows. 'You can come out.'

Yaizra walked towards him, a leather sling held in her right hand. She glanced at the bodies littering the ground and whistled.

'Thanks,' he said. 'Perfect timing.'

She shrugged. 'I was thinking about letting them beat you up, but when he said they were going to end you, well, I thought that seemed a little unfair.' She glanced at him. 'You're quick, ya big lump, quicker than you ought to be.'

'Do you believe me about Khora?'

'I don't care either way. Khora killed her own twin sister, Princess Niomi of Icehaven, and set fire to the palace, burning countless others to death. It wouldn't bother me if you had murdered her. You're probably a hero in Icehaven.'

'But I didn't do it.'

Yaizra shrugged.

There was a groan from the back of the wagon, and Achan appeared. He jumped down, clutching his head and emitting a low moan of pain. 'My head. I think I swallowed a gallon of oil.'

Yaizra snorted. 'If you had, you'd be dead, ya stupid Hammer.'

Achan walked round the side of the wagon, then stopped when he saw the bodies. 'Did I miss something?'

'No,' said Corthie, 'you're just in time.'

'For what?'

'For helping us clear this lot out of the way so we can get the wagon back to the refinery.'

Achan spat a lump of tar from his mouth. 'I should have stayed lying down.'

———

They found their two guards waiting outside the refinery gates after they had dropped off the last barrels of their shift.

'Evening, lads,' said Corthie.

They stared at the three prisoners as they approached.

'You might want to send someone back along the track,' Achan said. 'There appears to be a group of Sanders sleeping by the side of a tar pit. Lazy buggers.'

The two guards glanced at each other, and one ran off in the direction of the guard tower.

'Back to the camp,' said the other; 'come on.' He gestured to the prisoners to start walking, and they went up the path that ran along one side of the enormous refinery building. 'It's true what they say, then?'

'What?' said Corthie.

'What they've been saying about you; a Champion of the Bulwark?'

Corthie laughed. 'Is that why you left us back at the wagon, because you knew we could take care of ourselves?'

The guard glanced away, his eyes wide.

'No harm done,' said Corthie. 'I'd have done the same thing. No, now that I come to think of it, I wouldn't have, but there you go.'

'There were over a dozen of them.'

'There were nine,' said Yaizra.

'Yeah, alright, nine.' The guard shook his head. 'I'm not paid enough for this.'

Corthie glanced at him. 'You could always leave.'

'I can't; I'm paying off a debt.'

'So you're trapped here like the rest of us?'

Achan frowned. 'Corthie, why are you speaking to this... guard? He was one of those that beat you up ten days ago, when you were chained up outside in the snow. I saw him; he was there.'

The guard paled. 'I... I didn't have a choice, I...'

Corthie shrugged. 'He was just doing his job.'

'He's Gloamer trash,' said Yaizra, 'like most of the guards here.'

'Hold on,' said Corthie; 'that doesn't make any sense. I was told that the Icewarders and the Gloamers were basically the same; a bit like the Rosers and the Sanders. Is that not true?'

'It is,' said Achan.

'It's not,' said Yaizra, glowering at him. 'We're not the same; the Gloamers think they're so superior to us.'

'But they founded Icehaven.'

'So? That was nearly two thousand years ago, Achan, ya Hammer fool.'

'What about the folk of the Bulwark?' said Corthie. 'Where did they come from?'

'Descendants of Reapers and Evaders, mostly,' said Achan; 'all the excess population of peasants that had built up behind the Middle Walls, where the Circuit is now. They were all moved in with promises of freedom and prosperity, and then the Scythes and the Hammers were betrayed, and enslaved.'

Yaizra and the guard both looked away.

'See?' Achan said to Corthie. 'None of them like to talk about it. You could walk up to someone in Auldan and ask them how many tribes there are. Most would say six, and only a handful would even remember that the Bulwark exists.'

'That's not true any more,' said the guard. 'The Blades are all over Auldan now, thousands of them.'

Achan nodded. 'That almost makes me smile. At least the pampered inhabitants of Medio and Auldan will know about us.'

'You have no clue,' said Yaizra. 'Pampered? There's plenty of poverty in Medio; and no shortage of suffering. I admit that, until I met you, I had no idea how the Hammers lived, but don't imagine for a minute that things are all rosy in the rest of the City.'

They passed through a gate and entered the camp where the prisoners lived. The guard quietened as the track grew busier, and Corthie glanced around making eye contact with a few prisoners he had previously fought. A few nodded, their threshold for mutual respect having been reached, while others glared with hatred and a desire for revenge, and Corthie noted their faces for later. Their guard took them to the large building where they got cleaned up after every shift. They entered a changing room, and dumped their tar-coated clothing into large baskets, then Yaizra washed first while Corthie and Achan minded the door. When she had finished, they went in and stood under the freezing cold showers for ten minutes, scrubbing soap into their hair and skin. Achan was sick again, the black lumps in his vomit clogging the drainage hole. Despite scrubbing himself raw, Corthie's skin was stained in places from contact with the oil and tar, and he could still smell it on him after his ten minutes were over.

They grabbed dry clothes from the laundry station and dressed before venturing back outside into the freezing wind. They were greeted by stares as they emerged from the wash house into the shadows of the camp yard.

'Looks like they've heard about the Sanders,' said Achan.

'Yeah,' said Yaizra; 'ever wonder if we picked the wrong guy to befriend?'

There was a whoosh and a gust of flame belched upwards from the refinery, and for a moment the camp seemed transformed, lit up in a vibrant red, with the frost and ice gleaming like blood. The flaring dimmed and returned to normal, and Corthie set out across the yard, his two companions by his side. Prisoners and guards stared as they passed, their expressions hostile or wary.

Corthie halted in the middle of the yard, and slowly turned as he gazed out at the faces staring at him. He lifted his palms to show he was unarmed.

'Those nine Sanders attacked me,' he said; the yard silent against the background roar and noise coming from the refinery. 'I only did what any of you would have done to defend yourselves. They planned to drown me in a tar pit, but I left them all alive; beaten, but alive. I came to the City to kill greenhides, not people, but my patience is wearing thin, and I can't promise I'll be as generous again. If anyone has a problem with that, well, here I am.' He glanced around, making eye contact with every prisoner and guard brave enough not to look away.

'Clear the yard!' yelled an officer as guards streamed out from the barracks. They piled into the central space, their crossbows loaded and levelled at the crowd of prisoners.

The groups began to disperse, and Corthie turned towards the low building where he and his two friends slept.

'Not you, Holdfast; remain where you are.'

Corthie halted, and turned to the officer, keeping his arms by his sides.

'What do you think you're doing?' cried the officer in his face. 'Are you trying to start a riot?'

'No.'

The officer swung his baton and struck Corthie across the chin. 'That's "no, sir", boy.'

Corthie didn't react.

'You keep this up, boy, and it's only going to end one way.'

'Are you unhappy with my work rate, sir?'

The officer frowned. 'You think you're something special, but to me you're just another criminal piece of trash.'

'May I go to my room, sir?'

The officer glanced around the yard. The guards had cleared it of prisoners, and were patrolling the space by the accommodation blocks. He nodded, and Corthie turned and walked away.

Achan and Yaizra were waiting for him by the door of their block. He nodded to them and they went inside. They picked up a tray each from the food station and took them to their room. The other prisoners had been moved to other blocks, leaving them to share the three bunk beds between them. As soon as they were inside, Corthie shoved one of the heavy beds in front of the door, then they sat down to eat.

'This is not how I imagined my life would go,' Yaizra said, dunking a hard crust of bread into the gravy at the bottom of her bowl.

'No?' said Achan. 'You were a thief, weren't you? What exactly were you expecting?'

She grinned. 'Not to get caught. But that's not what I meant. I've been in prisons before, and have managed to keep my head down enough to survive. Here, I feel like I've painted a huge target on my back.' She glanced at Corthie. 'The big lump's going to get us killed.'

He smiled. 'The door's that way. I'll beat you both up a little bit if it helps, then you can join the rest of them.'

'Or how about you keep your mouth shut for a while, and stop antagonising folk? We can't walk ten yards in this place without some asshole niggling us, and you react to it, every time.'

'Come on,' said Achan; 'he's saved us from getting our heads kicked in on many occasions.'

'Yeah, but maybe it would've been better to have taken the beatings and then moved on. I have no desire to die in this Malik-forsaken dump. I have a five year sentence, and I feel like I'll be lucky to last six months.'

'You won't be here for six months,' said Corthie. 'Maybe another one, give or take.'

Yaizra laughed, the harsh noise filling the room. 'Because we're going to escape, yeah?'

'I'm running out of choices. If the prisoners have learned who I am, then it's only a matter of time before that news makes its way back to the City, and Marcus sends soldiers to kill me.' He smiled at her. 'Aye, we're going to escape.'

'Woah, Holdfast. Steady. Let's not get ahead of ourselves.'

Corthie glanced at Achan. 'What about you?'

'I have seventeen years left,' he said; 'a death sentence, in other words. If there's even the tiniest chance of getting out of here, I'm taking it.'

Yaizra shook her head at them. 'But none of us can sail a boat; are you expecting to swim to the City?'

'There's only one way,' said Corthie; 'we cross the icefields. We head sunward, and keep going until we reach the straits.'

'The western bank of the straits is infested with greenhides. Even if, and it's a massive if, we make it through the ice, we'll be exhausted by the time we reach sunlight again, and the greenhides will rip us to shreds.'

'I get it,' said Corthie. 'It's dangerous, but I have no alternative except to wait here for a shipload of Blades to arrive. You can stay here if you want to.'

'You stupid goat,' she said. 'What do you think will happen to me if you leave? You know how women are treated in this place; I wouldn't last a day. Wait, is that why you chose me, because I'm a woman? You think you're some kind of hero, rescuing me from the clutches of the evil guards and prisoners?'

Corthie paused for a moment. Among other reasons, he realised that she might have stumbled upon a part of the truth. He didn't think it had been a conscious decision, but he had watched how some of the other prisoners had been looking at Yaizra, and he had feared what would happen to her.

'You're tough,' he said, 'and smart, and you know how to use a sling.'

She glared at him. 'You didn't answer the question. And look at Achan. No offence to the little guy, but he's got "victim" written all over his face. Are you telling me that's it's a mere coincidence that the two folk you've chosen are the ones you think can't look after themselves?'

'It's about a mixture of skills,' he said. 'I can fight, and I'll keep the greenhides off us; that's my job. I'm a soldier, trained to kill in a hundred different ways, but I know nothing about tons of other stuff; how to hunt, fish, or what's good to eat. I figured a thief and a walking encyclopaedia would be handy.'

She glanced at him, suspicion lighting her eyes, and he wondered if she believed him. What he had said was true, but she had also been right; he felt a need to protect them, he couldn't help himself. He had promised his sister that he would use his powers to defend those weaker than him, and he didn't care if that made him appear foolish or misguided.

'Well?' he said. 'Are you in?'

Yaizra hung her head for a moment. 'Cross the icefields? You're insane.'

'Is that a "yes"?'

'Malik's ass, fine.'

He smiled. 'Then we have the personnel; and now it's time for the plan.'

CHAPTER 6
GREYLIN PALACE

Dalrig, Auldan, The City – 4th Monan 3419
   Bekha glanced up from the tavern table. 'Why does everyone here look so miserable?'

Aila shrugged. 'That's Gloamers for you. They've always been dour; probably comes from being ruled by Prince Montieth. We'll just have to put up with it; it's the price we pay for the relative safety of being in Dalrig. The prince refuses to allow any "foreign" troops to enter his territory, and not even Marcus is stupid enough to cross Montieth.'

A large gull landed by the table and began rooting round for food.

'Get away,' said Bekha, waving a hand at the bird; 'go on; shoo.'

'Quiet, Bekha. Remember, your Evader accent gives you away here. If I'm meant to be a Dalrigian merchant, then I would've hardly married one of your sort.'

Bekha rolled her eyes. 'Sorry, dearest husband; I forgot my place for a moment.'

'I like your hair that colour, it suits you.'

'No, it doesn't,' said Bekha; 'it's a mess. I'm cutting it short and letting my brown hair grow back in as soon as we're out of here.'

A waiter came over and dumped their food and drink onto their table without a word.

'So rude,' muttered Bekha. 'If someone in the Circuit did that they'd get a slap across the face.'

Aila glanced up at the clear pink sky. It was a beautiful morning, cold but sunny, and the outside tables of the tavern were getting busier, with Dalrigians stopping off for breakfast. The town's harbour was close by, and she could smell the scent of the Cold Sea. A few hundred yards away, the tall battlements of Greylin Palace were visible, rising above the streets and houses of the town like a fortress.

Bekha followed her glance. 'What does the prince do in there?'

'That's the big question,' she said. 'I don't think Montieth's left Greylin in a thousand years; I've certainly never met him.'

'What powers does he have?'

'I'm not completely sure, but I think he has the same range as the God-Queen.'

'You mean he could just point his finger at me and I would die?'

'Yeah, though I'd die too. In the Civil War I watched Prince Michael use his powers on one of Princess Yendra's daughters; it wasn't pretty. I think that's why Montieth's been left alone for so long; none of the other God-Children or demigods want their skin to blister or their blood to bubble and turn black.'

Bekha put down her fork and grimaced. 'I'm not sure I'm hungry any more.'

Aila laughed. 'In all the years I've known you, you've never been squeamish.'

'I guess I feel a bit strange here, in Dalrig,' Bekha said, her eyes narrow as she watched the locals go by. 'It's a weird place, filled with miserable, odd people, who, if they found you bleeding by the side of the road, would rob you rather than help you. The Roser militia in the Circuit were hated the most, but the Dalrigian soldiers were just as bad. I hope we're not here for long.'

'But where else can we go? It was impossible to stay in the Circuit any longer, and it was just as dangerous for us in Outer Pella. This is it, Bekha, there's nowhere else to go, unless we want to jump on a boat and sail to the ice lands. Vana's been after us like a hound this last month, and I'll bet she's already told Marcus that we're in Dalrig.'

Bekha's eyes narrowed. 'All the more reason we should leave.'

'I told you, Montieth won't allow soldiers from Tara or the Bulwark into Gloamer territory. If Marcus tries, there will be a civil war, and Montieth has two daughters who are supposed to share his powers. It would be carnage. Our biggest problem is if Marcus asks for us to be arrested or thrown out. Montieth is always careful to make it appear that his lands are part of the City; he pays his taxes, sends troops to Pella or the Circuit whenever asked, and makes sure Auldan is supplied with fish and oil and everything else they need from the Cold Sea.'

Bekha frowned. 'I hate to spoil the party, Aila, but what about those two guys?' She nodded at a table outside a tavern on the other side of the street. 'They've been following us all morning.'

Aila glanced over. The two men were of large build, and looked away as soon as Aila turned her head. 'Bollocks,' she muttered. 'Alright, so unless they're Dalrigian agents, Marcus might be a bit braver than I thought.'

'It's me, isn't it?' said Bekha. 'Even with the new hairstyle, it's me they recognise. You should have left me in Outer Pella.'

'It's too late for that. Your image has been posted up next to mine all over Auldan and Medio. "Accomplice to the renegade Lady Aila of Pella." You're famous.'

'Wanted throughout the City. My mother would be so proud.'

Aila finished her breakfast and pushed the empty dish to the side. She sniffed the mug of warm, malted milk, but decided to stay clear of it. She glanced back at the two men for a moment. 'Did they see where we stayed last night?'

'Yes,' said Bekha; 'they were waiting outside the hostelry when we left this morning.'

'We might as well say goodbye to our things, because I don't think we can go back there again.'

'But I paid for three nights.'

'Tough. If we go back, we'll be caught. We'll have to lose those two thugs, somehow.'

'And go where?'

She glanced at the dark, forbidding battlements of Greylin Palace. 'I think I have an idea.'

The houses of Dalrig were made of a dark grey granite, mined from quarries that had long been exhausted. The town seemed not to have changed in a very long time, and the people dressed in a style even more conservative than they did in Tara, with thick woollen coats buttoned from throat to ankle. Every woman seemed to have their hair in the same, severe bun, and the men all had oiled moustaches or trimmed beards. Compared to the free and easy ways of the Evaders, it was like a different world. Bekha's newly-dyed blonde locks stuck out, and she earned a few stares as they walked along a busy street.

'I knew this hair was a mistake,' she muttered after an old woman scowled at her.

'It seemed like a good idea in Outer Pella.'

'It was; just not so much here. It's alright for you, husband; you look just like the others; it's me they're all gawking at.'

'They're just jealous of my beautiful wife.'

They turned down a road to avoid the fish market, from where a strong smell was emanating. They passed some stalls selling silver jewellery and expensive lace and stopped to take a look.

'Are they still there?' said Aila under her breath.

'Yes, pretending to look at some fish.'

Aila picked up a shawl from the selection of clothes on the stall and handed over a few coins to the woman behind the table. She snuck it into her pocket, and they walked on. Aila waited until the street got busier, then glanced at Bekha.

'I'm going to make a distraction; when I do, put the shawl over your hair and I'll meet you by the corner of the road. I'll look a lot younger and have a wart on my nose.'

She passed the shawl to Bekha, then bent down as if to tie the laces on her boots.

You see me as a drunken old man.

She got to her feet, then fell into the side of a market stall, sending silver earrings and necklaces flying through the air. The woman behind the counter cried out as people started to grab at the fallen jewellery. Aila staggered off before anyone could accost her, then she ran through the crowded street, leaving a swarm of Dalrigians blocking the way behind her. She dived into a shop.

You see me as a young Dalrigian peasant man with a wart on his nose.

'Oops,' she said as the shopkeeper stared. 'Wrong shop, sorry.'

She strode back out onto the street and carried on, walking casually as she glanced at the wares for sale on the other stalls. Bekha joined her without a word as they turned left at the street corner, her hair hidden behind the black shawl.

'I preferred my earlier husband,' she muttered; 'this is a real step down for me.'

They picked up their pace as soon as they cleared the corner, and hurried down the street, taking another right at the next crossroads. Ahead of them, the enormous, dark bulk of Greylin Palace stood. It had been built right on the water's edge, next to the small bay where the harbour of Dalrig stretched. It had once been pink from the granite used in its construction, but hundreds of years had seen it slowly turn darker until it was almost pitch black. There were no windows visible from the exterior, and the battlements towered over every other building in the town.

'Are you sure this is the only way?' said Bekha. 'Just looking at it makes me feel queasy.'

'It's a gamble; I'm not going to lie. We're out of options, Bekha.'

'Will he even know who you are?'

'Good old Uncle Montieth? Who knows?'

'Can you make yourself look like him?'

'Eh, no. I need to be able to imagine my appearance before I get others to see me that way, and I have no idea what he looks like.' She glanced back down the street, but saw no sign of their pursuers. A deep, dry moat separated the palace from the rest of the buildings on its landward side, and they walked round towards the only bridge that crossed it, which led to a set of closed black gates. There were no guards by the bridge or the entrance, and the street opposite the gates was deserted. Aila gazed at the dark building. Arches and pillars engraved with twisting leaves and plants had been traced into the solid granite front of the palace, but without any windows the effect made it appear more sinister. They reached the bridge.

'I don't like this,' said Bekha. 'Who was the last of your cousins to visit?'

'I'm not aware that any have ever visited.'

Aila stepped onto the bridge, half-expecting some sort of alarm to be triggered, but nothing happened. She shrugged and walked up to the door. There was no bell or knocker that she could see, so she raised her knuckles and rapped on the solid wooden gate as hard as she could.

'Don't you think you'd better change your appearance?' said Bekha, joining her by the set of double doors. 'If anyone's watching, they'll think a peasant boy is trying to get in.'

Aila dropped her powers. 'Good thinking, though I don't know if they'd recognise me, either.'

She knocked again.

'This can't be the only way in,' said Bekha as she frowned. She glanced up and down the street, then her eyes widened. 'Aila, they're coming.'

Aila looked to her right, and saw the two men who had been tailing them. They had turned the corner of the palace and were hurrying up its flank towards them.

She knocked louder, thumping the door. Bekha unbuttoned her long coat, revealing a sword strapped to her belt.

Aila went to knock again, but before her fist could touch the door it slid open a foot.

'Yes?' said an old man.

'I want to speak to Prince Montieth, please,' Aila said, hearing the boots of the men running up the street.

The old man frowned. 'No.'

'Wait!' she cried as the door began to close. 'I'm his niece, Lady Aila. His sister, Princess Khora, gave me a message for the prince before she died.'

'And the fact that two men are chasing you is a coincidence?'

Aila leaned closer to the old man, her eyes narrow. 'They're Blade agents, sent into Dalrig by Marcus.'

The old man swung open the door. Behind him stood at least a dozen hulking warriors, all covered from head to foot in thick plates of steel armour; each wielding a mace almost as tall as Aila was. Behind her, she heard the two agents approach and she turned. The two men had halted at the edge of the bridge, their gaze on Aila and the warriors.

The old man stepped out from the entrance. 'What do you want here?'

One of the men pointed at Aila and Bekha. 'Those two are wanted criminals.'

'Wanted by whom?'

'Prince Marcus. If you work for Prince Montieth, it would be wise of you to go back inside and close the door.'

The old man squinted at them. 'Surely you mean Duke Marcus?'

'What?'

'You said "prince"; surely you mean "duke", for Marcus is a demigod, not one of the God-Children. How is it that he has usurped this title?'

'It was bestowed by the God-Queen herself, old man. Now, get out of the way.'

'Are you Blades?'

The two men glanced at each other.

The old man lifted his finger and the two agents crumpled to the ground, their eyes open but lifeless. Bekha gasped as Aila stared at the old man. He gestured to one of his warriors, who strode out over the bridge and picked up the two Blades, an ankle gripped in each hand.

'Can't have them littering the road like that,' the old man said. 'Blades in Dalrig?' He glanced at Aila. 'My niece, eh? Well, I suppose you'd better come inside.'

The old man escorted Aila and Bekha to a large room and sat them next to a fire roaring in a hearth. He sat across from them and pulled a cord that set off a bell somewhere in the depths of the building.

The old man picked up a poker and began prodding at the fire, as Aila and Bekha sat on a couch watching in silence. Without windows, the room felt smaller than it was, and the heat from the huge fireplace was making Aila perspire under her winter clothes. She took off her long coat and folded it across her knees.

'Staying, are you?' said the old man, turning to her.

Aila bit her lip. 'Eh... Should we have introductions? I'm Aila, and this is my friend Bekha.'

He frowned at the Evader woman. 'Is she one of Isra's brats as well? I don't remember her.'

'She's a mortal, uncle. Can I call you "uncle"?'

'A mortal? Is she a gift?'

'A what?'

He looked at her like she was stupid. 'Did you bring her as a gift for me?'

'No, she's my friend.'

'A mortal?'

'I think maybe we've already established that, uncle?'

'What did my sister have to say?'

Aila frowned.

'You said that Khora had a message for me; what was it?'

Aila paused to think. She had said that when she had thought the old man was a servant, not one of the most powerful beings in the City. 'There were a few things...'

The door swung open and a young woman walked in, dressed in

rich robes, and wearing a deep frown on her lips. She stared at Aila and Bekha. 'Who are you? What do you want?' Before Aila or Bekha could respond, the woman turned to the old man. 'Father, I leave you alone for ten minutes and you open the front gates?'

Montieth shrugged. 'They knocked.'

'And you let them in?'

'They're family, well, one of them is. The blonde girl's a mortal.'

The woman gave Bekha a look of utter contempt, then glanced at Aila. 'A cousin?'

Montieth nodded.

'Hmm. She'll either be Vana, looking for Aila, or Aila herself.'

'Very good, daughter; she is the second of those.'

The woman walked forward, staring at Aila. 'She should leave immediately. She is wanted by the authorities in Tara. Now is not the time to be stoking trouble with the God-Queen.'

'Let me handle my mother,' Montieth said. 'I haven't yet decided what to do with these delightful young ladies. There were two Blades chasing them.'

The woman looked enraged. 'Here, in Dalrig? Blades? Do we have proof?'

'Their bodies are lying in the guardroom by the gates. I thought you might want to take a look at them.'

'You killed them? Good. I shall send their heads back to Marcus as a present.'

'No,' said Montieth; 'I think it would be better if they disappeared.'

'Excuse me,' said Aila, her eyes on the young woman. 'Who are you?'

'This is my elder daughter,' Montieth said. 'Amber.'

Aila stood. 'Cousin Amber; it's nice to meet you at last.'

Amber glanced at her. 'There's no sanctuary for you here, Aila, if that's why you came. Dalrig cannot afford a serious rupture with Tara, despite Marcus's provocation.'

'But if the two Blades disappear,' said Montieth, 'then no one will know they are here.'

His daughter frowned. 'Perhaps we should speak alone for a moment, father.'

'I'd only just got settled by the fire, but I suppose you're right.' He got to his feet, then followed Amber out of the room.

Bekha turned to Aila as the demigod sat back down. 'I agree with Amber; we should leave.'

'And go where?'

'Anywhere but this place. Where is everyone? And that old guy's the prince? Why's he not young like you?'

'I don't know. Have you, umm, heard of salve?'

'The stuff the demigods use to look young?'

'Yeah. Well, I always thought the hills behind Dalrig had their own source of salve; not as big as the deposits in Ooste or Tara, but enough to have kept him looking young if he wanted to. Amber certainly uses it; she looks twenty-one, and she must be... I don't know, but a lot older than me if she's his elder daughter.'

'You don't look much younger than me, and I'm thirty. When did you last use it?'

Aila shrugged. 'A hundred years ago, maybe? Since then I guess I've aged a little bit, maybe a year or two? But I've only ever been given the tiniest amounts; a little sniff now and again. Montieth could bathe in it if he wished.'

'And he thought I was a gift; what does that mean?'

Aila sighed. 'I guess they don't think very highly of mortals.'

'And what are they talking about now?'

'I think Amber wants us to leave and Montieth wants us to stay.'

Bekha shook her head. 'Something else is going on; something's not right about this place.'

Aila glanced around the room. The paintings on the walls were so old that the smoke from the fire had completely blackened them, while the carpet was threadbare and bald in patches. Dust clung to the edges of the lamps and thick cobwebs sat in the corners of the ceilings.

Amber strode back into the room. 'Come with me.'

'Are you throwing us out?' said Aila.

'No, you can stay.'

They got to their feet and followed Amber from the room. The hallway was dark and badly-lit, and Amber led them towards a large staircase.

Aila caught up to Amber on the steps. 'About what your father said; it's not true. Vana will know that I'm here.'

'I know that,' said Amber. 'My father sometimes forgets the powers of his various nephews and nieces; for example, he has no idea that you can change your appearance at will. Vana's locating skills were one of the main reasons I had for not allowing you to stay, but my father is adamant. He thinks it's time we played a little game with the God-Queen and Marcus; see how much they really want you. After he explained it to me I tended to agree; by sending Blades into Dalrig, Marcus perhaps needs to be taught a lesson. Holding you here against their will gives us leverage.'

Aila stopped on the stairs. 'Holding us here? You can't hold us here.'

Amber laughed as she kept walking. 'You're free to attempt to escape any time you like, but you won't succeed. The guards have been instructed not to let you leave, and your powers won't work on them.'

Bekha and Aila turned, and saw a squad of armoured soldiers at the bottom of the stairs, their heads fully enclosed by steel helmets. Aila glanced up at Amber. 'Where are you taking us?'

'Your room, of course. You'll have servants, food, whatever you need; you are a demigod after all. And, there's no lock on the door. You're free to wander the palace, only don't interfere with my father's work; he can get awfully upset, and you don't want that, believe me.' She paused at the top of the stairs. 'Look, I can show you to your room, but I'm in a hurry, and if you're just going to stand there staring at me, I have better things to do.'

Aila glanced at Bekha, then back at the soldiers.

You see me as Prince Montieth.

'Get out of the way!' she cried to the soldiers, but none of them moved.

Amber laughed. 'It's a very good trick, you look just like him; but as I said, our guards are unaffected by your powers. I'm going to your room now; follow if you like.'

'What do we do?' said Bekha.

'I guess we have to play along, for now.'

They turned, and went up the stairs.

Their room was small, and looked like it hadn't been used in years. Two beds sat on opposite walls, with no windows and very little in the way of furnishings. A large fireplace dominated the space between the beds, and a servant came and lit it after Amber had left. The servant didn't speak to them, and kept his gaze averted at all times. Aila asked him for food and drink, and he gave an almost imperceptible nod and walked from the room.

Bekha paced up and down over the carpet. 'We should never have come here; this was a mistake. That old goat's going to sell us to Marcus, he's just holding out for a decent price.'

Aila reclined on her bed, sinking into the deep mattress. 'Relax. We just need to think it through. We're not in any immediate danger. They don't want to harm us; they just want to stop us from leaving.'

'How can you be so calm? We're prisoners. Those soldiers are massive and did you see that one pick up two Blades at the same time; and those lads weren't small.'

'I spent over two centuries under house arrest, remember? I know what this feels like, and I have no intention of staying here longer than we have to. But right at this moment, we don't have to worry about Blades catching us.'

The door burst open and a young woman, who looked a little like Amber, ran into the room. She stared at Bekha, then turned to gaze at Aila.

She raised a finger and pointed. 'It's you, isn't it?'

'It's me, what?' said Aila.

'You're my cousin. I have the same powers as my sister and father and I can tell the difference between a mortal and a demigod by sensing their life force.' She stuck her hand out. 'I'm Jade.'

Aila stood. 'Amber's sister?'

'Yes. I'm nine hundred and eight years old. How old are you?'

Aila shook Jade's hand. 'I'm, uh, seven hundred and sixty-seven.'

'Wow, you're so young; still under eight hundred? I'm glad I'm older than you; Amber's nearly five centuries my elder, and she's always reminding me about it. She says that's why she runs Dalrig, because she's older.'

Aila frowned. 'Amber rules Dalrig?'

'Oh yes, you didn't think it was my father, did you? He doesn't care about any of that; he leaves it all to us, but Amber gives me the dull jobs.' She smiled. 'This is nice, talking to an actual relative; you're the first one I've ever met. And I like your mortal too; is she a pet? Only joking, Amber said you called her a "friend", so, fine.'

Aila pulled her hand away and sat back onto the bed. Jade smiled again and joined her, sitting cross-legged on the covers.

'Have you ever left Dalrig, Jade?' said Aila.

Her cousin laughed. 'I've never left this palace, not since the day I was born.'

'You've never seen the sun?'

'Don't be silly, I have a beautiful garden on the roof that father let me build. I can see the whole town from the railings. You should see it; it's wonderful up there. I have apple and pear trees, and I grow cabbage and onions.' She stared at Aila. 'There was one thing I wanted to ask you, cousin, something I know my father is also very interested in. I read all of the news sheets about what's going on, and they said that you were at Cuidrach Palace when Auntie Khora was murdered. Did you see the champion?'

Aila started. Her mind had been so occupied since arriving in Dalrig that she hadn't thought about Corthie in a few hours, possibly the longest time since he had died. She lowered her eyes. 'Yes.'

'Did he really have battle-vision?'

'Yes, he did.'

'You saw him fight with your own eyes?'

'Yeah.'

Jade shook her head. 'And he was definitely a mortal?'

'He was, Jade, yes. Definitely.'

'He was from another world, did you know that, cousin? The champions are brought here from somewhere else; do you realise what this means?'

Aila shook her head.

Jade leapt to her feet and pointed to the ceiling, her eyes ablaze. 'Somewhere out there is a world where mortals have the powers of gods; and there's another world that has dragons, for where else would Buckler come from? We are not alone, cousin, though this City feels like a prison, it's not; it's just one place among many.' She sat back down and put an arm around Aila's shoulder. 'We shall live forever, cousin; one day we shall see all of those other worlds.'

Aila tried to draw away, but her cousin's grip was firm, and she could feel Jade's power tingle through her fingertips.

'I'm so glad you're staying; someone new to talk to at last.' Jade grinned. 'My father works on many projects; did you know he can change how old he looks from will alone? One day he looks eighteen, the next ninety, and that was the result of long experiments into the properties of salve. But he likes his privacy, so stay away from him when he's working.' Her grin disappeared and she stared into Aila's eyes. 'You understand, yes? Stay away. But don't worry, Amber told me to look after you while you're here, so you're in good hands.'

Jade hugged Aila again, then got up. She cast a look of disdain at Bekha, and left the room.

Bekha glanced at Aila, her eyes wide. 'We're screwed.'

CHAPTER 7
THE DRESS

Tara, Auldan, The City – 2nd Darian 3419

'Good morning, ma'am,' said Talleta as she eased open a set of shutters; 'it's time to get up.'

Emily rolled over and stretched on the enormous bed. It was so large that she could reach out with her arms and legs and not touch any of the sides.

'What would you like for breakfast, ma'am?'

Emily opened her eyes. Red sunlight was streaming through the open shutter, and the white sheets were reflecting the crimson glow.

'Do you need another minute, ma'am?'

'No,' she mumbled, her head a little sore from the wine she had drunk the previous evening; 'I'm fine.' She sat up. She knew the weather would be freezing outside, but the Aurelian house was always warm in winter. 'Are there any eggs?'

Talleta smiled. 'Yes, ma'am; the Aurelian larder never seems to run out of anything. The housekeeper has ordered in a new batch of herbal teas from the Sander hills; and he told me they were good for helping people wake up in the morning.'

'A subtle little comment aimed at me, no doubt.'

'Maybe, ma'am.'

'Of all the things I've had to get used to, the fact that the Aurelian household rises so early each day is perhaps the hardest; and I was never good in the mornings at the best of times. Late nights? No problem.'

'Would you like to try one of the new teas, ma'am?'

'Yes; might as well give it a go.' She stretched again. 'This bed is too damn comfortable.'

A hint of a smile touched Talleta's lips. 'The lieutenant has a pass from the barracks tonight, doesn't he, ma'am?'

'Yes, though you can remove that look from your face. You remember what happened last time?'

'Yes, ma'am. Sorry, ma'am.'

'I think I know what went wrong. With only one overnight pass every ten days, there's too much pressure when he does come home; I'm excited, he's excited; his mother's... excited. She plans a huge dinner every time, like it's his birthday or something, when all he wants to do is relax, and then we spend the whole night arguing.'

Talleta said nothing.

'Well, not the whole night,' Emily went on. 'We were just starting to get on last time, when he had to leave for the barracks. I know it's only temporary, but it's tiresome. It could be years before he's promoted to captain.' She shook her head. 'Years.'

Talleta smiled. 'His mother seems to think it won't be too much longer.'

'She says that to placate me. The Chamberlains hate the Aurelians, I mean us, but I don't think I'd realised quite how much; and they have the ear of the new prince. They can block Danny's promotion whenever they like, it seems. I wish Lady Aurelian hadn't gloated at the wedding. I'm sure it must have given her great satisfaction to see her son finally married, but Lord Chamberlain looked like he wanted to murder us all. If he tells the prince that Danny's useless, or a troublemaker, then he could be stuck at lieutenant for ages; maybe forever.' She glanced at her maid. 'I promised myself I wouldn't get maudlin, yet here we are.' She pulled the covers from her and slid out of bed. 'I'll wash, if you could get me some eggs, and a cup of that herbal tea?'

Her maid bowed. 'Yes, ma'am. Shall I bring breakfast here?'

'No, I'll take it in the morning room; that'll at least prove to his mother that I'm actually up.'

Talleta bowed again and left the room. Emily unbuttoned her white nightdress and let it fall to the warm, polished floorboards, then walked into the bathroom that adjoined the bedchamber. She opened a set of narrow shutters to let in some light, and turned on the tap by the deep sink. Warm water. She smiled. There was no doubt that life in the Aurelian mansion was luxurious, probably as fine as living in one of the City's palaces, and that compensated a little for the absence of her husband. She glanced at her reflection in the tall mirror as the room began to steam up. She had shadows under her eyes from staying up too late, but nothing so drastic that a little make up wouldn't fix. She stared at herself for a moment. She was a married woman. In some ways she didn't feel any different, but in others her life had altered completely. An enormous weight had been lifted from her shoulders, but it had been replaced by a different set of pressures.

She thought of her parents as she began to wash. She hadn't seen her father since the wedding, and with every day that passed she felt her anxiety decrease, and she realised that if she never saw him again, she would be fine with that. Her mother had visited a few times, and had been entertained by Lady Aurelian as Emily had sat quietly beside her like a dutiful daughter-in-law.

After washing she returned to the bedroom. Talleta must have been back in, as there was a fresh set of clothes laid out on the newly-made bed. Her maid was good at choosing outfits for her, and she barely had to give it a second thought any more. She pulled on the underclothes and dress, then sat and brushed her hair until she had restored some order to the tangle of blonde curls. She put on some make-up; not too much, just enough to make it look as though she hadn't put on any, but hiding the shadows under her eyes at the same time.

Talleta was waiting for her outside the bedroom door as she walked into the hallway.

'How long was I?' Emily said to the maid as they walked towards the morning room.

'About thirty minutes, ma'am. You're getting quicker.'

'I used to spend over an hour every day getting ready in the old house.'

'Yes, ma'am; I remember.'

Emily smiled. 'That's enough of your cheek.'

The maid's face fell. 'I'm sorry, ma'am, I didn't mean anything by that, I...'

'I was joking, Tallie. You're the only friend I have here, and sometimes I forget you're a maid.'

Talleta looked away, her face flushed.

Emily sighed. Had she just referred to a servant as a 'friend'? Her father would have... She stopped herself. She didn't care what her father thought any more, and she wasn't going to let his views dominate how she should think. Talleta *was* a friend, in a way; she trusted her, confided in her, and she was the only person in the mansion she could be honest with. But, at the same time she was only a Reaper, a member of a tribe whose main characteristic was servility towards their betters.

They entered the morning room, and found Lady Aurelian sitting in an armchair reading that day's news sheet, delivered each dawn by the Taran postal service. She put down her cup and glanced at Emily.

'Good morning, dear.'

Emily sat by a small table, where her breakfast was waiting. 'Good morning, my lady.'

'I have several folders of documents for you to look through and learn.'

'Documents, my lady?'

'Yes, the title deeds and contracts from our various land-holdings and other enterprises. I think it's time that you began to get a feel for the family business.'

Emily suppressed a grin. 'I'll start this morning. Thank you.'

She gave Emily an odd expression. 'You sound like you're actually looking forward to it.'

'I am. I want to help; I want to do something.'

'Let's see if you still feel that way after wading through countless pages of lawyerly footnotes. I'm going to gift you a small project to get you started; something fitting.'

'Yes?'

'In the marital exchange, we received a tract of residential land in the Circuit. I had a glance at the figures, and it seems that it makes a substantial yearly loss in income. Were you aware of that?'

Emily's face flushed. Had her family given the Aurelians something of no value? That sounded like the kind of thing her father would do. 'No, my lady; I wasn't aware.'

'I want you to look into it, and see what, if anything, can be done to make it profitable. As this is your first project for me, feel free to ask any questions, no matter how silly you may think them to be. By the way, have you tried the new tea yet?'

Emily picked up her cup and sniffed. 'I'm just about to, my lady.'

'Well, its vile. Apparently it helps one wake up in the morning, but as I've never had a problem with that, I think I might cancel the order. Unless, of course, you find it useful? I know that you struggle a little in the mornings, dear.'

Emily tasted the tea and grimaced. 'Perhaps it needs some honey?'

Daniel's mother frowned. 'Dear, I've noticed you've gained a tiny bit of weight since the wedding day. I'm not saying it's your fault, after all, you can eat whatever and whenever you choose, but, and I say this with all kindness, maybe you should go easy on the honey.'

Emily glanced down at her plate of eggs, her appetite evaporating. 'Oh.'

Lady Aurelian went back to reading the news sheet. Emily sipped the bitter tea, hiding her revulsion at the taste. Her father had often called her fat when she was growing up, and she had gone through a terrible time in her mid-teens as she had swayed between starving herself and bingeing; and she felt some of the old self-loathing that had dominated her mind at the time.

'Dear, oh dear,' muttered Daniel's mother; 'Prince Marcus is getting himself into a frightful tangle in his desire to arrest Lady Aila, and that idiot Chamberlain appears to be encouraging him.'

Emily glanced up. 'Is she still hiding in Dalrig, my lady?'

'She certainly is, though "being held prisoner" might possibly be a more accurate term. Prince Montieth claims that Blades have entered the territory of the Gloamers without permission, and he's threatening to cut off supplies of fresh water unless he is compensated. Dalrigian militia have been posted to the borders of Pella, ostensibly to protect against any further incursions by Blades, but it looks like he's preparing for bloodshed.'

'Why is the prince so anxious to arrest her?'

Lady Aurelian glanced over the top of the news sheet at her. 'You know, I wondered that myself. He seems to be paying attention to that one issue more than anything else. So, I did what any curious citizen would do, and bribed some servants in the palace.' She put down the news sheet, while keeping her gaze on Emily. 'What I am about to tell you is a secret, my dear. Are you good at keeping secrets?'

'I am, but my loyalty is to the Aurelians, and if I discovered something that you or Daniel needed to know, then I would tell you.'

Lady Aurelian smiled. 'A perfect daughter-in-law answer. I understand you were a knowledgeable student in political history; top of your class?'

'Yes.'

'Then you will know that both the quantity and calibre of the demigods and God-Children have deteriorated somewhat over the last few centuries. Prior to the Civil War, there were twenty-nine demigods residing in the City, and now there are only fourteen, and several of them are utterly useless. With the God-King and God-Queen seemingly irreconcilable, that means there will be no more God-Children coming. Prince Marcus thinks he has found the solution.'

'Is it the same solution that Prince Michael proposed in the year 3094?'

Lady Aurelian's eyes tightened a little. 'I forget that you have expertise regarding the affairs of our martyred prince. I regret that I am unfamiliar with any plan of his. Let me tell you what Marcus proposes and then you can tell me if it's the same. He intends to join different branches of the demigods together, in order that they, well, breed, and create a new generation of demigods for the City. He wishes to pair Lady Vana with Lord Naxor, Lord Collo with Lady Ikara, and Lord Kano with Lady Lydia; Prince Isra's surviving children with those of Princess Khora, in other words. Lady Aila, he wants for himself.'

Emily nodded. 'Yes, that's what Prince Michael wanted too, although I don't know what pairings he proposed. Princess Khora abandoned his plans when she became High Guardian.'

'Hmm. Do you approve?'

'No, my lady.'

'But I thought you were a devoted follower of Prince Michael?'

'I'm a devoted student, my lady; not follower. I admire some of what he did, but he also made many mistakes, and I think that was one of them. It's illegal among every tribe in the City for cousins to marry, and I think it hypocritical of the royal family to believe they are above the law.'

'My, Emily, you do surprise me. And what would your father, Lord Omertia, think?'

'He would think that anything that strengthened the royal family's rule would be a good thing.'

'So you would disagree with him?'

'Most certainly, yes.'

Lady Aurelian nodded, then went back to reading the news sheet.

Emily glanced away. Daniel's mother had made it clear on many occasions that she wasn't to be interrupted while she read. She sipped her tea. It wasn't so bad. She could get used to it without honey, she supposed. It was starting to work however, and she felt alert and ready for the day, despite the lack of breakfast.

'Poor Lady Lydia.'

Lady Aurelian frowned. 'What?'

Emily blushed. 'Did I say that out loud?'

'You most certainly did. "Poor Lady Lydia"? Why?'

'I, uh... I think that, maybe...'

'Spit it out, girl.'

'Lord Kano is a vile brute, and I pity anyone forced into his bed.'

'Interesting. Does this also make you feel pity for Lady Aila? After all, she is probably on the run to avoid having to share the new prince's bed.'

'I suppose so, yes.'

'Then you disagree with the concept of arranged marriages?'

'I do if either party has no way to refuse.'

Lady Aurelian smiled. 'I don't mean to disparage your parents in any way, but where in Malik's name did you get your brains from? I admit I wondered if your father had perhaps donated a small sum to your school in order to doctor your results, but I have seen over the last month that you earned your place at the top of the class. You're sharp, Emily, a good deal sharper than Daniel.'

'But Daniel is very clever, my lady, he...'

'He's not a dunce by any stretch of the imagination, but he doesn't apply himself like you do. Still, I like that you sprang to his defence; it bodes well. There will be a full house this evening; not only is Daniel coming home, but his father will be here also, so please dress modestly. I have a hard enough time coping with my son gazing at the beautiful eighteen-year-old living in the mansion without having to see my husband do it as well.'

Emily looked away, cringing with embarrassment.

'I don't hold it against you, dear. Men are easily distracted by such things, as I'm sure you are well aware. But you have a husband now; there's no need to dress like a Reaper bar maid any longer.' She stood, and placed the folded news sheet onto the table. 'Well, that was a lovely chat, dear. Don't forget those documents, I've had the housekeeper place them in Daniel's study for you.'

Emily sat in silence as Lady Aurelian left the room, then burst into tears. She felt a hand on her shoulder.

'Don't worry, ma'am,' Talleta said, passing her a handkerchief.

'Did you hear her? I'm fat, and I dress like a bar maid.'

'But she also said you were clever, ma'am. You know, I think she actually likes you.'

'What?'

'She likes you, but she's also a little jealous of you; that's why she said those things, ma'am; she knows how beautiful you are. For years, she's been the only Aurelian woman in the family, and now she has a little competition.'

'But I don't want to be in competition with her; I want her to treat me with respect.'

'Compared to the way she treats everyone else, ma'am, she does.'

Emily wiped her face, angry that she had let Lady Aurelian's words bite.

'Are you going to have the eggs, ma'am?'

Emily shook her head.

'You need to eat, ma'am.'

'I'm not hungry.' She stood. 'I'm going to the study. Have more of that awful herbal tea brought to me. I'm going to have to get used to the taste without any honey in it.'

The day passed quickly, with Emily burying herself in the enormous pile of documents and folders that had been left for her in Daniel's large and comfortable study. The shelves were bulging with the books that Emily had ensured were transported from her parents' home, and they sat next to Daniel's smaller collection. She pulled down one of her volumes on the law regarding land ownership, and began taking notes as she made her way through the documents.

Talleta brought her tea every hour or so, and she worked through lunch, only stopping when the daylight diminished, and the red glow of evening made it hard to read.

'Shall I light a lamp for you, ma'am?' said Talleta, placing empty tea cups onto a tray.

'No, I should stop. Danny will be getting here soon, and I need to find something... modest to wear.'

'I've taken the liberty of picking out a few outfits for you, ma'am.'

'I'll wear a sack if it stops Lord Aurelian looking at me.'

She got up from the desk and walked the short distance to the bed chamber. She glanced at the clothes her maid had laid out on top of the bed covers. Skirts that went down to the ankle, and long-sleeved, frilly blouses that buttoned to the neckline. She frowned. Danny would think he had married a Dalrigian if she wore any of those.

She glanced over at her wardrobe, where the rest of her clothes were hanging. Should she ignore the comments of Lady Aurelian and wear what she wanted, or would that risk disrupting the relative tranquillity of life in the mansion? After all, both Danny and Lord Aurelian would be gone by the morning, leaving Emily alone to deal with her mother-in-law. Maybe she was being tested. If so, what was the correct response? She opened the wardrobe and pulled out one of her usual dresses.

Talleta entered the room as she was finishing getting ready.

'What do you think?' said Emily, glancing at her reflection in the mirror. 'Too much like a Pellan bar maid?'

'I think you look great in whatever you wear, ma'am.'

'Thank you. Let's hope Lady Aurelian agrees.'

'Daniel has arrived, ma'am.'

'Yes? Where is he?'

'With his mother in the drawing room.'

Emily took a breath, then checked her hair again. 'Alright, here we go.'

She walked out of the bedchamber and along the hallway to the front of the mansion. She began to hear the voice of Lady Aurelian as she neared the drawing room, telling her son how good it was to see him again. Emily entered the room, her eyes looking for her husband.

Daniel glanced over to her and smiled.

'Danny,' she said, as his mother stopped talking.

'Hi, Emily.'

Lady Aurelian eyed Emily for a moment, but said nothing.

Daniel stood, and kissed Emily on the cheek. 'It's good to see you.'

'How have you been?'

'Stuck in the barracks doing nothing. To be honest, I'm bored and fed up with it. The Blades don't let us leave without written permission; it's like they think they own the place.'

Daniel sat back down on the couch and Emily joined him.

'What a delightful dress you've chosen,' said Lady Aurelian, presumably no longer able to hold it in.

'Thank you,' Emily smiled.

'A little inappropriate for dinner though, you'll agree?'

'Why?' said Daniel. 'She looks great.'

Emily resisted the temptation to smirk, keeping her expression even.

'Taran aristocracy has standards, son,' his mother said. 'It's what elevates us above the rabble.'

Daniel laughed. 'Are you calling my wife "rabble"?'

'Don't misconstrue my words, dear. You're both young, and I am merely trying to steer you safely into adulthood. We all make mistakes at your age, and I'm tolerant of them. Emily has yet to learn that she doesn't need to walk around half-naked to be thought beautiful.'

'Don't exaggerate, mother.'

'I'm not exaggerating. Her hem starts above the knee, and her arms and shoulders are bare. I think that amounts to half of her.'

Emily kept the smile on her face, but her heart was racing, and she had a tight knot in the pit of her stomach. Had she made a mistake? She began to feel a sense of dread, of what his mother would say to her once Daniel had left at dawn to go back to the regiment. At least he had stood up for her, she thought, grasping onto his words like a life raft.

Daniel shook his head. 'If it annoys you that much, I'm sure she won't mind changing into something else.'

She glared at him.

'Well, Emily,' said his mother, smiling, 'your husband appears to agree with me. Now that you've had the chance to remind him of some of your attributes, perhaps you'd better go and get changed? Dinner starts in twenty minutes, dear; please don't be late.'

Emily got to her feet. She glanced at Daniel, but he was avoiding her eyes, so she turned and strode from the room, Talleta hurrying behind her.

With no lamp lit, and all of the shutters open, the bedroom lay bathed in a red glow. In her old home, the view from her bedroom window had consisted of the rear wall of the next house along, but in the mansion, her new rooms all faced sunward, and had a clear view over the palace and the hills beyond.

The door opened and she blinked as lamplight spilled in from the hallway. It was Daniel.

'Come in and close the door,' she said.

He walked into the room, easing the door shut behind him. 'Why are you lying here in the dark?'

'Do you never do that? The light's beautiful; I often lie here and watch how it changes.'

He came over and sat on the bed next to her. 'Mother's asking where you are. Dinner's started.'

'Is that why you came here, because your mother asked?'

'What's wrong?'

Emily thought about saying 'nothing', but she turned away instead.

'Is it about what my mother said? About the dress you were wearing?'

'I'm still wearing it, Daniel, in case you hadn't noticed.'

He glanced down and peered through the gloom at her. 'Why didn't you get changed?'

'Despite what she said, I'm an adult, and I can wear what I want.'

'So we're having an argument about a stupid dress?'

'It's about respect.'

'Does this mean you're not coming to dinner? Pathetic.'

Anger surged through her. 'Pathetic? Let me tell you what's pathetic; a man who doesn't stick up for his wife; a man who laughs when someone insults her. You're a coward, Danny.'

He said nothing, his face obscured in the shadows of the room. Emily looked away. She knew that by not appearing for dinner she had invited a row. Lady Aurelian would probably think she was being melo-dramatic, but she felt as if something had snapped within her in the drawing room. Had she made a terrible mistake, not about the dress, but about Daniel?

'We still have time,' he said, breaking the silence. 'If you put some-thing else on quickly, we could go to dinner; and that'll show my mother that she hasn't got to you. Just smile and act as if everything's fine, and...'

'That's what I've been doing all my life, Danny; acting normally and pretending everything's alright. I'm not doing it anymore. I married you for a new life, not to get trapped in a different one.'

'You're not trapped; you're over-reacting. I'm sorry if my mother's been hard on you, believe me, I know what that's like.'

'Then you should understand how I feel.'

'And that's why you should go to dinner. You have to show her you're not beaten. She'll never respect you if she thinks you're hiding in a dark room, crying over a dress.'

'Alright,' she said; 'I'll go, if you'll stand by my side.'

He smiled, and put a hand on her waist. 'Of course I will.'

'And I'm wearing the dress I'm in now. Then, I'll go with you to dinner.'

'What? Do you think I want to spend my entire evening off arguing with my parents? If you walk back in there wearing that my mother will have a fit. Be reasonable, Emily.'

'That's the choice; take it or leave it.'

'No. I'm not going in there unless you change.'

'Then go, and leave me alone. And don't come back tonight, I wouldn't want the rest of your evening ruined by more arguing.'

'But... but what will I tell my mother?'

'Tell her what you like, and take your hand off my waist.'

He stood, and she could sense the anger and frustration simmering from him. Her body tensed as he glared down at her. She had never seen him lose his temper, and she wondered if he was about to do so at that moment.

'Good night,' he mumbled, and left the room, slamming the door behind him.

Emily lay still for a moment, then turned her head, so she could watch the swirling reds and dark purples of the night sky.

'Good night, Danny.'

CHAPTER 8
NON-ESSENTIAL

A rrowhead Fort, The Bulwark, The City – 3rd Darian 3419

'Dragons are the noblest of all beings,' said Blackrose as Maddie piled fresh straw round the edges of her sleeping area. 'A mixture of gods and the finest bodies of any creature that has ever existed; strong, majestic, enduring.' She raised her head as if addressing a crowd. 'When the gods first came to the world where I was born, there were no sentient beings among the animals or birds that inhabited it, so they entered into the minds of the best that was available. Once they had mastered those new bodies, they reigned supreme, harnessing their divine powers with that of the form of winged serpents, and the race of dragons was born.'

Maddie leaned on her pitchfork. 'Are you saying you're descended from gods?'

'Yes, but, alas, it was many millennia ago, and the bloodlines from those first gods have weakened over the long generations. The first dragons were almost immortal, but by the time I was conceived, our usual life span had dwindled to five or six centuries, and the range of our powers had narrowed at the same time. My ancestors could boast the ability to slay many at a distance, by will alone, and some had the power to generate earthquakes, or turn back the course of rivers. Now, we are limited to fire and a few vision tricks. And so, when the new gods arrived, we were defeated.'

'Wait, you were fighting gods?'

'Who else do you think would have the power to subdue a world ruled by dragons?'

'I suppose, if you put it like that. Were you queen of the whole world?'

Blackrose laughed. 'No, there were many realms. My world consists mostly of small archipelagos; islands scattered across a single, vast ocean.'

'It's good to hear you laugh. You've really been opening up to me about things these last few days, and I'm trying to remember it all. That stuff about the war you said to me yesterday, well, I had to write it all down when I got to my room. Actually, do you think you could check my spelling? Some of the names you mentioned sounded pretty weird.'

'And what are you going to do with all of this information?'

Maddie shrugged, and began levelling the straw with the pitchfork. 'I don't know. Learn it, I suppose. Once I've got the basics, then I'll know what to ask next. I already have one question.'

Blackrose lowered her head to Maddie's level. 'Yes?'

'Why didn't you mention the fact that the invaders were gods when you told me about the war yesterday?'

'I thought it was obvious.'

'Obvious to you, maybe. Secondly...'

'You said one question.'

'Yeah, but you know how these things work; anyway, you said that when the invaders, these new gods, came to your world, some of the humans living there helped you, and others sided with the enemy. If your rule was as benevolent as you've said it was, why would any human help an invader?'

'There are always malcontents; even a handful of dragons allied with the enemy. Our mistake was not to eliminate them before we were invaded.'

'Alright, my next question is... why are you telling me all this?'

'I do not think you will like the answer, little Maddie.'

'Try me.'

'Very well. For three months I have refrained from eating, and have only taken some water now and again. I am dying. I estimate that if I continue fasting, I may have another month, maybe two, before my body fails forever. I have a lot to say, I now realise, and you are the only one I have to listen. Perhaps I believe that if I impart enough of myself to you, then somehow I will live on, as a reflection in your memory, and I find that consoling.'

Maddie said nothing for a moment. She gazed up at the dragon's face, seeing the deep well of resignation in her eyes. 'You're right. I don't like that answer. Every day that I come in here, I hope more than anything that you'll have eaten something, but every day the trough is full. It's breaking my heart.'

'A part of you must wish for it to be over.'

'What do you mean?'

'I've seen it before in humans, when they care for the old or sick. Don't feel guilty about it; it's a natural reaction. You see someone you love in pain, and you want that pain to end, and so a part of you wishes for it to be over.'

'I get it, but it's not true in my case. I don't want you to die.'

'Maybe not consciously, but deep inside you do.'

Maddie flung down the pitchfork. 'No. No part of me does. Look at me, Blackrose; I want you to look at me and make me tell the truth.'

The dragon tilted her head. 'As you wish, though you may not like what you hear.' Blackrose stared into her eyes and Maddie felt a piercing pain behind her temples. 'It is done.'

'That hurt.'

'You knew the cost.'

'Alright then, ask away.'

The dragon kept her gaze on Maddie. 'Is there any part of you that desires to see me die, if only to end my misery?'

'No.' Maddie grinned. 'See? Ha! I told you.'

The dragon paused for a moment.

'That surprised you. Ask me another.'

'Are you, Maddie Jackdaw, utterly loyal to me, and to me alone? Am I your sovereign Queen?'

'Yes. Damn you. That's not fair.'

'You told me, commanded me, to ask you another question. Let's go on. Would you do anything to see me freed?'

'As long as it was possible. I couldn't fly to the moons, for example.'

'I'll consider that as a "yes". Would you kill Prince Marcus if it would set me free?'

'Of course I would. You didn't have to put the truth spell on me for that question.'

'What about Captain Hilde; would you kill her for me?'

Maddie's grin faded. 'Yes.' She hung her head. 'That's going too far. I want to stop now.'

'Look at me,' said Blackrose; 'lift your eyes.'

Maddie glanced up, and felt another pain behind her temples.

'I have lifted the compulsion to tell the truth from your mind. Know this, my rider; I will never question or test your loyalty again. This I swear to you.'

Maddie attempted a smile.

Blackrose lowered her head onto the fresh straw and closed her eyes. 'Now go; I wish to sleep. Come back this evening and I'll tell you more of my past.'

'Sweet dreams,' said Maddie, as she picked up the pitchfork and walked to the hatch in the black gate. She stepped through to the other cavern and leaned the pitchfork against the wall. It had been a good morning, and Maddie felt more hopeful than she had in a while, despite the dragon's stated reasons for wishing to talk to her. Blackrose wanted to live; she believed it firmly. She just had to be given a reason.

She went through to the hallway where she lived with Hilde.

'Good morning, Corporal,' said the captain. 'How did it go? Any changes?'

'Plenty of speaking, but still no food.'

Hilde nodded, her eyes shot with anxiety. 'There was a time I would have been jealous that she was talking to you and not to me, but I think I've moved past that. I'm starting to seriously worry, Maddie. Three months of no food? I can see her weakening.'

'She laughed today.'

'Did she?' Hilde smiled. 'That's good. What about?'

'I asked her a stupid question.'

'Good, keep doing that; anything to raise her spirits.'

Maddie nodded. 'Can I ask you a stupid question?'

Hilde's smile faded. She turned and walked to the kitchen, and Maddie followed her. The captain began unpacking a crate of supplies, placing the dried fruit, bottles, and salted meat into the kitchen cupboards.

Maddie leaned against the table. 'Well?'

'I suppose so, Maddie.'

'Alright, I want to know which of the following you would choose: Blackrose dies of starvation, or Blackrose escapes?'

Hilde stared at her. 'What kind of question's that?'

'A stupid one, like I said; but I still would like you to answer it. You got very upset before, when Blackrose thought she might be able to get out of the lair; and you're upset now, thinking that she might die. Which is worse?'

Hilde paused. 'On one hand, both outcomes mean the same thing for us; we lose Blackrose forever, and I don't want that. But if that was the only choice, then I'd pick escape. I'm not a monster.'

Maddie folded her arms and said nothing.

'Look, I didn't hear what Lord Kano said to you when he came here; how many times do I have to tell you? I was out-of-my-mind drunk.'

'I wish I could believe you, Captain.'

Hilde lowered her head. 'Me too. The truth is I can't remember what happened that night. There is, I guess... there's a possibility I heard it, but I don't remember, I swear. I'm sorry, I should never have left you to deal with Kano alone. I was very angry, but it's no excuse.'

'I accept your apology. I don't want to fight with you any more; we agree on Blackrose at last, and we need to work together to save her.'

'Well, if you have any ideas, I'm all ears.'

'We need to get her to back down.'

'In other words, we need to get her to do something she's never done before, except once, when she swore allegiance to Kano, and look how that turned out. But, I'm not sure if I can help; I see the way she looks at me. Apart from dying, the only thing she cares about any more is you.'

'I'm sure she still loves you, Captain.'

Hilde smiled, but it was forced. 'Thanks for saying so, but you know that's not true; not any more. She used to love me, but I failed the big test. When she had that spark of hope, I tried to snuff it out, while you fanned it. It'll take years before she trusts me again; and we don't have years.'

Maddie drummed her fingers on the surface of the table for a moment. 'Get her to do the truth spell on you. Get her to ask if you love her.'

'I can't; my mind's full of a hundred different thoughts and emotions, many of which are bleak. If she dragged them all out of me I think I'd want to crawl into a dark corner and die, like her.' She glanced at Maddie. 'It's different for you; your heart is clean and pure compared to mine. If anyone can save Blackrose, it's you.'

'But I don't know how.'

Hilde smiled. 'I still think you should take a few days off. You could visit your family, and Blackrose would still be here when you got back.'

'No way; I'm not leaving.'

'Then take fifteen minutes to clear your head; get some fresh air at least. I have a list of things I need picked up from the gatehouse.'

Maddie frowned.

'Girl, you haven't left the lair in ten days,' Hilde said. She reached over the kitchen counter and picked up a slip of paper. 'Here's my order chit. Go.'

'Fine,' Maddie muttered, taking the slip.

'And wrap up warm, have you seen what it's like outside?'

She shook her head as she walked to the hallway. She went to the front door and pulled on her winter coat and hat, then eased the bolts free. The door swung open and Maddie gasped. It had snowed overnight, and the castle forecourt was covered in a thick, white layer. She stepped outside, her boots crunching into the drifted piles of snow that had blown under the archways. Maddie smiled.

Forgetting all about the list of items to be picked up, she raced to the closest steps, and climbed them to the battlements. A few soldiers were standing up on the wall, and she joined them, peering out at the white landscape in front of the City defences.

Her mouth opened as she gazed out over the battlements, then she laughed as she saw a group of greenhides trying to cross the ice and snow. They were scrabbling about, slipping and falling over into the deep banks of snow.

'Look at 'em,' cried a soldier. 'Every year the snow comes, and every year they totter about like drunken fools.'

'They never learn,' said Maddie.

'Thank Malik for that, eh? If they did, they'd figure out how to build ladders and then we'd be screwed.'

A huge boulder was launched from one of the artillery platforms behind them, and they watched as it smacked down into a large group of greenhides that had strayed too close to the moat. The beasts tried to flee from the impact, but their legs kept slipping on the ice, and they scrambled about in a blind panic. Some raised their claws and they began to fight each other in their haste to retreat from the moat.

'Beautiful,' murmured one of the soldiers. 'I could watch this all day.'

Within minutes, the pure white snow was stained green with the blood of the eternal enemy, and the retreating beasts left at least a score of their own lying dead by the moat.

'Twenty down,' muttered another soldier; 'only about eight hundred million to go.'

'How come we never see baby greenhides?' said Maddie.

The soldiers glanced at her.

'They must breed somewhere,' she went on, 'but I can't tell the difference between boy greenhides and the girls, and I'm sure I'm not the only one.'

'I heard that there's a queen greenhide somewhere, far away,' said one, 'and she pops out thousands of them every day, but there are two types, not boys or girls, but her slaves, and the fighters.'

'Like ants,' said another.

Maddie frowned. 'Is that true? And how would we know?'

'When the God-Children left the City a thousand years ago, apparently they wiped out every greenhide for hundreds of miles, to give us enough time to build the Great Walls. I think I read somewhere that Prince Michael killed one of the greenhide queens; or maybe it was Princess Yendra.'

'So, in theory,' said Maddie, 'if we killed all of the queens, there would be no more greenhides? We'd just have to wait for them all to starve to death?'

'I guess so, but who would do it? It's not like we still have six God-Children to fight for us any more. Even Corthie wouldn't have got that far on his own.'

The other soldiers quietened at the mention of the former champion. Maddie glanced at the Blades standing next to her on the battlements, and she could see the disappointment and confusion in their eyes.

She lowered her voice. 'Do you believe what they say about him?'

'Lord Kano was there, wasn't he? He says he saw Corthie do it. What are we supposed to believe; that the Adjutant of the Bulwark is a liar?'

Maddie shrugged. 'He is a liar.'

The soldiers backed away from her a little, and some glanced around, making sure no officers were close by.

'Careful what you say, Corporal,' said one; 'there are some folk round here who wouldn't take too kindly to those words.'

Maddie turned her gaze back to the greenhides as the soldiers fell into an awkward silence. She took one last look at the clean, white landscape, then turned and headed back down the steps towards the fore-court. A row of wagons had been parked by the front of the Wolfpack Tower, their wheels having traced lines all over the snow in the courtyard.

Maddie walked past the wagons and turned for the gatehouse. She looked for the duty sergeant, but he wasn't standing in his usual place by the gates. She entered the entrance tunnel, and knocked on the door of the office. She pushed it open when there was no reply, and saw at least a dozen Blades inside, poring over the logbooks and personnel records.

'Hello,' she said.

An officer glanced at her. 'What do you want, Corporal?'

'I'm here to pick up a delivery for Captain Hilde, sir.' She passed him the chit.

His eyes scanned the piece of paper. 'Fine,' he said, nodding to a crate sitting in the corner of the office. He scribbled his initials on the chit and handed it back to her. 'Before you go, Corporal, what's your name?'

'Maddie Jackdaw, sir.'

He glanced over at a group of Blades going through the fortress records, and they nodded.

'Alright, Corporal, take your delivery to the captain, but under no circumstances should you leave Arrowhead, do you understand?'

She frowned. 'Yes, sir.'

She picked up the crate, grunted, then leant it against her hip. One of the soldiers opened the door for her, and she re-emerged back into the cold forecourt. Do not leave the fortress, she thought to herself, smiling. As if. She carried the heavy crate back to the lair, and let herself in.

'I'm back,' she yelled.

Hilde appeared in the hallway. 'What are all those wagons doing outside?'

'No idea,' she said. 'Where do you want this? My arms are getting sore.'

Hilde opened the door to a storeroom. 'Put it in there. Did you not think to ask what was happening?'

'I was going to ask the gate sergeant, but he wasn't there. His office is full of Blades, looking over the fortress records.'

Hilde frowned as Maddie set the crate down onto the floor of the storeroom. 'The sergeant wasn't there? That's the first time in ten years he hasn't been at his post. Something's going on; maybe you should go back outside and find out.'

Maddie rubbed the base of her spine as she straightened her back. 'I suppose so. Now?'

'Yes, Maddie; now, please.'

She nodded and walked back to the front entrance. She was about to reach for the handle when someone thumped on the door and she jumped. She glanced at Hilde, then opened the door.

Six soldiers were waiting outside, including the officer she had seen at the gatehouse.

'Corporal Maddie Jackdaw,' he said, 'you are now under my authority. Please step outside.'

'What? I mean, sorry, sir?'

Hilde raced up the hallway. 'What's going on?' She frowned as she saw the captain's insignia on the officer by the door. 'Can I help you?'

The officer nodded. 'Captain Hilde. Good morning. Your assistant has been re-categorised as a non-essential worker in Arrowhead, and I have orders for her redeployment.'

Hilde glared at him. 'Non-essential? You're joking, aren't you? Maddie makes a crucial contribution to the work I carry out. Do you know what we do here?'

'No, I don't.'

'Then on what basis has she been deemed non-essential?'

The officer reached into the pocket of his winter coat and withdrew a folded document. 'Her name is on my list.'

'Let me see that,' she said, snatching it from the officer's hands.

Maddie edged closer to Hilde, so that she could read it too. It was headed 'Arrowhead – Non-Essential Personnel for Re-Deployment', and consisted of a long list of names. At the bottom was Lord Kano's scrawled signature.

'Everyone on the list is being rounded up,' the officer said. 'More fighting-age Blades are needed in Medio and Auldan, and only those classified as essential to the defence of the Great Walls are being allowed to stay.'

'This can't be right,' said Hilde. 'There's been a mistake. Go back and tell Lord Kano that there's been a mistake.'

'You can write to Lord Kano and make your feelings known, Captain Hilde, but I am under strict instructions. I was explicitly told to make no exceptions.' He turned to Maddie. 'You got any gear?'

She stared at him. 'Like what?'

'Weapons, armour? Basic field kit?'

'Just what I'm wearing and a couple of spare uniforms.'

'Then let's go. I have another hundred names to find in this damned fortress.'

Maddie glanced back to Hilde. 'But...'

The officer shook his head. 'Are you disobeying a direct order, Corporal? Don't make me ask again.'

'This is wrong,' said Hilde. 'We can't strip the defences like this; what if the greenhides mount a serious attack?'

'In the snow?' laughed the officer. 'Don't worry about that; everyone will be back in time for summer.'

'And I'll get my assistant back then?'

'Provided she's still alive. Three months, that's it.'

Hilde took Maddie's hand. 'You have to go; there's nothing I can do. Take care of yourself, and you'll be back in no time.'

'But we don't have three months, Captain.'

'I'm getting tired of repeating myself,' said the officer. 'Corporal Maddie Jackdaw, you are ordered to step outside and follow me. Now.'

She took her coat off its peg, then glanced up the long hallway towards the door that led to the lair. Maybe if she screamed then Black-rose would hear her, but then what?

The officer sighed, then nodded to two soldiers. They moved forward, each taking a grip of one of Maddie's arms.

'Ow!' she cried. 'I'm coming.'

'Lord Kano will be hearing about this,' said Hilde, her face contorted with anger.

The two soldiers dragged Maddie out of the hallway and into the cold and snow. She turned her head, trying to get a last look at Hilde, but was swept round the corner and out of sight of the lair.

'Stick her in the lead wagon,' said the officer.

'Yes, sir.'

The soldiers hauled her past the long row of wagons. All were open-topped, except for the one in front, which had a large steel cage mounted on the back with a locked gate.

'Hang on, guys,' she cried. 'You don't need to put me in there.'

The soldiers ignored her. They reached the rear of the cage-wagon, and the officer unlocked the gate. He pointed to the interior, and the soldiers lifted Maddie by the shoulders and threw her in. She landed on the wooden floorboards, and turned her head to see the gate closed and locked.

She heard a low laugh. 'I might have known you'd cause trouble, girl.'

Maddie looked up. Seven other Blades were in the back of the wagon, sitting on the side benches, and among them sat the sergeant from the gatehouse. He stuck out his hand and helped Maddie back to her feet.

'Park yourself next to me, girl,' the sergeant said, moving along on the bench.

She sat. 'Why are you here?'

'Assholes say I'm non-essential,' he said, shaking his head. 'Ten years I've minded the gatehouse of Arrowhead, and in one morning they decide that I'm unimportant. What about you, lass? I can't imagine the Old Lady will be happy about you getting dragged off like that.'

She nodded. The sergeant knew about the existence of Blackrose, but she was sure that no one else in the back of the wagon shared the same knowledge. 'She doesn't know yet.'

The sergeant puffed out his cheeks and she noticed that a bruise was forming around his left eye.

'Did you give them cheek?' she said.

He laughed. 'You could say that. I might have called that officer something unpleasant.'

'What's going to happen to us; do you know?'

A Blade sitting across from them leaned forward. 'I heard Marcus is preparing to send Blades into Gloamer territory. Apparently Prince Montieth is refusing to hand over a rebel demigod that he's got locked up in his palace, so the new prince is going to invade Dalrig.'

'Dalrig?' said Maddie. 'Invade? But I don't know how to fight. I haven't held a crossbow or a shield in over a year.'

The soldier opposite shrugged. 'Same as the rest of us, Corporal. I've managed the laundry house for three years, do you think I want to be waving a sword at a bunch of rebel Gloamers?'

'Come on,' said the sergeant, 'we've all had basic training; we're all Blades. We stick together and watch each other's backs, and we'll be fine.'

Maddie glanced out of the gate of the cage. Behind them, the other wagons were filling up with the young and the old, as the auxiliary workers from all over the fortress were gathered.

The sergeant lowered his voice. 'I mean it, girl. You stay close to me, and everything will be all right; we'll be back here in a few months, yeah?'

She nodded, her heart pounding. She thought of her brother, posted somewhere within the streets of the Circuit, then she remembered her parents.

'Damn it, I should have asked Captain Hilde to send a letter to my family, so they know where I am.'

'Captain Hilde's a good woman,' said the sergeant. 'I'm sure she'll take care of it.'

Soldiers formed up around the convoy, and the lead wagon began to move, its wheels churning up the muddy snow. The Blades in the back fell silent as each gazed out at the interior of Arrowhead. As they entered the gatehouse tunnel, there was a rumble, and the faint echo of a roar from far away.

The sergeant glanced at Maddie. 'Something tells me the Old Lady's just found out what's happened to her favourite Blade.'

The wagon pulled through the gates, and took the road towards the Middle Walls, and the rest of the City.

CHAPTER 9
WHITEOUT

Tarstation, The Cold Sea – 21st Darian 3419

       Corthie, Achan and Yaizra pushed the wagon through the refinery gate, their boots sinking into the mixture of ice, slush and oily mud. The barrels on the back of the wagon were juddered by the movement, and some of their contents sloshed out over their arms as they shoved.

Ahead of them, guards were watching, their crossbows gripped loosely in their hands.

An officer approached. 'What's going on here?'

Corthie peered round the side of the wagon.

'Where are your oxen?' said the officer.

'Good question,' said Corthie, striding forwards, dripping oil from his hair and arms. 'I think we might have been the victims of a practical joke, sir.'

The officer frowned. 'Explain.'

'When we'd finished in the pit, we pulled ourselves out, but there were no guards, and no oxen.' He shrugged. 'We could've left the wagon I suppose, but we decided to bring it back.'

'You expect me to believe that you pushed this wagon all the way from the pits?' He grasped hold of some trailing cords. 'The reins have been cut.'

'Aye, that they have, sir.'

'So, where are the oxen?'

Corthie smiled. 'As I said, sir, we don't know.'

'You lost them? They're your responsibility, prisoner.'

'Maybe so, but what about the two guards; aren't they your responsibility? Where are they, sir? Have you lost them?'

The officer shook his head. 'You're going in the book for that, Holdfast; I'm sick of you questioning everything I say. Half rations tomorrow.' He glanced at Achan and Yaizra. 'That goes for them too.'

'But, sir,' said Achan, 'we only did what we thought was best. Someone stole the oxen, and we're being punished?'

'You're being punished for Holdfast's impertinence. Now, get out of here.'

Yaizra frowned. 'Told you they wouldn't thank us for pushing it all the way back.'

Corthie walked towards the rear of the wagon. 'I like giving them chances to be reasonable. Oh, and sorry about the rations.'

Achan leaned in as they walked out of the refinery gates. 'In four more days, we'll never have to worry about them punishing us again.'

'And in six more days,' Yaizra said, 'we won't need to worry about anything, cause we'll have frozen to death.'

As if to mimic her words, snow started to fall again, lightly at first, but growing thicker with every step they took towards the camp. Within minutes, the ground was covered in a thick fresh layer of snow, lying on top of the muddy slush that thousands of boots had turned the previous layer into. Only the refinery was unaffected; the heat radiating through its walls and roof keeping it clear. Every time the chimneys flared, the snow would turn a deep blood red, and the falling flakes looked like embers swirling down from the sky. There was no sign of their guards when they walked into the entrance of the camp, but several of the other prisoners were watching them with smug expressions on their faces. Most were standing under the shelter of an overhanging roof that shielded part of the yard, and Corthie noticed that it was the weaker and smaller prisoners that were being made to stand out in the snow.

They tramped to the wash house, and filed through the door.

'I know what you're thinking, big lump,' said Yaizra, as she pulled off her overcoat, 'but leave it. If you try to get back at the folk that took the oxen, you might end up in the cells again, and we can't risk it.'

'She's right,' said Achan; 'we're too close to take any chances.'

'Aye, but if I do nothing, then won't that look suspicious? Everyone will think, "Why's he not doing what we expected? What's he planning?" So maybe I should do something, to make them all think everything's normal?'

His two friends glanced at each other.

'I'll make it small,' said Corthie; 'tomorrow maybe. Nothing that'll get me locked up.'

'Alright,' said Achan. He walked over and peered through into the shower room. 'It's empty.'

Yaizra walked in, while Corthie and Achan waited on the bench in the changing room. The front door opened.

'Hey, it's occupied,' yelled Achan. 'Oh, sorry, sir.'

The guard walked in, glanced around, then closed the door. 'Holdfast, a word.'

Corthie got to his feet and followed the guard to the rear of the chamber.

'Keep your mouth shut about what I'm about to say, understand?'

Corthie nodded. 'Aye.'

'The prisoners who took your oxen today, that was just a distraction, a joke. They're planning something a bit more serious.'

'What?'

He leaned in close, and Corthie could smell the garlic on his breath. 'They're going to burn down your block tonight, while you're sleeping.'

'Have you told the governor?'

The guard frowned at him. 'No. The governor already knows about it. We've had word from the Grey Isle, everyone there's talking about how you're still alive in Tarstation, and it's only a matter of days before the City authorities send soldiers to pick you up. A fire would suit the governor down to the ground, as all evidence of you being here would vanish into smoke. I'm supposed to be on duty tonight, and I've been told to stay clear of your block; we all have.'

'Thanks for telling me.'

The guard nodded. 'Not all of us are assholes.'

'Come on,' said Corthie; 'there's got to be more to it than that. You're disobeying orders and risking your own freedom to help a prisoner?'

The guard shrugged. 'Fine, I hate the governor with all the passion I can muster, and I want to see the weasel arrested when the soldiers get here and discover that he's been harbouring a wanted criminal. That better?'

'Then you're not trying to help me at all; you don't care if the soldiers execute me.'

'No, you're a criminal, and if that's what you deserve, then the law's the law. What I don't like is that asshole governor thinking he can bend the rules to suit him. He's got rich sitting here, while the rest of us have bled our lives away in this dump. It's time he got some bad luck sent his way.'

Corthie said nothing.

'Believe me or not, it's your problem now.' The guard turned, and strode from the changing room, leaving through a side door.

Corthie went back to where Achan was sitting. 'Did you hear any of that?'

'Yeah.'

'What do you think?'

'Sounds like a trap to me.'

'That's what I thought, but wouldn't it be a lot easier just to burn us to death? I mean, why bother setting a trap?'

'I don't know. Maybe they don't want the hassle of having to build a new prisoner block; or maybe they're just bored and crave some excitement.'

'I should speak to the governor.'

Achan's eyes widened. 'No. Anything but that. And what would you tell him?'

The door leading to the shower room opened and Yaizra looked out. 'Shower's free, boys.'

The camp appeared almost deserted as they made their way from the wash house to their housing block. The low hut was at the edge of the camp, beyond which ran a palisade fence and a ditch, and then the ice fields.

'The wind's blowing from iceward,' Achan muttered as they walked.

Yaizra frowned. 'So?'

'Well, if Corthie's enemies are thinking of roasting us tonight, the wind will carry the flames away from the rest of the camp. It's the perfect time to do it, in other words.'

'I'm still not buying it. That guard was just having us on.'

'The part about the folk on the Grey Isle knowing that he's still alive, that sounded true to me.'

'Hey, big lump, what do you reckon?'

'I'm hungry; I reckon it's time for dinner. Grab as much as you can.'

'Why?'

'Let's keep our options open; we may have to improvise.'

They reached their hut and entered. Corthie glanced along the passageway that ran down the middle, but no one was around. They went down the hallway to the food station located at the far right of the building.

'Evening,' said Corthie to the old man behind the counter; 'what treats do you have for us today?'

The old prisoner attempted to grin, but anxiety was shining from his eyes. 'The same muck we have every day, lad.'

'I'm starving, so ladle in plenty for me.'

'Sure.' He stood and picked up a large serving spoon.

Corthie leaned on the counter. 'Quiet tonight. Is there something going on that we don't know about?'

The old man filled a bowl with a grey-coloured broth. 'Eh, like what? No, nothing, lad.'

Yaizra joined Corthie at the counter. She pointed. 'Is that a maggot?'

'What?' The old man turned to look, and Corthie leaned over the counter, slipped his hand into the man's pocket, then picked up a sack that had been lying by his feet.

'What are you doing?'

'What does it look like?' Corthie said. 'I'm stealing this sack of food. Are you going to report me?'

The old man stared at him.

Corthie smiled. 'It's a simple question.'

Achan leaned over and filled a bowl for himself and another for Yaizra, as the old man glanced away, his hands trembling.

'We're going to our room now,' said Corthie. 'Anything you want to say?'

The old man shook his head.

'I hope you sleep well,' said Yaizra, as they walked from the food station. They strode along the hallway to their room and went inside, Corthie with the sack, and Achan balancing three bowls. Yaizra lit a stub of a greasy candle and sat as Corthie closed the door.

'Alright,' she said, 'I believe it now. So, what are we going to do?'

'Eat,' said Corthie; 'we're going to need it.'

'Why?' said Achan as he sat and handed out the bowls of broth.

Corthie reached into the sack and pulled out some bread. 'We need to bring forward our escape to tonight. The fire could be perfect cover for us. We flee, and they think we burned to death.'

Achan frowned. 'I can think of at least a dozen problems with this plan.'

'Let me eat.'

They sat in the flickering glow of the candle, devouring the sour broth and the loaf. Corthie felt his spirits rise as his stomach filled, and he felt for his battle-vision. It thrummed into life, and his senses exploded with stimuli. Everything was sharper with battle-vision, his sight, hearing, reflexes. He listened carefully, and heard the old man wheel his food trolley out of the front door of the long hut, the wheels squeaking, but no sound was coming from the other rooms.

He eased off his powers, storing his energy for when he needed it.

'Yaizra,' he said. 'Do you fancy being sneaky for a minute and scouting the hallway?'

'I was thinking of that,' she said, getting to her feet. 'If the other prisoners are in their rooms, then we can probably relax; if not...'

She went to the door and slipped outside.

'Can we talk about your plan now?' said Achan.

'You're the cleverest of the three of us; what do you think we should do?'

'Well, we've got just about everything on the list we made up; the biggest exception is the sled. If we break out tonight, it'll still be in the repair yard, and that cuts the amount of supplies we can take. It also means you'll have to carry the tent.'

'I'm sure I'll manage.'

'The next flaw in your plan is that we were going to leave after work, before we were locked into our huts, which we will be by now. Right now, the old man will be heading back to the kitchens, where he might, or might not, report you for thieving.'

'He won't. He knows what's coming tonight; you could see it in his eyes.'

Yaizra came back into the room. She sat down, her lip pursed. 'There's no one else here. Place is empty.'

Achan's face fell. 'It's true, then.'

Corthie grabbed the sack. 'We need to leave, now.'

'But the outside of the front door will be barred. We'll alert the entire camp if we batter it down.'

Corthie held up the set of keys he had slipped from the old man's pocket. 'These might help.'

'Hey,' said Yaizra; 'I'm meant to be the thief of this crew.'

Achan squinted. 'Can I see them?'

Corthie handed the keys to Achan, then began stuffing things into the food sack; candle stubs, matches, the spoons from the broth bowls; while Yaizra pulled on a thick, woollen tunic.

'These are no good, Corthie,' said Achan as they left their room. 'There's a key for the food station, but not one to get outside.'

Corthie put his finger to his lips as they approached the front door of the hut. He could see the shadows of the two heavy bars on the outside through the cracks in the wood, then heard the sound of a boot treading on the steps. Corthie signalled to the others that someone was outside, and they crept along to the door to the food station.

'It's unlocked,' said Achan, turning the handle.

'Of course it is,' whispered Yaizra; 'Corthie stole the key.'

They went into the room at the end of the hall. The counter had been lifted, and pools of grease were staining the floorboards where the old man's trolley usually sat. Corthie pointed to the window. It had a thin mesh rather than glass for ventilation, and Achan went up to it.

'It's still quiet out there; can't see anyone.'

'They're waiting for us to fall asleep,' said Yaizra.

Corthie pulled a barrel hook from his pocket. He had stolen it almost a month previously, and had honed its tip into a sharp point. He went up to the window, and sliced through the mesh along the rim in four quick movements. He grabbed the mesh with his fingers, and pulled it free.

Yaizra frowned. 'Will you make it through there?'

'Aye,' he said, peering out. 'It's clear. You two first.'

He stepped back, and Yaizra placed an empty crate on the floor. She stepped up onto it, then pushed her arms through the window. She wriggled up, then through the gap and disappeared. Achan went next, Corthie holding his hands out so he could climb up more easily. He seemed to jam in the window, so Corthie gave him a shove and he fell through. Corthie then lifted the sack, and threw it through the hole in the wall. He peered through the gap, and saw Yaizra and Achan standing in the snow by the side of the hut.

'They're coming,' said Yaizra, 'I can hear voices.'

'Go,' Corthie said; 'I'll meet you at the second depot.'

Yaizra glared at him. 'Move your ass, big lump.'

Corthie watched as they ran across the gap between their hut and the next one along, and then they were out of sight. He glanced at the narrow window frame, then reached up and lifted himself into the gap. As he squeezed his shoulders through, he heard voices drift round from the front of the hut, and shadows flickered across the snow. Corthie heaved, getting his arms through and gripping the planks on the outside of the wall. With a final shove, he toppled through the hole, landing head first into the snow.

He glanced up at the window, and remembered that he had left the mesh lying on the floor of the food station. He swore, then scrambled into a crouch. He sprinted across the gap as boots turned the corner, and threw himself into the space between the base of the next hut and the ground. He burrowed through the snow, then turned. Smoke was starting to come from the front of the hut, and Corthie's nostrils filled with the smell of burning wood. As he was about to go, he saw four prisoners walk round the side of the hut, one holding a lit torch, while another was carrying a bundle of unlit brands in his arms. They stopped when they saw the open window, and another glanced at the series of boot prints in the snow.

They talked to each other for a few moments in lowered voices, then one of them shrugged and motioned to the man holding the brands. He lit two, then threw them through the window of the kitchen station. One of the prisoners started pointing at the foot prints and arguing with the others, and Corthie retreated through the snow that had drifted under the next hut along, until he reach the far side. He looked out, saw no one was there, then broke into a run.

Behind him, the sound of voices mingled with the roar of the fire as it took hold of the hut. He risked a glance backwards as he reached the side of the wash house. Flames were rising into the sky, and smoke was billowing upwards. A huge crowd had gathered in the courtyard, with every eye on the conflagration devouring the hut. At the rear stood a few guards, watching, but doing nothing, and among them Corthie saw the face of the guard who had warned him.

The champion gazed at the scene for a moment from the shadows, then turned and carried on. Snow started to fall again as he reached a row of workshops, and he saw Yaizra and Achan hiding in the narrow gap between the rear of a hut and the outer, palisade wall. By their feet was a ditch cut into the ground, where they had hidden their escape supplies.

'They'll be onto us soon,' he said as he reached them. 'A couple of guards saw the open window. You got everything?'

'Yeah,' said Achan. 'Your pack's here.'

The snow grew heavier, covering their heads and shoulders as they strapped the large packs onto each other's backs.

'We're going to wish we had that sled,' muttered Achan.

'At least we'll be alive to regret it,' said Corthie. He strode to the palisade wall, and began scanning for the mark he had left on one of the beams. It had been easy to see before the snow had begun at the start of the month, but it had drifted high, obscuring the bottom few feet of the wall. He cleared the snow, shifting armfuls at a time.

'Hurry, Corthie,' said Achan. 'Some of them are searching round the huts.'

'No screams,' said Yaizra. 'They know we're not in there.'

Corthie found the mark, and, using his barrel hook, he ripped the lower post of the wall out. He had cut through several of the beams, and once the first was out, he yanked the others free.

'There they are!' someone cried, their voice rising over the roar of flames.

Corthie pushed Achan through the hole in the fence as a mob of prisoners started running towards them. Yaizra went next, and Corthie readied his hook. At least a dozen prisoners rushed along the side of the workshop, halting when they saw Corthie holding the hook out.

'Holdfast,' said one of the Sanders he had put in hospital over a month before; 'you're a dead man. The only question is how you want to go; with a bit of honour, fighting us, or alone in the icefields as you slowly freeze and starve to death. Is that how you want to meet your end, lad?'

Corthie lunged forward, swinging his arm. The hook ripped through the neck of the closest Sander, and he fell, blood pumping from his throat. As the others took a step back, Corthie dived down into the gap under the wall and squirmed through. He glanced up. The blizzard was reducing visibility to a few yards, and he could barely glimpse the shadows of Yaizra and Achan ahead of him. He raced up, and ran to them.

'This is madness,' said Achan, his face covered in snow.

Yaizra pointed back at the camp, where even the roaring flames were hard to see through the thick snow. 'Go back inside if you don't like it.'

'Shut up and move,' cried Corthie, urging them on.

Weighed down by their heavy packs, the three prisoners turned, and began hurrying as fast as they could from the camp, the wind at their backs.

———

They walked until Achan collapsed, then Corthie picked up both him and his pack and they kept going for another few miles until they reached a high crest of rock where there was a little shelter from the wind. Corthie pitched the tent, and they huddled inside from the howling snowstorm, exhausted.

Corthie awoke as a grey light filtered through the thin canvas of the tent. To his right, Yaizra was sleeping fully clothed, with a blanket wrapped round her, while Achan was snoring to his left. Corthie eased himself to the front of the tent and opened the flap. Snow had risen through the night, and he had to tunnel his way to the surface. He pulled himself up and out, and stood on the fresh snow. The sky was as clear as it had been in days, and the sun was glimmering as it hung over the horizon. He smiled, and walked a few paces to get a better view of the high, rocky ridge they had stumbled across the previous night, then paused, his mouth falling open. A few yards away on the other side of the tent, the ground fell away into a high cliff, at the bottom of which raged the waters of the Cold Sea. He laughed. If they had taken another few steps the night before, they would have gone over the edge.

He heard a noise behind him, and saw Yaizra crawl through the snow tunnel from the tent to the surface. She stood and stretched, then she also saw the sea ahead of them.

'Amalia's ass,' she muttered. 'The God-Queen was smiling down on us last night.'

He nodded, his eyes on the enormous icebergs that were drifting across the surface of the Cold Sea. The weak sunlight was making them shine and glisten as they moved with the currents.

'Reckon they're chasing us?'

'I don't know,' he said. 'I'm hoping they think we died in the blizzard.'

'What's wrong?' she said. 'You're not the usual cheery big lump this morning. Has it finally dawned on you that we're screwed out here?'

'No.'

'Then what?'

'I killed someone last night, so we could escape.'

'So?'

'I should have just wounded him; I didn't need to rip his throat out. I acted without thinking.'

She stared at him. 'Are you soft in the head? They were trying to kill us, Holdfast. They burned our hut to the ground.'

'I know, but I want to be better than that. Killing greenhides was fine, but other people? I don't want to become like my brother. He slaughtered thousands when he was sixteen.'

'Hold on, was that the first person you've ever killed?'

'Aye, if you don't count gods or greenhides. I've broken plenty of limbs, but I've never killed another mortal human.'

'Do you feel different?'

'I don't know. I guess, partly, I don't want to let my sister down.' He glanced at her. 'She's opposed to killing folk, even her enemies, and I promised her I would try to be the same.'

Yaizra shrugged. 'I'm sure she'll understand.'

Corthie doubted that.

'And maybe she's changed,' Yaizra went on; 'I mean, it's been what, five years since you saw her? Maybe she's got a bit meaner in that time.'

'Aye, maybe.'

They heard a groan from behind them 'Are we there yet?'

Corthie smiled. 'Aye, Achan; we've made it.'

He stumbled out of the tunnel, shaking with cold and exhaustion. Yaizra grimaced at the sight of him as he got to his feet.

Achan glanced around then his eyes widened when he turned and saw the Cold Sea stretching out before them. 'The sea!'

'Yes, Achan, well done,' said Yaizra.

'But, if we'd gone just a few more...'

'Yes, Achan, we know.'

He pointed. 'Ships.'

Corthie and Yaizra turned, following the direction of Achan's raised finger. Sailing in a spread out line were four large ships, all heading in the direction of Tarstation, their sails full in the wind.

'They're Gloamer boats,' said Yaizra, 'but they're flying Blade standards.' She turned to Corthie. 'We were right to leave; this proves it.'

'And now we have the coastline to help,' he said. 'With that to guide us when the sun's not shining, we should be able to make our way sunward.'

Achan sagged. 'I'm never going to make it. I'm so tired, and that's just after one night.'

'We'll make it,' said Corthie, 'even if I have to carry you all the way. Come on, we'll have some breakfast, dig the tent out, and we can be moving in thirty minutes.'

Achan groaned.

'Remember,' said Corthie, 'every day we travel, it'll get a little bit lighter, and a little bit warmer.' He smiled. 'We're already through the worst of it.'

Yaizra scowled.

'What's the matter with you?'

'I think I preferred it when you're miserable.'

CHAPTER 10

LIFE AND DEATH

D alrig, Auldan, The City – 26th Darian 3419

The town of Dalrig lay blanketed in snow as Aila and Bekha gazed down from the roof of Greylin Palace. As the only place in the building that felt open and light, they had found themselves going to the roof as often as they could, and had even chosen to sit out in the rain rather than face the humid claustrophobia of the palace interior.

In the harbour below them, fishing vessels and ships laden with oil sailed in and out between the two vast breakwaters as gulls circled over their masts; their harsh cries echoing through the air. Along the promenade, the ladies and gentlemen of the town were taking their morning walks, and Aila thought she could spot the tavern where she and Bekha had sat before deciding to go to the palace. The trees of the roof garden were bare, their branches swaying in the cold breeze.

'It's so peaceful up here,' said Bekha. 'If we're still trapped by the time summer comes, it'll be great; we could lie out in the sun all day.'

Aila frowned. 'Doing what?'

'Nothing; just lying. Relaxing.'

'You could do that in bed. Do you think we'll still be here in summer?'

Bekha frowned. 'Who knows? It depends on whether Marcus or

Montieth are bluffing. Every day I wonder if we'll see Blades march through the streets below us; and when I see that they haven't, the next thing I worry about is that Montieth will hand us over.'

'I feel a little weird,' Aila said, 'thinking that a war might break out because of me.'

'When's the last time Marcus actually saw you?'

'Malik's ass, I'm not even sure if I can remember. It would have been during the Civil War, before he became Commander of the Bulwark. I think it was a few days after Prince Michael killed my father. Marcus was in Cuidrach Palace then, and I was there too.' She shuddered. 'I remember he tried to come into my room; he was pretending he was sorry about what had happened to my family, and he was telling me he would protect me from his father, but I could see through his lies. I told him what he could do with his fake sympathy and he stormed off. That was probably the last time.'

'And, after three centuries, he still loves you?'

Aila glared at Bekha. 'That's not love; he doesn't love me. He wants to own me, and after I've rejected him so many times, he probably wants to punish me too. He's the kind of guy that thinks, if only I realised how much he wanted me, then I would fall into his arms. I guess he's not used to people saying "no" to him.'

'Enjoying the view, girls, on this glorious winter day?' came a voice from behind them.

Aila and Bekha turned, and saw Lord Montieth standing in the garden a few yards away. He had adopted his middle-aged persona, what Aila and Bekha privately referred to as 'suave-Montieth', as opposed to appearing as an old or a young man. His personality and accent seemed to alter with whichever age he had chosen, and it was clear that he relished his mastery over his appearance.

'Yes, uncle,' said Aila. 'We don't see you up here often.'

'I had to vacate my laboratory this morning, so it could be cleaned and thoroughly ventilated following a slight mishap. On my way upstairs I ran into Amber, and she informed me you were in Jade's roof garden.' He smiled, his waxed moustache crinkling. 'She also gave me this morning's news. Have you heard?'

'I've not seen my cousin this morning, uncle.'

Montieth strode forward to the railings and gazed out over the town. 'A delightful vista; I particularly enjoy snowy days like this one.'

Aila joined him by his side. 'The news, uncle?'

'Ah, yes. I'm afraid it concerns your sister, Lady Vana. As you know, she has been living in Maeladh Palace with Duke Marcus, supplying him with the whereabouts of the rest of the Royal Family. At some point yesterday morning, she was seen walking in the grounds of the palace with a few courtiers, when there was an incident.'

Aila's eyes widened. 'Is she alright?'

Montieth arched an eyebrow. 'For an answer to that, you'd need to ask your cousin, Lord Naxor.'

'Naxor was there?'

'The palace is suppressing the news, but I have spies in Tara who confirmed it for me. A fire was started in one of the palace out-buildings, presumably as a distraction, and then Lady Vana simply disappeared. She was there one moment, then Lord Naxor was next to her, and then they were both gone. Curious.' Montieth looked into her eyes. 'You wouldn't have any guesses as to how such an impossible thing may have occurred?'

Aila shrugged. 'Sounds like the eyewitnesses are confused. Maybe there was smoke from the fire you mentioned.'

'Prior to this episode, Lord Naxor was last seen in your company, my little niece.'

'That was in the Circuit, and I've not seen him since.'

'And now he has Lady Vana. Without her, Duke Marcus is blind to the movements of the divine beings of the City. You are safe to leave Greylin Palace at last, well, you would be if I were prepared to allow your departure.' He smiled. 'Naxor's little stunt leaves me in a powerful position. Even more so, if you consider those who were killed in the fire.'

'I thought that was just a distraction; were people killed?'

'Lord Naxor never does anything by accident. He is easily the brightest and most cunning of all the demigods. Inside the building he chose to burn to the ground were two dozen of the highest ranking officials in the Taran militia and government, out of which only four survived. The Rosers have ordered three days of mourning in their territory following the slaughter. I really must thank the little fire-raiser if I ever meet him; with this one act he had benefitted me greatly.'

'And Vana could be anywhere.'

He narrowed his eyes. 'What do you mean, "anywhere"? Does Lord Naxor possess something that would allow him to go "anywhere"?'

Aila shrugged. 'I don't understand; I meant he could have taken a ship somewhere, or he could be in the Bulwark. Who knows?'

He kept his gaze on her for a moment longer, but Aila knew he had no vision powers. He could kill her with a snap of the fingers, but he couldn't see inside her mind.

'I have more news that may interest you,' he said, breaking off the glance and gazing back out over the City. 'The most notorious mortal in the City might not be dead after all.'

Aila gasped. 'What? What mortal?'

'The Champion of the Bulwark we all believed to have been executed; he lives.'

'Corthie?'

'If that is his name. What has my attention is the battle-vision he possesses. I would give a lot of gold to examine him closely in my laboratory...'

'He's alive?'

Montieth frowned. 'Don't interrupt, niece.'

'Where is he?'

Her uncle raised a finger and pointed off to the left. 'About two hundred miles that way. Duke Marcus is incandescent with rage; this truly has been a most wonderful morning of news.'

Aila stared at him, unable to get a grip of her thoughts. Corthie was alive? But she had seen him, lying on the gravel outside Cuidrach Palace, his blood staining the ground. She had reached for him seconds before Naxor had used the Quadrant to take them away, and the image was imprinted in her mind. Had he been alive?

'How?'

Montieth smiled at her. 'How what?'

'How could he be alive?'

'Still on that, are we? I don't know, but Lord Salvor has been summoned to Tara to explain himself, so he may very well be implicated. No matter how it occurred, what is clear, is that word spread here from the Grey Isle, with sailors and returning guards all swearing they had seen the champion slaving away as a prisoner in far-off Tarstation. It's under my control, you know; it's a Gloamer colony, but I haven't given it any thought in a hundred years. Duke Marcus has sent ships to apprehend him, and...'

'Ships? From where? Tara can't send ships into the Cold Sea.'

He frowned. 'If you interrupt me again, niece, I will throw your mortal friend over the railings and into the bay below.'

'Sorry, uncle.'

'Blade troops are occupying the harbour of Fishcross in Icewarder territory, so Duke Marcus can indeed access the Cold Sea. Several ships filled with Blades have sailed off to Tarstation in order to correct Lord Kano's error. Maeladh Palace has found this news harder to suppress, of course, as its source is out of their control, and the whole affair is causing Duke Marcus much embarrassment. That, allied to the work you did in the Circuit before you came here, spreading the story that it was Kano who murdered Khora, is already undermining the duke's rule. I must say, you have been very helpful.'

'Then will you let me go? You could tell Marcus I'm still here.'

'No, niece. The game I'm playing is a long one, so make yourself as comfortable as you can, because this will be your home for quite some time to come. You are a valuable asset, for as long as Marcus desires you.' He smiled. 'I think I shall descend to the lower floors to see how the clean-up in my laboratory is going. My hands itch to be back at work.'

He gave a slight bow, then turned and walked away.

Bekha shook her head. 'I prefer old-man Montieth. That one's just creepy.'

Aila glanced at her. 'Did you hear what he said about Corthie?' She rubbed her head. 'Oh, damn it, what am I going to do?'

'What can you do? Your uncle also said that he wasn't going to let us leave.'

'Yeah, I know, but since when did I take advice from my family? There's got to be a way out of here.' She glanced over the railings. 'Can you swim?'

Bekha frowned. 'That water's freezing. If the fall didn't kill us, the temperature would. Let's face it, we're trapped. The only way out is locked and protected by huge soldiers that don't speak, and who are not affected by your powers.'

Aila nodded. 'We need someone to help us.'

———

'What do you think is a fair price for a demigod?' said Amber at the dinner table as she glanced at Aila.

'What?'

'If you were in my place,' Amber went on, 'and it were you who had to decide what it would take to avoid a war; what would you ask Marcus for in exchange for handing you over? A tract of territory? Gold? He's under pressure right now, so we could push the price quite high, I feel.'

'Luckily it's not up to you,' said Jade. 'Father decides.'

Amber laughed. 'Father's attentions drifts from one day to the next. You could ask him the same question on consecutive days and get completely different answers. Today he thinks that keeping Lady Aila here is a fine idea, but by tomorrow? Have you noticed that I never try to dissuade father of any opinion he happens to hold? I merely wait for his opinion to align with mine, and then I act. In this case, I have felt it prudent to open a channel of communication with the authorities in Tara, in advance of my father's inevitable change of mind, so that when it does occur I shall be prepared.'

Aila shook her head. 'That was a lot of words to say that you've gone behind your father's back.'

'I wouldn't expect you to understand the pressures of my job, cousin Aila. Dalrig is stable and prosperous, and I will do nothing to imperil that.'

'Even if it means bowing before Marcus?'

'Why not? We bowed before Princess Khora, and to Prince Michael before her. From a distance, naturally, but bow we did. This is all about negotiating the terms of our relationship with the new regime. We want no interference in our affairs, and no foreign military presence.'

Jade pursed her lip. 'What did they offer to give us for Aila?'

'A full year's tax relief,' Amber said. 'So far.'

Her sister's eyes widened. 'Does father know?'

'Not yet. He was so enthused about the latest humiliations to land at the door of Marcus that he wasn't in the right mood to discuss anything else. I'll bring it up when he's being more reasonable.'

Jade turned to Aila. 'A whole year's tax is an awful lot of money. Duke Marcus must really want you.'

'And what if your sister decided to sell you?' Aila said, trying to control her anger. 'What do you think you'd be worth?'

'More than that, I'd imagine. Umm... at least five years of tax. Yes. I have healing and death powers, whereas your demigod ability basically amounts to carrying around a box of masks.' She turned to a bouquet of flowers resting in a vase in the middle of the table and raised a finger towards it. She smiled as the flowers withered and died, their petals blackening and falling to the table. 'See? You can't do that.'

'Jade,' said her sister, shaking her head; 'what have I told you about that? Those were fresh flowers. And was it you who killed the roses I cut from the garden?'

'You didn't ask me if you could cut them. It's my garden, and they were my roses.'

'So you killed them?'

Jade shrugged. 'They're for me, not you.'

'Seems fair,' said Aila. She glanced at Amber. 'You should have asked. It's not right to take other people's things, just as it's not right to sell someone against their will. Isn't that right, Jade?'

'Uh, yes. I suppose so.'

Amber shook her head. 'Don't listen to her, sister; she's trying to divide us. There's no right or wrong when it comes to power; either you have it, or you don't. Aila is feeling powerless, and the powerless are always jealous of people like us. She came in here, to our home, uninvited, pleading for our help. Have we not helped her? Is she not safe? Does she not now owe us something in return?'

'Yes,' said Jade, 'but selling her?'

'We're not selling her, sister. What you're saying is impossible, for we cannot sell what we do not own. Duke Marcus owns her. That might seem unfair, but it's the law of the City. Imagine you had a pet cat, and it went missing. Wouldn't you give a reward to the person who found your cat? That's all we're doing; negotiating our reward. Do you see?'

Jade gazed down at the table. 'I think so.'

Amber smiled. 'Good.'

'Can I get a pet cat?'

'Certainly not.'

Jade glanced up at Bekha. 'What about this mortal? Once we've handed Aila back to the duke, can I keep her?'

'We'll see. Father might have an opinion about that, so I can't promise anything.'

'That's not fair; father gets all the mortals. I've not had one to play with in a hundred years.'

'I said "we'll see". That means I'll ask father. He likes them young, so this one might already be too old for him.' She glanced at Bekha. 'What age are you, mortal?'

Bekha glanced round the table, her eyes wide. 'You're letting me speak?'

Amber sighed. 'Have I not gone over these rules with you? You are allowed to speak if asked a direct question. Well?'

'That's none of your business,' said Aila. 'Leave her be.'

'It's fine,' said Bekha. 'I'm thirty.'

'See?' said Amber to her sister. 'She's probably too old for father. He likes them to be under twenty, if possible.'

'And what does he do with them?' said Aila, dreading the answer.

Amber laughed. 'If I told you that, you'd have to remain in this palace for the rest of your life.'

A servant walked into the room, his head bowed. He began to clear away the dinner plates, white gloves covering his hands. It was the same old servant that Aila had seen many times, but not once had he uttered a word in her presence.

Amber got to her feet. 'If you'll excuse me, I have a meeting with the Dalrigian Guild of Merchants scheduled for this evening.'

Aila watched as she strode from the room, then turned to Jade. 'Does she leave the palace for all these meetings she attends, or do they come here?'

Jade narrowed her eyes, as if she were trying to ascertain if Aila was tricking her. 'I don't think I should say.'

'Are there lots of things you've been told not to mention to us?'

'Oh yes, plenty. Sometimes I forget what I can say, and what I can't.'

'And what do you think about selling me to Marcus? You can't think that's right?'

Jade frowned for a moment, then her expression switched into a smile. 'My sister is very clever. She's always right.'

'Even when she steals your roses without asking?'

Jade stood. 'Why are you treating me like I'm a child? I know what you're doing. Amber said it herself; you're trying to divide us. We've been nothing but kind to you and your pet since you arrived here; why would you do such a thing?'

She strode from the room, and Aila groaned.

'That went well,' said Bekha. 'They're completely...'

Aila put a finger to her lips and nodded at the silent servant loading dishes onto a tray.

'They're completely lovely,' said Bekha. 'I don't know why I ever thought that demigods were arrogant or cruel.'

Aila began to laugh, then stopped as soon as the servant had left the room. 'We have to get out of here.'

Bekha's calm features dissolved, and her eyes shone with fear. 'How? I always thought that I'd be going with you, but there's no way I'm staying here to be Jade's pet. I'd rather jump off the roof.'

Aila leaned in closer to her. 'Amber and Montieth are both busy this evening. This might be our last chance. If they accept Marcus's offer, then it's over. Listen, there must be another way out of the palace. Amber keeps having these meetings, and Montieth's mortals must come from somewhere, right? But we've never seen the front gates open since we arrived.'

'Boats,' said Bekha. 'It's the only alternative. There must be an entrance with access to the harbour where barges or small boats could berth.'

'Shall we take a look?'

'But those guards are everywhere.'

'If we don't try, we're well and truly screwed.'

They got to their feet and left the dining room. Two of the fully-armoured soldiers were standing outside in the hallway by the door.

Aila paused in front of one of them. 'Hello. What's your name?'

The huge soldier did not respond.

Aila raised her knuckles and rapped on the steel breastplate. 'Anyone home?'

'You're wasting your time,' said Bekha.

'Fine,' she muttered, and they walked along the passageway towards their room. They reached a narrow flight of stairs that led to the ground floor. A guard was standing motionless at the top of the steps and Aila stopped next to him.

'Remember what we did to that Blade sergeant by the bakery in the Circuit?'

Bekha frowned for a moment, then her eyes widened. 'Are you sure?'

Aila didn't answer, instead she approached the guard. 'I'm lost,' she said to him as Bekha edged round his armoured bulk. 'Can you help me? I've completely forgotten where my room is.'

The guard said nothing, while Bekha crouched down behind him.

'Is it this way?' said Aila, swinging an arm out. 'Or this...?' She shoved the guard with all her strength, and his top-heavy armour sent him back a foot, where he tripped over Bekha. With a great clatter, the guard tumbled backwards down the stairs, banging off each step, and colliding with the ground at the bottom, his helmet flying off and bouncing across the marble floor.

'Oops,' said Aila. 'I hadn't quite realised how loud that would be.'

Bekha said nothing, her eyes staring at the guard at the bottom of the stairs as he began to lift himself up. She pointed. Aila turned her eyes to the soldier, and her mouth opened. His face was a grey, rotten mask of flesh; his nose a shrunken hole in the front of his head, his lips gone, his eyes red and blank. He leaned over, picked up the helmet from the ground, and pulled it back over his head.

Bekha screamed.

'Run,' cried Aila, as the guard began climbing the steps towards them.

They sprinted down the hallway away from the guard, then ran down another flight of steps. A pair of guards were standing in the marble hallway, and Aila swerved past them and kept running, her mind filled with the image of what she had seen. They turned a corner, and went down another flight of stairs, entering the basement. They paused in the shadows of a dark passageway.

'Did you see?' sobbed Bekha. 'What was that thing?'

Aila panted, her hands on her knees.

Bekha stared at her. 'Was it alive?'

'Yes. No. I don't know. The God-Queen can do... things. She can kill, and she can...'

'What?'

'She can bring mortals back from the dead.'

Bekha's face froze.

'I've never seen her do it,' Aila went on, 'but that's what my father told me. She can revive people who die, but if they've been dead for too long, then, it doesn't work properly and you end up with a... monstrosity. And if Montieth and his daughters have the same powers as her, then...'

'You mean all of the guards are like that?'

'And that old servant too, I think.'

'Why did you not say anything to me before?'

'My father used to tell those stories to frighten me at bedtime. I never really took them seriously, until now.' She glanced around. 'Where are we? I don't think we've been in this part of the palace before.'

There was a dim light flickering at the end of the corridor, and Aila took Bekha's hand and they crept along towards it. A door was slightly ajar, and lamplight was coming from within. Aila peered through the gap, and saw another passageway lead off, the light coming from the end. She pushed open the door and they stepped through. Bekha opened her mouth, and Aila placed her hand over it to stop her from crying out.

On either side of the passageway were rows of cages, and each one contained a person. Chained and gagged, the bodies were lying curled within the cramped cages. Some opened their eyes at the sound of Aila and Bekha, and terror and panic shone out from their faces. Men, women, children. A few appeared dead, their flesh grey and mottled, while others looked fresh, as if they had only been placed inside the cages a short while before. One began kicking the bars.

'We should go back,' whispered Bekha. 'I can't stand this.'

Aila shook her head. 'I need to see.'

She forced herself to keep walking, drawing ever closer to the light at the end of the corridor. The door was lying open, and there were tables loaded with equipment, where liquids were bubbling in glass vessels. Aila reached the end of the passageway and looked inside. A woman was lying on one of the tables, leather straps securing her body to its surface. On a desk next to her were a selection of knives and metal saws, and a vial of milky-coloured liquid. Aila walked over, her feet seeming to move without any conscious command, her curiosity over-riding her revulsion and fear. She picked up the vial, gazing at its contents as they swirled within the glass.

The woman on the table struggled against the straps, her eyes staring with terror at Aila.

'Aila!' cried Bekha from the door. 'Someone's coming!'

She slipped the vial into her pocket, then her hands went to the straps. Her fingers tried to release them, but her hands were shaking.

'Step away, niece,' came a low voice, the rage barely contained. 'Step away.'

Aila turned. Montieth was staring at her, a look of anger contorting his middle-aged features. He raised his hand towards her.

'I should kill you now,' he said; 'you have been warned to stay away.'

'Sorry, uncle. I got lost.'

'Get out!' he screamed.

Aila ran past him, pulling Bekha along with her. They fled past the cages and back out into the dark passageway. Without knowing where they were going, they ran, until they came to a dead end with a store-room. Aila and Bekha sank down to the ground, hugging each other as they listened.

'I think you might have been right about the roof,' said Aila as her heart raced. 'I'd rather jump off than stay here.'

'There is another choice,' said someone from the shadows.

Aila jumped. She turned, and saw Jade crouching in the corner of the storeroom. 'What are you doing here?'

'I followed you,' she said, 'but as soon as I saw you go into father's laboratory, I knew there would be trouble, and I hid in here.'

'But why were you following us?'

'What you said at dinner; I've been thinking about it. It's not right to sell you to Marcus, and I'm sick of being told what to do all the time by Amber. I hate her.'

Aila swallowed. 'Then will you help us?'

'To do what?'

'To get out of here. Please.'

Jade said nothing, her eyes hidden in the shadows. 'I have one condition.'

'Yes?'

'I have always wanted to leave the palace, but my father and sister have never given me permission. I will help you escape, but only if you take me with you.'

'Agreed. I have a condition too.'

'What, cousin Aila?'

'We do it now. I mean, right now.'

'But I haven't packed any of my things.'

'I'm sorry, but you'll have to leave them here. If we manage to escape, I'll show you the entire City. You'll get to see all of the things you've missed.'

'And, can I get a cat?'

'Yes, I'll buy you one, I swear it.'

'Can I call it Nathaniel?'

'You can call it whatever you like.'

'Promise?'

'I promise.'

Jade stood. 'Alright. Follow me.'

Aila helped Bekha and they got to their feet. Jade moved quickly through the corridors of the basement, and they kept up with her. They stopped at a door, and Jade unlocked it, using a key from a large set she took from a pocket. Two guards were standing on the other side of the door, but at a glance from Jade, they parted to allow them past.

They turned a corner, and Aila caught the scent of the sea. Ahead of them was a stone walkway, lying next to a channel of water leading to an arched opening. Beyond was the night sky, and Aila's heart skipped a beat at the sight.

Jade pointed to a small vessel that was tied up by the walkway. 'Get in. Do you know how to row?'

'I do,' said Bekha. She glanced at Jade as she stepped into the small boat. 'Thank you.'

Jade smiled as she and Aila boarded. Bekha picked up two oars from the bottom of the craft as Jade freed the ropes, and the boat drifted away from the stone wharf. Bekha placed the oars into the slots on either side, and began rowing, the water splashing as the little boat began to move. They reached the archway, and pulled out into the dark, still harbour of Dalrig.

Aila glanced back, looking up at the featureless side of the dark palace as the boat moved further away with every stroke of the oars.

Jade laughed. 'Father is going to be so angry.'

CHAPTER 11
ACTING

Tara, Auldan, The City – 27th Darian 3419

Emily gazed out of the carriage window. The snow had all gone, but a fresh frost lay upon the grass by the side of the road, and it was glimmering in shades of pink from the morning sunshine.

'It's a beautiful day for it,' said Talleta, sitting on the warm bench opposite her.

Emily frowned. 'Be careful who you say that to; it might sound callous to some.'

'Sorry, ma'am. Should I stay in the carriage when we arrive at the palace?'

'Yes. Apart from the relatives of those slain, it's officers and their spouses only. There's going to be a memorial at the academy tomorrow, and the general population of Tara can attend to pay their respects. Prince Marcus wishes for this to be a more private affair. Poor Prince Marcus; I almost feel sorry for him.'

'Almost, ma'am?'

'He wanted power, and now he's got it. But what's he doing with it? Threatening to invade Dalrig because of a single demigod? With all his focus on capturing Lady Aila, he's let other things slip. First, the Champion of the Bulwark turns out to be alive, despite Lord Kano saying he had executed him, and now this? His Blades were responsible for palace security when the attack happened. He keeps saying that they're the best soldiers in the City, but the Taran militia have never once let terrorists get into Maeladh Palace.'

The carriage slowed as they approached a queue leading to the palace gates. Emily glanced out of the window. Soldiers in Blade uniforms were stopping every vehicle and searching it before letting them pass through. Behind them, in a courtyard at the side of the palace, Taran officers were standing around in groups, waiting to greet the arriving civilians.

Talleta turned to look. 'Do you see your husband, ma'am?'

'Not yet.'

Her maid shot her an anxious glance. Emily ignored it, concentrating on removing the knot from her stomach. She hadn't seen Daniel in fifteen days. The last time he had been home, they had argued again, and Daniel had retired to his study to drink a bottle of gin while Emily had gone to bed alone. On the day of his next ten-day pass, he had sent a note excusing himself, saying he had been invited to a dinner party with the senior officers of the militia, and couldn't refuse. Emily had been livid and relieved at the same time, and the extended gap had seen her relationship with Lady Aurelian improve. Without the presence of her son to complicate matters, Emily had found she shared a lot in common with his mother. They still disagreed about certain things, including the clothes Emily chose to wear, but a slow respect was building.

For that day's ceremony, Emily had selected an outfit that reflected the occasion; conservative, and dark. Her hair was covered by a black veil of lace, and the rest of her clothes matched the colour.

The carriage moved again, and then stopped, and a soldier rapped on the window. Talleta leaned over and opened it.

The Blade peered inside, her eyes scanning the interior. 'Invitations?'

Talleta withdrew a card from her shoulder bag and handed it to the soldier. She read it, then nodded and passed it back. The carriage moved off and they passed through the gates, the wheels crunching on the gravel. The officers standing in the courtyard were all wearing their full dress uniform, with sabres buckled to their belts, and leather boots that went to the knee. Emily caught sight of Daniel among the crowd, and their eyes met. He nodded to his colleagues and stepped forwards as the carriage slowed to a halt.

'Good morning,' he said as he opened the side door, inclining his head a little.

She took his offered hand. 'Good morning, Daniel.'

He helped her out of the carriage, and they walked a few paces away as the door was closed and it moved off again.

He glanced at her. 'How have you been?'

'Well, thank you. You?'

'I think I'm still in shock, to be honest. It's hard to believe we've lost so many officers. I was at dinner with several of those who were killed; I knew them.'

'Must be hard.'

'It is. Thanks for coming.'

She nodded. There had been no choice about going, she thought; the invitation from the palace had read more like a summons. She would have gone regardless, to represent the Aurelians, and to present a front that all was well with their marriage.

She smiled. 'It's nice to see you.'

'Is it? That's not what you thought the last time I went home.'

'You weren't pleased to see me either, Daniel, so don't pretend it was all one-way.'

'I'm not pretending; don't put words in my mouth.'

'You hardly speak to me and your letters have dried up, so I'm left to interpret your meaning from the few grunts and groans that comprise your normal conversations.'

'I'm speaking to you now.'

'And what do you have to say to your wife?'

He glanced at her. 'That's she's looking beautiful.'

'Thank you. I tried to be more... appropriate today.'

'So you mean my mother didn't force you to wear that?'

'I thought you'd learned by now that your mother doesn't control how I dress; I do. But don't drag your mother into this; she and I have been getting on a lot better without you.'

He glanced away. 'Could we not do this today? I know you'll think it unmanly of me, but my head's a mess. Can we please not argue?'

'Alright; let's be civil. If we saw each other every day, then this wouldn't happen.'

He half-smiled. 'That's funny. A few days ago I was seriously considering resigning my commission.'

'Why?'

'For a few reasons, but mostly so I could see more of you. If we had our own place to live, it wouldn't be so bad, but having my parents there every time I come home... it's not helping.'

Emily watched him as he spoke. She remembered back to the excitement she had felt before their wedding, and how she had counted down the days. She had barely known him before becoming his wife, but one trait she had believed to be true was his strength of will. What he had done in the Circuit had seemingly proved that to her, but the way he always sided with his mother, and his desire for a peaceful life, even if that meant Emily's needs had to be put aside, all of it filled her heart with resentment.

'I can't resign now, of course,' he said. 'Not after what happened.'

Emily lowered her eyes. 'I know; it would look terrible.'

'It would do more than look terrible, it would be a dereliction of duty. I've never been a very good subordinate; I've always found it hard to obey orders I don't like, but, right now, I have to stand with the militia.'

'Of course, yes.'

A large group of grieving relatives began moving into the building, leaving the officers and their spouses in the courtyard. A senior Blade called out, and the Taran officers formed into a long line, stretching across the yard. Prince Marcus emerged from the building with Lord Chamberlain by his side, and he started to make his way down the line, stopping to speak to each as he went. Emily stood to Daniel's right as they waited. She noticed Lord Chamberlain whisper in Marcus's ear as they went down the line, and she wondered what he would say about the Aurelians. The demigod towered above the waiting Tarans, his shoulders massive and broad. His eyes seemed disconnected from the rest of his face as he smiled at the officers, as if he were suppressing a tide of other emotions.

The prince reached Daniel. Lord Chamberlain whispered something, and the prince nodded and stuck his hand out.

'Lieutenant Aurelian,' he said as Daniel shook his hand; 'I've heard much about you. Your record in the Circuit and in Pella speaks for itself. The Taran militia has need of officers like you, now more than ever. I hope you're ready to step up to meet the challenge?'

'Yes, my lord.'

The prince gave Daniel a cold smile, then he turned his gaze to Emily, and his eyes roved over her for a moment. 'And this must be your young bride, Emily?'

She curtsied as Daniel said, 'Yes, my lord.'

The prince kept his eyes on her, and Emily squirmed. 'You'll need to keep your eye on this one, Lieutenant,' he said; 'beautiful and cunning, a deadly combination for any young wife.'

Marcus moved on, and Emily forced herself to continue smiling. To her left, she could feel Daniel's anger simmering, but she wasn't sure at whom it was directed. She wanted to think it was solely aimed at the prince, but she suspected he might be annoyed at her for embarrassing him. Maybe she was imagining it, but based on the way he had acted when his mother was around, she couldn't shake the feeling that it might be true.

They stood in silence as the prince continued greeting the surviving officer corps of the Taran militia. It seemed to take forever, and Emily could feel her spirits decline with every minute that passed. Why had the prince called her 'cunning'? It must have been something Lord Chamberlain had whispered to him, for how would the prince know anything about her? Was she cunning? What did it mean? Sly and devious? A liar?

A cold wind gusted over the courtyard as the prince reached the end of the line. A Blade officer called out, and the side doors to the palace were opened. The officers began to file through, and Emily kept pace with Daniel, replacing her fixed smile with something more sombre as they passed into a large hall. The relatives of the dead were packing the first few rows of seats, and the officers spread out behind them. Daniel took a seat by the centre aisle and Emily sat next to him, and they watched as Prince Marcus and Lord Chamberlain strode between the rows of seats towards the platform at the end. The prince took his place upon a raised chair, and Lord Chamberlain turned, and lifted a hand for silence.

'Ladies, gentlemen, officers of the Taran militia, good morning,' he said to the packed hall. 'The circumstances in which we meet today are heartbreaking, for we are gathered to mourn the senseless and cowardly murder of twenty officers. Colonels, majors, captains; almost the entire command structure of the militia, cut down in their prime by enemies who seek to destroy our way of life.

'Justice will be coming for the craven terrorists who carried out this heinous act, and for their supporters, for we shall root them out of their hiding places, wherever that may be; they will never be allowed to rest for a single moment in the knowledge that the wrath of the Rosers is coming for them; this we, the government of Tara, vow to you.

'As sure as we are that vengeance will come, today is about celebrating the noble lives of those taken from us. The Taran militia is honourable, and brave; a shining beacon of enlightenment amid savagery; but there is a cost that comes from defending our freedoms, and sometimes that cost is high.'

Lord Chamberlain paused, and withdrew a document from his robes. His eyes went down it, and he began to read out the names of those who had been killed in the fire, as the sound of weeping rose from the front rows. Emily glanced around, seeing the raw anger on the faces of the surviving officers, their eyes burning. She heard Lord Chamberlain read out the name of Daniel's commanding officer; a major who had been mentoring him since Pella, and she took her husband's hand. When the last name was read out, Lord Chamberlain took a seat next to the prince, and the hall sat in silence for a few minutes.

Prince Marcus rose, his features dark, his rage barely contained.

'Beyond the Great Walls of the Bulwark,' he said, 'lie the eternal enemy. For three hundred years I have fought them, while to my rear, the City that I love slowly started to rot and fall into decay. I knew then that I had to act, to restore the City to its rightful position of power and grandeur, but I have found our internal enemies to be more treacherous and cunning than the greenhides.' He paused, his eyes gazing over the crowd. 'Disloyal and cowardly Evaders, selfish, discontented Reapers, and the treacherous rulers of Dalrig; these are the internal enemies we face, and all are conspiring against the noble and pure purposes of my government. We do not yet know to which of these groups the terrorists belonged, but we can be sure that they were all involved in some way.

'They are laughing at us amid our tears; taking joy from our loss, exalting in our grief.' He paused again, allowing the anger among the crowd in the hall to grow. He gestured to a courtier, who carried forward the prince's great sword. Marcus took it, and raised it with one hand. 'I am the High Guardian of the City, but I am also the Prince of Tara, anointed by the blessed God-Queen herself, and as the head of the Rosers I swear to you on the sword of my martyred father that our vengeance will be swift and devastating. Anyone who stands between the Rosers and their appointed place as the first tribe of this City shall feel my wrath, and the edge of this sword. Rosers!' he cried. 'Are you with me?'

The crowd roared out its response.

'On your feet,' Marcus said, his calm features dissolving into a mask of rage and hatred. 'Are you with me?'

'Yes!' the crowd roared, standing as one. 'Yes!'

'We shall show our enemies no mercy,' Marcus thundered, 'just as they stood by and let our officers burn. Remember their screams, imprint them into your minds, and use them as your rallying cry when we take our revenge. Death is coming, and we shall wade in their blood.'

The crowd roared again. Emily glanced around, seeing the faces twisted with rage, then she looked back at Daniel. Her husband was silent. He wasn't joining his voice with the others; instead, he seemed a little bewildered by the cacophony of rage exploding within the hall. He caught her gaze for a moment and she squeezed his hand.

'Wine, ma'am?' asked a waiter carrying a tray in one hand.

Emily took a glass of white from the tray, and turned back to the small group of wives she had been talking with. The officers had all been taken into a different room after the speeches, leaving an assortment of husbands and wives in the hall.

'My cousin was one of the first on the scene,' one of the wives was saying, 'but there were no terrorists around by the time he arrived. Someone had sealed the doors after setting the fire.'

'Cowards,' said another; 'sounds like exactly the kind of thing Evaders would do. They have no honour.'

'But how could Evaders even get into Tara?' said the first. 'The soldiers along the Union Walls are stopping them crossing into Auldan. My money's on a group of Reaper servants. They have access to the entire town, and they're inside each one of our homes, but how can we trust any of them after this?'

'It might have been Reapers who carried it out,' said the second, 'but they haven't got the intelligence to plan such an act. The gold and the brains behind it were Dalrigian, mark my words. Old Montieth is jealous of our prince's success, and he wants him to fail.'

One turned to Emily. 'What do you think?'

'Without any evidence, I wouldn't like to speculate. I do worry, however, about where all this will lead. The City hasn't been this close to civil war in three centuries.'

'You never struck me as a pacifist; your father certainly isn't.'

'Who said I was a pacifist? I merely feel that there's a difference between the pursuit of justice and a call for bloody revenge.'

Some of the wives glared at her. 'The Rosers have been insulted by this atrocity; insulted and provoked,' said one, 'and you think we should meekly submit? We have long lived with the knowledge that some of the other tribes of this City could be better described as savages, and we have tried to be patient with them for centuries. Enough, I say. It's time to show them all who the first tribe is. We are Rosers; we are the City.'

'Hear, hear,' muttered several of the others.

Emily wished she had kept her mouth shut as the others cast glances in her direction. She had heard such language come from her father all her life, and she had even said similar things herself, but something about the prince's oration had stuck in her throat. It might have been as trivial as his use of the word 'cunning' to describe their enemies, so soon after he had called her that to her face, but, regardless, it had left a slightly nauseous feeling in the pit of her stomach. The pain of the people around her was being transformed into hatred before her eyes.

'Good afternoon, ladies,' said Lord Chamberlain as he approached, a glass of sparkling wine in his hands. 'I hope I'm not intruding?'

'Of course not, my lord,' said one of the wives as they all curtsied.

'Such a sad day,' he said, 'but one also tempered by hope when I see the resilience and determination in everyone's faces; it has quite uplifted me.'

'I only wish everyone felt the same, my lord.'

The Lord Chamberlain raised an eyebrow. 'But surely none here disagree?'

A few of the wives glanced at Emily, and the lord turned to her.

'Mistress Aurelian,' he said, 'do you have anything to add?'

'Only, my lord, that I hope it is still not too late for peace. Our fallen officers would not thank us if, in our desire to see justice, we destroy the City.'

'Ah, so you're an appeaser, eh? One of those who think we should negotiate with the cowards who carried out this attack? It's no wonder you get on so well with your husband; I think he has some similar ideas.'

The others laughed as Emily's face flushed. She thought about replying, but knew it would only make it worse.

Lord Chamberlain took a step closer to her. 'I had no trouble thinking about what to say to the prince when we reached you and your husband in the line outside in the courtyard. I told him the Aurelians were ambitious, grasping, and were suffering from the grip of a delusion, imagining that they should be the rulers of Tara.' He leaned even closer. Emily took a step back, but she was close to the wall as he leered down at her. 'I had hopes that an Omertia joining the family might have introduced some sense into the Aurelians, but I appear to have been wrong. You seem just as pathetically deluded as the rest of them. Make no mistake, I will see you fall. I've been looking into your past, girl, unearthing your secrets.' He whispered in her ear. 'You can hide nothing from me.'

'Step back from my wife, Chamberlain,' said Daniel, appearing by the side of the lord; 'before you make an even bigger fool of yourself.'

The group of wives fell silent as the lord turned to face Daniel.

'I am the most powerful mortal in the City,' Chamberlain said, his eyes tight. 'You have no right to address me thus.'

'I'll do more than that if you harass Emily again.'

The lord laughed, but it was forced. 'Are you threatening me, Lieutenant?'

Daniel smiled. 'Yes.'

'You try my patience on a day like today? The arrogance of the Aurelians truly knows no bounds. If you and you wife leave in the next few minutes, then, for the sake of those here who are grieving, I shall overlook your insubordination this time. Do you understand?'

Daniel turned to Emily and extended his arm. 'Shall we?'

She glanced at the faces of everyone around them; their stares boring through her. She took Daniel's arm, and they walked through the hall in silence, as the others parted to make way for them. A Blade opened the door for them and they stepped outside into the crisp air.

Emily put a hand to her face. 'I don't think I've ever felt so humiliated.'

Daniel turned to her, his eyes lit with fury. 'Would you rather I'd done nothing?'

'That's not what I meant. I feel sick.'

'It'll take ten minutes to get a carriage,' he said, starting to stride away. 'We'd be quicker walking to the mansion.'

She glared at his back, then caught up with him, her boots crunching over the frost-covered gravel. 'You're coming back to the mansion?'

'Yes. We've all been given a pass for the night, but I'll go back to the regiment if you want me to.'

Emily said nothing. She didn't know what she wanted. She had assumed that he would be returning to his barracks after the ceremony, and knew his mother hadn't been planning for his presence.

'I'm a disappointment to you,' he said.

'What?'

'I'm clearly not what you were hoping for as a husband.'

Emily said nothing as they approached the gates of the palace, the Blades on duty eyeing them as they passed. They stepped from the gravel of the palace driveway onto the road that led to Princeps Row and the Aurelian mansion.

Daniel slowed his pace and turned to her. 'What did he say to you?'

'That he'd told Prince Marcus not to trust us, and that he was looking into my past.'

Daniel frowned. 'Your past?'

'Yes. I don't know why, though; I have nothing to hide.'

'There are no Omertia secrets?'

'My father being an oaf is not a secret, but maybe there are some things you should know, in case you hear of them from other sources.'

'Such as?'

Emily sighed, and glanced away as they walked. 'He used to beat me and my mother.'

Daniel halted on the road, his fists clenching. 'What? That asshole hurt you?' His eyes drifted down the cliffside, in the direction of the Omertia family home. 'Say the word and I'll kill him.'

'No, Daniel. I'm free of him, and I've left that old life behind.'

He shook his head. 'I can't bear the thought of it. I wanted to punch Chamberlain for the way he was pawing at you in there, and now the thought of your father hurting you... I... What should I do? Tell me.'

'I don't know, Daniel.'

'And when did you stop calling me "Danny"? You hate me, don't you?'

'No.'

'But you don't love me either.'

'Do you love me, Daniel?'

'I don't know how I feel. I miss you when we're apart, but we fight whenever we're together.'

She nodded. 'That's how I feel too. Did we make a mistake?'

'I don't want to think that way,' he said. 'I want to make this work.'

'I'm not sure I believe you. You haven't written, and you didn't come home for your last ten-day pass. That doesn't look like someone trying to make it work.'

He nodded, his eyes dark. 'I have news, from the meeting with all of the officers. Things are going to change again, and you have a choice to make.'

'What choice?'

'I've been assigned back to Cuidrach Palace in Pella.'

'Oh.'

'But I'll be going as an acting-captain this time, which means that you're allowed to come with me if you want. There are apartments for married officers in the palace, with a view of the bay.'

'Pella?'

'Yes. What do you think?'

'Do you want me to come?'

He took her hand. 'Yes, more than anything. We can't go on in the same way. We might end up hating each other, but this way, at least we will have tried.'

She glanced up at him, unsure of how she felt about his proposal. She would miss the luxury of the mansion, but he was right, if they didn't try, then they might as well give up.

'I'll come,' she said.

He smiled, and they started walking again, their hands still entwined.

They turned up the driveway of the mansion, and entered through a side door. A Reaper servant bowed as they walked into the warmth of the interior. They passed the kitchen, where his mother was talking to the housekeeper. Her eyes darted over when she saw her son.

'Daniel, what a lovely surprise; are you staying?'

'Yes, mother. I have a pass until tomorrow morning.'

'Marvellous. I'll arrange everything, just leave it all to me. It'll be wonderful to catch up with you, dear.'

'Another time, mother,' he said, squeezing Emily's hand. 'I want to be alone with my wife.'

CHAPTER 12
THE ROADBLOCK

Reaper-Gloamer Frontier, Auldan, The City – 28th Darian 3419
'Good morning, Corporal,' said the captain; 'how did the night pass for you and your squad?'

'Quiet, sir,' said Maddie. 'No one approached the border.'

The captain gazed out over the empty fields that marked the frontier between the two tribal territories. An ancient ditch marked the line, and the suburbs of Outer Pella went right up to it, while on the Gloamer side there were two miles of farmland before the town of Dalrig began. In the distance Maddie could see a Gloamer patrol, standing a quarter of a mile away, facing the Blade defences that lined the frontier.

The captain nodded. 'Get yourself some rest, Corporal. Dismissed.'

Maddie gave a weary salute and trudged away from the observation platform. She had a tent she shared with her squadmates, and was looking forward to wrapping at least a dozen blankets round her and getting some sleep. The Blades had constructed palisade walls along the frontier, and several towers watched over Gloamer lands for any sign of their local militia. For days, Maddie and the rest of the Blades had been waiting for the order to attack, but their plans had been delayed due to a fire in Tara that had wiped out most of Prince Marcus's Roser commanders. Maddie understood little about the politics of it all, and cared even less. To her, the tribal rivalry in Auldan was squalid and petty compared to the eternal war against the greenhides, but she was a Blade. She felt no loyalty to Marcus, but she would fight for her comrades.

She crossed a wide road, which led all the way from Dalrig before heading off through Outer Pella to the Union Walls. The road was the reason her company had been based there. Before the siege of Gloamer territory had begun, it had been one of the busiest thoroughfares in Auldan, carrying goods back and forth, including much of the food supply that the Circuit depended upon. With every day that the road lay empty and blocked by Blade soldiers, the Evaders were one step closer to starvation.

She entered the company's camp, where four wooden walls surrounded a score of tents. It stank after a month of occupation, and was busy with soldiers working or resting. She made her way to the open kitchen, and was handed a bowl of seaweed and a piece of flatbread. She grimaced at the smell, then walked to her tent. The rest of her squad were already there, sitting by the entrance, eating their breakfast.

The sergeant noticed her and beckoned. 'Did you report to the captain?'

'Yes, Sergeant,' she said, sitting down next to him.

'Thanks, Maddie. He give any orders?'

'Nope, just rest. I don't think we'll be attacking today.'

'Thank Malik for that,' muttered one of the squad.

'Indeed,' said the sergeant. 'Prince Montieth's a crafty old bird; he'll not want to go to war over a demigod. He'll negotiate at the last minute, you'll see.'

'But what if it was Montieth who organised the fire in Tara, Sergeant?' said the private. 'Marcus might not want to negotiate with him.'

'But he'll never attack,' said another soldier, 'not if Montieth has the death powers.'

'He doesn't,' laughed the sergeant; 'that's just an old myth. And besides, he hasn't left his palace in a thousand years.'

Maddie chewed her seaweed as the squad argued about the course events might take. She had been in the camp for twenty-one days, following a short stay in a fort on the Middle Walls while the company had been assembled. In that time, no news had come to her of Blackrose, and her worry had increased day by day. The only good news had been the rumour that Corthie might still be alive, but it remained a rumour, only that, and not many of the Blades wanted to discuss the disgraced former champion.

She put down the empty bowl, feeling a bit sick and wondering how so many in the City survived on such strange food.

A lieutenant approached the squad. 'Good morning.'

The sergeant nodded. 'Morning, ma'am.'

'I need two volunteers, Sergeant. We're a little short-handed.'

'Doing what, if you don't mind me asking, ma'am?'

'Guard duty.'

'But we were on guard duty all night, ma'am.'

'It's only until lunchtime.'

The sergeant frowned, and glanced over the members of the squad, who all looked away.

'Malik's sweaty crotch,' muttered Maddie; 'I hate being corporal. Fine. I'll do it.'

'Good lass,' said the sergeant. 'Who else?'

'I'll do it,' said a private named Hagan. 'I can't sleep during the day anyway.'

The sergeant nodded up to the officer.

'Thank you,' she said, and Maddie and Hagan got to their feet. They were still dressed for duty, with crossbows slung over their shoulders.

They followed the lieutenant out of the camp, and she gestured to the left, along the road leading into the suburbs of Outer Pella.

'Watch the roadblock up ahead; you'll be relieved at noon.'

Maddie saluted. 'Yes, ma'am.' She nodded to Hagan. 'Let's go.'

They trudged along the road, the wooden palisade wall of the camp on their left, and the first houses of Outer Pella on their right, all of which had been commandeered by Blade officers and their staff. The roadblock they had been assigned to was at the opposite end of the camp from the one they had stood at all night, and was designed to keep any overly-curious Reaper civilians from approaching the frontier. It was deserted when they reached it and Maddie and Hagan settled down by the barrels filled with rubble that had been laid across the road in a double line.

'Just five hours of boredom to go,' muttered Hagan as he leant against a barrel.

'I'd rather have that than any actual... you know, fighting.'

The private eyed her. 'Can I ask you something, Corporal?'

'Yeah?'

'This might sound cheeky, but it's not meant to be; how did you become corporal?'

'I can think of several answers to that. Firstly, it's none of your damn business; second, how was that not meant to be cheeky? It was cheeky. Third, I don't like your tone. Fourth...'

Hagan laughed. 'Alright, I get it. I saw your arm, you know, when you were coming out of the showers a few days ago.'

'You've been watching me coming out of the showers? Is that why you volunteered to do guard duty with me? Well, you can forget it, buddy; it ain't happening.'

'I was talking about your tattoos.'

'Yeah, of course; I knew that. What about them? You jealous of my varied career?'

'You seem a little young to have been in so many different units.'

Maddie sighed. 'I understand. You think I'm too young, and too... whatever to be a corporal. I didn't ask to be made one, and now that I am one I don't like it. I hate being responsible for making decisions that might get people killed, but, I suppose, I wasn't much use at following orders either. The infantry booted me out, then I quit an arbalest course, and then I got kicked out of a support battalion, on my first day.'

She glanced at him, and noticed he was staring into the distance. 'Boring you, am I?'

'What? No, look. There's a wagon coming along the road from Dalrig.'

She squinted down the road. Thirty yards ahead of them was the main roadblock, where the squad had been posted the previous night. It was situated on the line of the frontier, and the ancient ditch stretched out on either side of the filled barrels that barred the way. Beyond that, the road led away between the fields of Gloamer territory. Along it, a carriage was approaching, a team of ponies speeding over the flag-stones. The squad on day duty was getting into position, pulling their crossbows from their shoulders as their sergeant stepped out onto the road, his arm raised.

Maddie walked out from her post and strode forwards to get a better view. The wagon slowed as it neared the roadblock. There were three figures sitting on the driver's bench, but they were too far away for Maddie to hear the words they were exchanging with the duty sergeant. From the gesturing, they seemed to be demanding the removal of the roadblock, but the Blades were under strict orders to detain anyone trying to cross the border. Raised voices drifted through the air, attracting more soldiers, who emerged from the entrance to the camp.

'Who is it, do you think?'

Maddie turned to see Hagan standing next to her. 'I don't know. Shouldn't one of us be guarding our own roadblock?'

'I want to see what happens. No one's ever approached the frontier before. Look, they're getting down from the wagon.'

She turned back. The three figures had gone from the driver's bench, lost amid the gathered Blades. There were more shouts, then screams, and Maddie froze as a dozen Blades fell, their bodies thrown backwards in a circle around the three figures. More Blades rushed them, and one of the figures raised a hand, and the soldiers toppled over, collapsing in heaps by the entrance to the camp. Maddie felt panic rise. She and Hagan were the only Blades left alive on the road. She could hear cries coming from the camp as the three figures started to run towards her. The woman raised her hand again, and more Blades by the entrance fell, and screams rose up from within the camp, piercing the air.

Maddie shoved Hagan. 'Run.'

The three figures got closer, and Maddie saw that they were all women. The one who had raised her hand and killed the Blades had long, braided black hair, and her eyes were shining with exhilaration. The other two women were staring at her in shock, and one with brown hair was shouting.

'Why did you do that?' she cried. 'You didn't need to kill them.'

The woman with the braids saw Maddie and Hagan, and lifted her hand again as she ran.

The brown-haired woman reached out as if to restrain her. 'No, Jade!'

Maddie stood frozen, her crossbow still slung round her back. Hagan stepped in front of her as the power left the woman's hand. Maddie felt it hit them like a wave of pain, and Hagan's body seemed to wither and crumple before her eyes, his skin peeling off in dry strips. They fell to the flagstones, Hagan dead, Maddie writhing in agony. The body of the private had shielded her, but she was still dying. Pain consumed her, and she vomited blood down her uniform, while her guts felt like they were on fire. She tried to take a breath, her vision blurry.

'I told you not to do that!' cried an angry voice.

Maddie lifted her arm. 'Don't walk away,' she gasped, 'don't leave me like this.'

'That one's still alive,' said the blonde woman, horror on her face as she glanced at Maddie.

'Malik's ass, look what you've done to her, Jade.'

'Don't leave me to die like this,' Maddie said, her voice sounding gargled as blood trickled down her chin.

The woman with the braids stopped and stared at her. 'I'll put the mortal out of its misery.'

'She's just a girl,' said the one with brown hair. 'Heal her.'

'What? I don't waste my power on mortals, and you already have a pet.'

'We're not monsters, Jade; heal her, or you can forget about Nathaniel.'

Jade scowled. 'Fine.' She raised her hand again, and Maddie felt a great force surge over her, filling every inch of her body. At first she panicked, but then realised that she liked it. The feeling ripped through her, healing and repairing all the damage that had been inflicted by Jade's death powers, and then fixing every niggle and ache and pain she had ever had. She felt as if she were drunk, her mind reeling in the wave of well-being and health. She opened her eyes. She had never felt so good in her life; had never felt so alive. From her hair to her toes, and over every part of her skin; it felt like she was glowing.

The brown-haired woman ran over to her. 'Are you alright?'

Maddie giggled, her mind overwhelmed by what she was feeling. 'I feel great. Wow, oh wow; this is amazing...'

The woman frowned. 'What's wrong with her now?'

Jade shrugged. 'I'm not used to healing mortals. I might have over-done it a bit.'

'When will... this wear off?'

'I don't know.'

Maddie stared at her palms as if seeing them for the first time. Had something bad happened? She couldn't focus, as if everything was blurry and vague at the edges. Where was she? She glanced around. 'Blackrose? Are you there?'

The brown-haired woman stared at her. 'What did you say?'

'We need to go,' said the other woman, 'more soldiers will be coming.'

'Wait,' said the brown-haired woman. She turned back to Maddie. 'What did you say? Do you know Blackrose?'

'She's my dragon,' Maddie said, grinning. 'I look after her. I even rode on her back once as she flew through the air. Wheeeeeee! I'm her rider.' She glanced around, her eyes wide. 'Well, I used to be. Where are we; what's happening?'

'You're her rider? They have riders?'

'We don't have time for this,' said the other woman; 'we have to run.'

'Then we're bringing this girl with us.'

'No way.'

'I made a promise, Bekha; a promise to Corthie.'

'Do you know Corthie?' said Maddie. 'Is he here too? I like him; he remembered my name.'

'Help me lift her,' said the brown-haired woman. 'Come on. Now.'

Maddie felt hands grab her under the shoulders, and she was pulled to her feet.

'Can you run?' asked the brown-haired woman.

'Blackrose broke my leg,' she said, gazing down at it, 'but it feels nice now.' Everything went dark. 'Hey, is it night?'

'Does she need to wear a hood?' said a voice.

'She does if we plan to let her go.'

Maddie started moving, guided by a strong arm round her shoulder.

'Come on, follow me,' the voice said. 'I know a safe house less than a mile away where we can hide.'

Maddie felt her legs move under her but despite the hood, she felt safe. How could anything be wrong if she could feel so good?

They ran for what seemed a long time to Maddie, then they went down some stairs and Maddie was placed onto a soft bed, where she fell into a warm, comfortable sleep.

She awoke in a panic, the hood over her head. Her hands had been tied while she had been sleeping, and she nearly fell off the bed as she struggled to free herself. Her memories were groggy, but the events on the road had come back to her as she had awoken, and the image of the Blades lying dead on the flagstones burned in her mind. At the same time, her body felt wonderful, and for the first time since Blackrose had injured her, she could feel no aches or pains anywhere.

'Help,' she cried, her voice muffled through the hood.

She remembered the faces of the three women who had taken her. The one with the braids had looked at her as though she were an insect to be trod upon, but the other two had seemed angry and upset with the deaths of the Blades; and the one with the brown hair had made the one with the braids save her. Hagan's last act flashed through her mind. She was only alive because that idiot had sacrificed himself for her. She felt tears well in her eyes, and she sobbed into the hood. She had been his corporal, it should have been her who had saved him, and now she was captured.

'Hello,' said a voice. 'I'm going to remove your hood, but you must promise me that you won't cry out or try to escape.'

Maddie wriggled on the bed, trying to turn towards the source of the voice. 'Who are you?'

'Do you promise?'

'Are you going to kill me?'

'No, I only want to talk to you.'

'Is Jade here? I don't want to see her.'

'She's not here, and I've told her to stay out of this room. You're safe.'

Hands went to her head, and she felt the knots of the cord being untied. The hood was pulled from her face and she glanced at the brown-haired woman. She was crouching by the bed, unarmed. Maddie glanced around the small room. It had earthen walls and no windows, and apart from the bed, there was no other furniture. The woman had a mug in her hands, and she held it out.

'Drink?'

'What is it?'

'Just water.'

'Have you poisoned it? How do I know you haven't poisoned it?'

'Easy. If I wanted you dead, I could just call Jade back in here. Listen, back at the road, you were giddy, like you were drunk, and you were saying some things that caught my attention.'

Maddie narrowed her eyes. 'Yeah? I don't remember that. What about?'

'Blackrose.'

'What? I, uh... No, I don't know what you're talking about, sorry.'

The woman smiled, and placed the mug onto the earthen floor. 'You said you were her rider.'

'I said that? Oh, bugger.'

'You also said you knew Corthie, and that he remembered your name.'

'Oh. Well, like you said, it was as if I was drunk. I must have been babbling the first things that came into my head. I've never even heard of a Blackrose.'

'Come on, drop the act. You know about the other dragon, there's no way that just popped into your head from nowhere. Look, I'm a friend of Corthie's and I made a promise to him about Blackrose; a promise that I couldn't keep.'

Maddie squinted at the woman.

'And...'

'Quiet,' said Maddie; 'I'm thinking.'

The woman quietened as Maddie tried to recall everything Corthie had said to her.

'I'm good at guessing,' she said after a moment, 'and I bet I can guess who you are. You're Lady Aila, you must be, that's why you were running from Dalrig; you must have escaped, but you don't want to be caught by the Blades either, or you'll be sent to Marcus.' Her eyes widened. 'It was you, wasn't it? Blackrose said that Corthie was in love, but he wouldn't say who with. And when he went to steal the Quadrant, you were there.'

The woman blinked. 'How do you know that?'

'Because Corthie visited Blackrose the day he went to Pella. Poor Blackrose, she blames herself for Corthie killing Princess Khora... Oh, wait, did you hear the rumour that he might still be alive?'

'Listen, I need you to pass on a message to Blackrose for me.'

Maddie frowned. 'And how am I meant to do that? Does it look like I'm still assigned to her? I got rounded up and sent here. How does it feel to have a war start because of you?'

'I'm hoping there won't be a war, not now that I've managed to get out of Dalrig.'

'And Marcus? Why does he want you so much?'

Aila met her eyes. 'Are you loyal to the new Prince of Tara?'

'I swore an oath like all Blades, so yeah, technically I am; but if you're asking me if I like him, then no. He's a disgusting brute, just like Kano, and I hate being here. The Blades are not supposed to be used to sort out the petty squabbles of Auldan; we're supposed to be defending the City from the greenhides. If you're running from Marcus, then I sympathise, I guess, but at the same time I wish you'd all stop dragging us into your problems.'

'I couldn't agree more. What's your name?'

'Maddie Jackdaw.'

'Alright, Maddie Jackdaw, listen to me. I understand that you've been re-assigned, but you're still the first person I've met who can possibly help me reach Blackrose. If you get back to the Bulwark, you must pass her a message.'

'Do you love Corthie? Did I guess right?'

Aila smiled. 'Yes, I do love him.'

'Awwww; that's sweet. Have you kissed?'

'Yes.'

'Is he a good kisser?'

'Yes,' she said, her face flushing a little, 'but that's not my message.'

'And he's alive? Is that true?'

'I think so, but Marcus has sent soldiers off to Tarstation to kill him.'

'Tarstation? Where's that?'

'It's about two hundred miles iceward, across the Cold Sea.'

'He's out of the City? Wow, I didn't know that was possible. So, what's your message?'

Aila caught her eyes. 'He didn't kill Princess Khora.'

'What? I knew it! I told that stupid dragon, but she wouldn't believe me. I knew Corthie wouldn't do that. Ha! Who did?'

'My brother, Kano.'

'That asshole's your brother? Oops, sorry, but he is an asshole.'

'I know. He wasn't always that way.'

Maddie frowned. 'He's a beast. He once... never mind. What he did is not the sort of thing a sister wants to hear about her brother.'

'Did he hurt you?'

'He tried, but I threatened him with Blackrose. She's quite protective of me, well, she was, if she's still alive.'

'What do you mean?'

'She was so ridden with guilt over Corthie, and so depressed about him not getting the Quadrant... Do you know what I'm talking about when I say the "Quadrant"? I don't really know what it is, myself, I just heard Corthie and Blackrose talk about it. Could you untie my hands, please? My nose is itchy.'

Aila pulled a knife from her belt, and leaned round behind Maddie. She sliced through the ropes, and Maddie rubbed her hands together.

'That's better,' she said scratching her nose. 'Anyway, where was I? Oh yes, Blackrose decided that she was going to starve herself to death, after we heard that Corthie had been executed, and as far as I know, she hasn't eaten anything since. She wants to die.'

'Then it's even more important that you get my message to her. Corthie didn't forget about Blackrose. He made me and Khora promise to help her escape; but Khora was killed, and there was nothing I could do.'

'Where is the Quadrant?'

'Someone has it; I can't tell you who. Sorry.'

'I bet I can guess.' Maddie thought for a moment. 'Lord Naxor?'

'How in Malik's name did you know that?'

'He's the other rebel demigod we were told to look out for. He's also the one that brings the champions to the Bulwark. It wasn't that difficult. How are we going to find him?'

'There's no "we", Maddie. After this, we're letting you go, and you'll be able to return to your unit. Plenty of Reapers saw us drag you away, so you should be safe. You were a hostage, taken in case we were followed; that's what you can tell the Blades. '

Maddie frowned. 'What's left of them. How many did that crazy Jade kill? She's a demigod too, isn't she? A daughter of Montieth?'

'Yes.'

'Why did you bring her? She's a maniac. How many people did she kill on the road?' she paused, feeling the pain of her memories return. 'Hagan. He died for me, did you see?'

'That soldier who stepped in front of you? Yes, I saw. I'm sorry; I'm really sorry. Jade... she's...'

'Out of control?'

Aila leaned in closer. 'Taking her was the only way I could get out of Greylin Palace. I had no idea she would react that way when we came to the roadblock. I had a plan worked out, but she panicked when she saw the Blades aiming their crossbows at her, and before I could stop her, they were all dead.' She rubbed her face. 'And now everyone will know that one of Montieth's daughters is on the loose in the City. We'll have to lie very low for a while.'

'Where's Naxor?'

'I don't know,' she said. 'When he left me in the Circuit, he told me he would return, but I've not seen him since.'

'Did you mention to him anything about getting Blackrose back to her home?'

'No. I'd just watched Khora die, and I thought Corthie was dead too. I was a mess.'

'Alright,' said Maddie, 'here's what we do. I'll try to get back to Blackrose, to tell her that Corthie's innocent and alive, and that you're trying to help. You're going to have to find Naxor, and tell him we need the Quadrant. But you'll need to keep Jade under control, because the Blades will be looking for you after what she did.'

Aila nodded. 'And what about Corthie?'

'I've seen him fight the greenhides; a few boatloads of Blades shouldn't be much of a problem for him.'

'It was Blades who filled him with crossbow bolts at Cuidrach Palace, Maddie. I saw what they could do to him.'

'Then we say a prayer to Malik and hope.'

Maddie stumbled forward, the hood blocking her vision, her hands tied behind her back again. The woman named Bekha was pushing her along an uneven track, and she tripped over the loose cobbles. An arm guided her, then pushed her down, and she sat on the ground.

'Don't move,' whispered Bekha's voice in her ear. 'There's a sheer drop to your side, and directly ahead of you. If you move, you'll fall over the edge. I'm going to cut the ropes round your wrists, but stay completely still until I say, then you can remove the hood. Understand?'

'Why are you leaving me here? I don't want to fall.'

She felt the ropes by her hands drop away.

'You won't fall if you do exactly as I say,' said the voice as it grew fainter. 'Not yet. Stay still. Another minute. I'm watching you.'

The voice fell silent as Maddie waited. She moved her head to listen, but could hear nothing. After another minute had passed, she raised her hands to the hood. Silence. She pulled the hood off and realised that she was sitting in a narrow alleyway. She frowned; there was no drop. Bekha had tricked her, but she didn't mind.

She stood, rubbing her wrists. She was alive, and in better health than she had been in years, maybe ever. She glanced around, seeing the tight lanes and red sandstone houses that made up most of Outer Pella. It was still daytime, but the alleyways were covered by thick, cotton awnings, and only a dim light was seeping through from the sky.

They had taken her crossbow, but she didn't care. She thought back to Aila and Jade; both demigods, but completely different from each other, and she smiled at the plan. She had told a demigod what to do, and the demigod had listened. Corthie and Aila; they suited each other. Now all she had to do was somehow get back to Blackrose before it was too late.

First though, she had to return to the camp, and the roadblock. Her smile fell away, and she began walking.

CHAPTER 13

THE STRAITS

The Western Bank – 15th Yordian 3419

'I've decided it's my birthday today,' said Corthie.

Yaizra raised an eyebrow at him across the low campfire. 'Yeah?'

'Aye. I hope you both got me a present.'

Achan leaned up from his blanket. 'I didn't know your birthday was in Yordian.'

'It's not,' said Corthie. 'There's no month called "Yordian" where I'm from. There are no months either; well, there are, but we call them "thirds". We don't give them names; it's just the First Third of Spring, that sort of thing.'

Yaizra poked the fire with a stick. 'Why don't you call them months?'

'No idea.'

Achan pursed his lip, his face reflecting the flames. 'Do you have a moon where you come from?'

'No.'

He shrugged. 'Then that's why. Month comes from moon. No moon; no months. So, it's not really your birthday today?'

'In my world, it falls in the middle of the last month of winter, which is today, aye? I've no idea what date it is where I'm from, but here, I'm claiming today.'

'Happy birthday,' said Yaizra. 'How old are you?'

He smiled. 'Nineteen.'

Her face fell. 'What? I've been taking orders from a nineteen-year-old?'

'An eighteen-year-old,' he said, 'before today.'

'I thought you were the same age as me, big lump, and I'm twenty-four.'

Achan nodded. 'I'd have never have guessed that you were still a teenager.' He shook his head. 'You were killing all those greenhides when you were eighteen?'

'Never mind the greenhides,' said Yaizra, 'he carried you across half the ice field.'

'Don't exaggerate; it wasn't half,' Achan smiled; 'maybe a quarter...'

Corthie shrugged. 'It wasn't as bad as everyone had made out it was going to be.'

'What?' said Yaizra. 'Are you insane? Twenty days of ice and blizzards? And the cold?' She shivered. 'I'll never forget it.'

'Aye, but look at us now, having a campfire in a forest, with no snow anywhere. And it's been getting lighter; you must sense it. To me the light here's the same as it is in the City; we must be close.'

'The City might only be a few miles away,' said Achan.

Yaizra and Corthie stared at him.

'But it makes no difference,' the Hammer went on, 'not while we're on the other side of the Straits. The currents are crazy, and it's impossible to swim across, even though the distance between the two coasts narrows to only two miles in places.'

Corthie raised an eyebrow. 'Two miles? I could swim that.'

'Did you not hear what I said about the currents? The Straits are where the Cold Sea meets the Warm Sea, and the water foams and churns, and there's nearly always a fog lying thick over it. It's called the Clashing Seas. No ship can cross, did you know that? It's impossible to sail from the Cold Sea to the Warm Sea, and it's the same the other way around. The big bay where Ooste, Pella and Tara sit is sunward of where the two seas meet, but nothing can go iceward of there.'

'But we have to get across somehow.'

Yaizra nodded. 'And preferably before the storms of Freshmist begin. Once that happens, we'll be stuck here until summer, and then the bank will be infested with greenhides.'

'Yeah,' said Achan, 'that's why I was thinking we should go down to Jezra.'

'Jezra?' said Corthie.

'It's the ruins of an abandoned town on the western bank. Thousands of years ago, before the greenhides arrived and wiped it out, it was part of the alliance with Tara, Pella and the rest of the original towns. There might be something there we can use to get across.'

Yaizra shook her head. 'But that'll mean we'll be on the sunward side of the Clashing Seas, and the closest place will be Tara. We can't go there. We need to cross the Cold Sea; we can hide in Icehaven.'

Corthie smiled. 'Yaizra doesn't want to go to Jezra. Is that because it sounds like your name?'

'I'm named after the town, you idiot.'

Achan laughed. 'Jezra has a strong place in the mythology of the City; our lost town, one day we shall reclaim it, blah, blah, that sort of thing. It's a common name among the Hammers too.'

Yaizra frowned. 'Are you saying I'm common?'

'No, thankfully there's only one of you. Anyway, I wasn't thinking of going to Tara. If you go past Port Sanders, there's a harbour in the Bulwark; Salt Quay. There's a Blade garrison, but it'll be depleted with all the trouble going on. And right behind it is the territory of the Hammers. We can easily hide there, and we'll be among my folk, who'll be able to help us.'

Yaizra shook her head. 'What, and get stuck inside the Bulwark? No way. If we've reached Jezra, then we're already too far sunward. We should go back a bit, and try to cross the Cold Sea to Icehaven.'

Corthie watched as they glared at each other. He hadn't given too much thought to what they would do after they had escaped; his sole motivation had been to make sure they all crossed the ice fields alive. He frowned. It was time to think about what he was going to do when he got back to the City. Finding Aila was the key; find her, and then get to Blackrose. Aila would know what to do. His thoughts drifted to her, as they often had during the journey across the ice. She had been with Naxor the last time he had seen her, but over four months had elapsed since then and she could be anywhere.

'Are you listening to me, Holdfast?'

Corthie glanced at Yaizra. 'What?'

She sighed. 'Dreaming again? I asked if you had an opinion about where we should go.'

'Inside the City; beyond that I don't care. Achan, how far are we from Jezra?'

'An hour's walk, maybe.'

'Then we should go there. There might be no way across, but it's worth trying before we double back to the Cold Sea.'

Yaizra glared at Achan. 'You planned this; you knew how far sunward we'd come.'

'I honestly didn't think it would be a problem,' he said, spreading his palms. 'It never occurred to me that you'd want to go back to Icehaven; wouldn't you be recognised and arrested?'

'I could say the same about you and Salt Quay, ya Hammer fool.'

They packed up their things and began trekking through the rough terrain of the forest. They had run out of their food supplies a few days previously, and had been living on whatever they could forage and hunt, with Yaizra's sling providing them with more than one meal.

'Why is the land so uneven?' Corthie said, as they traversed a high ridge.

'The ruins of Upper Jezra lie beneath our feet,' said Achan. 'The town was in two halves; the narrow coastal strip at the bottom of the cliffs where the harbour lies, and the land at the top, where we are now. Three thousand years ago this was all streets and houses.'

'And everyone died when the greenhides came?'

'Not everyone; some got away by ship. Then, three hundred years later, before the God-King and God-Queen started having children, the town was re-occupied. For two centuries it held out, but it was too small and had to be re-supplied constantly, and in the end it was abandoned again, for good. I can't wait to see what remains of the lower town by the coast. There was a massive fortress down there; I wonder if any of it's left.'

'Listen to him drool,' said Yaizra. 'It's just a bunch of old rocks.'

Achan frowned. 'This is our history. We might be the first people to walk here for a very long time.'

They carried on over the broken land, rising and falling with its contours. They scrambled up an embankment, and before them spread a view of the Straits and, in the distance, was a faint line of cliffs, marking the edge of the City. Below them, the Warm Sea was a pale blue, sparkling in the pink light of morning, while to their left the Straits were obscured by a thick blanket of fog drifting over the surface of the water. Far to the left, the end of the fog was visible, and the dark waters of the Cold Sea began.

'The Clashing Seas are under all that fog,' said Achan. 'Any boat that enters, never comes out again.' He pointed ahead. 'Ooste lies directly opposite us.'

Corthie nodded. 'And where's Salt Quay from here?'

Achan pointed to the right. 'Sail sunward past Tara, then turn east towards the Bulwark.'

'I sailed there from Port Sanders when I first arrived in the City. There was a big wall separating the harbour from the land of the Hammers.'

Yaizra chuckled. 'I told you his plan was stupid.'

'We may have to fight,' Achan said; 'and when I say "we", I really mean you two. Come on, let's find the edge of the cliff and see if there's a way down.'

He hurried off in the direction of the Straits as Yaizra glanced at Corthie.

'He wants you to lead the Hammers in revolt; you do know that, yeah?'

Corthie nodded. 'Aye, and who knows? Maybe I'll do it.'

'What, and destroy the City in the process?'

'It's not right that they're treated like slaves. And what's the alternative? What would we do if we followed your plan and went to Icehaven?'

Yaizra smiled as she started walking. 'Hide.'

Achan called to them, and they caught him up by the edge of the cliffside. Corthie put a hand on a boulder to steady himself and looked down. Below them were the ruins of a town, built upon a narrow shelf of land at the bottom of the cliffs. Exposed to the winds, and the waves from the sea, the walls of the ancient settlement had long since crumbled away. A few huge stumps of rock remained that might once have been great towers, and the street layout was still discernible in places, but the majority of the town had been reclaimed by nature.

'I think I've found a way down,' said Achan.

'Why?' said Yaizra. 'There's nothing there.'

'Much of the town was burrowed into the cliffside to make up for the lack of space; it's worth a look, and if we find nothing I'll admit defeat and we'll go with your plan.'

Corthie glanced in the direction Achan was pointing, and frowned. He strode over and crouched down to look at some markings on a large boulder.

'What is it?' said Yaizra.

'I'm not a tracker, but these look like the claw marks made by greenhides. I've seen the same beyond the Great Walls.'

'Like they're marking their territory?'

'Maybe.' He stood and scanned the forest, using his battle-vision to listen. 'I can't see or hear any sign of them, but that doesn't mean they're not around. Keep your eyes open.'

They began to descend the cliffside, following the steep path that Achan had found. Yaizra made no sound, but Achan's foot slipped on a loose rock, and it slipped down the face of the cliff, sending a cascade of other stones with it, and they fell with a low rumble and clatter that echoed across the small bay.

'Donkey brains,' Yaizra muttered.

Achan gave a guilty-looking smile, and they carried on. Corthie heightened his powers, trying to catch any movement within his field of vision. Something glistened for a second down by the ruined harbour and he crouched, stilling himself.

Yaizra glanced back, lifting her head to listen.

Corthie leaned close to her. 'I thought I saw something move down in the ruins. Maybe it was the water shining off the rocks, I don't know.'

Achan stopped and turned. 'What's the hold up?'

'Nothing,' said Corthie as he stood. 'Keep going.'

They set off again, and descended a long stretch that clung to the side of the cliff, Corthie keeping his eyes on the treacherous path. They came to a wide platform three-quarters of the way down, and rested. The ground was uneven but seemed to be the remnants of a massive building that had once dominated the cliffside.

'This must be the Roser Palace,' said Achan, his eyes wide as he gazed at the ruins.

'Was Jezra a Roser town?' said Corthie.

Yaizra snorted. 'No. It was shared by the three original tribes. I don't know why the palace would be called that.'

'The town was shared,' said Achan, 'but it was also divided. The Rosers held this bit down here, and the harbour, while the Reapers took Upper Jezra and the farms on the plateau. The Gloamers had to make do with a small harbour on the Cold Sea two miles away. It was linked by a wall, but it was almost like a separate little town. Even back then they were squabbling.'

Corthie pulled his pack off and sat, his legs dangling over the edge of the ancient palace, breathing in the cold sea air. The three miles of water separating the ruins from the City seemed to mock him. He had crossed mile after mile of the ice fields, but now a tiny gap barred his way. Despite what Achan had said, he reckoned he could swim it, but he doubted that either of his friends would be able to withstand the currents, and after all they had been through, he didn't want to abandon them.

He pulled a small bag of roots and berries that he had collected from a pouch on his belt. They were vile-tasting, but edible, and Achan had been useful in identifying what they could eat. He picked at the knot that closed the bag, then his fingers slipped and he dropped it into a thick clump of bushes on a ledge a few feet below them.

'Bollocks,' he muttered as Yaizra laughed next to him.

'That's your lunch gone, ya clumsy big lump.'

'No way.' He eased himself to the edge and dropped down to the bushes.

As he moved, something long and dark shot through the space where he had been sitting, and a moment later it struck the cliff face behind them in an ear-splitting crack, sending a mass of stone fragments showering over the ruins of the palace. Corthie glanced up from the ledge wide-eyed.

'Ballista!' cried Yaizra. She was pointing across at the large stone ruins that sat by the harbour.

'Get down,' he called up to her. 'Where's Achan?'

She glanced back and around. 'I'll find him.'

Corthie watched as she scampered away out of sight, then he turned to the harbour. He crept along the ledge, the thorns on the thick bushes scratching his arms and legs. He caught a flash of something shining in the sunlight, close to where he had seen movement before, and saw the bolt-throwing machine, its end poking out through a small gap in the mass of ruins.

It was pointed right at him.

It loosed, and he threw himself off the ledge, hearing the impact a moment later. Chunks of ancient masonry exploded as the four-foot-long steel bolt smashed into the ruins, and fragments hit Corthie as he fell. He landed on the remains of a low wall twenty feet below the ledge, rolled off it and toppled into the dense undergrowth. He lay still for a moment, winded and bruised, gazing at the pink sky overhead.

His view of the harbour was blocked by trees and more ruins, and he struggled to his knees. His pack was still up on the ledge with Yaizra and Achan, but his sharpened barrel-hook was on his belt, and he gripped it in his right hand as he crawled forward. He peered through a mass of thorns at the harbour. Soldiers were running down from the ruins from where the ballista had been loosed, their shields and cross-bows held in their arms.

Blades.

Corthie swore; they had been lying in wait for the fugitives, and he realised why they hadn't seen any signs of pursuit over the land journey they had taken. The Blades hadn't bothered chasing them over the long stretches of the ice fields, instead, they had sent a company to Jezra.

His right leg was aching from the fall, but he knew he had to move. The Blades were fanning out into the ruins, keeping their lines together in small, disciplined squads as they hunted for him and his two friends. He glanced back up at the remnants of the palace, but there was no sign of Yaizra or Achan. He turned, and tore through the undergrowth, working his way round the base of the palace ruins, as he heard the boots of the Blades approach. His heart sank as he looked for a way to avoid being cornered, then he noticed a dark opening close to the uneven ground. He crouched down, and pushed the branches of a bush to the side. The opening led inside the palace, so he pushed his legs in, then turned and squeezed his body through the gap. He dropped a few feet, then felt ground under his boots. Outside, the Blades were continuing their search, scanning the ledge and the area where Corthie had fallen. He remained still and silent, and they passed by his hiding place.

Something sharp grazed his ankle and he looked down. By his feet were weapons, most rusted or broken, but some still held their edges. There was also armour, the leather rotted, but steel cuirasses and plate armour remained. He frowned, then saw the bones spread out behind him. Heaps of human bones, piled up and scattered for as far as he could see in the dim light of the palace interior. He knelt, and picked up a skull. Corthie had no idea how to date it, but it didn't look like it had been there for thousands of years; maybe ten, but not thousands. He searched among the weapons for something useful. Most of the swords were beyond repair, but he saw a heavy mace lying amid the bones, its handle sturdy and long, and its head still solid and intact. He wiped the dirt and grime from it, and felt its weight in his hand.

He glanced back through the gap to the outside, and saw Blades everywhere he looked, so he turned towards the heaps of human remains and powered his battle-vision, his eyesight picking out the details of the interior. He began walking, picking his way past the bones as the light grew dimmer. Ahead of him, he noticed a series of large, rounded boulders. He frowned. There were dozens of them packing the space under the palace. He glanced at one on his right, and noticed a green shimmer to it in the fading light.

He froze as he realised he had walked into the middle of a mass of greenhides. They were motionless, each curled up and presenting only their thick armoured backs, just as Corthie remembered them sleeping on the plains in front of the Great Walls, but they were covered in dust and grime, as if they had been there for years. He was wondering if maybe they had starved to death when one of them moved. A slight motion, just a small rustle before settling again. Corthie listened to the growing noise outside as the soldiers searched for him. The louder it got, the more likely the greenhides would awaken and, sensing the flesh of the humans, they would go wild to get it.

Corthie took a slow breath, and kept walking, the mace gripped in his hand as he stepped between the dark green mounds. Another moved to his left, its claws scraping off the ground as it began to stir, and Corthie quickened his pace. He came to the end of the greenhides, and saw the entrance to a narrow tunnel leading off. It was in complete darkness, and he crept into it then stopped and turned.

He picked up a stone, feeling its size and weight in his hand. He felt bad about what he was going to do, but he could see no other way. It was that or death, he told himself, and he wasn't about to die in the ruins of some stupid palace. He stared back at the small opening he had crawled through, aimed, and threw the stone. It soared over the backs of the green mounds and cracked into the wall by the piles of rusted armour and broken swords, sending an echoing clatter through the cavern.

At once, over a dozen greenhides stirred, their heads coming up from where they had been sheltering under the armoured backs as they looked for the source of the noise. Corthie remained silent by the tunnel entrance, holding his breath as more greenhides awoke. The sound of the Blades outside caught their attention, and the first one got to its clawed feet, and let out a howl of enraged hunger. The floor seemed to move as the rest of the greenhides rose, every one of them staring at the small opening from where the sound and scent of human flesh was coming. As one, they took off, running towards the hole that led to the outside. Their claws ripped at the rock and the undergrowth, and they squeezed through, one after the other. Shouts and screams arose from the ruins, and Corthie listened, feeling guilty about the ordinary Blades who were about to die. They were trying to kill him, he told himself, but sending greenhides against anybody seemed wrong. He watched as the last of the beasts scuttled through the gap, leaving the cavern empty.

He retraced his steps, and peered up through the gap. The sound coming from outside was awful, as Blades were ripped to pieces by the greenhides. He pulled himself up and through the gap, then ran down the slope through the undergrowth. Bodies of dismembered Blades lay strewn across the ruins. A few greenhides also lay on the ground, their fronts riddled with crossbow bolts, but there were at least six dead Blades for every fallen greenhide.

The bushes to his right rustled, and a greenhide sprang at him. Corthie swung his mace two-handed, the heavy tip smashing through the beast's face. There was a sound behind him and he lifted the mace again.

'It's me, ya big lump!' cried Yaizra, her arms up to protect herself.

'Where's Achan?'

She glanced away. 'Dead.'

He stared at her.

'Come on,' she said, 'we need to move.'

They ran through the ruins, heading left by the harbour. Dead bodies lay everywhere, bloody and ripped. They turned a corner and saw a group of greenhides feasting upon the corpses of Blades, their claws and faces stained red. They were so engrossed in their meal that they ignored Yaizra and Corthie, who skirted past them. They ran on, leaving the scenes of carnage behind them. At the end of the bay the cliffside came down in a sheer wall, but there was an ancient staircase cut into it, and they started to climb, the sounds of the screams fading away behind them. They reached a point where the stair switched back, and Corthie turned to gaze upon the ruined town. A few Blades were still alive, but the greenhides were chasing them down.

Yaizra pointed. By the ruined fortress a ship was moving away from the harbour. It had been hidden out of sight within the ruins, and Corthie could see the crew on board staring at the greenhides. Its sails were up, and the wind was pushing it out into the Straits. A few greenhides tried to leap across the distance, but fell flailing into the water.

'They were waiting for us.'

'Who?' said Yaizra. 'The Blades or the greenhides?'

'Both.'

She shook her head. 'That's the first time I've ever seen those things. The way they ripped through the Blades...'

'How did you get away?'

'I came looking for you. The Blades were all shouting, and I stayed quiet and hid, and then I saw you kill one of those beasts. Where did you get the mace?'

'What happened to Achan?'

She looked away.

'What got him?' said Corthie. 'The ballista?'

'No, the greenhides. He was running with me to look for you, and one of them jumped at us. It was only luck that it got him instead of me.' She shuddered. 'It ripped him to pieces.'

Corthie closed his eyes, a nauseous feeling forming in his stomach.

'Where did they come from?' she said. 'One minute there were none, and the next they were everywhere. I don't understand.'

'It was me,' he said. 'I... disturbed a nest of them when I was hiding under the ruins of the palace.'

She put a hand on his arm. 'It wasn't your fault. Achan wouldn't have felt a thing; it was over in a second. And,' she went on, her eyes scanning the ruins, 'they got the Blades. Horrible to say it, but we'd all be dead if the greenhides hadn't attacked.'

Corthie gazed down at the blood-filled streets of the harbour. The greenhides had reached the ballista, and a group were eating the Blade crew that had been operating it. He wondered if any of the soldiers had been based at Arrowhead. Shame filled him.

'Hey,' said Yaizra, 'come on, we've plenty of time to mourn. Right now, we have to run.'

She took his hand and began pulling him towards the next set of stairs. Corthie tore his gaze from the harbour, and followed her.

CHAPTER 14

SEAFOOD DIET

Port Sanders, Medio, The City – 16th Yordian 3419

Aila gazed at the clear blue sky overhead and smiled. It was cold, but the sun was shining upon Port Sanders, and the water in the harbour was sparkling. Beyond, the sheets of mist that hung over the Warm Sea gave way to peaches and pinks at the horizon, and she marvelled at the sight, relaxing for the first time in days. She was disguised as a Sander citizen of the town, and no one had glanced in her direction for the entire shopping trip, as she filled her bags with fresh food and bottles of the local wine.

A few Blades were on duty down by the quayside, but their eyes were on the boats arriving and leaving, not on the small market that ran alongside the harbour front. She glanced at the food on offer. She and Bekha had tastes that were easily satisfied, but Jade was more picky. For nine centuries she had eaten fish caught in the Cold Sea, and bread baked from Gloamer wheat, and the goods on offer in Port Sanders had so far failed to please her. Seaweed, seafood, rich sauces, citrus fruits, honey; all of it seemed foreign to Jade, but the blockade of Dalrig had meant that nothing from her home town had made it to the market-places of Port Sanders.

She caught sight of a row of squid hanging from hooks, but after seeing Jade's reaction to her bringing home a lobster, thought better of buying any. She moved on to the next stall, and purchased a bag of beans and pulses, then checked her bags. There was enough for a few days, she thought, but didn't want to return to their hideout. It felt great to be able to walk the streets, and it was a relief not to have to be with Jade.

She handed over a few coins to a girl selling news sheets, and walked to a bench that overlooked the harbour. Sitting, she glanced at the headline that had caught her eye. Prince Montieth had denounced his daughter Lady Jade as a renegade, and was refusing to accept any responsibility for the deaths of the Blades on the frontier. She smiled as she read on. Montieth was still claiming to have Lady Aila in custody, and was threatening 'the duke', as he insisted on calling Prince Marcus, with her execution if Blades crossed the border.

Aila could sense Amber's hands all over the words of the statement, and she wondered if Montieth had even read it. She skimmed over the other stories, but there was nothing about Corthie, so she folded the sheet and put it into one of the bags for Bekha to read.

No mention of Corthie could only be good, for if he had been caught or killed, then she was sure that it would have been the main headline. Her worry remained, though. There had been enough time for the ships sent after him to have reached Tarstation and returned with the news, but nothing had been made public.

She had been hopeful after meeting Maddie Jackdaw, but eighteen days had passed since then, and she was painfully aware that she had not fulfilled her part of the plan. She was supposed to find Naxor, and so she had dragged Jade and Bekha all the way to Port Sanders, but there had been no sign of her cousin anywhere. She wondered if Maddie was having any better luck getting back to Blackrose. She remembered Maddie's words about Corthie, and how the dragon had sensed that he was in love. If a dragon could sense it, then it must be true, she thought, smiling as she gazed over the waters of the harbour.

Conscious that for every minute she was away, Bekha would be cursing her name, she lifted the bags and stood. She turned away from the harbour, taking a street that led up the gentle slope upon which the town was built. She took a detour to the right, past the expensive quarter, where the wealthiest merchants and town notables lived. As always, there was a squad of Blades standing outside the mansion belonging to Lord Naxor, and she walked past them without glancing in their direction. She made her way to a poorer part of town, where clusters of small apartments sat by the old town walls, and she changed her appearance to match that of the old lady that the neighbours recognised as living there. She entered the hallway of a cramped apartment block and took her keys from a pocket as she climbed the stairs. An old man was standing on the landing outside a row of apartment doors.

He glanced at her, then glared. 'Those daughters of yours have been screaming the place down again.'

Aila frowned. 'Sorry.'

'You said that last time. Tell them to keep quiet, or I'm fetching the town wardens. This is a respectable block, and we had no noise or trouble before you moved in.'

'I'll tell them.'

The old man glared at her again, then went back inside his apartment, which was the next along from theirs. She gave the front door three taps to let Bekha and Jade know it was her, then walked into their apartment, locking it behind her.

She hung her coat up in the hallway, dropped her disguise, then walked through to the main room. There was only that, a bedroom and a tiny bathroom, and the small size contributed to the tension in the air. Jade stared at her as she walked in.

'Did you get food?'

'Yes, Jade. Two bags full of it.' Aila placed the bags onto their kitchen table.

'Thank Amalia's sweet breath,' said Jade. She got up and delved into the bags. She held up a bundle of seaweed. 'What's this? I'm not eating this filth. Ahh! What's that?'

Aila sighed. 'Crab claws.'

'Claws? And what about this thing that looks like a snail?'

'It's seafood, Jade.'

'That's not food; those disgusting things are insects of the sea. Vermin and salty weeds, that's what you've brought me. Do you want me to starve; is that your plan? I'd rather eat your pet mortal than this garbage.'

Aila glanced around. 'Where is Bekha?'

'I murdered her.'

'What?'

Jade laughed. 'You should see your face. No, I haven't murdered her, yet, but the day is coming if she keeps provoking me. And at least then I'd get some red meat. If you can't find me any Dalrigian beef soon, then I'm afraid she might be the next best thing.'

'I keep telling you, Jade, we can't buy any Dalrigian produce at the moment.'

'What utter rot. We're demigods, we can get anything we like.' She burst into tears. 'Look at me, I have been reduced to this; living in squalor while I'm slowly starved to death. You said you would show me the whole City, but you won't even let me leave this apartment.' She stamped her foot. 'I should be in charge, not you; I'm much older. If you don't let me out today, I shall make the flesh on your mortal's face rot until it stinks.'

Aila held up a jar. 'I got you some honey. You like that, don't you?'

'I vomited the last time I ate that.'

'Yes, but that was because you finished the entire jar in two minutes. Just have a spoonful.' She twisted the lid off the jar and dipped in a spoon as Jade's eyes lit up. She passed the spoon to Jade and she put it into her mouth, smiling.

Aila edged away as Jade sat down licking the spoon. Bekha walked through the door of the bathroom, a look of seething frustration on her face.

She noticed Aila. 'Enjoy your walk?'

'Yes, thanks, it was lovely. The air was crisp and clear, and the views by the harbour were delightful.'

'Screw you,' Bekha muttered as she fell into a chair.

Aila glanced at her two housemates. 'Listen, you're going to have to stop all the shouting. The old man that lives next door was complaining again.'

'Let him in the next time he says anything,' said Jade. 'I'll fix him so that he never complains again.'

'And by "fix him", you mean...?'

'I mean I'll kill him, cousin, slowly and painfully while I watch.'

'But we're trying to hide, and we have to keep quiet. If the town authorities or the Blades find out we're staying here then we're finished.'

'And then I'll kill them too,' said Jade. 'Problem solved.'

'Is killing your answer to everything?'

Jade laughed. 'Of course not. If it were, I would have slain your pet a long time ago.'

'We should go our separate ways,' said Bekha. 'I'm going to the Circuit. I'd rather take my chances with the Blades than put up with Jade for any longer.'

Aila stared at her. 'But we have to find Naxor.'

'We've been stuck here for half a month, Aila, and there's been no sign of him. Maybe he's never coming back. I could be doing a lot more in the Circuit than I can hiding in Port Sanders.'

'But I made a promise.'

'I know, but it was your promise, not mine.'

'Are you saying that you're leaving us?'

Bekha shrugged. 'Can't see what good I'm doing here.'

'But your "wanted" posters will still be up on every corner of the Circuit, and the streets are crawling with Blades.'

'And yet I'd still feel safer there. Funny, that.'

Jade stared at Bekha. 'You ungrateful mortal. I knew Aila was soft-hearted to have allowed you to tag along.'

'Yeah?' said Bekha. 'Well, you should be pleased, because I won't be tagging along any more.'

'Oh, I won't miss you,' said Jade, 'but you're not walking out of here alive.' She turned to Aila. 'I know what to do with this wretched girl. It's what we used to do to the servants in Greylin Palace; it makes them very

CHRISTOPHER MITCHELL

docile and compliant. Best of all, it'll only take a few minutes. All I need to do it shut off the blood going to her brain for a while, then turn it back on again. After that, she'll do whatever we say.'

'No, Jade,' said Aila; 'we're not going to kill her.'

'She'll only be dead for a few minutes; any longer than that and she'd be completely useless.' She raised her hand towards Bekha.

Aila rushed forward, to stand between them. 'No, Jade. If Bekha wants to go, then we're not going to stop her.'

'But she knows everything! She'll tell Marcus where we are, and thousands of soldiers will come, or maybe even the God-Queen herself. You can't trust her, cousin; she's a weak mortal.'

'Then why don't you leave?' said Bekha.

'Don't speak to me like that, you worthless wretch. I'm staying with Aila; with my own kind. You're the odd one out among the three of us. You're a slave in the presence of gods.' She stood. 'In fact, you should kneel before us, slave, and beg for your life.'

Bekha stood and faced Jade, her hand going round to her back where she kept a knife. 'I'm never kneeling before you; you're living proof of what's wrong with demigods ruling the City. We should get rid of them, so that we can get on with our lives in peace.'

Jade smirked at Aila. 'Did you hear that cousin? She wants to get rid of us, you included. There's no way we can let her live after that.'

Aila stared at Jade's hand. 'No.'

'Get out of my way, cousin; I don't want to hurt you too.'

Aila readied her powers. She needed to shock Jade, but not make her lash out and kill them both.

'This is your last chance, Aila,' said Jade, her eyes lit with a terrible glee.

'Hello girls,' came a voice from the kitchen. 'I'm glad to see you're all getting on so well.'

They turned. A man was sitting at the table.

Aila blinked. 'Naxor?'

'Wait,' said Jade; 'is this our cousin?'

'Yes,' he said. 'Nice to meet you, Jade; now go to sleep.'

186

Jade collapsed on the couch, her eyes closed. Aila and Bekha stared at her, and the mortal took a step forward and prodded Jade's shoulder.

Naxor laughed. 'She's definitely asleep. My powers work on everyone; well, everyone apart from one person, but we'll come to that later.'

'But won't her self-healing powers revive her?' said Aila. 'She has the same powers as the God-Queen.'

'She's sleeping, dear cousin, not ill; her powers will do nothing, because there's nothing wrong with her.' He took a bottle of wine from the shopping bag and opened it.

Bekha laughed. 'Peace at last; this is great. How long will she be sleeping for? Oh, and pour me a glass.'

Naxor glanced at her. 'Certainly, Miss... Bekha. About ten hours or so?'

'How do you know my name?'

Aila frowned. 'He has vision powers; he can read our minds.' She leaned over and pulled Jade's legs onto the couch, then slipped a cushion under her head.

Naxor shook his head as he filled three large glasses. 'Why in Malik's name did you bring Jade along?'

Aila strode over to the table. 'How long were you watching us for?'

'I saw you close to my apartment, and recognised the little old lady; you've done her before. I stayed outside until Jade became a little threatening, and acted when I thought she was actually going to kill you both.'

'She was,' said Bekha, taking a seat and picking up a glass.

'I know; I could see it clearly in her mind. It wasn't the only thing I saw in there, but again, we'll come to that in time.'

'It's good to see you,' said Aila, 'but you're an asshole. Your last words to me in the Circuit were "I'll be back soon," and it's been six months. Where have you been?'

He glanced at Bekha. 'Not in front of the mortal, cousin.'

She glared back at him. 'You *are* all the same.'

'We can trust her,' said Aila. 'Anything you can tell me, you can tell her.'

Naxor shook his head. 'It's not a matter of trust. Miss Bekha might be the most loyal and trustworthy of friends, but secrets are secrets for a reason. There are things you and I know that need to remain between us. But that can wait. Let's enjoy our wine together before we get down to business. So, you were in Dalrig?'

'Yes, for nearly two months, held prisoner by Uncle Montieth.'

'You were prisoners?'

'It was more like house arrest, to be honest, and we weren't harmed or anything, but we couldn't leave.' She took a sip of wine. 'His guards...'

'I know.'

'You do?'

'Yes, I was in Greylin Palace, looking for you. That's where you're supposed to be, so that's where I looked first. I saw some things there...' He grimaced. 'At some point someone will have to deal with Montieth and what he's doing in the palace.'

Aila nodded. 'Yes. I feel like a coward for not doing anything while I was there, but when we discovered his laboratory we just ran, we were so terrified.'

'The same thing happened to me,' Naxor said, frowning. 'I always suspected he was up to no good. Amber's a danger too; she's much more focussed than her father, and just as ruthless. If it weren't for the inevitable carnage that would ensue, I'd quite like to watch Marcus and Montieth tear each other to shreds.'

Aila took another sip. 'How's my beloved sister Vana?'

'Safe. I always knew that she would have to be the first thing I took care of, so that I, and you, could be free to move about the City without being detected.'

'She's alive?'

Naxor laughed. 'Yes. I whisked her off her feet and bore her away. And then, after failing to find you in Greylin Palace, I had to whisk her all the way back here to locate you. But don't worry, I've put her back; she's safe again.'

'Where?'

Naxor glanced at Bekha and shrugged.

The mortal woman got to her feet. 'Fine, I'll go and sit in the bedroom, and let you higher beings talk about things a mere mortal like I could never understand.'

Naxor smiled. 'Thanks, Bekha.'

She glared at him, then took her glass and the half-full bottle of wine from the table. Naxor took another bottle out of the bag as she walked away.

He glanced at Aila as he opened it. 'Lostwell. I was on Lostwell, and that's where I've put Vana.'

'You left her alone on a different world?'

'She's not alone; she's living in a great big castle, with servants, and the person to whom the castle belongs.'

'And who's that?'

'I can't tell you, sorry.'

'What? But we're alone now, like you wanted.'

Naxor refilled their glasses. 'I'm not sure your head could cope with it. Why don't I tell you some good news instead? Your boyfriend's alive.'

She frowned at him. 'I know Corthie's alive; I heard about it ages ago.'

'Yes, but here are two things I bet you didn't know. Firstly, it was Salvor who saved him; can you believe it? Salvor? Secondly, he escaped from Tarstation before the Blades sent by Marcus could arrive to apprehend him. He's gone.'

'He escaped?'

'Yes, and from that grin on your face I assume you like my news? It's not all good, though; they're still after him. Salvor told me that Marcus has sent Blades to Jezra, to kill him if he turns up there.'

'So you've been using this Quadrant thing to get around?'

'From here to Lostwell and back, yes.'

'Can I borrow it?'

Naxor's mouth fell open, and for a moment he was speechless. 'Ah. What?'

'Can I borrow it? Or can you use it to do something for me?'

'Such as?'

'Take Blackrose home.'

'Whoa, steady. Blackrose? You've met her, have you? She has a way of getting into your head.'

'I've never met her, but I promised Corthie I would help her escape.'

'And why would you make such a promise?'

'Your mother promised too; we both did. Corthie sacrificed himself for us; he charged a company of Blades so that we could try to escape. Khora knew what he was going to do, and so did I; so we promised him.'

'No.'

'What? Is that it? Just "no"?'

He shrugged. 'You have no idea how close I was to not coming back at all. I mean, what do I have to live for here? They slaughtered my mother. Kano may have wielded the sword, but the God-Queen and Marcus ordered it. And who can stand up to the God-Queen? The God-King? You and I know the truth of that. So tell me, why should I care about the City that murdered my family and cast me aside; that hunts me as a rebel?'

'Sounds like you're describing my life.'

'Yes. I now realise how you've felt for all these years, dear cousin. But you never had a choice, whereas I possess the Quadrant. The only being I would be prepared to rescue from the City is you, Aila.'

'Me?'

'Yes. If you wish, then say the word, and we could be there in seconds. Vana will be there, and the other person I mentioned.'

'Who? You have to tell me; if you're being serious, you must tell me.'

'Very well, it is your eldest brother Irno.'

Aila stared at him, her mouth open. 'But he died in the Civil War.'

'Did you see his body? He was supposedly consumed in the fire that ravaged Pella, but I rescued him. He and I were close friends before the war, we still are, and I couldn't stand to watch him burn, so I took him to Lostwell. I'd only been there a few times by that point; my mother had not long arranged permission for me to use the God-King's Quadrant. I helped him settle there, and he became my main contact when I started bringing champions to the City. He is extraordinarily wealthy by any standards; my trade in champions for salve has enriched him greatly. Vana was so happy to see him she burst into tears. Vana, crying; not a sight I thought I'd ever see.'

'Irno's alive?'

Naxor laughed. 'I'll give you a moment.'

Aila felt tears roll down her face. Of all of Prince Isra's children, Irno had been everyone's favourite brother before the war, and his loss had devastated the family. To think that he had been alive all that time; and Naxor had never told her.

'Why didn't you tell me?'

'He wanted it to be kept secret. At first it was because he didn't want Prince Michael to learn that he was alive, and after the war, he decided to begin again. So, what do you say, Aila? Will you return with me to Lostwell, and escape the madness here?'

She thought about it. The idea that two of her siblings and Naxor would be there was tempting; and she felt the pull of curiosity to experience a new world. And she could leave the chaos of the City behind her. She smiled; it was hopeless. There was no way she was abandoning Corthie, not unless she knew for certain he was dead; and her promise to him about Blackrose niggled at the back of her mind. And then there was Bekha, and the masses of mortals living in poverty and fear. She belonged to the City; it had made her. Did she not owe a debt to the people who lived there?

She shook her head. 'I can't. Use it to take Blackrose to her home, and Corthie too if you can find him, and if he wants to go, though I'd rather he stayed.' She bowed her head. 'Sorry.'

'I thought that would be your answer,' he said, a half-smile on his lips. 'When I read your mind in Cuidrach Palace, I saw how much you loved the champion. There's no way I can find him, though, not even if Vana was with me. The ice fields alone cover hundreds of square miles.'

'And Blackrose?'

'No.'

'Why not?'

He shook his head. 'You have no idea what unleashing her upon

Lostwell would do, and as for the idea of sending her back to her home world? The war among the gods is over; do you think I want to restart it?'

Aila raised an eyebrow.

'She was a queen, and she fought against the winning side in the war. She can never go back.'

Aila nodded. She glanced at his tunic. The Quadrant was most likely hidden there, under his jacket. If she could distract him for a moment...

Naxor laughed. 'Really? Distract me how? Turn into Prince Marcus before my eyes? Even if you did steal the Quadrant, you have no idea how to use it; it took me months to learn. You could always ask the God-Queen, as she probably retains the ability to construct one. In fact I'd be surprised if she hasn't already got one hidden away in Maeladh, ready to use if the greenhides ever get as far as Tara.'

'What are we going to do?'

'There's no "we", Aila. I'm going back to Irno's castle. You can... do what you feel is best.'

'You're abandoning the City?'

'It abandoned me when my mother was murdered; just as it has abandoned you. One last chance, Aila; come with me.'

'No.'

He sighed. 'Alright. Before I go, I want to remind you that I read Jade's mind. She really was about to kill you when I arrived. She's decided that you are of no further use to her; and there was something about a broken promise regarding a cat named Nathaniel? If I were you, I would leave before she wakes up.'

Aila lowered her eyes. 'Damn it. Thanks for the warning. Take care, I'll miss...' She raised her eyes, but he was already gone; the seat empty. She turned to the bedroom door. 'Bekha?'

The mortal appeared in the doorway. 'Yeah?'

'Grab your things; we're going.'

CHAPTER 15
LAW AND ORDER

Pella, Auldan, The City – 19th Yordian 3419

Emily stretched her arms then pulled on her dressing gown. She could see from the shadow through the shutters that Daniel was already out on their balcony, so she tied her hair back to neaten it and slipped outside to join him.

'Good morning,' he said glancing up from the news sheet he was reading.

She gazed out at the view. It was the best in the City, or so Daniel reckoned, and she found it hard to disagree. The dawn light had transformed the bays into pinks and reds, and the buildings of Ooste were shimmering. To the left, she could see Tara in the distance, and the great statue of Prince Michael that dominated the headland.

'How did you sleep?'

'Well,' she said, hiding the truth that she had spent most of the night awake, her head buzzing with work and plans. She took a seat at the little table, a cold breeze chilling her bare ankles.

'I made you a cup of that horrible tea,' he said, gesturing at the table.

She nodded, her mind still sluggish. 'Thanks.'

'Until we started living here,' he said, 'I had no idea you were so sleepy in the mornings.'

She picked up the cup, trying to think of a response. She took a sip, and smiled. 'Honey?'

'Yes, dear?'

'No, I meant you put honey in the tea.'

He laughed. 'Yes. I tasted it without any, and it was rank. I thought you liked honey? Should I not have put any in?'

'It's much nicer with, but I need to watch my weight.'

He raised an eyebrow. 'You? Why? You're in great shape.'

Emily thought better of bringing his mother up, so she just smiled again and sipped the tea. It did work, though, and she felt her lethargy start to lift. She stretched again, trying to shake off the last of the sleepiness. 'Anything in the news?'

'Lady Jade is still on the loose. She was last seen heading in the direction of the Circuit. The Blades have been ordered to shoot on sight.'

'Good. The sooner she's killed, captured or sent back to Dalrig the better.'

'I know. She could do untold damage in the Circuit. The place is already boiling over with rumours of another uprising; it'll only take a single spark, and the slums will explode.'

'And then the fools will burn down their own houses again. I understand protest, but riots help no one, and it's the poorest who suffer.'

Daniel nodded. 'But what else can they do? When they protest, no one pays them any attention, and when they riot, everyone in Auldan tells them they should be protesting. They can't win, no matter what they do.'

'Are you sympathising with Evader rioters? Even after serving there with the Taran militia?'

'There were bad folk among the rioters, but most of them were just ordinary people, angry and fed up with how the City's treated them.'

'And they think that burning down their own communities is going to help?'

'It might be the only way they can get the rest of the City's attention. I'm hearing reports that the Blade occupation has been brutal; they've implemented martial law with curfews, searches, raids, mass arrests. Beating up peaceful protesters is not going to solve anything.'

Emily put down her empty cup. 'I just don't understand how the Evaders think. They came to the City as refugees, and we took them in and housed them and fed them, and they behave like this? You'd think they'd be a little more grateful. And I hope you're being careful about who you give these opinions to. I imagine that the commanders of the militia might disagree with you strongly on this.'

'Yes, they do. Some of them consider the Evaders to be barely human.'

'That's ridiculous. They're different from us, but they're still human.'

Daniel nodded, his eyes on her. 'And what about your father's plan? I take it you're familiar with it?'

She frowned. 'Yes.'

Daniel paused, and she could see that he was debating in his mind if it was a good idea to press on with his line of reasoning. They had been getting on much better since living in Pella together, but the potential remained for a rupture between them as they grew to learn each other's hearts and minds.

'I don't agree with it,' she said. 'What he's advocating basically amounts to mass murder. And how would the rest of the City force hundreds of thousands of Evaders onto boats in the first place, let alone transport them all to the western bank of the Straits? My father is an idiot, Danny, and I hope you don't think I go along with his ideas.'

'But you do think the Evaders are different from the rest of us?'

'They are different. Their customs and traditions; their way of life, their laws, or should I say, their disregard for laws. The proportion of criminals among them is far higher than any other tribe, and their level of literacy is the lowest, despite all the money that's been spent building them schools that they burn down every time there's a riot.'

'But if you or I had been born there, we'd act the same.'

She frowned at him. 'No. Sorry, husband, but I cannot agree with that, and I don't think you'll find many other Rosers who would.'

He nodded. 'I guess we'll just have to disagree.'

'You know that I've been working on a project for the Aurelians?'

'Investigating the land we got from your family in the exchange?'

'Yes. Ten acres of the Circuit, that last year made a loss of over two thousand sovereigns. I think I've worked out a way to make it profitable.'

He smiled. 'How?'

'A combination of things. We redevelop part by knocking down some of the slums, and we bring in a better firm of debt-collectors. Then, with rent rises and some evictions of the worst offenders, it should break even.'

Daniel glanced out over the bay. 'We should give it away to the people who live there.'

Emily laughed, then realised he was being serious. 'Give it away? I don't understand.'

'One of the problems with the City is that Rosers own so much of it. The Evaders hate being tenants on some aristocrat's land, it's part of the reason they don't care if they burn the place to the ground. If they owned it themselves, then they might look after it better.'

'It's not as simple as that, Danny. Alright, say that we wanted to do as you say, and gift the land to the tenants who live there? It sounds noble, but legally speaking, the Aurelians would be liable for the enormous bill that would accrue, as it's against Roser law to gift land that is indebted.'

He shrugged. 'We're rich enough to cover it.'

'Let me get this straight. You want me to go to your mother and tell her that not only are we giving away ten acres of land for nothing, but we'll also have to pay a bill that'll amount to tens of thousands of sovereigns? She commissioned me to make the land profitable.'

'It's up to you,' he said, 'but if we're not part of the solution, we're part of the problem. To me, the rent-collectors of the Circuit are a plague on the City, achieving nothing but to make the rich even richer, and the poor even more miserable than they already are.'

Emily puffed out her cheeks. 'I had no idea you were such a... radical. You want to throw away thousands of years of property law and impoverish the very families that made the City great in the first place?'

'The foundations the City were built upon are fundamentally unfair. Why should the Rosers dominate land ownership, and the positions of government? Why are the Reapers all labourers, peasants and servants? Why are the Sanders so much richer than the Evaders, who only live a few miles from them? I want to see the City united and peaceful, but that will only happen if the different tribes are all treated fairly.' He stood. 'I'd better go to work. The colonel said it looked like there might be trouble brewing in Outer Pella, and we're going to be deploying troops out on the streets.'

She glanced up at him. 'Take care.'

They kissed, and Daniel strode from the balcony as Emily turned back to the view. She thought through his words. They were admirable in a way, but hopelessly naïve, like trying to fix a leaky roof by destroying the entire building. Still, at least they had reached a stage where they were able to argue without falling out over it. She could live with them having differing opinions if there was a basis of respect between them. It was the absence of his mother that had made the real difference to their lives, and she was enjoying the intimacy that being together had brought.

There was a knock on the door, and she got up to answer it.

Her maid, Talleta, bowed as she entered. 'Good morning, ma'am. I saw Captain Aurelian depart. Are you ready to get dressed? Would you like some breakfast?'

'Yes to both,' she said, 'and then I would like to be undisturbed; I want to finish my proposal for Lady Aurelian today.'

Talleta bowed again. 'As you wish, ma'am.'

―――――

Her desk groaned with the piles of heavy volumes on law and case history, each studded with dozens of bookmarks to note the pages she had referred to. She spent an hour looking into the feasibility of transferring the ten acres of the Circuit to the tenants; not because she thought it was a good idea, but so she could say to Daniel that she had at least tried. It was useless. The laws were strict, and there was no way the Aurelians would be able to wriggle out of their expensive liabilities. The more she looked into it, the more she became convinced that the laws had been written to prevent such transfers of land from the owner to the tenants, and she could see how unfair it was, but the existing law was all they had to work with. Besides, nothing came for free, and it rankled that those who had defaulted on their rent might in any way benefit from the generosity of the Aurelians.

She took a break when it was nearly lunchtime, and strolled through their quarters to stretch her legs. The other officers' wives usually met each day to drink wine and chat, but Emily had avoided such social contact, preferring to remain within her tight circle of Daniel and Talleta, regardless if that made her a target of gossip. She wandered out onto the balcony, filling her lungs with sea air. The markets by the harbour front were busy with Reapers shopping or walking, and she watched them for a while, trying to imagine what it would be like to be one of them. For her entire life, she had been told that the Reapers had servile natures that made them unfit for leadership, but perfect as servants or as labourers who worked the fields belonging to the Rosers and, until recently, she had never questioned it.

She watched a Reaper family walk along the promenade and wondered if they were happy. Was she? She was married to an officer and living in a palace, and it seemed ridiculous to imagine that she could be unhappy, but there was so much more she wanted from life. But doing what? She was good at law; perhaps she could think of making a career out of it. She imagined becoming a property lawyer, and helping Daniel's downtrodden masses. That way, they could be rich, and her husband's conscience would be salved at the same time.

There was a thump-thump-thump at the door. A little loud for lunch, she thought as she walked from the balcony. She opened the door, expecting to see her maid with a food trolley, but Talleta was standing by herself, a stricken expression on her face.

Emily frowned. 'What's wrong?'

'Your husband has been arrested, ma'am.'

'What?'

'Blades have taken him into custody.'

'Come in,' Emily said, glancing down the hallway as she let Talleta squeeze past. 'Tell me everything.'

'I was in the kitchens, ma'am, getting your lunch ready, when I heard a commotion. A wagon pulled in through the back gates and Blades got out and led your husband into the palace. His hands were tied, but there was no hood, and all of the servants around the kitchen could see it was Master Daniel.'

'And what is he accused of?'

'I heard someone say he struck his commanding officer, ma'am, but I don't know if that's true.'

Emily took a breath to calm her racing heart. 'I'm sure it's all just a mix-up.' She glanced at Talleta. 'I'd better go down and sort it out. Do you know where he is?'

'There are cells under the kitchen wing, ma'am. I think they took him there.'

'Right.' Emily nodded. She went to the mirror, to make sure she looked presentable, and to check that her face appeared calm and confident.

She felt Talleta's hand on her arm. 'I'm sure it'll be alright, ma'am.'

'You did the right thing, coming to get me. Thank you.'

Her maid smiled as Emily strode towards the door. She opened it and went out into the hallway. No one was around, but she knew that the other officers and their spouses would soon learn what had occurred. If she could fix it all before it got out, then maybe it would fade before the gossips had a chance to turn it into a major scandal. She hurried down the hallway and descended to the ground floor. She passed the palace library on her right, then entered the wing where the large kitchens lay. A Blade soldier was standing at the top of another flight of stairs and she approached him.

'Excuse me. Are the cells down there? My husband is being detained and I wish to speak with him.'

The soldier glanced at her. 'Name?'

'Mistress Emily Aurelian.'

He nodded. 'Wait here.'

The soldier disappeared down the stairs and Emily suppressed a desire to follow him. She paced back and forth for a moment, then stopped in case anyone saw her. A couple of servants walked past and she lowered her eyes, aware that every Reaper in the building probably knew that Daniel had been arrested.

The soldier came back up the stairs, accompanied by a Blade officer, who glanced at her.

'Miss Emily?'

'Yes?'

'You can talk to the captain for five minutes. Come with me.'

She followed him down the stairs and into a long corridor. Several Blades were standing outside the cells that ran down one side of the passageway, while others were filling a guardroom. The officer took her past the first few cells then halted.

He glanced back at her, eyeing her up and down. 'You're not carrying any concealed weapons, are you?'

'No.'

'Then you won't mind if we search you first?'

'I'm wearing a dress. Where exactly could I have hidden a weapon?'

The officer frowned, then took a key from his belt and unlocked the door. 'I'm leaving this door open so we can keep an eye on you. Five minutes.'

She glared at him, then entered the dark cell, her eyes taking a moment to adjust.

'Emily?'

She saw Daniel, lying on the bench at the rear of the cell. She strode over to him, then paused. His face was covered in bruises, and blood streaked his chin from a cut in his lip, while one of his eyes was closed over by swelling. She crouched by the bench and took his hand, noticing that he also had blood on his knuckles.

She gazed at him, feeling her eyes well. 'They beat you?'

'I resisted arrest.'

'What happened?'

He pushed himself up into a sitting position, grunting from the effort and clutching his side.

'I deployed my company, as ordered,' he said. 'We were in Outer Pella, on market day. There was a big crowd, and when they saw us, they started chanting. You know, "go home", and all that. We blocked the road to the old town, to prevent any from going that way, and the crowd grew. They were getting angry, but they weren't attacking, so I kept back from them. Usually they blow off some steam, and then go home of their own accord, but the colonel appeared out of nowhere and demanded to know why I hadn't dispersed them.' He shook his head. 'That's when it got ugly. He ordered me to give the word to the crossbow teams to loose at the crowd, and I refused. Two hundred crossbows against an unarmed crowd? I couldn't do it. He ordered me again, then struck me when I refused again. That's when I hit him back. The next thing I knew I was being bundled away by Blades. I punched one of them. That was a mistake; you can see what they did to me in return.' He put his head in his hands. 'The worst thing was, when I was being dragged away, I could hear the company shoot into the crowd. There were children there, families out shopping in the market.'

A tear rolled down his cheek as Emily crouched in silence next to him.

'I guess you think I'm an idiot,' he went on. 'I've ruined everything. The Blades are going to transfer me over to the Taran military authorities.'

'That's good, isn't it? Better the Tarans than the Blades.'

He let out a low laugh. 'Lord Chamberlain sits on the militia's court-martial tribunal.'

Emily put a hand to her mouth.

'I've finally given him the excuse he's been looking for, Emily. Sorry.'

'For what?'

'I thought you'd be angry with me.'

'Oh, I'm angry, Danny, but not with you.'

'You don't think I made a mistake?'

'Punching that Blade was a mistake. Disobeying an illegal order was not. Danny, I know you think I'm hard-hearted about these things, but do you believe I'd want my husband to order a company to shoot into an crowd of civilians?'

'I was responsible for a massacre in the Circuit, remember? Everyone thought I was a hero for that, and you seemed to agree.'

'That seemed different; far away. If I thought that, then I was wrong. This is not over, Danny. The court martial will have to consider all of the evidence, and if we can prove the order you were given was illegal, then they'll have to acquit you, regardless of the tribunal's membership.'

He smiled at her. 'Thank you. You've no idea how happy it makes me to know that you're on my side.'

'We're married, that's what we do; we stick up for each other.'

She leaned forward and kissed him, careful to avoid the cut on his lip.

'Right,' called a voice from the door; 'time's up. The prisoner is being put on a wagon bound for the military prison within Maeladh Palace in Tara.'

Emily stood, still holding Daniel's hand. 'May I accompany my husband in the wagon?'

'No, you may not, miss. This is the last time I'll ask politely; please vacate the cell.'

She glanced back at Daniel as she released his hand. 'I'll see you in Tara.'

Emily rushed back up the flights of stairs to their quarters and packed a bag as quickly as she could, while Talleta assisted by standing by the door, to ensure no one came round to pry. When she had filled her bag full to bursting, she nodded to her maid. They pulled their winter coats on, and Talleta took the bag. Emily almost broke down by the entrance, but she suppressed her tears and stiffened her resolve, and opened the door.

Outside in the hallway, a few of the other officers' wives were standing. They fell silent as Emily appeared, but their glances and barely-disguised smirks told her all she needed to know.

'My husband is innocent,' she said as she locked their quarters behind her, 'and I am not ashamed.'

The wives remained silent as Emily and Talleta walked past them. They descended the stairs and made their way to a large courtyard where most carriages were stationed. Blade soldiers were loading Daniel into the back of a wagon parked in the middle of the yard, but the door was slammed shut and locked before Emily could call out to him.

Talleta hailed a free carriage, and paid the driver from a purse of coins Emily had given her. They boarded the carriage, and it took off, following the wagon with Daniel inside.

'Why didn't you tell me about his face?'

Talleta lowered her eyes. 'Sorry, ma'am. I didn't want to upset you.'

'I don't like surprises. Please remember that.'

'Yes, ma'am. Sorry, ma'am.'

The carriage reached a junction, and the four ponies turned left onto the main road leading to Tara. On their right, the huge bay spread out, shining in the cold sunlight. Emily stared at the view, trying to block out her other thoughts, but her anger simmered. She knew her life would be much simpler if Daniel had obeyed orders, but she didn't want a hypocrite as a husband; a man who talked about the plight of the poor and powerless, but who then went out and massacred them the same day. She tried to think of the worst outcome; Daniel would be dishonourably ejected from the militia, perhaps with a jail sentence attached. From her previous reading of the law, she reckoned he might get two years if found guilty. Two years. The best outcome would be acquittal, but would he want to return to a service that asked him to kill the innocent? Either way, it looked as though his career in the Taran militia was over.

The carriage pulled into Tara after a slow journey round the bay, and Talleta instructed the driver to climb the hill to Maeladh Palace.

'When we stop,' said Emily, 'go straight to the Aurelian mansion and let Daniel's mother know what's happened.'

'Yes, ma'am.'

The carriage ascended the steep road then came to a halt before the gates of the palace. The driver opened the door and Emily and Talleta stepped down to the road. Talleta slung the bag onto her shoulder, then ran off down Princeps Row, while Emily turned towards the closed gates.

'Excuse me, officer,' she said to a Blade standing on guard. 'I'm looking for my husband. Has he been brought here?'

The soldier ignored her.

'I'm speaking to you,' she called through the thick bars of the gate. 'My name is Emily Aurelian, and I'm looking for my husband; is he being held here?'

The soldier frowned, then gestured to an officer, who emerged from the guard post by the gates.

'What does she want?'

'She's whining about her husband, sir.'

The officer frowned and approached the gates. 'Yes?'

'Thank you, officer. Is Captain Daniel Aurelian being held in the palace?'

He shrugged. 'Not that I'm aware of.'

'Wait,' she said as he turned away. 'We were following him in a carriage. He would have only just arrived. Could you please check for me?'

The officer groaned. 'I've got better things to be doing with my time. What did you say his name was?'

'Daniel Aurelian. He's a captain in the Taran militia.'

The officer smirked. 'Those pretend soldiers? Fine, I'll go and check.'

Emily took a breath as she watched him walk away towards the palace buildings.

'Emily?'

She turned, and saw Daniel's mother approach, Talleta and another servant following.

'What in Amalia's name is going on? Has Daniel been arrested? Your maid here was telling me that the Blades gave him a beating. Is this true?'

Emily nodded.

Lady Aurelian placed a hand on her brow, and for a moment Emily thought she was going to explode. Instead, she took her daughter-in-law's hand. 'What did he do?'

'He disobeyed an order to shoot unarmed civilians, then punched a colonel.'

Emily's eyes widened as her mother-in-law laughed. 'That fool. Somehow I always knew this day would come; I knew that Daniel's silly notions would get him into trouble.'

'I think the order may have been illegal. We need a good lawyer.'

'Don't worry about that, I know a few. Illegal, eh? Are you sure?'

'No, not sure, but I think the militia need reasonable cause before ordering troopers to attack unarmed civilians, and Daniel said that wasn't the case.'

'And how bad was the beating?'

'Quite bad. He also assaulted a Blade. I think...'

'Wait. Look who's coming out to speak to us.'

Something in Lady Aurelian's voice made her uneasy, and she turned. Lord Chamberlain was striding across the palace driveway towards them, a squad of Blades flanking him as he walked.

'Ah,' he beamed. 'Lady and Mistress Aurelian. How may I assist you on this beautiful day?'

'You know why we're here,' said Daniel's mother. 'Where is my son?'

'He is currently sitting in a cell under the palace, no doubt pondering the error of his ways.'

'Is he being court-martialled?'

'Naturally. He disobeyed a direct order and has two further counts of assault against his name. Striking his superior officer, dear, oh dear.'

'When is he being released, pending the start of the trial?'

'He isn't, I'm afraid.'

'Why not?' said Emily. 'The law clearly states that he should be released until the trial.'

Chamberlain smiled. 'Unless he is deemed a threat to the tranquillity of the City, and I have decided that he is.'

'You have no right to do that.'

'I have every right, little miss Aurelian, as I am the chair of the court-martial tribunal. If you recall, Daniel threatened me in front of witnesses on the day of the memorial for the fallen officers. I most certainly deem him to be a danger.' He eyed her through the bars. 'And, let's not forget the secrets you're hiding, eh, Mistress Emily?'

'But...'

'Don't, dear,' said Lady Aurelian. 'Let's not humour him any longer.' She turned to Lord Chamberlain. 'This is not over; we will fight this with everything we have.'

'I'm sure you will, however it is my duty to inform you that the court martial will be held behind closed doors, with no outside legal representation permitted, so your money will be of no use to you.' He smiled again. 'Farewell, my dear Aurelians. You may rage, you may weep, but it will avail you nothing. I will crush your family, just as I always promised I would.'

He turned, and strode away, leaving Emily and Daniel's mother standing by the closed gates.

'Don't cry,' said Lady Aurelian. 'If you must, save it for the privacy of the mansion; I want no signs of weakness out here on the street. Come; it's time we went home.'

Emily lowered her eyes and followed her as she strode towards Princeps Lane.

'One more thing,' Lady Aurelian said as they walked; 'what did he mean by "secrets"? Are you keeping something from us?'

'No. I don't know what he means. He said something similar after the memorial service, but I can't think of what it could be.' Her heart sank. 'Unless, it's to do with my father. He, uh...'

'He has a violent temper?'

She hung her head. 'Yes.'

'Lift your chin, girl; you've absolutely nothing to be ashamed of. Don't ever let what that brute did define you. Unfortunately, however, Lord Omertia's behaviour is well known in aristocratic circles, so I doubt Lord Chamberlain was referring to that. Are you sure there's nothing else?'

Emily nodded. 'I'm sure.'

'I hope you're right, because we'll need to pull together to get through this, and the last thing I want is any unpleasant surprises.'

'I understand.'

Lady Aurelian nodded. 'Good. Now, let's go home and figure out how to get our boy acquitted.'

CHAPTER 16

AN ANSWERED PRAYER

R eaper-Gloamer Frontier, Auldan, The City – 19th Yordian 3419

Maddie rinsed her mouth with water and spat into the ditch. 'Hey,' she shouted at the sergeant, 'do I still have seaweed in my teeth?' She bared them.

The sergeant frowned. 'Eh... no, I think you got it all.'

'Comes from having to eat weeds like a cow,' she said. She went back to scrubbing her armour on the bank of the ditch, a broad smile on her face. She felt great, the effects of Jade's healing lasting far beyond the few moments the demigod had taken to do it. She had never felt fitter, or stronger, and her hearing and eyesight had improved. And her hair, it shone, and felt gorgeous. A few lads in the company had even glanced at her in a funny way, which she had found a little disturbing. She had no time for boys, not when Blackrose continued to dwell in her mind.

She thought back to Lady Aila; she had been nice, and because of that, as well as the fact that they had shared what they knew of Corthie and the dragon, Maddie had left her name out of the reports she had been made to write following her abduction by the renegade Lady Jade. Without names, the Blade authorities questioning her had assumed the two women to be Jade's mortal servants or slaves, and Maddie had let them continue to think that.

She felt someone's eyes upon her and she glanced up to see a couple of Blades turn away. She was getting that a lot. As the only person who had been close to Lady Jade and had survived, most of the soldiers in the camp knew her face. Some looked at her with suspicion, but most were curious about the Blade that Jade had mysteriously let go.

'Ignore them,' said the sergeant, catching her glance.

She shrugged. 'They're a good distraction from what we're doing later today.'

'Don't think about that either.'

'Can I see your list?'

'Eh, what list?'

'The list of things I'm allowed to think about, Sergeant? I presume you have one.'

He frowned at her. 'You like guessing. Take a guess what I'm thinking right now.'

'No, thanks; I don't want to know what floats around that mind of yours. It'll be something unsavoury, no doubt. Tell me a happy story of your childhood instead. What was it like growing up a hundred years ago?'

'You should have asked Lady Jade that when you had the chance.'

'What makes you think I didn't? And she's over nine hundred years old; I looked it up. Nine hundred years of crazy. I'm still waiting for that story of yours.'

He shrugged. 'I don't think I have any.'

'Come on, you were hanging around the gates of Arrowhead for a decade; you must know tons of stuff.' She leaned in closer. 'I mean, you knew about the old lady.'

'I'll tell you one thing if it'll shut you up.'

She grinned.

'Ten years ago, I didn't work at the gates.'

'That's a rubbish story.'

'I used to work somewhere else.'

'Obviously.'

'Will you close your gob for one minute?' He shook his head. 'Anyway, I used to work with a certain Lieutenant Hilde. That's how I learned about you-know-who; she got the job while I was dating her.'

Maddie started to laugh.

He frowned. 'It's not that funny.'

'She once told me about this,' Maddie said, 'but she didn't mention your name. Were you going to get married?'

'We'd talked about it, but her new job took over her mind completely, and we never discussed it again, and eventually we ended it. I've seen what that job's done to her over the years, and I worry it'll have the same effect on you.'

'You worry about me?'

'I'm your sergeant, of course I worry about you. Especially today. Do me a favour and stick close by, no matter what happens.'

'I'll be fine; it's only an invasion.'

'Don't joke about it, lass; hundreds will have died by the time the sun sets this evening; Dalrigians and Blades, and for what? Nothing.'

Maddie resisted adding that what he had said was literally true. Everyone believed that Lady Aila was still being held in Dalrig, and the ostensible purpose of the invasion was to rescue her from the clutches of Prince Montieth. None of the Blades believed that was the real reason. For four months, Dalrig had refused to submit to the rule of Prince Marcus, and had continued to address him as 'duke' in every statement issued by Greylin Palace. It was wounded pride that had led to the decision to invade, not any noble aim about rescuing a demigod.

Another consideration too weighed upon the minds of the Blades as they assembled by the border with Gloamer territory. With barely ten days left until the storms of Freshmist were due to arrive, if they didn't invade at that moment, it might be too late, for as soon as the short season of Freshmist was over, the greenhides would return in strength to face the depleted garrisons of the Great Wall. Many believed it was already too late, and that Blades units should be on their way back to the Bulwark; instead, ever more were still entering Medio and Auldan.

'Whether we win or lose today,' the sergeant said, 'as long it's decided quickly.'

She frowned at him. 'You think there's a chance we might lose?'

'There always the chance of that; nothing's ever certain, but yes. If they have anyone else with the powers of that Lady Jade, it could be a dark day indeed.' He glanced along the line of the ditch, where the rest of the squad were cleaning their equipment. 'Right, you lot; that'll do.'

He stood, and Maddie joined him. From a standing position, she could see the huge force the Blades had gathered by the border. Thousands of soldiers were lining the ditch, and spreading down the embankment on the Reaper side of the frontier. Shields and armour were piled high by each company and squad, while stacks of crossbow bolts were being distributed from great baskets that were being carried down the line.

'Check you've got everything you need,' said the sergeant, 'and discard anything you don't. No matter what happens today, if you survive you'll be eating in Dalrig tonight, or else we'll be back here by our tent. Bear that in mind, and bring nothing that will slow you down.' He walked along the section of the ditch where their squad was getting ready, helping them adjust their straps and checking they had everything. An officer was hurrying by on the Reaper side of the ditch. 'Five minutes, five minutes,' she was calling out to the sergeants as she was passing.

'You heard the captain,' said the sergeant. 'Shields.'

The squad lined up in the bottom of the ditch, facing the land of the Gloamers, and Maddie could see other squads and companies doing the same thing as the first wave readied itself. Out of sight behind the ridge of the ditch, the other two waves were also ready, and would be launched minutes after the first was away.

'Stay together,' called out the sergeant. 'It's only a few miles to Dalrig. Shields up at all times, watch each other's backs, and stay low. The Dalrigians have got ballistae, catapults, the works, all hidden in the farms ahead. Remember, it's not a race, even if we only make half a mile in an hour, we'll still be at Greylin Palace before sunset.'

Maddie took a breath, her heart pounding. She gazed at the slope of the ditch. In a minute she would be running up it, and into the expected hail of artillery and crossbow bolts. She gripped the handle of her shield in her left hand.

'Malik,' the sergeant called out; 'protector of the City, watch over us this day, we pray; guard the lives of your faithful Blades, we beseech you.'

It must be bad, Maddie thought, if the sergeant was praying. She swallowed, waiting for the whistle.

'Is there a Corporal Maddie Jackdaw here?' cried a voice behind them. 'Maddie Jackdaw?'

The sergeant frowned, and turned. 'Hey, she's down here.'

The scout skidded to a halt, and looked down. 'Corporal Maddie Jackdaw?'

'That's me,' she said. 'What do you want?'

'You have orders to report to camp. The commander wants to see you.'

'What? Now? But we're about to attack.'

The sergeant began pushing her out of the line. 'Don't argue with the boy, lass; go.'

She stared at the rest of the squad. 'But I can't leave you guys, no way. If you run up that ditch... then I... I should be there.'

The sergeant shoved her back a step. 'Don't you understand, girl? Malik's just answered my prayer. You don't belong in the front line, Maddie, and it would break me if I had to carry your corpse home.'

'But...'

'Don't question it, Maddie; just go.'

She glanced at the squad, guilt and shame freezing her to where she stood.

'Corporal?' said the scout. 'We, ah, need to get out of the way of the advance.'

She followed him up to the ridge of the embankment, then looked back down at the squad.

'This is wrong,' she said. 'What does the commander want me for? Am I in trouble?'

'No idea, Corporal.'

They turned away, and ran down the slope on the Reaper side of the ditch, passing through the lines of the second wave. A whistle blasted out behind her, and she halted, turning. She could hear the shouts of the first wave as they climbed the ditch, but couldn't see them through the ranks of the second.

'Come on,' cried the scout, as he quickened his pace. They ran across a gap, and then through the thick lines of the third wave.

They reached the entrance to the camp. Maddie felt almost giddy with guilt and relief as she glanced around at the empty tents.

'Drop your kit off here,' the scout said.

She stacked her shield by a pile of others, then hung her crossbow up on a rack. In a month and a half, she had yet to loose it, and hoped she never would. She dropped her belt and pack off by her tent, then rejoined the waiting scout. He led her to one of the large houses that lined the road to the frontier, and they entered, passing soldiers posted at the door. The front room of the house was busy, with staff officers standing over large maps of the area, where little flags marked the positions of each unit that had been gathered for the invasion. The scout walked up to a senior officer, saluted, then whispered to her.

She turned to Maddie, an irritated expression on her face. 'Follow me.'

Maddie's heart sank as she kept up with the officer. Aila; it must be. They had discovered that Aila had escaped, and Maddie would be blamed for the entire invasion. The officer led her into a quiet side room.

'Take a seat, Corporal.'

Maddie sat, while the officer gazed out the window for a moment.

'I have some news,' she said without turning her head.

'Yes, ma'am?'

'I received a communication from the office of Commander Kano, Lord of the Bulwark, this morning. You have been recategorised as an essential worker, and are being sent back to the Bulwark with immediate effect.'

Her eyes lit up. 'Back to the Bulwark?'

'Yes. Unfortunately you are needed there, and I have to lose a corporal.'

'Am I going back to my old job, ma'am?'

'It seems so. Return to the camp and retrieve your possessions; a wagon has been organised to transport you this afternoon. That is all. Dismissed.'

Maddie stood, saluted, then left the room. She suppressed a desire to yelp with joy as she ran from the house and onto the street. She was going back to Blackrose; why didn't matter.

It took Maddie five minutes to gather her things, and then three hours to wait for her wagon. In that time a trickle of wounded returned from the front lines; soldiers with crossbow bolt injuries, or with broken limbs from being struck by projectiles, and she watched as they were carried into a roped-off area of the camp. Smoke was rising along the horizon in the direction of Dalrig, and she guessed that the Gloamer farmhouses were burning, but no one stopped to give her any news as she waited by the side of the road. Each minute dragged, and her impatience bubbled up, making her almost sick with nervous anticipation. When the wagon finally arrived, she jumped up onto the back, and sat next to a group of wounded Blades. Some were laid out on stretchers along the bottom of the wagon, while the others squeezed onto the benches that ran down each side. A lieutenant sitting on the driver's bench turned and nodded to her, and the wagon set off, the oxen pulling it through the streets of Outer Pella.

Groups of Reaper civilians watched as the wagon made its slow procession towards the gate in the Union Walls, while some of the Blades clutched their crossbows, aware of the angry stares they were getting. A crowd of youths began following the wagon through the streets, shouting out abuse and challenging the soldiers on board.

'The first rock that comes our way,' muttered one of the Blades, a bandage across his thigh, 'and I'm shooting.'

'Steady,' said the lieutenant. 'Keep your heads down.'

'What's riling them today?' said Maddie.

The lieutenant turned. 'Our noble colleagues in the Taran militia opened up with crossbows on an unarmed crowd close to the old town this morning. Over fifty Reapers were killed, including several children.'

'Taran idiots,' muttered a Blade.

'Yeah,' said another; 'fifty's not enough, they should have killed them all.'

'Quiet,' said the lieutenant, 'I want none of that. We're transporting the wounded; let's just hope they respect that.'

Maddie glanced back at the crowd. Older Reapers among them were trying to restrain the younger elements, and arguments were breaking out. The wagon turned left at a large crossroads, and the Union Walls reared up ahead of them. Maddie glanced at them, willing them to be closer as the crowds bayed and called out for their deaths. She had never felt so exposed. If the crowd wished, they could overpower the few fit and armed Blades on the back of the wagon in seconds. Groups of young Reapers were rushing forward to block the road ahead of them, and Maddie heard the lieutenant curse under his breath.

The wagon started to slow down as the crowd ahead of them grew, and a chant of 'go home' rose above the red sandstone buildings.

The lieutenant got to his feet and stood on the driver's bench. 'This wagon is full of the wounded and sick, and we are returning to the Bulwark.'

A cheer rose up at his last words.

'You want us to go home?' the lieutenant cried. 'Then let us pass.'

At first it seemed as if his words had changed nothing, and the few armed Blades in the back of the wagon readied their weapons. Then, gradually, the crowds parted, leaving a clear way through towards the Union Walls. The wagon pulled off, creeping along between the masses of staring Reapers. Maddie glanced at the hatred in their eyes. Were these the people the Blades had been defending for a thousand years? A young woman spat at the wagon as it passed, and Maddie felt like jumping down and asking her why, why would they turn on their protectors? Did their millennium-long sacrifice mean nothing? Instead, she lowered her eyes and stayed still.

It was Marcus, she thought; he was responsible for the mess the City was in. It was he who had ordered the Blades to break with the past and occupy Medio and Auldan, tearing up the settlement that had kept the City safe for a thousand years. She hated him.

They approached the fortress on the Union Walls, and the gates opened to allow them in. Blades took the harness of the ponies and led them through while the gates were closed to the angry crowds beyond.

'Thank Malik that's over,' muttered Maddie.

The lieutenant frowned at her. 'That was the easy part. To reach the Middle Walls, we still have to get through the Circuit.'

It was sunset by the time their wagon entered the safety of the huge gatehouse on the Middle Walls. They had traversed two miles of the Circuit before reaching a road that had taken them through the relative calm of Icewarder territory, but the pace had been slow throughout. The Evaders had been just as hostile towards them as the Reapers had been, and stones had been thrown at the wagon several times before they had made it out of the Circuit. She thought about Tom. Her poor brother was stuck in that awful place. Maddie had never imagined how bad the Circuit could be, and the sight of the massive, sprawling concrete slums had shocked her.

Once at the Middle Walls, the wounded were carried to a hospital in Blade territory, and Maddie was left to make her own way to Arrowhead. She managed to get a lift on a cart that carried her the four miles to Stormshield on the Great Walls, and then she walked the remaining four miles to Arrowhead, her legs tired, but her spirits rising with every step she took. The Bulwark was quiet, with the roads almost deserted, but it felt like she was home again.

The fortress of Arrowhead was silent and still as she approached. A soldier was at the main gates, but he barely glanced at her as she passed through into the interior. She smiled when she looked up and saw Buckler's eyrie, the familiarity almost bringing tears to her eyes. She hurried to the front door of the lair, but it was locked. She went along to the narrow windows that opened into the kitchen, and into Hilde's office, but there were no lamps lit within. She knocked and knocked, but there was no response.

She glanced around, starting to get cold after her long walk through the winter evening. It must be near midnight, she thought. Captain Hilde would most likely be in a drunken slumber, oblivious to her banging on the door. There were lights coming from the Wolfpack common room, so she went in to get warm.

The large chamber was nearly empty, with just a few soldiers drinking and talking. She spotted a table where a few higher-ranked Blades were sitting and walked over.

'Hello,' she said. 'I'm looking for the officer on duty.'

A woman put down her glass and frowned. 'That'll be me. What do you want?'

'Hi, I've been re-assigned from Auldan to the Fourteenth Support Battalion, Auxiliary Detachment Number Three, under Captain Hilde.'

The woman shrugged. 'Is any of that supposed to mean something to me? The Fourteenth Support Battalion was transferred out over a month ago.'

Maddie frowned. What was she supposed to say, *I need to find my dragon*?

Another officer frowned. 'Captain Hilde did you say?'

'Yes, sir.'

'Are you her replacement?'

'She can't be,' said the woman; 'she's a corporal. Since when did we replace captains with corporals?'

'What do you mean "replacement"?' said Maddie.

The man glanced at her. 'She got injured, and has been invalided out of duty.'

Maddie collapsed into a chair next to the officers. 'What? Is she alright?'

'I don't know,' said the man, 'and I didn't say you could sit next to us, Corporal.'

'What happened to her?'

'No idea, sorry. Now, I don't mean to be rude, but bugger off; we're trying to have a quiet drink.'

Maddie glared at him as she got to her feet.

'Wait a minute,' said the woman. 'I'm remembering something... Wasn't there a letter from Commander Kano about Captain Hilde? Something about a girl called Jackdaw?'

'I'm Maddie Jackdaw,' she said, her eyes widening. 'There was a letter?'

The woman sighed and stood. She glanced at her colleagues. 'Get me another brandy, I'll be back in two minutes.'

Maddie followed her out of the common room and into a guard post. The officer opened a drawer and began rifling through a stack of paperwork. She smiled when she found a large envelope, and ripped it open. A set of keys fell out and dropped to the floor.

'Those are for you,' the officer said as she read the letter.

Maddie leaned over and picked the keys up.

'Right,' said the woman, glancing at her as she put the letter down. 'Corporal Maddie Jackdaw, you are to return to your earlier duties immediately. You'll be working alone, due to the injuries sustained by Captain Hilde. However, Commander Kano says that you have one month to show him some results, or the entire project will be cancelled permanently.' She smirked. 'I hope you understood all that, because it means bugger all to me.'

'One month?'

'That's what the letter says, Corporal.'

'And I'll be working alone? Who do I report to?'

The officer glanced at the letter again. 'You're to report directly to Commander Kano from now on. He wants written updates every few days. If I were you I'd keep to that, Corporal, otherwise the commander might feel he has to come to Arrowhead in person, and to be frank, no one wants that.'

She nodded.

'Are we done? Can I go back to my brandy now, Corporal?'

'Yes, ma'am; thank you, ma'am.'

The officer snorted and walked from the guardroom. Maddie clutched the keys and ran all the way to the entrance to the lair. She unlocked the door and entered the cold, still darkness of the interior. She kept her coat on as she lit some lamps. The kitchen was in a dire mess, with unwashed dishes and mugs, and a cluster of empty wine and brandy bottles littering the floor. Further on, Hilde's office looked the same as it always did, with papers strewn across the desk. She went to her own room at the end of the passageway and dumped her bag on the bed.

She sat in silence for a moment, trying to collect her thoughts. Whenever she had pictured the lair during her absence, Hilde had always been there, and the place seemed desolate without her. Was she expected to live alone?

But she wasn't alone. If Blackrose had died, then she would never have been recalled. She stood and left her room. The door to the cavern was closed. She pushed it, and it swung open. She picked up a lamp and walked into the huge cavern, sensing the odour of animal. She lifted the lamp. The enormous gates, both red and black, were shut. She stole across to the black gate and opened the hatch.

She heard a low growl in the darkness, then it stopped.

'Maddie?'

'Yes, it's me.'

She walked into the lair, and lit a few more lamps as the dragon watched her.

'You have returned.'

Maddie nodded and gazed up. Blackrose looked strong, much stronger than when she had last seen her, and she was gazing down. Maddie put the lamp on the floor and ran over. She put her arms round the beast's forelimb, feeling tears come to her eyes as she buried her head into the dark scales.

The dragon lowered her massive head and gently nuzzled her. 'Why are you crying, little one?'

Maddie glanced up into her eyes. 'I thought I'd never see you again.'

'When you were taken from me I raged for days,' Blackrose said, 'but then I realised something. I wanted you back more than I wanted to die.'

'So you started eating again? Thank Malik.'

'Yes, but do not thank him; you have no reason to be grateful to that useless god. I haven't eaten in four days, however, and I am very hungry.'

'Four days?' said Maddie. 'Is that when...?'

'Yes. That's when Captain Hilde was injured, and I haven't been fed since.'

'Is she badly hurt? How did it happen?'

The dragon glanced away. 'It was me.'

Maddie took a step back. 'What? You did it?'

'Yes.'

Her hands started to tremble. 'Why?'

'Her spirit was broken after you were taken, and she became insufferable company. She would come into the lair and castigate me about all manner of things. Following one particularly unpleasant argument, I lost my temper.'

'What did you do?'

'She was cleaning out my feeding trough, and I swiped at her. She fell down the refuse chute all the way to the midden at the bottom. Her screaming alerted some guards, and I could hear her being carried away. Her back is damaged, and she is lying in hospital.'

'Were you trying to kill her?'

'Truthfully, I cannot say; my mind was clouded with anger. I am, however, glad that she is alive.'

Maddie shook her head. 'Did you realise I'd be recalled?'

'It crossed my mind at the time, I admit. Tell me, Maddie, for I value your opinion and my conscience is troubled; did I do a terrible thing?'

'It sounds like you came close to it. Poor Hilde. I knew she was unhappy, but I always hoped she'd come around and help me to help you escape.'

'Oh, Maddie. There is no escape for me. There is only vengeance; it's all I have left. Vengeance on Kano and Marcus and the City that has imprisoned me. Now, here's a question; are you prepared to help me to gain my revenge? Shall we burn the City together?'

'Wait. Things have changed.'

The dragon laughed. 'Really? How?'

'Corthie is alive.'

Blackrose fell silent.

'And I have a demigod helping to find the Quadrant for us. Lady Aila, she's the woman Corthie's in love with; she loves him too and is going to help us.'

'But Corthie was executed for killing Khora? This had better not be a twisted joke, girl; do not anger me.'

'It's not a joke. Kano thought he was dead, but he wasn't, and he was taken away to a place far iceward of here. And he didn't kill Khora; it was Kano. They set him up.'

Blackrose tilted her neck and let out a roar that sent Maddie tumbling backwards clutching her ears. The noise exploded throughout the cavern, shaking the ground under Maddie's feet.

Maddie stared from where she had fallen as the cries echoed and began to fade.

'That filthy wretch Kano,' Blackrose said, her voice boiling with rage; 'I will kill him if he enters this lair again.' She swung her head down to Maddie's level. 'He came here, the day after Hilde was injured. He told me I had a month to prove I was prepared to fight for the City.'

'And if you don't?'

'Then he said I would be walled into this lair and left to starve. I should have killed him then, but I was... upset over Hilde, and I did nothing. And now, what? We wait again, hoping that Corthie and this Lady Aila come?'

Maddie stood. 'I'm going to the storeroom. I'll bring all the food you can eat tonight, and then tomorrow we'll swing the black gate open again.'

Blackrose stared at her. 'Why?'

'We have a month to get you fit and ready to fly, and I don't want to waste a single minute.'

CHAPTER 17
GREY ISLE RAIDERS

The Western Bank – 19th Yordian 3419

Corthie and Yaizra ran through the undergrowth, the bare branches of the forest above them. Somewhere to their right lay the cliff's edge and a hundred foot drop into the Cold Sea, but it was hidden by a thick mass of trees and bushes.

From behind them came the noise of the pursuing greenhides, their claws ripping through the undergrowth. The forest echoed to the sound of them, and Corthie powered his battle-vision, using it to guide his steps as he scanned around for a place to turn and fight. Beside him, Yaizra was racing along. She had lost her pack, as had he, when they had been ambushed that morning. Greenhide claws had ripped their tent to shreds and Corthie had barely been able to grab his mace before their camp had been surrounded. They had broken through the ring, leaving a dozen dead greenhides lying amid the trees, and since then they had been running. The dense forest had slowed the pace of their pursuers, and they had managed to keep ahead of them, but whenever they had rested, the horde would catch up and they would be forced to run again.

He glanced at Yaizra as they ran. 'I think they're tiring.'

She glared at him. 'My legs are about to give way. I need to stop.'

She skidded to a halt, her hands on her knees, panting. Corthie glanced behind them, his eyes searching between the trees. He could hear the greenhides approaching, but couldn't see any.

'Alright, take a minute.' He opened his water skin and offered it to her.

She took a drink and splashed her face. 'Thanks, big lump.'

He drank what was left in the skin and tied it to his belt. 'Can you climb trees?'

She shrugged. 'I can climb buildings, so, probably.'

He looked around the broken ground. 'We need to find you about a hundred stones, then you can go up a tree and I'll stand at its base; that'll give us a chance at least.'

'What are you talking about?'

'We're going to have to fight.'

She squinted at him. 'Forget it. There are hundreds of the damn things after us.'

'So what do we do?'

'We run.'

'How far? We're heading in the direction of the icefields again.'

'Yeah, but we'd almost circled back to Jezra yesterday. Do you remember Achan mentioned that tiny harbour that once belonged to the Gloamers? We should be close to that.'

'And how would that be any better than fighting them in the forest?' He noticed movement in the undergrowth. 'We'll talk about it next time we stop, come on.'

They sprinted off again, racing through the thick bushes. The mention of Achan's name darkened Corthie's thoughts as he ran. He hadn't told Yaizra that he had deliberately stirred up the nest of greenhides in Jezra, and the guilt was weighing on him. And neither he nor she had mentioned the obvious fact that, had he remained alive, they would not have been able to outrun the beasts. Yaizra was a strong runner, and Corthie's battle-vision could power him all day, though at some point he would need to rest and eat, and his reserves were low after so many days of fighting and running.

They ran for another two hours, until Yaizra started to flag. Corthie looked around for the next place to stop. It needed to be somewhere defensible that would allow Yaizra to get out of range of their claws so she could use her sling, though he doubted the stones would have much impact upon the hard outer shells of the greenhides.

The ground rose a little before him. He raced up it, and nearly fell over the cliff that lay beyond the ridge. He reached out and grabbed hold of a branch as his feet slipped on the loose stones that sat by the edge. Below, the ground fell away in a sheer drop, at the bottom of which the Cold Sea frothed and churned.

Yaizra slid to a halt next to him and they gazed down into the crashing waters below, then out at the Cold Sea stretching all the way to the horizon. The bay to the left of them curved, and on the far side they saw the small harbour that Achan had mentioned.

Yaizra pointed at something, but was panting too much to be able to speak.

A ship was anchored in the bay.

Corthie laughed. He turned back to listen for the greenhides, and heard them in the distance, but it would take them a few minutes to catch up.

'Come on,' he said; 'not far to go. Can you still run?'

She nodded, her eyes on the ship below them. Corthie took off again, turning left along the edge of the cliff, and they raced round the curve of the bay. As they ran, Corthie kept his eyes on the ship. When they were half way around the bay, it unfurled a single sail and began moving closer to a long stone pier, where people were standing. On the short wharf behind them, piles of timber were lying, the trunks stacked.

'Grey Isle raiders,' said Yaizra.

They paused for a moment to catch their breath.

Corthie frowned. 'Raiders?'

'Yeah. They sail to the western bank to plunder what they can; timber, deer, even stone for building. Anything the City's short of.'

'They risk the greenhides to collect some wood?'

She eyed him as if he was stupid. 'Have you any idea how much wood sells for in the City? Every damn tree that grows behind the walls is counted. A few boat-loads would set you up for life.'

'This is our chance,' he said. 'We have to get on that boat.'

'If we go down there, they won't be best pleased that we've got a few thousand greenhides following our scent.'

'We'll worry about that when we get there.'

They set off again, their boots pounding along the edge of the semi-circular bay. The cliff was lowering as they ran, and they scrambled down a low slope of scree, the noise attracting the attention of several workers on the wharf, who turned to look. Many were holding long saws and axes, and they gripped them as Corthie and Yaizra approached.

A woman strode forward from the pier. She pointed at them, and several workers picked up crossbows from there they had been stacked by the wharf.

Corthie and Yaizra slid down the last section of slope and descended a path by the forest. A small area had been cleared of trees, and fresh stumps covered the ground. They came out of the forest and stepped onto the wharf.

'Stay where you are!' cried the woman, as half a dozen crossbows were pointed at them.

'We're stranded on the western bank,' Corthie called out to them. 'Can you help us?'

The woman frowned. 'Stranded? I recognise you from the description posted up on the Grey Isle. You've escaped from Tarstation. Why should we help you?'

'Because I'm innocent. I didn't murder Princess Khora.'

'But you're not denying that you're the renegade champion?'

Yaizra glanced behind them at the slope. 'We don't have time for this.'

'Help us or not,' Corthie said to the woman on the wharf; 'I have to warn you, there are greenhides on our trail. I advise you to get on your ship and get out of here as soon as possible.'

The workers' eyes widened and they glanced around the bay.

'You heard him, move!' cried the woman. 'Get the timber loaded!'

A crane on board the ship was already lifting the first of the shorn tree trunks from the wharf onto its wide deck, and the workers ran back to help, leaving the woman with a handful of guards.

Corthie slung his mace over his back and stepped forward, his arms raised.

'I told you not to move,' said the woman. 'That's my ship, and only I can say if you get on board or not.'

'I have a deal for you, ma'am,' he said. 'I'll hold off the greenhides while you get the timber and your crew safely on board, and then you let me and my friend join you.'

'And then what? You're a wanted fugitive. The authorities on Grey Isle will arrest you as soon as we land.'

He shrugged. 'One problem at a time.'

The hillside erupted in noise. The people on the wharf turned to stare as the first greenhides came into view.

'Move these to block the pier,' shouted the woman, pointing at a pile of tree trunks.

Corthie and Yaizra ran to help. They and the workers dragged three thick tree trunks across the wharf, and laid them down at the end of the pier, while everyone else got behind the makeshift barrier.

'That won't stop them,' said the woman, 'but it might slow them down a bit.' She drew a short sword from her belt. 'Here they come.'

The greenhides poured down the slope, rushing headlong through the trees. They spilled out onto the wharf, and Corthie gripped his mace. He jumped over the barrier they had made and charged into them. His battle-vision reserves were low, but he powered up everything he had left. He battered the first greenhide with a mace blow across its face, then jumped onto its back as it fell to the stone wharf. He swung out, striking anything within range as the greenhides lunged up at him, his speed reaching them before their claws could strike. Bodies started to pile up around him, and he lost track of time, and even forgot for a moment where he was, his concentration on one thing only; killing.

'Pull back!' he heard a voice cry, as if from far away. He lashed out with a boot, kicking a greenhide into the freezing waters of the bay, where it thrashed around before sinking.

'Corthie!' cried the voice again.

He turned, and saw Yaizra waving at him, both arms in the air. He jumped down from the back of the dead greenhide and ran, a set of claws grazing his back and tearing through his clothing. He barrelled forward. The ship's captain, Yaizra and the handful of guards were behind the barrier of trunks, and Corthie vaulted it, the greenhides only yards behind.

'Run!' he cried as the greenhides swarmed over the barrier.

Two greenhides jumped onto one of the guards and tore him to shreds in seconds, their claws bloody. The captain stared, her mouth open, and a greenhide leapt at her. Corthie sprang forward as the green-hide swung its claws at her, and he brought the mace down, breaking its skull. It fell forwards onto the captain, and he pulled the body from her and threw it into the waters of the harbour.

He grabbed the captain's arm and they ran for the gangplank. The ropes securing the ship at bow and aft had already been loosed, and they sprinted up the narrow gangplank as the ship began moving away from the side of the pier. A greenhide leapt the distance, and Corthie smashed it in the face, sending it falling from the side of the vessel into the dark waters. The ship drifted a few yards back, and the entire crew stood on deck, staring at the mass of greenhides crowding the pier. They were roaring and shrieking in frustration at the sight of so much human flesh just out of reach. Some tried to jump, but they all fell into the bay, while the others roiled like a seething mass along the wharf.

Corthie dropped the mace onto the deck and staggered, exhausted. Yaizra grabbed his arm to steady him as the crew gathered round. A mug of ale was pushed into his hand and he drank as the crew slapped his back.

'That was amazing,' said one, 'you tore them up.'

'Give our guest some space,' said the captain, shoving her crew aside, 'and get back to work.' She reached Corthie and stuck out her hand. 'I'm Captain Hellis, and I owe you my life.'

He shook her hand.

'I'm not forgetting that you brought the greenhides down upon us,' she went on, 'but to get out of that with only one casualty was nothing short of a miracle.'

Corthie nodded as he slumped down to the deck.

'Then you'll take us to the Grey Isle?' said Yaizra.

'I will,' said the captain, 'though you've put me in a tricky situation. I can hardly hand over the man who saved us to the authorities now, can I?' She frowned.

'Are there Blades on the Grey Isle?'

'There were a few last time we docked; staying in the castle with the Gloamer garrison.' She crouched down by Corthie. 'I want an honest answer from you, lad.'

He nodded. 'Aye?'

'There's a rumour been spreading all winter that it was someone else who killed Khora. Tell me the truth; who was it?'

'The rumour's right,' he said. 'I was there. Kano killed her.'

The captain nodded. 'That's what I heard. I also heard that the Blades are arresting anyone who repeats the rumour, which only serves to make me think there might be some truth to it. Damn Blades. First they besiege Dalrig, and now this.'

Yaizra frowned. 'They've besieged Dalrig?'

'Yeah. Something about a rogue demigod; Lady Aila, I think.'

'Aila?' said Corthie.

'Yeah. She's wanted by Duke Marcus, and our prince is holding her in Greylin Palace; though what he's doing in there with her is anybody's guess.'

Yaizra frowned. 'Prince Montieth has her?'

Corthie glanced at the faces of Yaizra and the captain. 'Why are you both looking like that? It sounds like this Prince Montieth guy is protecting her from Marcus.'

'No one's seen him in a thousand years,' said the captain; 'it's his daughter, Lady Amber, who runs Dalrig. She might be a ruthless witch, but she's our ruthless witch, and she's always done what's right for Dalrig and the Gloamers.'

Yaizra muttered something.

The captain glared at her. 'You're an Icewarder, eh? I should have guessed from that miserable expression on your face. Tell me, girl, would you rather have been rescued by Rosers or Blades?'

'But Aila's safe?' said Corthie.

The two women looked at him. 'Why you so interested in a demigod, eh?' said the captain.

'She's a... friend.'

'What have you been keeping from me, Holdfast?' said Yaizra. 'Are you involved with a damn demigod?'

'Why are you not answering my question? Is she safe?'

The captain shrugged. 'She's alive, that's all I know. No one knows what goes on inside Greylin Palace, so I can't promise any more than that.'

He nodded.

The wind picked up as the boat sailed out of the bay and into the Cold Sea.

'We'd best get you two below,' said the captain. 'The sea's rough this time of year, with the storms of Freshmist just round the corner.'

Corthie pulled himself to his feet. 'Is there any food?'

The captain laughed. 'Sure. We'll put you with our other... passenger, and I'll have something warm brought to you.'

'You have another passenger?'

'Yeah. We picked him up a couple of days ago from the coast. He was in a bad way, but he'll live. He's resting below decks.'

The captain led the way, and they followed her past the stacks of timber to the rear of the deck and descended a flight of narrow stairs. She took them to a cabin by the stern, knocked on the door, and opened it. Inside, a man was lying in a hammock, groaning with the movement as he swung back and forth.

He raised his head as they walked in. 'Guys! You made it. Malik's ass, I'm glad to see you two.'

Corthie's mouth opened. 'Achan?'

'You know this man?' said the captain.

'I know them, boss,' said Achan from the hammock. 'They're good people.'

The captain nodded. 'I'll leave you to it, then. The food'll be ten minutes.'

She left the room and closed the door.

Corthie turned to Yaizra, his eyes narrow. 'Well?'

She stared from Corthie to Achan.

Achan sat up. He had bandages across his right arm and his torso. 'Is something going on between you two?'

Yaizra lowered her eyes. 'I... uh...'

Corthie shook his head. 'She told me you were dead.'

'Look, I'm sorry,' Yaizra cried. 'I panicked and I'm sorry. He was surrounded by greenhides; if I'd gone back to help him...'

'But he's alive.'

She nodded. 'Yes. Clearly. Though Malik alone knows how.'

'I fell through a hole in the roof of the Roser Palace,' he said. 'I did see you, you know. I watched you run back to help me, and then you stopped when you saw all of the greenhides. Then you ran away. If I'm being honest, I might have done the same. I ran, but they were everywhere. Then I put my foot through the roof and fell thirty feet onto a huge pile of bones. I remember looking up, and seeing all these greenhides staring down at me through the hole, but none of them could squeeze through the gap; it was too small for them. I crawled away, and eventually came out by the cliff side. After a couple of days of hungry wandering, I saw the ship, and jumped into the water, screaming for help, and they saw me.'

Yaizra sat down in the corner of the cabin, her head in her hands.

Achan glanced at Corthie. 'Don't be too hard on her. It was the first time either of us had been face to face with those beasts. They're like something from a nightmare.'

Corthie turned to her. 'I know something that might make you feel better.'

She glanced up, wiping the tears from her eyes. 'What?'

'I have a confession too. I told you I'd disturbed that nest of green-hides under the palace. Well, I lied. I did it deliberately. I woke them up and unleashed them on the Blades.'

'You did what?'

'I didn't think about either of you when I did it. I'm sorry.'

'You asshole,' said Yaizra. 'You're right though; I do feel a little better. At least I wasn't the only one who made a mess of things.'

'We're through it now,' said Achan, 'and look at us; we're all alive and on a boat. Let's face it, things could be a lot worse.'

One of the crew brought them a basket of food and a jug of ale, and then Corthie slept, his need for rest over-riding everything else.

He awoke with Yaizra's hand on his shoulder.

'The boat's slowing,' she whispered. 'I think we're close.'

Corthie sat up and glanced around. The cabin was in near darkness, and he could hear gentle snores coming from Achan's hammock.

'You two didn't kill each other, then?'

She frowned. 'I actually wish Achan had been angry with me.'

'I know what you mean. There should be no more lies between us.'

He got to his feet and peered out of the porthole, but the glass was filthy, and he could see nothing but dark grey. 'How long was I asleep for?'

'A couple of hours.'

'So the sun's not long set? Why's it so dark?'

'I don't know. There could be rain coming.'

'I'll go up on deck and take a look. See you soon.'

He stepped out of the cabin and climbed the narrow steps to the deck. A strong, cold wind was gusting from iceward, and he felt the chill whip though his clothes. Overhead, the sky was thick with heavy, dark clouds, and a few drops of rain touched his face. Sailors were working on the sails and rigging, and he looked around for the captain. She was standing by the helm on a raised platform at the stern, talking to a group of sailors, so Corthie made his way past the stacks of timber lashed to the deck and climbed up to join them.

'Here he is,' said the captain as he approached, 'our protector at the quayside. Are you rested?'

He noticed the glances of the sailors turn to him. 'Aye. Thanks for the food.'

'We'll be docked in under an hour,' she said. 'We're coming up to Grey Isle now.'

She pointed ahead of them and Corthie squinted into the murk. A darker grey body rose above the horizon in front of them, high cliffs that towered over the waves. The captain nodded to the sailors and took Corthie's arm.

'A word,' she said, pulling him along as she went down the steps to the main deck. She led him to a door that went under the stern platform, unlocked it, and they went inside to a small room lit with an oil lamp burning against the wall.

'This is my private room, take a seat. Wine?'

Corthie sat on a cushioned bench by a table as she picked up a jug and began pouring.

'I have a dilemma,' she said as she handed him a mug. 'On the one hand, I loathe Duke Marcus, and like the idea of depriving him of your head, if only to annoy him.' She smiled. 'Of course, there is also the small matter of you saving our lives at the quayside. Mine, in particular. On the other hand... well, there is no other hand, but there is a problem.'

He tasted the wine. 'Go on.'

She kept his gaze. 'Sailors talk.'

'And they've all seen me.'

'Precisely. I run a pretty tight-knit crew, but I can't control thirty tongues. Someone will talk, it's inevitable, even if it's only to their girlfriend or neighbour, or a drunken guy in the tavern. There's no way I can keep this a secret from the castle authorities. The Grey Isle is a small place, and as a ship's captain, I'm well known among the soldiers in the garrison, the Gloamer ones anyway; the Blades are a different matter.'

Corthie nodded. 'So I stage an escape as soon as we land? Push a few folk over and run for it? Is there somewhere on the island my friends and I can hide, or, even better, is there another boat I can get that'll take me to the City?'

'There will be no boat to take you the City, not now that the storms are coming. I can feel it in the wind; winter is over. It's a little early this year, but the seasons never fall exactly when the calendar says they should.'

'Are you telling me that, by tomorrow, the weather will be too bad to sail?'

'That's exactly what I'm telling you. Why do you think we're sailing back with our hold only half-full? As soon as I saw the clouds this morning, and felt the direction of the wind change, I knew it was time to get back to the safety of the Grey Isle. You were very lucky you caught up with us when you did, lad. One more day, and you'd have been on the western bank for Freshmist.'

'Is it as bad as Sweetmist?'

'The same, but colder. A lot of ice and hail, and winds from iceward that could peel your skin off. It calms a bit in the second month like it does in Sweetmist, but there's no equivalent Fog of Balian, so sailing can sometimes restart then.'

'So what do we do?'

'Don't worry, lad; I've got it all figured out.'

An hour later, Corthie was handling the oars of the ship's small rowing boat, pulling it across a small bay while being lashed by the wind and freezing cold rain. Achan lay huddled in the bottom of the boat, sodden and miserable, while Yaizra sat at the rear, staring grimly ahead.

The captain had asked Corthie to break a hole through the side of her own ship, and had given him an axe with which to do it. He had

234

done so, hacking a small breach above the water line from inside their cabin, and then they had crawled through it, dropping into the rowing boat below. The captain had made sure the crew were up on deck moving the timber around while they were escaping, to cover the noise, and to make sure no one saw them.

Rowing gave Corthie a perfect view of the small harbour town that lay beyond the ring of cliffs that encircled the island. There was a small break in the circle, that opened onto the sheltered bay. A sturdy castle with a tower and a keep sat to the left of the settlement, which backed up onto more cliffs, from which waterfalls gusted and sprayed wildly in the wind.

'A little to the right, big lump.'

Corthie nodded, his arms beginning to ache. He was going to need to sleep for a good eighteen hours whenever they finally stopped for the day. As long as it was warm and dry, he thought as the rain smacked against his face.

'There he is,' she said; 'I see the lantern. Keep going.'

'Do you think I'm likely to just stop?'

'Save your breath for rowing.'

The ship and harbour had faded into the distance ahead of Corthie, and he wondered if Blades were starting to search the island for him.

'Alright, Holdfast. Get ready.'

'For what?'

The rowing boat collided with the rocky shore, the keel grinding and tilting to the left.

'Over here!' called a voice. 'Bring the boat.'

Corthie pulled the oars in. The water was shallow around them, so he jumped in as the wind sprayed them.

'I'll take Achan,' cried Yaizra. 'You get the boat.'

She picked Achan up and slung him over her shoulder, bowing under the weight. Corthie helped her out of the boat, and she waded off towards the man standing above them on the shore. Corthie tied the oars to the bottom of the boat, then lifted it out of the water, his knees bending as he staggered. He placed it upside down over his head, and stumbled forward, the surging waters slowing him. He struggled up the slope, and almost fell into a wagon.

The man put down the lantern, and helped Corthie push the boat into the back of the wagon. Corthie leaned against a wheel, panting.

Yaizra patted him on the back. 'Good job, big lump.'

Corthie glanced up, and saw the man who had been waiting for them.

'Good evening,' he said. 'I am Takon, the husband of Captain Hellis. I understand she owes you her life? For this I am in your debt. Climb aboard; we don't have long before the garrison is sweeping the island for you. Fortunately, I have an excellent place where you can hide.

'Thank you,' said Corthie. He clambered up next to the boat, and out of the rain under the canvas covering. Yaizra helped Achan up, and then climbed in beside them. A whip cracked, and the wagon started moving, heading along a track away from the castle and settlement.

Corthie lay down as the wagon bumped along the track. Exhaustion seeped through his body, and he was asleep within seconds.

CHAPTER 18
UPRISING

T he Circuit, Medio, The City – 28th Malikon 3420

For thirty-six days without cessation the storms of Freshmist had pounded the City, and nothing had moved. The streets were empty of traffic, and each house was shuttered and closed amid the freezing wind and torrential rains. At the height of the storms it had been impossible to tell when day merged into night, so thick and black were the clouds that hung overhead.

In the Circuit, every Blade had been confined to their barracks to wait it out, and the rebels had been busy in their absence, preparing for the day when the storms lessened. The cramped indoor conditions were perfect for the fostering of gossip and rumour, and the Circuit simmered with anger and anticipation.

On the twenty-sixth day of Malikon, the first month of 3420, the City awoke to an eerie stillness. Rain was still falling, from the Bulwark to Tara, but the storms had passed, and the rebels of the Circuit went into action.

Within two days, insurgents had occupied over a quarter of the territory of the Evaders, ejecting the Blades from their strong points and pushing them out of the centre, where a strange euphoria had descended upon the populace, who gathered in the wet streets to celebrate their freedom.

For Aila, it was reminiscent of the Civil War that had caused so much carnage and destruction three hundred years previously. Then too, rebel Evaders had gained control of much of the Circuit, only to see Prince Michael and the Blades invade, and Aila could remember how that had turned out. She and Bekha had hidden for the first ten days or so after arriving in the Circuit from Port Sanders, but had slowly emerged to take part in the plans that were sweeping through the territory, Bekha as herself, and Aila as Stormfire.

'I'm going to tell them the truth today,' Aila said to Bekha as they walked along one of the many secret tunnels that ran under the Circuit, connecting the different areas of the territory together.

'The truth about what?'

'About me. It's time the Evaders learned they have a demigod on their side.'

Bekha frowned in the shadows of the tunnel's lamplight.

'Why not?' said Aila. 'I keep hearing from the rebels about how the Royal Family all deserve to die, and, to be honest, although I kind of agree with the sentiment, I don't particularly want to be burned at a stake myself, or beheaded, or anything of the other things they'd like to do to us.'

Bekha continued to frown.

'I see I haven't completely convinced you,' Aila went on, 'but I remember back to the days of Princess Yendra, and how popular she was with the Evaders because she was on their side.'

'So you want to be popular?'

'That's not what I meant; only that it might be good for morale, you know, for the ordinary citizens.'

Bekha sighed.

'What?'

'You don't even realise how arrogant you sound, do you? You think that the people will be singing for joy because you're helping them? No offence, Aila, but maybe if you had the death powers of Jade, or the battle-vision powers of your brother Kano, or even the vision powers of Naxor, then maybe, from a tactical point of view, the rebels would welcome you with open arms, but, as the delightful Lady Jade herself said, your power is the equivalent of carrying around a box of masks...'

'Screw you,' Aila muttered.

They reached a ladder leaning against a wall of the tunnel and climbed. A rebel soldier was waiting at the top, a Blade-issue crossbow across her knees as Bekha and Aila pulled themselves through a hatch.

The guard stood and saluted. 'The commanders of the central district are in the back room.'

'Thanks,' said Bekha.

Aila scowled. She had been used to insults about her powers, or lack of them, from her siblings and cousins all her life; did the mortals think of her in that way also? The fact that she had kept her one skill a secret didn't help, and it occurred to her that perhaps the mortals of the City thought she was as useless as her brother Collo, who had no powers at all, other than the ability to keep living.

They walked through to the back room of the ground floor apartment, where a dozen rebel commanders were assembled around a table, poring over maps and plans.

'Good morning, Stormfire, Bekha,' said the overall commander as they walked in. 'Sit. We were just going over today's plan.'

Aila nodded. 'Has it changed?'

'A few details, but the gist is the same: the Great Racecourse and Redmarket Palace. We occupy them, then fortify them against the inevitable Blade counter-attack.'

'I have concerns about Redmarket,' said another commander. 'Wouldn't it make more sense to burn it to the ground?'

'Yes,' said another, 'preferably with Lady Ikara still inside.'

The rebels round the table laughed, and Aila caught Bekha's eye.

'That's no good,' said the main commander; 'we need to execute her somewhere the people can see it happen, otherwise they might not believe it.'

'Remember, she's supposed to have battle-vision.'

'Yeah, but has anyone ever actually seen her use it?'

They laughed again.

Aila frowned. 'I have.'

They turned to her.

'Ikara's battle-vision is pretty feeble, but I've seen her use it.'

The commander frowned. 'When?'

'Oh, about three hundred and thirty years ago, give or take.'

The table fell into silence.

One of the officers raised an eyebrow. 'Are you claiming to be immortal, Stormfire?'

She dropped her disguise, and gasps echoed round the table. 'Do you know who I am?'

'Lady Aila? But...'

'I fought in the last Civil War, alongside Princess Yendra. If anyone here doubts my loyalty to the cause of the Evaders, speak up.'

One of the officers stood, a hand on the hilt of his sword. 'You're one of *them*. We can't trust her! She'll betray us at the first opportunity. She's worked for Lady Ikara for a hundred years, doing her dirty work. My cousin was sent in chains to the Bulwark two years ago, and this bitch's name was at the bottom of the document ordering his deportation.'

'And during that time I was also Stormfire,' she said. 'I was imprisoned for two centuries following the end of the Civil War, and I was being constantly watched by the government. If they'd caught me doing anything, I would have been put straight back into house arrest in Pella. Listen to me, I can get into Redmarket; you all saw what I can do, I can change my appearance to look like anyone I choose.'

The commander glanced at Bekha. 'Did you know this?'

'Yes. Like you, I was shocked when I found out Stormfire has been Lady Aila all along, but I vouch for her; we can trust her.'

'But she's a demigod. She sees every one of us sitting here as worthless mortals.'

Aila smirked. 'Not every one of you. Just some.'

'She's supposed to be in Dalrig,' said another officer, 'and we need Prince Marcus to continue believing that. If he finds out she's in the

Circuit, he could divert the thousands of Blades from the siege of Gloamer land to here.'

'Good point,' said Aila, 'so I advise that what I've told you today doesn't leave this room. I'm putting myself at your disposal, it's up to you how you deal with it.'

The commander nodded. 'Please leave the room, Lady Aila. Wait in the hall outside until we decide what to do next.'

She stood. 'I understand why you hate my family; I hate most of them too. Do you know the biggest mistake our enemies make? They see the mass of the Evaders as a single entity, and they treat them as if they are one, faceless group, instead of realising that, like everyone else, they are made up of individuals. Please don't make the same mistake.'

She left the room, changing her appearance back into Stormfire as she did so. She wandered into the kitchen, where a couple of Evader rebels were preparing food. They nodded to her as she leaned against a window frame and peered through the gaps in the shutters at the dark clouds outside.

'Are you Stormfire?' said one.

'Yup.'

'I heard about you a lot when I was growing up. You look younger than I'd imagined.'

She smiled. 'Thanks. Tell me something. What do you think about the demigods?'

'I despise them. They treat us like slaves and are bringing the City to its knees.'

'All of them?' Aila said. 'Aren't there any good ones?'

'Not since Princess Yendra,' said the other rebel, 'and her daughters, of course; the three sisters.'

'What about Lady Aila? She's not quite as bad, is she?'

'Nah,' said the first. 'She's alright, I guess.'

'No, she ain't,' said the second. 'She's worse. She knows what's wrong with the City, and does nothing about it. She went crawling back to the others at the end of the Civil War, begging for forgiveness. At least with Kano, Ikara and Marcus, folk like that, we know where we stand.

They've always been the enemy, and always will, but Aila's a treacherous back-stabber; a traitor who should have died when Yendra did.'

'You're being a bit harsh there, mate,' said the first. 'Wasn't she in jail for like, two hundred years or something?'

'So? Two hundred years is nothing to those freaks. I ever saw her, I'd have no problem cutting her head off and mounting it on the gates of Redmarket. I'd put it right next to Jade's and Ikara's, and we won't stop until we've got them all.'

'Come on,' the first went on, 'you can't compare her to that maniac Jade.'

'They're all the same, that's what I'm telling you. They're a poison polluting the City, and the sooner we kill them all the better.'

Aila stood. 'Well, it's been lovely chatting to you, boys. I think I'll get some fresh air.'

She left the kitchen and made her way to the back door of the apartment. A rebel guard was watching the door, but let her pass as Stormfire. She slipped outside into the rain, then ran.

'Elsie!' cried Nareen as Aila walked into the Blind Poet. The bar was deserted, and Aila had needed to pound at the door for several minutes in the pelting rain before the owner had unlocked and opened it up.

'I confess,' said Nareen as she locked it behind them, 'I thought you must be dead. It's been months since you were round here.'

'Just been keeping my head down,' she said. 'Any chance of a drink?'

'Well,' said Nareen, waving her hand at the empty tavern, 'as you can see, we've been shut for a while, ever since the brewery next door was damaged in a riot.'

Elsie took a seat by the bar. 'Then how come you're still here? How are you affording to eat?'

Nareen smiled. 'I had a mysterious benefactor, who gave me enough gold to tide us by. Brandy any good for you?'

'Yeah, that'd be great. Someone gave you gold?'

'By Yendra's holy breath, I swore not to tell anyone, but why not, eh? It was that strapping young champion that you were so cosy with; he gave me and the husband enough to live on for a year.'

'Corthie?'

'That's him. What an awful shame to hear he had been executed, especially as he was innocent; did you hear? It's all over the Circuit. The Blades are lying – no surprise there – they're covering up for that beast, Kano.'

'I heard, yeah.'

Nareen filled a glass with brandy and slid it over the counter to Aila. 'If you've been lying low,' she said, 'then today's a funny day to come out of hiding. There are rumours everywhere that the rebels are about to mount a big offensive, right in the middle of the Circuit.'

'Is that right?'

'Aye, so if it all goes mental outside, you can stay in here with me and the husband until it calms down, alright?'

'Thanks.'

'No bother. Have you heard the latest about that Lady Jade? Supposedly she's living like a queen near the Sander border; she's taken over a whole block herself, and apparently she's got all these servants and guards to look after her. I don't understand it; I mean, who'd want to work for her? Anyway, the locals down there are giving the place a wide berth, and even the Blades refuse to get too close.'

Aila nodded. The daily news sheets at one point had been listing every sighting of the rogue demigod as she crossed from Sander territory into the Circuit. By accident or design, the rebels were finding her presence a strategic advantage, as her location was blocking the main routes for reinforcements trying to push up from Port Sanders. She had, however, also left a trail of corpses behind her, and Aila doubted any of her guards or servants were willing helpers, or even if they were still alive.

She sipped her brandy, while trying to work out what to do next. She was out of ideas. Bekha had been right; she should never have revealed her identity to the Evader rebels. It was clear that they hated all demigods, and saw their aim as the complete eradication of the Royal Family, even the ones who were harmless, or who tried to do good. There weren't many of them, she admitted to herself, but tarring them all with the same brush meant putting her into the same category as Marcus.

A low rumble of noise seeped in over the sound of the rain.

'Sounds like folk are on the move,' said Nareen, peering towards the door. She sighed. 'It's a pity the demigods of the Circuit aren't a bit more like Jade.'

Aila frowned. 'What?'

'You know, then they could defend us the way Jade's sister killed the Blades when they attacked Dalrig. She showed them. If Lady Ikara or Lady Aila could do that, and if they were actually on our side, instead of just licking the boots of whoever's in charge, then we'd kick the Blades out of here in no time.'

'But Lady Aila's on the run from the Blades, just like the rebels are.'

Nareen frowned. 'Is she? I remember something about her being in Dalrig? I could never understand the point of her, to be honest, she was just there to help Ikara as far as I could see. What's she wanted for?'

'She was helping the folk of the Circuit. It was her putting all those posters up, telling everybody that it was Kano who killed Khora.'

Nareen raised an eyebrow. 'And how would a swine trader know about that?'

Aila swallowed. 'Umm, it's what I heard.'

'You seem to care about this Lady Aila; you're very defensive of her all of a sudden.'

'I just think, ah, that she, uh, doesn't deserve to be lumped in with the rest of them.'

Nareen shrugged. 'They're all bad. I can agree that some might not be as bad as the others, but they're all the same deep down, and it's time the City was done with them.'

Aila lowered her eyes. It was clear to her; with the exception of Yendra, the Evaders' hatred of the ruling family knew no bounds, and Aila was deemed to be the same as the others. All her years of work, mostly as Stormfire, but using countless other faces as well, had been in vain if she had hoped the people of the Circuit would look more kindly upon her as a result. That wasn't why she had done it, she told herself. She had helped people because it had been the right thing to do, not for any applause or thanks. Still, part of her felt anger at the ingratitude of the mortals for whom she had given up her freedom. Chased from one end of the City to the other; hunted like a criminal, trapped in a palace, all because she had refused to go along with the will of her family. She remembered feeling the same three centuries before, when faced with the choice to help Princess Yendra, or return to her comfortable house arrest in Cuidrach Palace. She hated Yendra for making her feel compassion towards the mortals; she should have hardened her heart as most of her cousins had. It was pathetic for a god to feel sympathy towards a being that flamed for so brief a time; then she remembered Corthie, and a tear rolled down her cheek.

'Are you alright, love?' Nareen said. 'Do you want a hanky?'

A thought popped into Aila's head from somewhere, and she knew what she needed to do. 'No. I think I'll just go home.' She dipped into her pocket, but Nareen shook her head.

'It's on the house, Elsie. It was just nice to see you again. Come by when things have calmed down.'

Aila nodded. Nareen unlocked the front door and peered out into the rain. 'Street's quiet. All the sounds coming from the right, over by the racecourse.'

'Thanks, Nareen. Take care.'

Aila walked out onto the street, and heard the door closed and locked behind her.

You see me as a fellow Evader who might be a rebel.

It was a little vague, she thought, but she needed something flexible, that could be accepted by whoever she might come face to face with. She set off, heading towards the rumble of noise. Ahead of her, the Great Racecourse reared above the concrete tenement blocks, the dark clouds overhead almost seeming to touch its roof. Aila veered a little to the right. She had told Nareen she was going home, and she was. If the rebels were going to burn down Redmarket Palace, then she wanted to see it one last time.

———

The streets surrounding both the racecourse and the palace were heaving with people. Groups of wounded Evaders were being tended to at each junction, and the bodies of several Blades were being loaded onto wagons. The Circuit had used its best weapon, the vast population, and faced with such overwhelming numbers, the remaining Blades had withdrawn from the district, leaving only a loyal garrison to protect the palace. Rioters were roaming free, looting the few mansions in the small merchant's quarter, and Aila circled round behind them to approach the palace from the direction of the canal that served it. The gates by the canal were guarded by loyal militia, and Aila emerged from the shadows looking like one of them. She ran towards them, and the gate slid open to let her pass.

An officer approached as the gates were re-closed and barred.

'The rioters are still in the merchant's quarter sir,' Aila panted, 'but there are more at the front gates of the palace, and they'll be here any minute.'

'Report to the front gates, trooper,' the officer said. 'We have enough here to hold them off.'

She saluted. 'Yes, sir.'

Once inside the rear doors of the palace, she sprinted down a hall-way, then turned for the stairs that led to her private quarters. She ducked into a dark alcove on the way.

You see me as a palace servant.

She darted back out, and reverted to walking, keeping her ears open as the sound of the mob outside grew. She went up another flight of stairs, and turned into the hallway where her rooms lay. She hurried along, taking keys from a pocket. She unlocked her door and went in, sighing with relief. Home at last.

She blinked, her mind clearing. What was she doing? Was she

insane? Why had she gone back to her rooms in the middle of the worst uprising in three hundred years? She began to sweat as panic rippled up from her toes.

A tap on the door made her jump and she turned. The door opened, and a man in leather armour glanced at her, a sword in his hand, and a scarf covering the lower half of his face.

'Lady Aila?'

She remembered she still looked like a servant.

'If that is you,' he went on, 'then you must come with me. We have only moments before the palace is infiltrated, and your life is in danger.'

'Who are you?'

'That can wait. Are you her?'

'Yes.'

'Then come.'

He made off down the hallway, and she watched him for a second, then followed. Who was he and how had he known she was going to be there? And why had she gone there in the first place? She recalled the idea entering her mind as she had sat inside the Blind Poet. It had felt right at the time, and she had acted on it without thinking through the consequences.

The man slowed then halted by the top of a flight of stairs as raised voices drifted up from the landing below.

'We must leave now, my lady,' cried someone.

'What do you think I'm trying to do?' Aila recognised Ikara's voice as she edged to the wall behind the man. She glanced down, and saw the back of her cousin's head as she rushed down the stairs.

'What'll we do about her?' whispered Aila.

'Nothing. My orders were concerned with you alone.'

'And who gave you those orders?'

The man turned to her. 'Make yourself appear like me; ambiguous, but edging towards rebel.'

She frowned at him, then went back to the vague might-be rebel she had been before.

'Perfect,' he said, then began to descend the stairs.

Aila followed him to the landing, then they waited until Ikara had disappeared down a hallway to the left.

'Where are we going?' said Aila. 'The canal?'

'Too obvious,' said the man; 'besides, that's where Lady Ikara's going.'

He set off again. Aila glanced at the direction Ikara had taken and wondered if that was the last time she would ever see her cousin. Aila loathed her, but she was still family, and a larger part of her than she had imagined hoped she would make it out of the Circuit alive.

She went down the stairs after the man, looking for her chance to lose him. She didn't trust him, and felt as if she had been tricked somehow. A roar of noise came from their right that sounded to Aila like the front doors being smashed in. Awful memories of the last time she had been in Redmarket Palace when it had been invaded by a hostile force surged through her, and she halted when she saw the man head in that direction, towards the noise.

A mob was approaching, swarming through the wide central hallway at the heart of the palace, entering the rooms on either side, and rushing up the grand staircases, their way lit by enormous sparkling chandeliers.

The man turned, and saw that she hadn't moved. 'Blend in,' he hissed. 'I have transport waiting for us.'

'No,' she said. 'I'm not going with you. I can blend in on my own, change my appearance a dozen times in this crowd. You'd never find me.'

His expression darkened. 'I don't have time for this.'

'Tough.'

'Wait! If I tell you who sent me, and why, will you come?'

She shrugged. 'That depends.'

He ran towards her, then past her. He turned and kicked in a door. 'In here.'

Aila glanced at the mob as they cheered and chanted. Paintings were being ripped off walls, and an ancient statue of the God-King and

Queen was toppled over, shattering into a cloud of a thousand fragments sent flying across the marble floor.

She went over to the door. The man was inside a large storeroom. She stepped inside and he closed the door, a red light coming from the flames of the rioters through a window. The shadows flickered over the man's face as he frowned at her.

'You are my cousin,' he said.

'What? I admit, that wasn't what I was expecting. But, you're a mortal.'

'I am.'

'Then you're the child of a demigod?'

'I'm still your cousin.'

She folded her arms. 'Alright. Whose child are you?'

'I am the son of Chancellor Mona of Ooste.'

She squinted. 'Mona? I've not seen her in over a hundred years. And how did you know I was in here?'

'My mother has a vision skill; she can implant suggestions into people's minds.'

'She forced me to come here?'

'No, she can't force anyone to do something against their will; their mind has to be receptive to the idea. She guessed you'd want to visit your old home, and guessed you would be in the centre of the Circuit.'

'But how did she know where I would be tonight?'

'She's been sending out her vision powers over the Circuit ever since the storms stopped a few days ago, and I've been here, waiting for her signal.'

'I barely know your mother. What in Malik's name does she want with me?'

'She was a beloved friend of Princess Khora, and still mourns her death. The princess told my mother that she saw great promise in you, and she is offering you sanctuary within the Royal Academy. Her word is law there, and you will be safe from Prince Marcus.'

Aila frowned. 'No, thanks. I've already been imprisoned inside a Prince's palace. I have no desire to walk into captivity again.'

'You'll be free to leave any time you wish; I swear it on the life of the God-King, my great-grandfather. Just listen to what my mother has to say, then if you don't agree, you can go, but give her a chance, please.'

Aila recalled Princess Khora telling her that Mona was one of the few people who knew the secret of the God-King. Aila had been surprised at the time, as the Chancellor of the Academy was almost never seen in public, and who knew how long it had been since she had left Ooste.

'How do I know you don't work for Marcus?'

He widened his eyes. 'What?' He pulled down his sleeve, to show he had no tattoos.

'That doesn't prove anything.'

'Alright,' he said, 'no one working for Marcus has vision powers. My mother does, and I have some vestigial powers of my own. It's not much, but I can summon my mother's attention. Hold on a moment.'

Aila took a step back as his eyes glazed over. She had heard of some powers seeping through to the children of demigods. Never self-healing, but occasionally a spark or echo of the divine parent's abilities.

Lady Aila, echoed a voice through her head.

She started. 'What?'

I am in your mind, cousin Aila. I am Mona. My son says you doubt his word. This does not surprise me, for it is a time to be wary. Come to Ooste, Aila; my son has arranged the journey. There is much I wish to discuss with you, regarding the betterment of the City.

Aila's first instinct was to refuse, her suspicion twisting a knot in her chest. Then she thought back to the words she had heard all day from the mortals of the City. She was a demigod whether she wanted to be or not, and the Evaders didn't care about Stormfire, or anything else she had done.

'Alright,' she said, hoping Bekha would forgive her; 'I'll do it.'

CHAPTER 19

A LITTLE SCRAP OF PAPER

Tara, Auldan, The City – 30th Malikon 3420

Emily stared out of the window as the rain continued to fall. It was a miserable view, but at least the storms had stopped and she could open the shutters. The first month of Freshmist had been gruelling and claustrophobic despite the size of the Aurelian mansion, and Emily had never seen so much of Lord Aurelian, who, like the others, was trapped in the house for the duration of the terrible storms.

They had received no word from Maeladh Palace in that time, and were in the dark about the progress of Daniel's case, or even if there had been any progress. As soon as the storms had lessened, his mother had sent a flurry of letters to the court-martial tribunal, but none had been answered.

To pass the time, Emily had buried herself in the family accounts, learning all she could about the sources and status of the Aurelian's vast wealth. Their spread of land holdings was wider than she could have ever imagined, with estates, farms and industrial concerns across much of Auldan and Medio. It was a magnificent portfolio, but was also more fragile than it first appeared, with huge losses accumulating from the recent troubles. The blockade of Dalrig, the chaos in the Circuit, and the strikes in Pella were all contributing to the steep fall in income. Prince Marcus was insisting that every tribe pay their share towards the maintenance of the Blade garrisons, and the Aurelian's bill was enormous. It was right that the rich should pay more, Emily knew, but without a quick resolution to the crisis, the family would be forced into selling assets to cover the cost.

Compared to that, her work on the small parcel of land in the Circuit had paled into insignificance. It was situated within the districts occupied by the rebels, and the tenants had paid no rent for months, while the repair bill for the damage caused by the riots mounted steadily. The Omertias would be suffering more, as the majority of their wealth came from the rent they squeezed out of the Evaders, and she was glad that she didn't have to hear her parents rage and rant about the savages of the Circuit.

Lady Aurelian was harder to read. She had the ability to switch from stoic to enraged and back again in the blink of an eye, and Emily had grown used to watching her mother-in-law closely, to pick up the signs of when her anger was about to tip over. She had taken most of her fury out on the Reaper servants that staffed the mansion, though her husband had been on the receiving end of more than a few barbed comments. Lord Aurelian knew his wife well, and would retreat to his study for hours at a time whenever he sensed an impending row.

To Emily's surprise, Lady Aurelian had been patient and courteous with her, treating her as an ally in the fight to free Daniel, and seeming to respect her opinions. They had spent days discussing the family accounts without a single cross word being exchanged. Emily also kept her temper with the servants, and they had started to come to her if they wanted to pass on information that might elicit an unfavourable response from Lady Aurelian. If it weren't for Daniel's incarceration, Emily would have been pleased with the progress she had made in winning Lady Aurelian over, but her husband's absence reminded her daily of the struggles they had yet to overcome.

'Don't stare out of the window like that, dear,' said her mother-in-law as she walked into the reception room where Emily was sitting. 'If anyone outside sees you, they'll think I'm holding you hostage.'

Emily turned and smiled.

'Our old friend Nadhew is due to visit this morning,' Lady Aurelian went on. 'He has connections through his lawyerly circles with two members of the militia tribunal, and he had arranged to meet with them last night, on an informal basis, of course.'

'Do you think they would tell him anything?'

Lady Aurelian sat, and took a glass of wine that a servant was holding out for her. 'Probably not, but it's worth a try. Lord Chamberlain has made them all take oaths of secrecy, but Nadhew is good at eking out clues. He helped get the charges against Daniel dropped after the incident in the Circuit last summer.'

'Is he expensive?'

'Yes, dear; very. He is coming round today as a favour, however, and we pay him an annual retainer, so I don't expect to see a bill to pop through the front door.'

Emily nodded.

'Don't look so worried, dear. The accounts are what they are. The Aurelians have weathered far worse in the past, and we shall sail through these current difficulties as well.'

'I am worried. I've never seen the City like this. The Evaders are burning effigies of the gods and demigods in the Circuit...'

Lady Aurelian raised her hand. 'Enough. I do not wish to discuss what those barbarians are doing. The Evaders have made it clear that they do not wish to be associated with the rest of the City. They wish to rule themselves! The Royal Family has protected this City for thousands of years, and those stupid savages...' She took a breath, then sipped her wine. 'Anyway, enough about them. They and the Dalrigians, and every truculent Reaper that is refusing to work; damn them all.'

'And what about the Blades?' Emily said. 'They were supposed to leave Auldan before the end of winter, then Freshmist came early, and they were supposed to leave as soon as the storms finished. Well, they finished five days ago, and there's no sign of any Blades going.'

'Prince Marcus is cutting it fine. If he pulls the Blades out now, he'll have nothing to support his power.'

'But the Great Wall needs them back in time for summer.'

'I have made no secret of the fact that I dislike Marcus; however I find it hard to believe that someone of his experience would take any chances with the safety of the City. I'm sure there are plenty of soldiers left in the Bulwark to garrison the outer defences. Quelling the uprising in the Circuit is the first priority, closely followed by any acceptable agreement with Dalrig to get trade moving again. It was terrible what Lady Amber did to those Blades, but they did invade Gloamer territory, so what were they expecting? No, Marcus will have to back down from his wild threats towards Dalrig, especially as Lady Aila does not seem to be in the town any longer, if she was ever there in the first place. Prince Montieth has played Marcus with flair, but it's time for a settlement.'

A Reaper servant walked into the room, her head bowed. 'Ma'am, there is someone at the front door.'

'If it's Nadhew, girl, I hope you let him in and he isn't standing outside in the rain.'

'It's not Lord Nadhew, ma'am.'

Lady Aurelian frowned. 'Then who is it?'

'Soldiers from the palace, ma'am.'

Daniel's mother and Emily shared a glance as they stood.

'Fetch my husband,' said Lady Aurelian to the servant. 'He should be here for this.'

'Yes, ma'am.' The servant bowed and left the room.

Lady Aurelian nodded to Emily. 'Shall we?'

They walked through the mansion towards the front entrance. There was a small room just off the main doors, and Emily saw three very wet Blades standing inside, warming their hands by a fire.

'Good morning,' said Lady Aurelian. 'How may I help you?'

One of the three Blades was an officer, and he turned to face the two women as they approached.

He bowed. 'Lady Aurelian. We are here on the instructions of the court-martial tribunal regarding the case against your son, acting-Captain Aurelian.'

'Yes?'

'The tribunal has requested your presence at the palace, ma'am, that you might hear the result.'

'What do you mean "result"? We weren't informed that it had even begun.'

'As far as I understand it, ma'am, the case was completed yesterday.'

'And so you come round here and expect me to drop everything at a moment's notice? Why wasn't a letter sent yesterday?'

'I think there was an administrative oversight, ma'am.'

'An oversight, you say. When are we expected?'

'Right away, ma'am.'

Lady Aurelian's face darkened. 'Return to the palace, and inform your superiors that we shall be along shortly, as soon as we are properly attired and our carriage is ready.'

The officer nodded, looking relieved to be leaving. 'Yes, ma'am.'

The soldiers saluted, and a servant showed them to the front door.

Lady Aurelian glanced at Emily. 'I could say something very rude right now, but I think I'll save it for the palace. Come, we don't have long to get ready.' She turned to a servant. 'And where is my husband?'

'Lord Aurelian took a carriage into town earlier this morning, ma'am.'

'He did, did he? Right. Well, Emily, it looks like it'll be just me and you today.'

Twenty minutes later, Emily and Daniel's mother stepped out of the mansion's side door and into a carriage, while servants held out umbrellas to keep them dry. The rain was pelting down onto the roof of the carriage as it took off down the driveway.

Lady Aurelian glanced at Emily as the carriage pulled onto Princeps Row. 'No matter what happens in the palace today, do not break down. I'd rather you be thought harsh than weak, do you understand?'

'Have you ever seen me cry?'

'No, Emily, I haven't. However, Daniel has been imprisoned within a cold, dark cell for over a month, and he may be a little worse for wear. If that is the case, and he glances at us, then I don't want him to see two weeping women; I want him to see that we are being strong for him, that we are fighting for him. If the positions were reversed, imagine how you would want Daniel to look.'

Emily glanced out of the window. 'If they give him two years, I might not be able to help myself.'

The carriage climbed the gentle slope to the gates of Maeladh Palace, and the Blades on duty in the rain waved them through. The ponies trotted across the gravel and swung round before a side entrance, where a courtier was waiting with an umbrella.

'Lady and Mistress Aurelian,' he said bowing as the carriage door was opened. 'Please come this way.'

They walked into a grand entrance hall and a servant took their rain coats.

Lady Aurelian frowned. 'When do the proceedings commence?'

'They have already begun, my lady,' said the courtier.

'Another oversight?'

'It appears so, ma'am, apologies. This way.'

They followed the courtier along the ornate hallways of the palace, ascending a wide flight of stairs to an upper level. The courtier knocked on a tall door and entered. Lady Aurelian and Emily stepped inside after him, into a grand hall, with huge windows overlooking the Straits. On a clear day, the western bank was visible from the hall, but the dark grey clouds loomed over the skies and rain was streaking the glass.

A long table was sitting on a platform in front of several rows of empty seats, and a man was speaking. He glanced up from the table and frowned as the courtier gestured to the seats. Lady Aurelian walked up the front row, her head held high, and sat directly in front of Lord Chamberlain, who was sitting at the centre of the table.

'These proceedings started ten minutes ago,' he said, as Emily took her place next to Daniel's mother.

Lady Aurelian smiled. 'You may continue.'

The man who had been speaking raised a sheaf of papers and

scanned them. 'Where was I? Yes, the accused, acting-Captain Daniel Aurelian entered a plea of not guilty to the charge of disobeying an order from a superior officer in the field, and the tribunal took this into consideration when judging the severity of the sentence to be handed down.'

'Sentence?' said Lady Aurelian. 'What happened to the verdict?'

Lord Chamberlain gave a wry smile. 'You missed it. Let me recap; Daniel Aurelian was found guilty of all charges. It was a unanimous decision.'

Emily frowned. 'But the orders he received were illegal.'

Lord Chamberlain raised an eyebrow. 'Are you a lawyer, Mistress Aurelian?'

'No, but I can read.'

'Oh, I'm sure you're a very clever girl. I'm sure you could probably quote case history to me, but I'm afraid in the current crisis such niceties can no longer be afforded. In such a time of unparalleled upheaval, there can be no excuse for disobeying an order. Now, shall we get back to the sentencing?'

The other man nodded. 'The first aspect of sentencing the accused involves his membership of the Taran militia. With immediate effect, acting-Captain Daniel Aurelian is dishonourably discharged from said militia, and his service record will reflect that. As such, Daniel Aurelian is not permitted to use any titles or ranks he accrued while in the service of the militia, and all payments to pensions and other such benefits shall cease forthwith.

'The second aspect involves punitive measures. It was felt by the tribunal that a custodial sentence would be counter-productive, and it is therefore decreed that Daniel Aurelian shall pay a fine of fifty thousand gold sovereigns to the Taran treasury within the next thirty days.'

Emily puffed her cheeks in relief. Fifty thousand was a fortune, but Daniel would not be going to jail.

Lord Chamberlain nodded to the other man. 'Thank you. These proceeding are closed.' He gestured to a guard standing by a side door. 'The accused is now free to go.'

The guard opened the door and disappeared inside as the members of the tribunal got to their feet. Lord Chamberlain stepped down off the platform as he walked towards Emily and Lady Aurelian, who both stood.

Chamberlain smiled. 'A most satisfactory outcome, you'll agree? Apart from Mistress Aurelian's little outburst, which was rather unbecoming for a young Roser lady.'

'She was showing loyalty and principle,' Lady Aurelian said, 'concepts that you seem unfamiliar with.'

Lord Chamberlain laughed long and hard for a moment. 'My, it does please me to see the way you leapt to her defence; we'll see if that lasts, eh? Now, Daniel will be along in a moment or two, so I'll leave you alone for your little reunion, but don't go anywhere just yet; I have a surprise.'

He strode away, still chuckling to himself.

'What's he playing at?' muttered Lady Aurelian.

'At least Daniel's not going to jail.'

'I wouldn't say that just yet; we still have to rustle together fifty thousand in gold.' She turned to Emily. 'You've seen the accounts. It won't be easy. We might need to sell some land, and right now we'll be lucky to find any buyers. Start working on it right away; I want to know what all my options are.'

Emily nodded. 'Of course, yes.'

'Good, thank you. For the record, I do not regard your interruption as unbecoming. On the contrary, we Aurelian women have a proud history of standing up for our rights; a tradition that we are duty bound to uphold. You did well.'

Emily smiled. 'Thank you.'

'And I was worried you might cry.'

A door opened and they turned. Emily's eyes widened as she saw her parents walk into the hall, escorted by a courtier. They were dressed in their finest clothes, and her mother smiled as she saw her daughter.

'Emily, dear,' she cried as she hurried over. 'So lovely to see you. What are you doing in the palace?' Before Emily could answer, her mother turned to Lady Aurelian. 'And my greetings to you, Lady Aurelian. A pleasure to see you again.'

Daniel's mother smiled, but Emily could see the lines by her eyes.

'A pleasure to see you both, Lord and Lady Omertia,' she said. 'Emily and I are here today for the outcome of Daniel's court martial.'

The faces of the Omertias fell. 'Oh,' said Emily's mother. 'Have you heard anything yet?'

Lady Aurelian sighed and nodded. 'A fine, and he'll have to make his career in some other field.'

'How unfortunate,' said Lord Omertia, shaking his head. 'I heard he punched a colonel clean out. A bit of a young hothead, it seems; reminds me of my own youth. It's a pity, you know; after his exploits in the Circuit last year, I had high hopes of him becoming an accomplished officer. Still, the militia needs its discipline, for without discipline where would we be, eh? We'd be no better than the Evaders.'

'He's strong and independently-minded,' said Lady Aurelian, 'and as such, he's never particularly enjoyed being told what to do. I always feared his free spirit might not be a perfect fit for the rule-bound militia.'

Emily suppressed a smile at her mother-in-law's words. Instead of trying to deny any of it, she had come out fighting. Her parents would have learned what had happened anyway; it was better therefore that they heard it spun into something almost righteous by his mother.

Her father turned his eyes to her. 'My little Emily, I hope you've been behaving yourself?'

'She's settled right in,' said Lady Aurelian before Emily could open her mouth. 'She's a wonderful addition to the Aurelian household, and you can both be very proud of her. I practically rely on her these days; unlike Daniel, you only have to tell her something once and she remembers it.'

The Omertias laughed, while Emily's frustration started to grow. She wished her parents would leave; what were they doing there? Her father's eyes kept glancing at her, as if he could tell how much she despised him, while her mother hardly looked at her at all. She had never felt more like an Aurelian, and the thought that she would never have to return to the Omertia house filled her with a quiet joy.

'And what brings you to the palace today?' said Lady Aurelian.

A door opened ahead of them, and Daniel walked into the hall. He was unshaven, and his hair was coming down to his shoulders, and he was dressed in prison clothes, his uniform presumably having been taken. He glanced up, and his eyes fell on Emily. He smiled. She ran forward and into his arms, pressing herself against him, her head buried in his chest as his arms folded round her.

She held him tightly, surprised at how much she had missed physical contact with him, and from the way he was holding her, it was clear he felt the same.

'I missed you,' he murmured in her ear.

Her ear tingled and she laughed. She pulled away to get a better look at him. His bruises had healed, and all that was left of the cut on his lower lip was a small scar. She touched the month-old beard.

'This'll have to go.'

'It'll be the first thing I do when I get home.' He pulled her closer. 'Well, maybe the second thing.'

A cough came from his mother behind them.

'Hello?' said Lady Aurelian. 'You two? There's a time and a place for everything.'

Daniel glanced over, as if noticing the others in the hall for the first time. He and Emily broke off their embrace, but he kept a grip of her hand as they walked forwards.

'Lovely to see you in one piece, my dear,' his mother said. 'Did they feed you alright in there?'

'Yes, mother, it was like being back in barracks, except less marching around.'

'I spent a few nights in the town cells in my youth,' said Lord Omertia; 'I was a little touch boisterous back then.'

Daniel half-smiled, but his eyes remained cold as he looked at Emily's father.

'It was indeed a pleasure to see you both again,' his mother said to the Omertias, 'but perhaps we should be going home. We have Daniel's whole new career to plan.'

'Well, good luck, old chap,' said Lord Omertia.

Emily's mother leaned forward and kissed her daughter on the forehead. 'Take care, dear.'

The Aurelians turned for the main doors, and strode past the rows of chairs. Ahead of them, two Blades were standing at the entrance, and they moved to block the way.

Lady Aurelian frowned as they came to a halt. 'By this, am I to assume we are being held here against our will?'

'Lord Chamberlain's orders, ma'am. No one's to leave until the lord returns.'

'More games? What a frightful bore.' She turned to Emily and Daniel. 'Do either of you know what this is about?'

'No,' said Emily as Daniel shook his head. She glanced over to her parents, who were standing where they had left them. Whatever it was, it involved them too, and she was the only connection that could bring the two families together. She frowned as she tried to figure out what it could be.

A side door opened and Lord Chamberlain walked in, a smile on his lips. He walked up to Lord and Lady Omertia and greeted them, then turned to the Aurelians.

'If I may beg your indulgence for a moment, please?' he said.

'You don't need to beg,' Lady Aurelian said as they walked back to the front of the raised platform, 'you have armed soldiers to enforce your will.'

'Yes, I do,' he grinned, 'and it's always nice to be reminded of it. Take a seat, all of you.'

Emily sat down by Daniel, with Lady Aurelian and her parents to his left. Lord Chamberlain reached into his robes and produced a rolled up document.

'The news I bear,' he said, donning a sombre expression, 'has caused me no end of sleepless nights, as I pondered what to do with such information. I struggled, yes, but have come to the conclusion that being open and honest is the only honourable course left to me.'

Lady Aurelian sighed. 'Oh, for Malik's sake, get on with it.'

'If I could bottle this moment, I would,' Lord Chamberlain said, grinning, before making his features more serious again. 'I have evidence of a subterfuge, a gross deception, a nest of lies that must be uprooted. The Omertias, it is clear to me, have played a most foul trick upon the Aurelians.'

Lord Omertia stood, his eyes flashing. 'How dare you? What trick? There has been no trick; that piece of land in the Circuit was perfectly profitable when the Omertias were looking after it.'

'My dear lord, sit, sit. We are not here to discuss a mere parcel of land. Alas, I wish we were.' He turned to Lady Omertia. 'By your silence, my lady, and your husband's outburst, I begin to suspect that perhaps Lord Omertia is an innocent party in this sordid affair. Perhaps you never revealed the truth to him.'

Lady Omertia's eyes widened as she clutched a bag on her knee. 'I don't know what you're talking about.'

'No?' He unrolled the document and thrust it in her face. 'So this is not your signature at the bottom?'

She gasped, and put a hand to her mouth, as Lord Chamberlain pulled the document away.

Lord Omertia stared at his wife. 'What is it?'

'Yes,' said Lord Chamberlain, his eyes on her. 'You should be the one to tell your husband.'

Lady Omertia glanced from her husband to her daughter as tears stared to edge their way down her face. 'Emily's adopted.'

Emily's mouth opened. She stared at her mother.

'Impossible,' said Lord Omertia; 'I saw you pregnant. What are you saying?'

'I faked the pregnancy, husband. We had been trying for so many years, and I thought you were going to leave me if I didn't produce a child for you. That's why I went to my mother's for the last few months. It was getting too difficult to deceive you, and that's where I got Emily. She was only a few days old, and I brought her back home as ours.'

Lord Omertia's face had grown redder with every word that had come from his wife's mouth, and his fists were shaking. 'You brought someone else's child into our house? All these years have been a lie?' He stood, and leaned over her. 'You disgust me.' His fists hovered over her for a second, then he strode away, and began pacing the floor by the platform.

'Even for you, Lord Chamberlain,' said Lady Aurelian, 'this is a new low. Cruel, petty, spiteful; which pretty much sums up your character. Is this what we waited here for, for you to spread tittle-tattle about the private affairs of a family?' She turned to Emily. 'You're an Aurelian; this nonsense means nothing.'

Emily nodded, but her mind was buzzing. Amid the shock, she felt almost ashamed that her first feeling had been relief; she wasn't related to her father after all, he was no part of her, and for that she was glad.

Lady Aurelian glanced back at Lord Chamberlain. 'Since when did being adopted change anything? There are many, many adopted children in Tara and the wider City; do you intend to go around holding people hostage while they are forced to listen to you reveal their parentage? You truly have brought shame to your noble position.'

Lord Chamberlain nodded. 'Finished? Good. I was expecting this range of reactions, and so we move onto the part I have been most eagerly anticipating. I have a further document, not signed by anyone present, but that is only because Mistress Emily's dear old grandmother couldn't join us today.'

Lady Omertia glanced up through her tears. 'What does my mother have to do with this?'

'It was your mother that procured baby Emily, was it not?'

She nodded. 'Yes.'

Lord Chamberlain smiled. 'You wouldn't believe how much effort it took to retrieve this little scrap of paper,' he said, taking a small document from a pocket. 'This precious little piece of paper, that has so much to give.'

'What is it?' said Lady Omertia.

'It details the death of a young mother. Died in childbirth; how tragic. Gave birth to a little girl, who was then placed into the custody of your mother, who had to sign her name at the bottom to confirm she had received the aforesaid baby. Now, who is going to ask me why it took so much effort to get this little scrap of paper? Anyone?'

Lord Omertia glanced over. 'Why?'

'Thank you,' Lord Chamberlain grinned. 'It took a lot of effort to get this from the hospital records, because the hospital in question is located in the Circuit.'

He paused, as the words slowly settled over the people sitting in front of him.

'I'll clarify,' Lord Chamberlain said; 'Legally speaking, Emily is an Evader. Furthermore, by marrying Daniel, the Aurelians can no longer claim to be of true Roser stock. Three and a half thousand years of history have come to an end with this marriage.'

No one said anything, the silence deep and still. Emily felt Daniel squeeze her hand and, at that moment, it meant everything.

'Of course,' Chamberlain went on, 'the scale of this deception gives the Aurelians just cause to have the marriage annulled. Seems such a shame to break up a happy couple, but the Aurelians have always placed family pride above sentiment.'

Daniel clenched his fists and jumped to his feet. Emily grasped his right arm, and his mother took hold of his left as they tried to pull him back.

Lord Chamberlain laughed. 'If you strike me I'll see you rot in a cell.'

Daniel spat on the floor at Chamberlain's feet.

'Guards,' said Chamberlain, 'please escort these people from the palace.'

The Aurelians turned and headed for the front doors. Emily felt Daniel's hand slip back into hers as they walked, but on his other side, his mother glanced away, not meeting her eyes. Emily tried to think about the words Chamberlain had said, but they seemed unreal, as if dreamt. Surely she would wake up and realise it had all been a dream.

She couldn't be an Evader. It wasn't possible; she was Roser through and through. Yet, from her own mother's face, she had seen the truth. She broke down in tears as the front doors were opening, and, as Daniel's arm went round her shoulder, his mother glanced at her, her eyes dark.

'I told you not to cry.'

CHAPTER 20

THE BOND

Arrowhead Fort, The Bulwark, The City – 30th Malikon 3420

The hospital was the busiest part of Arrowhead Fortress. While most of the barracks were deserted, and with many of the auxiliary staff also having been sent into Auldan and Medio, the wards were packed with injured Blades. Maddie had never seen so many wounded people before; they filled the halls and corridors of the hospital, while others had been moved into the empty barracks next door. The entire place was chaotic, with nurses and medical staff running around, and no one seemed to know where Captain Hilde was located.

She took a wrong turn into the burns ward, and left immediately, her eyes seeing too much, and her heart sickening at the maimed soldiers lying on the tightly packed rows of beds. She cursed the Evaders, knowing that most of the wounded had been sent back from the Circuit, where the worst outbreak of fighting was taking place.

After a weary search, she entered a small ward in the basement, and saw the captain lying on a bed at the end of the long room. She walked past the other beds and sat in a chair next to the captain. Her eyes were closed, and her face seemed fixed with pain.

'Are you sleeping?' Maddie whispered.

Hilde opened her eyes. 'Maddie?'

'Yes, it's me. Did I wake you? Sorry.'

'No, I can't sleep. The pain... What day is it?'

'The last day of Malikon.'

'Already?'

'Yes. Sorry it's been a while since I visited. I didn't know they had moved you to the hospital in Arrowhead, so I've been going back and forth between here and Sector Five looking for you. But it's good news, it means I'll be able to come round more often now that you're here. I'll cook you something nice and bring it over tomorrow, would you like that?'

'I can't think straight, Maddie. My back... I never knew anything could hurt so much.'

'Blackrose is very sorry about what she did.'

'Don't lie to me, girl. That evil beast knew what she was doing. She was trying to kill me.'

Maddie nodded. What could she say? She had been over what had happened with the captain before, and no amount of talking could persuade her that Blackrose hadn't tried to end her life. At least the captain was lucid, she thought. On some visits the captain had been given so many opium-based painkillers that she had been rambling and incoherent, or just lying in a soporific daze staring at the walls.

'I found out from the doctors in Sector Five why they'd moved you,' Maddie said. 'It's because the wards there are being used to treat the fresh casualties coming in from the rest of the City. You were not classified as an emergency case, so they put you back here in the recovery ward. That's good, I think.'

'It's because there's nothing they can do for me,' Hilde gasped. 'Surgery would only make it worse. They told me that. So they just drug me and hope that eventually I'll get better.'

'You will get better. It'll just take time. Remember when I got injured? It took months to get better.'

'But at least you were in the lair; at least you were home. I hate this hospital even more than I hated the last one. Down here, I can't even look out of a window.' She glanced at Maddie, her eyes heavy. 'Did you find out what happened to the gate sergeant?'

Maddie smiled. 'Yes. He's alive. Our squad, I mean, his squad, were lucky; they stayed on the outskirts of Dalrig, so they weren't slaughtered when Lady Amber came out from Greylin Palace. She killed over four hundred Blades in two minutes.'

'Where is he now?'

'In the Circuit.'

Hilde closed her eyes, a tear rolling down her cheek.

Maddie took her hand. 'He'll be alright. He's smart; he knows how to survive, and he'll be back here when things return to normal. All the Blades will come back, and then things will be the way they were before.'

'There's only one month left before summer starts.'

'I know, but that's still plenty of time to recall all of the regiments from Auldan and Medio. And Buckler's still here. Even Marcus balked at using a dragon on the rebels.'

Hilde snorted. 'The rebels would shoot him from the sky. Buckler only looks good because the greenhides don't have ballistae, or even crossbows. Blackrose could do it; she's a full adult, and her skin's thick enough to withstand arrows and bolts.'

'Umm, I don't think I'll be suggesting that to her. I think she'd like the idea of burning the City. Once she started, she might not stop.'

'Wait,' Hilde said; 'if today's the last day of Malikon, then you've had longer than a month. Has Kano forgotten his promise?'

'I don't know, and I don't want to ask, in case he has. I keep sending him my little reports, each full of the progress we've been making, but I don't know if he reads them. Maybe he's so busy, he has other things on his mind. Every day I don't hear from him is a good day.'

'He's always hated the dragons. Next to him, even Marcus seemed reasonable, but with the new prince being in Tara, I fear that Kano will use this time as an opportunity to get rid of Blackrose. You can't trust him.'

Maddie nodded. 'You don't need to tell me that; I hate him. If I had the chance to stick a rusty fork into the eye of just one person, it'd be him. I'd probably enjoy it, too.'

Hilde closed her eyes again, and Maddie could see the waves of pain that were rolling over her.

'Shall I get a doctor?'

'What's the point?' groaned Hilde. 'They'd only give me more opium, and that just makes me sick. Maybe this is a punishment for everything I've done wrong; maybe I deserve this.'

'Don't be silly. You saved me from the Rats, remember?'

'There's nothing wrong with the Rats, girl. You...' She clenched her face tight as her words trailed off. 'Leave me. I... I can't speak right now.'

Maddie squeezed her hand and stood. 'I'll be back tomorrow, and I'll bring you some warm soup.' She leaned over and kissed the captain on the cheek. 'See you soon.'

The captain nodded, and Maddie released her hand. She turned from the bed, and saw a doctor checking the notes of another patient.

'Doctor,' she said as she approached.

The woman glanced up. 'Yes?'

'I'm a friend of Captain Hilde.'

'Who?'

Maddie pointed to the bed where the captain was lying.

'The back injury?'

Maddie nodded. 'Yes.'

'What about her?'

'How's it looking? Is she getting any better?'

'Her spine has been damaged, I'm afraid. There's nothing we can do but manage her pain for now.'

'But will she get better?'

'Probably. That's the best I can say. The idiots that transferred her here weren't exactly gentle, and that's put her recovery back by about a month, I'd guess. In all honesty, I'd like to transfer her back to wherever she lives, as we need the bed, but I don't want to risk moving her again.'

Maddie nodded.

The doctor smiled. 'We'll know for sure in another month or so.'

'Alright. Thanks.'

'At least she has someone like you to come and visit her; that always helps.'

Maddie tried to smile, but her face seemed frozen into a frown. She turned, and walked from the ward, her heart heavy. Outside the hospital, the rain was hammering down onto the forecourt of Arrowhead Fortress, and Maddie ran past the empty barracks blocks all the way to the lair. She unlocked the door and slipped inside, shaking the rain from her hair as she stood in the entrance hall. She hung up her coat and walked to the kitchen, trying to ignore the mess. She had been a bit lazy about keeping the place clean and tidy, and Hilde would probably faint from the shock if she could see how little housework Maddie had done since she had returned from Auldan. All her time seemed to revolve around organising enough food for Blackrose to eat. She had inherited the captain's authority when it came to requisitioning supplies, and had marvelled at how much a hungry dragon could get through.

She considered giving the kitchen a good clean, then shuddered at the thought, grabbed an apple and wandered to her room. She made a half-hearted attempt to gather up the dirty clothes from the floor, then lay down on the bed to eat the apple, her thoughts turning to Hilde. Her memories of her own recovery were still fresh in her mind, though she hadn't told the captain about how Jade's powers had completed her recovery. The effects of that healing were still strong within her, and if Hilde had been in less pain, then she was sure the captain would have noticed. If only she could somehow bring Jade to visit the captain; she would be able to heal her in seconds. In fact, if the demigods of the City cared at all about the mortals, then Jade and her equally-powered sister Amber should be healing the sick and wounded, not using their skills to go round killing people. Maybe the Evaders were right, maybe the City would be better off without them.

· · ·

Apart from Aila; she was nice. She wondered if the demigod was any closer to getting hold of Naxor and the Quadrant. Maddie had fulfilled her part of the bargain, and had got back to Blackrose with the news that Corthie was alive, it was surely time that the demigod also did her part.

A loud knocking grabbed her attention, and she got up from the bed. She went into the hallway, and realised that the banging was coming from inside the lair, to her right. She opened the door to the cavern and stepped through.

'Is that you making that noise, Blackrose?'

The black gate was lying open, and the dragon's head appeared round the corner.

'It's coming from the red gate,' she said. 'If it's Buckler, tell him I'm not in.'

Maddie frowned, and walked over to the huge red gate. She took her keys from her belt and unlocked the small door cut into the gate. On the opposite side was a woman that she had seen before, working in Buckler's lair.

'Hello,' said Maddie.

The woman nodded. 'Got something for you.'

'Yeah?'

She gestured to a crate behind her. 'Yeah. Courtesy of Buckler. He ordered it up from an armoury.'

Maddie glanced at the crate. 'What is it?'

'No idea. He just told me to deliver it to you. Want to give me a hand with it? It's a bit heavy.'

'Alright.'

Maddie stepped through the hatch and looked down at the crate. 'How is Buckler?'

'Fine.'

'And, uh... how many of you working in the lair know about, eh...'

'Know about the old lady? Just me and a couple of others.'

'I'm on my own in here now, did you know that?'

The woman frowned. 'What happened to Captain Hilde?'

'She's in hospital. She hurt her back.'

'Oh. Send her my wishes.'

They each took an end of the crate and carried it to the hatch. Maddie lifted her legs through, then the woman helped her lower the crate onto the floor on the other side of the gate. The woman glanced over in the direction of the cavern where Blackrose lived, but there was no sign of her.

'She's avoiding Buckler,' Maddie whispered. 'She loves him really, though; tell him that from me, and tell him thank you.'

The woman frowned, then nodded. 'Right then, I'd best be going back. Good luck.'

She stepped back through the hatch and Maddie closed and locked it behind her.

'What was that all about?'

Maddie turned, and saw Blackrose's head peering round the corner of the black gate.

'We have a gift.' Maddie said.

'From the young red dragon? Why?'

Maddie started to drag the heavy crate across the stone floor. 'I don't know; maybe he was just being nice. Some people are like that, they do nice things for each other, like get each other presents.'

'I'm not sure I can accept it. I would feel like I owed him something in return, which, no doubt, was his intention.'

'Don't be like that,' Maddie said, grunting as she hauled the crate along. She pulled it over the groove in the floor where the black gate would sit when closed, and into the lair. 'I wonder what it is?' she said as she stopped. 'What kind of presents do dragons give each other? Hats? I'd like to see you with a hat on.'

She crouched down by the crate, looking for a way to open it. It had been branded with the symbol of the Hammer tribe, but there was no writing or any other markings on it. Blackrose was feigning a lack of interest, and was grooming her wings as if Maddie wasn't there. She grappled with the lid of the crate, and after a struggle it loosened and she placed it to the side. Inside the crate were piles of leather with metal rings and buckles. She picked up an end, but it seemed as if the whole thing was connected together, so she tipped the crate over and dragged the contents out.

'What is it?' she said.

The dragon said nothing.

'Do you recognise it?'

Blackrose sighed. 'Yes.'

'Well?'

The dragon brought her head closer. 'It appears that this gift is meant for both of us. I know what it is, though I haven't seen one in a very long time. And the red dragon has made a few mistakes in his design, but as he has never been on my home world, that is not surprising.' She turned her head to glance at Maddie. 'It is a rider's harness.'

'Wow, really? You mean like a saddle on a pony?'

Blackrose's eyes flamed. 'Never compare me to a pony again.'

'You know what I mean.' She leant down to examine part of it, and found herself unravelling it on the ground; spreading it out so she could see where all the straps went. She found the seat, a wide, padded cushion of leather, and judged that to be the centre. She grinned. 'Shall we put it on?'

'No.'

'But we have to check if it fits.'

'No.'

'It'll be fun.'

'No, it won't.'

'Look,' she said, picking up a large, sturdy hoop made of leather, 'I think this part goes over your head, and then...'

'Very well, if it will stop you haranguing me.'

Maddie yelped and lifted the hoop. 'Is this right; am I doing it right? Where does this bit go? Oops, did I just poke you in the eye? Lower your head a bit... right. You know, I've never noticed how big your ears are; they're enormous.'

The dragon groaned. 'I knew this was a mistake.'

An hour later, after much confusion and restarting, Maddie stood back to admire her handiwork. The black leather straps fitted over the dragon's shoulders, in front of the wings, and straps came down and then buckled round the base of each forelimb. A series of handles ran down both flanks, that allowed Maddie to climb on and off the dragon's back, and as well as the cushion, there were grips for her feet to rest against, and a thick leather bar to grab onto while in the air.

Blackrose had grumbled throughout, but Maddie knew from her tone that she was enjoying the attention, and the company. She went through to the living quarters and pushed a wheelbarrow of food through for Blackrose.

'Lunch,' she said, tipping it out into the trough before the dragon.

'Maybe you should remove the harness before I eat.'

'Leave it on, it suits you. And it took so long to get it on, that I feel I need to look at it for a bit longer. Is it uncomfortable?'

'Only when you were choking me earlier.'

'Yeah, sorry about that; the straps were a bit tight. I was thinking, do I need a new name, you know, as your rider? You've got more than one name, so maybe I should as well.'

'In my world, the human riders are reared, and named, by dragons. A dragon will get to know their next rider while they are young, and while their current rider is still with them.'

Maddie frowned, surprised at the disappointment she felt. 'You mean you've had riders before?'

'My girl, I am a queen. I've had many riders over many years, but you are the only one of this entire world that I would choose. Don't look so forlorn. Maddie. You and I are bonded until death separates us.'

'We are?'

'Yes. As soon as I made you my rider, and as soon as you accepted, the bond was made. It cannot be unmade except by death. If I had explained this to you before, would you still have accepted?'

'Yes, of course. Are you joking? I'm bonded with a dragon, for

Malik's sake, and not a puny little red dragon, a proper queen dragon. Malik's ass, I wish my brother and sister could see this.'

'If you must swear, I'd rather that you wouldn't use the name of that worthless creature. But, on the subject of your kin; bring them here. The family of my rider is welcome to visit.'

'You know I'm not allowed to do that.' She pursed her lip for a second. 'Well, maybe. My sister's good at keeping secrets, and who would know? Captain...' She struck her forehead. 'Damn it, I got completely sidetracked by the harness and forgot to tell you. I found Captain Hilde. She's been moved to Arrowhead, and there was me going off every morning to search Sectors Five and Six for her, and she's been here for the last few days.'

'How is her recovery?'

Maddie puffed her cheeks. 'Slow. I'm going to make her some soup.'

'Will that help?'

'I'll bring the pot through when I'm making it, and you can give it a quick stir with a claw, and then I can tell her that we both made it for her.'

'You seem to be endowing this soup with miraculous healing powers.'

A thump came through from the other cavern.

'That'll be the goat,' Maddie said. 'It's getting delivered today. It upsets me, I'm not going to lie, but if you must, I suppose.'

'Don't try to make friends with it this time. Just bring it to me and close the door.'

Maddie grimaced and turned for the entrance to the main cavern. She crossed it and entered the living quarters, the thumps getting louder.

'I'm coming,' she yelled.

She went to the front door and opened it. Lord Kano was standing outside, with at least two dozen soldiers.

She frowned. 'Bollocks.'

Kano brushed past her into the hallway without a word, and began striding towards the lair, the soldiers trooping in behind him as Maddie stood wide-eyed, her hand still holding the door open. She waited until the last soldier had passed through the hallway, then closed the door. She glanced at the backs of the armed Blades as they climbed through the hatch-door leading to the cavern at the end of the hallway, then she heard a low growl from Blackrose rumble through the ground beneath her feet. She began walking, then picked up her pace. She stepped through the hatch to see the soldiers standing in two lines by the entrance to the lair, with Kano out in front. She ran to the open gateway, but the soldiers moved their shields to stop her passing.

Ahead of them, she heard Kano's voice.

'I said you could have a month, and I've been generous. I hope you've used that time well, to reconsider your earlier foolishness. The last time I asked you to swear allegiance to the City, I was too kind, too indulgent of your emotional instability, and I let you be unchained without making you kneel, or even say the words of the oath properly.' He glared at the dragon. 'I cannot be so kind-hearted again; not after you went back on your word. Your chains will remain in place unless you give me all that I require of you.'

Blackrose lifted her head. 'That was quite a speech, vermin Kano, did you practise it before you came here today? It seems that you are under some false illusion that I wish to swear allegiance to the City. What gave you that idea? If you have come here to discuss the terms of my freedom, then I am prepared to listen. I am not so foolish as to turn my back on you if you have a deal we can consider.'

Kano spat on the ground. 'Here's the only deal on offer, lizard Blackrose. You prostrate yourself before me and recite the oath, and then the soldiers behind me will release the shackles that bind you to this cavern. After that, I have a job for you.'

Maddie struggled behind the double line of soldiers to get through, but they shoved her back. She peered between their shields, and caught a glimpse of the dragon's head, hovering a few feet over Kano. She looked down at him, her eyes as black as coal.

'What job?'

'Something that I know you'll like. Burning humans.'

Blackrose laughed. 'You wish me to kill your own kind?'

'They're not my kind; they're mortal scum. Fit to burn. The target area lies between the Union and Middle Walls; a vast concrete wasteland called the Circuit.'

'I am aware of it, yes.'

'This area is filled with irreconcilable rebels, and you can show no mercy. Sweep the region from end to end; devour it with flames, and then you can return here to a life of luxury, a life like Buckler leads, with no chains, and the freedom to fly where you please when you are not helping with the defence of the Great Walls. Well? It's a good offer; better than some might think you deserve.'

Maddie gasped as she listened to the words. A quarter of a million Evaders lived in the Circuit, and Kano wanted Blackrose to kill them all?

'It is a grand proposal,' said Blackrose, 'and the thought of slaking my thirst for vengeance on the inhabitants of this City fills me with a cold joy. It's only a pity that you demand the bowing and swearing of oaths first, otherwise I'd be tempted.'

Kano shook his head. 'Even now you spurn my kindness, my generosity? You stupid reptile. Do you understand that this is your last chance?'

'Oh yes? And what do you intend to do if I rebuff you?'

'If you refuse to bow, then you will die in this cavern.'

The dragon glanced over at the soldiers. 'Then you should have brought a bigger army.'

Kano clenched his fists in frustration. 'Why are you being so obstinate? I realise you loathe me, well, the feeling is mutual. I, however, can look beyond that, to a future where we can work together despite our feelings for each other; a future where you are alive. Do you not wish to live?'

Blackrose said nothing for a moment, her great head slightly tilted. 'I do not bow before vermin.'

'Damn you, lizard. This is the end, be under no illusion. I'm going to walk out of here, and as soon as I pass through that door, it's over.'

Kano turned, and began striding away from Blackrose.

'You are mistaken,' said the dragon, 'for I will not let you walk out of here.'

Kano glanced back, his eyes wide as the dragon reared up in the cavern behind him, then he broke into a run. Blackrose opened her jaws and a stream of red hot fire burst from her mouth, engulfing the demigod and the Blades surrounding him. Several soldiers fell screaming as the flames covered them. Others pulled Kano's burning body away from the dragon, and one grabbed hold of Maddie's arm.

'Let go of me,' she yelled as the soldier pulled her away.

The soldiers ran, their shields up as Blackrose sent another burst of flame into the cavern. Three more soldiers went up in flames, howling in agony, their skin and hair alight. Maddie was hauled through the door hatch and the soldiers dragged her down the hallway. Lord Kano's smouldering body was lifted through and the door was closed.

'Move back, back!' cried one of the Blades, and they hurried down the hallway, bundling Maddie with them.

The hatch exploded into the hallway, flames and fragments of wood flaring in from the cavern as the soldiers stared. Lord Kano spasmed, then began to struggle, and the soldiers set him down onto the floor. Maddie watched with both arms held behind her back as the demigod's self-healing powers got to work. The blisters and burnt flesh faded, and fresh, new skin appeared in their place. His hair re-grew over the scalded patches, and his eyes blinked open. He sat up, then glanced at the burnt-out hatchway.

'We're out of her range, sir,' said one of the Blades. 'Are you alright?'

Kano stood, his uniform hanging in tattered and burnt strips from his massive frame. 'Of course I'm alright.'

'We lost seven Blades, my lord.'

Kano nodded. 'Could have been worse. Wall up the lair. Fetch masons, carpenters and bricklayers; everyone that is required. Wall it up from the outside so that no one knows what dwells in here, and then do the same to the tunnel that leads from Buckler's lair. The name of Blackrose shall never be mentioned again, and she will die, alone.'

A great roar rumbled through from the lair, shaking the ground.

Several of the Blades glanced back at the broken hatch as if they expected to see the dragon appear, but Maddie knew her shackles were unbreakable. Kano stared at the cavern for a moment, then glanced away, his eyes cold.

'You asshole!' cried Maddie, struggling in the grip of the soldiers.

He turned, as if noticing her presence for the first time.

A Blade grunted. 'What will we do with the corporal, sir?'

Kano frowned for a moment, then a smile crept across his young-looking lips. 'I know just the thing for Maddie Jackdaw.'

She glared at him with all the contempt she could muster.

Kano strode off, laughing. 'Send her to the Rats.'

CHAPTER 21

THE SMUGGLER'S CAVE

G rey Isle, Cold Sea – 2nd Amalan 3420
'We need to get off this damn island,' said Yaizra as she paced up and down the old smuggler's cave. Light was entering through a natural shaft that opened out on the vastness of the Cold Sea, and a grey glow lit the interior of the cave where Corthie and Achan were sitting.

'The storms are over,' said Corthie. 'How far away is the harbour at Dalrig? Maybe we could swim it?'

'The currents are so strong,' Yaizra said, glancing at him, 'that we'd be pulled into the Clashing Seas and end up drowned or back on the western bank. A ship's the only way we're getting off this rock. And as we've been told, Dalrig is under siege by the Blades; if we go there, we'll be trapped again.'

Achan frowned. 'She wants us to go to Icehaven.'

'It's the only sensible choice,' she said; 'it's the only place where we can be safe. Like Dalrig, there will be no Blades there, but Marcus would need the entire Blade army to besiege Icehaven; it's impossible.'

'But how are we supposed to help the revolution from there?' Achan said. 'The rest of the City is in the middle of an uprising, and you want to hide until it's all over?'

Yaizra glared at the Hammer. 'You don't have to hide; you're welcome to head off and follow your heart. All the way to your death.'

'Don't you want to be a part of something bigger? You heard the captain a couple of days ago; the Circuit is being occupied by rebels, Pella's on the brink, and Dalrig's fighting back. This is it! This is when the people shake off their chains of servitude and free themselves.'

'Screw you, Achan,' she said. 'You're dreaming. All it would take for your glorious revolution to collapse is for the God-Queen and God-King to leave their palaces and show their power for a few minutes. Then every mortal would scurry back into their holes.'

Corthie shook his head. 'Stop bickering; my head's aching with your stupid arguments. There is no boat, and until there is, what's the point of fighting?'

Yaizra shrugged. 'Bugger all else to do.'

'She's right,' said Achan, 'and I look forward to my daily tussles with her. I'll win her round one day, I'm sure of it.'

'Yeah, right,' she said. 'Dream on, little man.'

Achan raised his hands. 'I can see it now; "Yaizra, scourge of the demigods", "Yaizra, Queen of the Revolution".'

She laughed. 'I prefer, "Yaizra - drunk, rich and living in peace".'

'That's for after the revolution,' he said; 'after we've booted out the demigods.'

'You can't "boot them out",' said Corthie. 'Where would they go?'

'We could exile them here, to the Grey Isle,' said Achan. 'Did you know that this island used to be a prison, long ago?'

Yaizra rolled her eyes. 'Time for another history lesson.'

'The City built a prison here,' he went on, ignoring her, 'for political prisoners, after there was a rebellion among the princes. The God-King and God-Queen wanted their own children to become the princes and princesses of the City, but there was a problem; there were already mortals in those positions, the descendants of long hereditary lines. The Prince of Tara, for example, could trace his lineage right back to Year One, can you imagine? Naturally, they didn't want to hand their power over to the brats of the two Gods, and some of them put up a fight.'

Corthie nodded. 'The Gods won, I assume?'

'Easily. The princes of Dalrig, Pella and Ooste submitted, and their authority was handed over to the Royal Family. The only one that held out for a while was Prince Aurelian of Tara. He refused to abdicate, and there was a brief siege of Maeladh Palace. He was captured, chained and sent here, to the Grey Isle. He became the first, and last, prisoner ever to be held in the brand new prison they built.'

Yaizra shook her head and glanced away.

'It's true,' said Achan. 'You can look it up in any history book. Apparently, and this is the bit I like best, there still exists in Tara a branch of the Aurelian family that can trace their line all the way back to the last mortal prince, and among the Hammers there's a legend that one day they will return to power, and sweep the gods and demigods out of the City once and for all.'

'What a load of donkey dung,' said Yaizra. 'If anyone's coming along to save us, it ain't going to be some aristocratic asshole from Tara. You almost sound like a Redemptionist.'

'I knew a few of them,' said Corthie; 'they thought I was their saviour. They used to follow me around the Bulwark, chanting and praying; and when someone once tried to kill me, they tore his body to shreds.'

Yaizra squinted at him. 'They sound like a lovely bunch.'

'I only mentioned it as a legend,' said Achan; 'I didn't say I believed it. No one's coming to rescue us; it's a foolish dream that has contributed to generations of apathy and inaction. Why rise up, when you can simply hope instead? It is donkey dung, you're right. The only people who can save the City are the ordinary folk who live in it; not the gods, not the demigods, and certainly not some mystical saviour.'

Yaizra nodded. 'At last we agree on something.'

A low noise came from a tunnel behind them and they turned.

'Here they come,' said Corthie. 'Let's just hope they have news of a ship.'

They watched as torchlight flickered off the walls of the tunnel, then two figures emerged and walked into the cave.

'How are you all today?' said Captain Hellis, putting down a large, covered basket. Her husband also held one, and he placed it on the ground next to them.

'We're fine,' said Corthie. 'Any news?'

'Lots,' said the captain, coming over and taking a seat on an old crate. 'Some good, some bad. Which do you want to hear first?'

Corthie shrugged. 'The bad.'

The captain took a breath, and her husband glanced away, staring out of the shaft at the rain pelting down outside.

'There's no boat,' she said; 'not for a while yet.'

Corthie felt his nerves ripple with frustration. 'Why not? The storms finished days ago. Surely the sea is safe to sail?'

'Oh, it's perfectly safe. However, the harbour on the island is most certainly not. Two companies of Blades have arrived, to assist with the sweep of the island, and every ship is being searched before departure. Two warships are constantly patrolling the waters between here and the mainland, in case you manage to slip away.' She frowned. 'I'm working on a plan, but it'll take a while.'

The cave fell into silence as the three fugitives let the news wash over them.

'Do you want to hear the good news?' the captain said.

Corthie nodded.

'Your hiding place here is secure. The entrances to this network of caves are too well hidden, and it's so close to the town that they'd never believe you'd be here. Every day the Blades climb the cliffs behind the settlement, where there are hundreds, if not thousands of caves. They'll be searching there for years. Even better, the Gloamer inhabitants of the island are thoroughly sick of the Blades trampling all over the place and issuing orders as if the locals were slaves. The Grey Isle is technically ruled by Dalrig, and you know how they feel about Duke Marcus, the pretend prince. No one here on the island is helping the Blades in any way, and folk's sympathy is firmly with the ex-Champion of the Bulwark.'

'That's great,' said Yaizra, glowering, 'but what do we do now?'

'Well, everyone, the Blades included, is expecting them to be recalled to the Bulwark before the end of the month; before the start of summer. If that's the case, then all you have to do is wait them out. As soon as they've gone, we can get you on a ship.'

'I thought you were working on a plan?' said Corthie.

'I am, but it's dangerous, and should only be used if we really need it. The safest option by far is to wait.'

'What does it involve?'

'It involves me trying to strike a deal with the owner of the fastest ship on the island; one that could out-run anything the Blades have. If I succeed, then we might be able to do something sooner, if we have to.' She smiled at them. 'I know you're disappointed. I've put a couple of bottles of brandy in your baskets today that might serve to lessen the frustration. They're a gift from a Gloamer merchant that wanted to show support.'

Corthie nodded. 'Fine. Thank them from us, please. And keep working on getting that fast boat; I'd feel better knowing there's another plan besides us sitting here hoping the Blades will leave.'

'They'll leave,' said the captain. 'They have to, otherwise who will defend the Great Walls?'

Corthie nodded, but said nothing. Like many others, the captain assumed that Marcus would withdraw every single Blade from the rest of the City long before summer arrived. He wished he shared their confidence, but everything he knew about Marcus pointed to his lust for power, and he wondered if the new prince would care about losing half of the City so long as he retained his authority over the rest.

'We'll leave you to eat in peace,' the captain said, rising. She gestured to her husband, and they left the cave, disappearing back down the tunnel.

Achan got up, and began rummaging through the two baskets. 'There's some good stuff in here; fresh bread that must have come straight off a boat from Dalrig, and some nice smoked fish. You guys hungry?'

Corthie nodded, but Yaizra got up and wandered over to the window-shaft.

'Another month in this place?' she said. 'I think I'm going to go crazy.'

'It's better than Tarstation, or the icefields,' said Achan; 'or the western bank. Damn it, I should have asked the captain about getting some more books; I've finished all the ones she loaned me.'

Yaizra scowled at him. 'For Malik's sake, ask her tomorrow. At least you're quiet when your head's in a book.'

He scowled back at her. 'At least I can read.'

'At least I don't want to get myself killed in some stupid revolution.'

'Yeah? Well, at least I don't leave people to get killed by greenhides.'

Yaizra stared at him, her eyes narrow.

Achan's face fell. 'Sorry, that went too far.'

'I've had it,' she said; 'with you guys, with this place. I can't take it any more.'

'Then why don't you wander off somewhere?'

She glanced at Achan, her expression changing. 'What are you talking about?'

'Do you think me and Corthie are completely stupid? We know you've been going off at night. Why don't you tell us where you've been?'

She looked over at Corthie, who shrugged.

'Every night,' Achan went on, 'after you think we've gone to sleep, you sneak out of the cave. Corthie doesn't want me to ask about it; he said it was none of our business what you did, but I disagree. If you're endangering our hiding place, then we should know.'

Yaizra sat on a crate. 'I'm not endangering our hiding place.'

'Then where are you going?'

'Forget it,' said Corthie. 'If she says she's being careful, then leave it at that.'

'No,' said Achan. 'How about she tells us, and then we judge if she's put us in danger? You'll have to forgive me if I'm a little suspicious, but Yaizra has proved she's capable of lying.'

'I've apologised for that a hundred times,' said Yaizra; 'but alright. I'll tell you; I've got nothing to hide.'

Achan nodded. 'Let's hear it, then.'

'The network of caverns is vast,' she said, 'and I'm bored and curious. I started off exploring in case we were found; I wanted to have a rough idea of the layout, you know, if we had to run for it.'

'You happy now?' said Corthie to Achan. 'I knew it would be something like this.'

Yaizra smiled. 'I hadn't finished, big lump. I found a tunnel that leads somewhere quite interesting.'

Achan frowned. 'Interesting, how?'

'You guys aren't going to get angry with me, are you?'

Corthie laughed. 'That depends.'

'I can't help myself sometimes,' she said; 'remember, I'm a thief, a good one. I can sneak into just about anywhere.'

'Go on.'

'Well, I discovered this big outflow pipe; a small tunnel drops you right into it. It hasn't been used in years, I reckon, and it's all dried up. Anyway, I followed it away from where it opens out into the sea, and found where it leads.'

'Where?' said Achan.

'Think about it,' she said. 'If you go along the bay from here, what's the next building you come to?'

Corthie frowned. 'The fortress?'

'Well done, big lump; got it in one.'

Achan stood, his arms raised. 'You've been sneaking about in the one place on this island that's full of Blades? You stupid Icewarder, are you trying to get us killed?'

Yaizra folded her arms. 'This is why I didn't tell you. I knew you'd react like that.'

'But you haven't been seen?' said Corthie.

'Of course not. I'm good at what I do, and besides, the dungeons of the fortress are pretty much deserted.'

'You've been in the dungeons?'

'Not exactly. The old sewage pipe goes under these empty cells, but there's a grille that I can look through. I saw the cells, but there are no guards.'

'It sounds like you were in the ancient prison I was talking about before,' said Achan, his attention perking up. 'Wow. I guess the reason there are no guards is because there are no prisoners, and haven't been since the last mortal Prince of Tara.'

Yaizra chuckled. 'That's not entirely true.'

'What?'

'Almost every cell is empty. One isn't.'

'There's a prisoner?' said Achan. 'It can't be the ancient prison then. You must have found the town jail.'

'No,' she said. 'I told you; there are no guards. I've been there a dozen times now, and never seen a single person apart from that one prisoner.'

Achan raised an eyebrow. 'I assume the prisoner is dead? I mean, if no one's bringing any food or water...'

'No, she's alive.'

'She?' said Corthie.

Yaizra sighed. 'This is another reason I didn't want to tell you. I knew that as soon as the big lump found out that the prisoner was a "she", then he'd want to rescue her.'

'I didn't say anything about a rescue.'

'No, but I can tell what you're thinking. You picked me to join the escape from Tarstation because you thought I was a weak woman who needed rescuing. I see you're not denying it.'

Corthie glanced away, knowing that any denials would sound false. He had picked Yaizra and Achan because he had thought they would be vulnerable in Tarstation without him there to protect them. He thought through what his reaction would have been if Yaizra had pronounced the prisoner to have been a man, and he realised there might be some truth to her words.

'It's not the worst trait in a man,' she said, 'but not every woman needs you to rescue them, and some don't deserve rescuing.'

'And what about this woman you saw in the fortress?'

Yaizra shrugged. 'How do I know? I've no idea why she's in there. She could be a mass murderer.'

'She must be eating and drinking something,' said Achan. 'Guards must come and go at times when you've not been there.'

'Yeah, maybe.'

Achan nodded. 'She must be important, if that really is the ancient prison you found. What does she look like?'

Yaizra smiled. 'Want to come and see for yourselves?'

'Yes!' Achan cried. 'I mean, is it safe?'

'Perfectly, as long as you can be quiet.'

'You're not the only one who's good at sneaking about,' Achan said, his eyes glowing; 'I managed to evade the greenhides on the western bank after you two... eh, never mind. Wow, the ancient prison on Grey Isle. I remember reading about it when I was a boy, and now I might actually get to see it?'

'Don't wet your knickers,' Yaizra said, 'it's a sewage pipe and a grille.' She turned to Corthie. 'Are you up for it, big lump?'

'Aye,' he said, pulling one of the food baskets closer to him; 'after I've eaten something first.'

Once the three fugitives had finished breakfast, they laced up their boots and got ready to go. Corthie insisted on bringing his mace; the weapon had served him well on the western bank, and he was growing used to the weight and feel of it in his hands.

Yaizra led them down the tunnel that the captain and her husband had used that morning, but then took a fork to the right that narrowed and led down. Achan lit a lantern, and followed her, while Corthie stayed at the rear, ducking his head as they went. He noticed tiny etchings scratched into the stone by his side, and Yaizra saw him glance at them.

'That's my little code,' she said, 'so I don't get lost down here.'

Achan frowned at it. 'It's just squiggles. How does it work?'

She snorted. 'As if I'm going to tell you. Tell you what, let me know if you think you've cracked it; no one else has. Come on.'

She set off again, Achan's lantern sending flickering light around the tight tunnel. Corthie kept his head low, and was almost crouching in places as he squeezed through behind the others. Yaizra seemed to know where she was going, avoiding several turns, then heading right and descending again. They came to a hole in the ground, through which a dull grey daylight was rising.

'Down here,' she said. 'This is the old sewage outlet I was talking about.'

Achan smiled. 'Something about this place remind you of home, did it?'

'Don't push me. I could run down that tunnel right now, and you two would be lost in here forever. Holdfast, you go first.'

Corthie crouched down by the hole in the ground. Below was another tunnel, but grey light was entering from the right hand side, and he could hear the faint murmur of the sea. He lowered his legs in, then dropped. He crouched as he landed, the top of the tunnel lower than his height. He stepped to the side and gazed towards the source of the light. In the distance he could make out a large circle of brightness at the end of the tunnel.

Yaizra landed next to him, followed a few moments later by Achan.

'That's the sea,' she said, pointing towards the light. 'We could get out that way if we're ever cornered; it's a ten foot drop to the water.' She turned to face the other direction. 'And the fortress is this way.' She frowned. 'Listen, before we go on, there's something I have to tell you.'

'Aye?' Corthie said.

'It's about the prisoner. Just so you don't get a surprise when you see her, you should know that she's being tortured, somehow.'

Corthie raised an eyebrow. 'Now you tell us. I thought nobody else was there; how is she being tortured?'

'She has this weird mask strapped onto her head, covering her eyes. There's blood coming down from it, streaking both of her cheeks. She also has chains, lots of chains, like they've captured a wild beast rather than an old woman.'

'She's old?' said Achan.

Yaizra glanced at him. 'Yes. Does that make a difference to you?'

'Eh, no. Why would it? We're not thinking about rescuing her, are we?'

'We couldn't,' Yaizra said, 'even if we wanted to. The grille's tiny, you'll see. We'd have to break down walls before we could get anywhere near her.' She gestured to Achan to extinguish the lantern, then put her finger to her lips. 'From now on, we move quietly, like little mice.'

She crept up the tunnel, and the others followed her. Corthie kept his eyes on the dark ground, his eyes adjusting to the gloom. They continued for a hundred yards as the tunnel slowly bent to the right. Light started to come from ahead of them, through a series of narrow holes and grilles. She stopped by one, and glanced up.

Corthie and Achan raised their eyes and saw the bottom of an ancient toilet above their heads.

'I'm glad this prison was never used,' Achan whispered.

Yaizra gestured to them and they followed her to the wall. She stood up on her toes and peered through a small, metal slat near the ceiling, then turned.

She nodded. 'She's there.'

Corthie looked next, his height meaning he had to crouch to see through the grille. It looked out onto a lamplit stone corridor that ran from left to right. On the wall opposite were barred doors every few yards leading to cells, and the one directly across from the grille was occupied. The prisoner was an old woman, just as Yaizra had said, but her age was impossible to tell due to the heavy iron band that was attached to the upper part of her face. It covered the woman's eyes completely, and fresh streams of blood were seeping down from its lower edge, staining her sunken cheeks. Her frame was almost skeletal, and she had shackles fixed to her neck, wrists and ankles. She was groaning and writhing in pain, and mumbling something that Corthie couldn't make out. He felt sick looking at her, her agony unbearable to watch, but he couldn't pull his eyes away. Her rags, and the cell floor, were filthy, and a sour stench floated over to the grille.

He felt a hand on his sleeve. 'My turn,' said Achan.

Corthie turned away with an effort, and sat down on the tunnel floor next to where Yaizra was crouching.

He shook his head. 'What are they doing to her?'

'Some barbaric punishment, I'd guess,' she whispered. 'Who knows what she did?'

'Who cares? No one deserves that.'

'Don't get all dreamy-eyed about it.'

Corthie got back up and started walking away down the tunnel the way they had come, as anger slowly grew within him. Whoever she was, and whatever she had done, the punishment seemed too savage. From the rust and grime on her chains, she looked like she had been there a long time, and he couldn't bear to think about how much suffering she had endured in that time. Yaizra had been right, though; no rescue could be attempted via a two-inch high grille.

He walked closer to the light until he could hear and see the waves crashing into the cliffs beneath him at the lip of the outlet pipe. He glanced to the left, and saw the high battlements of the fortress rise up from the rock. The standard of the Blades was flying from a tower, and Corthie realised how much he had come to hate a symbol he had once loved. He recalled the faces of the individual Blades he had known in Arrowhead, and tried to reconcile that to what Marcus had unleashed upon the City. People like Quill and Maddie Jackdaw were Blades too, and he had to remember that.

He heard footsteps behind him.

'Are you alright?' said Achan.

He turned his gaze back to the sea. 'Aye.'

Yaizra leaned against the side of the outlet. 'Maybe I shouldn't have brought you here. I didn't realise how squeamish you were.'

'I'm not squeamish,' said Achan. 'I'm fine.'

'I wasn't talking about you, little Hammer, I was meaning the big lump here.'

Corthie turned to her.

'Let me guess,' she said, 'your manly instincts have been activated and you feel the need to rescue a complete stranger?'

'It's not right what they're doing to her.'

'Life isn't right,' she said; 'life isn't fair. Life kicked each one of us in the face when we got sent to Tarstation. All the same, I'm fond of my life, and I'm not throwing it away on a prisoner who might very well deserve to be punished. We need to get off this island before you can be all heroic, so I can hide before you start ripping the place up. We either escape, or we die trying to rescue this stranger; you can't have both.'

'That's not entirely accurate,' said Achan. 'We could rescue her, then escape.'

Corthie smiled. 'Exactly. Who says we can't have both?'

'I do,' said Yaizra, shaking her head.

They started walking along the outlet towards the hole in the roof that led back to their cave.

'It'll take a bit of planning,' said Corthie.

'You leave that to me,' said Achan. 'I've already got a few ideas.'

Yaizra glared at them. 'I can't take you boys anywhere.'

CHAPTER 22

THE SCENT OF POWER

P ella, Auldan, The City – 3rd Amalan 3420
     The rain was hammering down as Aila stepped off the gang-plank into the harbour of Pella. Behind her walked the son of Lady Mona, dressed as a Reaper merchant. Aila was disguised similarly, and they had posed as husband and wife when they had embarked upon the ship at Port Sanders that morning.

A line of carriages was stationed at the far end of the quayside, and they hurried through the downpour, their umbrellas flapping in the wind. To their right stood the great bulk of her old home, Cuidrach Palace, the flag of the Blades fluttering from its front entrance. It was the last place she had seen Corthie, she thought, and it was where Princess Khora had died. She had so many memories wrapped up in that one building; her father had also died there, slain by Prince Michael, and it was where she had escaped from to join the rebellion of Princess Yendra.

They reached a carriage, and Mona's son gestured as the driver opened the side door.

'After you, dear wife.'

Aila frowned as she boarded. Her half-cousin had enjoyed the various disguises they had been forced to adopt in their flight from the

293

territory of the Evaders. It had taken them five days to escape from the Circuit, and they had only got out by travelling perilously close to where Lady Jade had taken up residence, and then slipping over the border into Sander territory. After that it had been simple; a carriage to Port Sanders, and a boat to Pella, and within a few hours, their journey was nearly complete.

Mona's son got into the carriage and the door was closed.

'Only an hour to go and we'll be there,' he said. 'I'll almost miss all this. I wouldn't say it's been fun, but it's had its moments.'

'It's a civil war,' said Aila. 'I know it hasn't been officially pronounced, but that's what it is. And I should know. Only last time it was a war between two factions of gods and demigods, while this time it's the mortals against all of us.'

'Except half of the mortals are on the side of the gods, and you are not.'

'And which side is your mother on?'

'That will be one of the things she wishes to speak to you about. Still suspicious? I have been honest with you, but I'm not going to second guess all that my mother might say.'

Aila narrowed her eyes. 'Alright, which side are you on?'

He smiled back at her. 'My mother's.'

Their carriage pulled into the rainy streets of the old town of Pella, the beautiful red sandstone mansions obscured by the mist that rose from the bay. It was clammy in the carriage, and she loosened her raincoat when the window became so steamed up it was impossible to see anything. She rubbed her head, trying to figure out what she was doing. She had been so focussed on trying to find Naxor, and then with helping the rebellion, that she felt empty; her plans in ruins. She was no further forward in getting her hands on the Quadrant, and the Evaders had made their feelings plain. Stormfire had been acceptable to them before they had known it was her, but as the demigod Lady Aila, she was no longer welcome in the Circuit. It hurt, but she was beyond angry. The five days of hiding and running to reach Port Sanders had been terrifying, and there had been more than one occasion when she had thought her life was going to end at the hands of an Evader mob.

Mona's son yawned. 'I'm looking forward to my bed; my own bed at last.'

'Does your mother often send you out on little jobs?'

'Sometimes, when she needs things done.'

'And what about siblings; do you have any?'

'None that are alive. My mother has had many children over the course of her long life, including the ancestor of the line that became the Chamberlains in Tara. She tends to have one every century or so.'

'And what about your father?'

'From the hints my mother's dropped, I think he might have been a soldier. I've never met him as far as I know.'

Aila shook her head. 'This is one reason why I've never had children. Dealing with mortals can be so... messy.'

He gave her a strange look. 'But you're in love with one.'

'How in Malik's name did you know that?'

'When my mother went into your mind, she read your memories; then she told me.'

'It's none of your damn business. Mona had no right to ransack my mind, and even less of a right to tell you about it. How am I supposed to trust you if you play tricks on me like this?'

He sat back, frowning. 'It wasn't a trick, it was a necessary precaution. My mother is very concerned about Prince Marcus discovering her true feelings, and she needed to know that you wouldn't betray her.'

Aila glared at him, feeling the anger in her rise. She remembered Princess Khora reading her mind in Pella, but that had been after Aila had threatened to kill her, so her reasons were at least understandable. Naxor, too, had never read her thoughts without warning her first, or without a good excuse. Mona's intrusion felt different, especially as she hadn't known her memories were being read. She would have no secrets in Ooste, no way to hide her true feelings, and no way she could lie to protect herself.

'She only did it once,' he said. 'I don't know why you're being so defensive about it.'

'They're my memories and feelings,' she cried, 'no one else's. Mine. What's so difficult about that to understand? I guess she's been in your mind ever since you were born; you're so used to it that you can't see why someone might be upset. What else did she tell you?'

He shrugged.

'If you don't tell me, I'm stopping this carriage and getting out. You'll never find me in the rain, I'll have changed my appearance a dozen times, and then you'll have to go to Ooste alone and explain to your mother why I'm no longer with you. Is that what you want?'

He narrowed his eyes as he listened to her, then frowned. 'My mother is aware that you have an ulterior motive for meeting with her.'

She paused. 'I do? Enlighten me.'

'You want to use my mother to find something that will help a dragon escape.'

Aila laughed. 'Oh yeah, that. I made a promise.'

'I know, to the Champion of the Bulwark; it's quite prominent in your mind, I gather.'

'Alright, what else?'

'That was the main thrust of it. She also told me that you were unhappy, but that seemed quite obvious to me; and that you hated Marcus, again, not a great shock. It was your love for a mortal that most surprised her. My mother had assumed that you had forsworn any such romantic involvement with mortals a long time ago, and she wondered if this new interest was because you wanted to have a child with a mix of your powers and his powers. He is an exceptional mortal, by all accounts.'

'A child? Malik's ass, that hadn't even crossed my mind. Well, it had crossed it, but it wasn't something I was obsessing over. In fact, the idea makes me sad. It would be bad enough watching the man I love grow old and die in front of me, but a child? You would need to have a heart of stone to watch your own child wither before your eyes... Oh. I, uh... Sorry.'

He wiped some of the condensation from a window and glanced out of it, his eyes dark. Aila watched him for a moment, then lowered her eyes, perversely relieved that he had shut up for a while.

'The gods and demigods,' he said after a long silence, 'have a differing set of morals from mortals. Their unlimited life spans make this inevitable. They wouldn't be able to function if they shared the same weaknesses as those whose lives are so short in comparison.'

'You call love and empathy a weakness?'

'Yes, if they prevent you from doing what's necessary and right. The puzzle that I have is why you don't seem to fit in with the other demigods. '

Aila gave him a wry smile. 'I blame Princess Yendra.'

He raised an eyebrow.

'When I was young,' she said, 'and by "young" I mean under three hundred years old, my attitude was much the same as the others. My brothers and sisters were sleeping with mortals, and having fun without any moral qualms, and so was I, for a while. But then I was sent to the Circuit, and Princess Yendra mentored me for a few years, and everything changed. She actually *cared*. To her, if the luxury and riches of the demigods came at the expense of the mortals, then it was wrong. Children were suffering, starving, in the vast slums, while the demigods were having endless parties and congratulating themselves on how well-run the City was. Prince Michael was the worst. To him, the mortals were no better than cattle, and you don't give cattle the right to vote, or the right to live in freedom; they are there to serve you and for no other purpose. Then the Civil War started, and I returned to Pella, fired up. I joined my father when he decided to side with Yendra and the rebels; I was so proud of him for choosing that path, when he could so easily have kept neutral, or even helped Michael. Of course, it all went wrong, and my father was murdered by Michael in front of me, along with most of my brothers and sisters.'

'You saw Yendra kill Michael, didn't you?'

She smiled. 'Yes. It was horrible, but also glorious. I'll never forget it. At that moment, I thought we'd won.'

'And then Yendra was killed?'

'Yes. She was taken away by the God-King and God-Queen first, who had arrived in a flash of light a few moments after Michael's death. A huge crowd of Evaders had witnessed Michael's death, and the God-King didn't want them to see another God-Child be killed before their eyes. I assume they executed her in Ooste; I never heard the details.'

'The two mightiest God-Children, dead in a single day.'

'The best and the worst.'

'Michael's supporters would say the same.'

'Yeah, no doubt. So, it's Yendra's fault I'm the way I am. She filled my head with the foolish notion that each mortal's life is worth the same as any demigod's. That was her legacy to me. Sometimes I hate her for it, and wish I could be as hard-hearted as my cousins and siblings, but others times I thank her that I'm nothing like them.'

'Nothing like my mother, you mean?'

Aila shrugged. 'I don't really know your mother. She stayed out of the Civil War, and as far as I know, she never leaves the Royal Academy. But, based on the way she plundered my mind without asking, yeah, possibly.'

He rubbed the window again. 'We're nearly there.'

She glanced through the smeared pane of glass. To their left was the beach that ran between Pella and Ooste, deserted and rainswept, while the first houses of Ooste were appearing ahead of them. In the distance, she could make out the white façade of the enormous Royal Palace where the God-King dwelt, while the green domes of the Royal Academy spread out beneath the high cliffs that protected Ooste from the storms of the Clashing Seas.

'Your mother was one of my tutors when I was a little girl,' she said. 'I spent eight years in the Royal Academy.'

'I think every demigod was schooled there. And so was I.'

The carriage pulled through the wet streets of the town, passing grand mansions and huge public buildings, where much of the administrative business of the City went on. Many of the buildings seemed closed, and the streets were deserted.

'It's been a lot quieter here since Prince Marcus moved the seat of government to Tara,' said Mona's son. 'I hear Maeladh Palace is packed out with staff now. Every City official who needs a signature or a decision now either has to get the boat to Tara each day, or move there. How I wish the God-King would say or do something.'

Aila glanced at him, but said nothing. His mother hadn't told him the truth about the God-King, she thought. Or perhaps he was testing her.

'It baffles me,' he went on, 'and my mother seems to have no good explanations either. Why would the God-King sit in his palace and do nothing as Marcus wrecks the City? It makes no sense. Does he fear the God-Queen?'

'I'm not sure he fears anything.'

'Exactly. So why does he do nothing? Did the death of Princess Khora mean so little to him? And what about Prince Montieth's daughters using their death powers on mortals; has he nothing to say about that?'

She nodded. He seemed genuinely angry, and so she guessed that he was unaware of the truth. That made her feel a bit better. Princess Khora had threatened to kill Aila if she had revealed the truth about the God-King, and she was glad that Mona wasn't spreading the news around.

The carriage pulled into a large forecourt, enclosed on three sides by the huge buildings of the academy. Taken together, the complex was as large as any palace in the City, with spreading wings and tall towers, bound together by the profusion of round domes. The carriage went under an archway, and continued on, towards the private area occupied by Chancellor Mona. She had an entire keep to herself, a strong, almost fortress-like structure at the rear of the academy, where it nestled under high, overhanging cliffs. A waterfall sparkled at its back as it tumbled down the rocky cliff, before joining a stream that wound between the academy buildings. Little gardens and bridges followed the path of the stream, creating a beautiful green ribbon that snaked through the heart of the academy. The carriage came to a halt in front of the keep, and the driver opened the door.

Mona's son paid him, and then he and Aila ran through the torrential rain, climbing the steps to the keep. A pair of Reaper guards were on duty, wearing the uniform of the academy staff. They recognised Mona's son, and opened the tall doors to let them in. A Reaper courtier was waiting in the entrance hall for them.

'Greetings, my lord,' he said, bowing low. He straightened his back and glanced at Aila.

Mona's son nudged her. 'You're still in your merchant's disguise.'

'Am I? Damn it, I forgot. Should I, uh...?'

He shook his head and turned to the courtier. 'This is the guest my mother asked me to bring to the academy. Please tell her that we have arrived.'

'Your mother, the honourable Chancellor Mona, is already aware of your approach. She has asked me to show our... guest to the quarters where she will be residing during her stay here.'

Mona's son nodded. 'Fine.' He turned to Aila. 'I'll see you at dinner.'

Aila watched as the driver brought their bags in. Mona's son picked up his luggage, nodded to her, then walked off down a hallway.

'Is this your only bag?' said the courtier, gesturing to the small satchel she had brought.

'Yeah.'

The courtier picked it up. 'Follow me.'

They walked along a wide, marble-floored hallway, then ascended a carpeted flight of stairs, where paintings and tapestries adorned the walls. Aila glanced at the portraits as they climbed. Most were of the God-Children and there was a space on the wall where she presumed a picture of the disgraced Yendra would once have hung. After that, the portraits changed to the demigods, and she frowned at the painting that had been made of her. She remembered sitting for it when she had been a troublesome and arrogant one-hundred-year old, and the artist had captured the boredom and contempt she had felt at the time.

'What are the rules?' she said to the courtier as they reached the landing and began walking along a wood-lined corridor.

'Rules, ma'am?'

'Yes. Are there... laboratories or anywhere else I'm not supposed to go sniffing around? Or any weird, silent guards I'm not allowed to talk to?'

'There are no places here forbidden to you, ma'am, though of course I would ask you to knock before entering the chancellor's private rooms.'

'And I can leave whenever I like?'

The courtier frowned. 'Of course, ma'am. You are free to walk out of the front door whenever you wish.'

Aila nodded. 'Alright. Her son mentioned something about dinner?'

'Yes. Dinner is in two hours' time. I shall come and collect you ten minutes prior to that, and would ask that you please be ready.'

'Will Mona be there?'

'The chancellor shall indeed be present at dinner, ma'am. Please dress formally.'

'You've seen the size of my bag, just how many fancy dresses do you think I'm carrying in there?'

'A wardrobe has been put together for you, ma'am, and you may select something appropriate from that.'

To the hundred-year-old Aila that would have sounded like something exciting, but to the Aila who had lived for nearly eight centuries it was just another formal dinner to endure.

They came to a tall, white-panelled door and the courtier pushed it open. 'Your quarters, ma'am.'

Aila smiled as she entered. The chamber was high-ceilinged, with tall windows overlooking the town of Ooste. There were comfortable couches and chairs, and a table next to a large hearth. Mirrors and paintings hung from the walls, and the whole room was light and airy.

'Your bedchamber is to the left,' said the courtier, placing the bag onto the thick carpet, 'and the bathroom leads off from there. Is this to your satisfaction?'

She nodded. 'Yeah, it'll do.'

Aila went into her bedroom once the courtier had left. Everything was clean and neat, and the sheets on the huge bed were freshly laundered. She dropped her bag onto a seat and opened the bathroom door, seeing a large ceramic tub amid the white tiled floor. She smiled, then turned the taps on. Hot water came gushing out, and steam rose to fill the air. She pulled off her stained and worn travelling clothes as soon as the water level was high enough, then got in, sighing as the temperature turned her skin a bright pink.

An hour later, she stood in front of a full-size mirror, trying to decide what to wear. The clothes in the wardrobe were all in her size, but there was an eclectic mixture of styles and fashions, as if the collection had been put together over many years. In the end she decided on a simple black dress, and left her shoulder-length hair loose instead of tying it up as she usually did. She slipped on the pair of high-heeled shoes that went with the dress and practised walking about her rooms for a while, her ankles wobbling.

She sat on the bed to give her feet a rest and noticed her bag lying next to her. She picked it up from the bottom and tipped the contents out. She had left most of her things behind in the Circuit when she had walked out on the rebels, and she shook her head at the meagre possessions she had been carrying about. Something glistened for a moment beneath a pile of worn clothes. She picked it up, puzzled for a second, then remembered. It was the vial of silvery liquid that she had slipped into her pocket in Prince Montieth's laboratory. It was small, about as long as her index finger, and the contents swirled and shimmered.

She almost put it back down onto the bed, but curiosity got the better of her and she pulled the stopper off so she could smell it. It had no odour, so, disappointed, she pushed the stopper back in, then stood. As soon as she had got to her feet she felt light-headed, and she stumbled, almost falling over as a wave of dizziness struck her. She glanced at the mirror, and her mouth fell open. Her face was changing as she stared at the reflection, growing younger-looking. She gasped as her appearance morphed, from late-twenties to early-twenties in a few seconds, the lines around her eyes disappearing, and her skin almost shining with life.

Stop, stop, she prayed. *Please stop before I get to my teens.* Her features settled at what she guessed appeared like a twenty-one year old and she sat back onto the bed. She picked up the vial.

It was pure, concentrated salve. Not the weak and diluted tinctures that she had been given every few decades as a reward for behaving herself, but the real stuff. The stuff that had sent the God-King mad; the stuff that made her idiot brother look like an eighteen-year-old; the stuff that was so valuable, Naxor could exchange it for dragons to bring to the City. It had paid for Corthie too. She swore. What would he think when he next saw her? She had liked looking as if she were in her late twenties, it had made her appear a little more mature than the demigods like Kano, who over-indulged in the stuff and ended up looking like teenagers.

She repacked her bag, burying the vial at the bottom, after making sure the stopper was firmly in place. She stood again, and gazed at her younger reflection. It wasn't so bad, she thought; give it a few decades and she would be back to her old self.

A tap sounded at the door. 'Ma'am? Dinner will shortly be ready.'

She went to the door and opened it. The courtier's eyes widened slightly at her, then she remembered that she had still looked like a Reaper merchant the last time he had seen her. *At least he doesn't think I've been sniffing salve*, she thought.

She followed him through the warm, carpeted hallways of the keep, until they reached a large room, with a huge table that could fit twenty people round it. The walls were panelled with oak, and the ceiling was alive with carvings of birds and animals. Stained glass windows coloured the light as it entered the room, sending greens, reds and yellows across the table and walls. At the head of the table a woman was sitting, dressed in flowing white robes, with a silver tiara on her brow.

She stood.

'Welcome, Lady Aila. Please sit.'

Aila glanced around the table, then walked up so that she was close to the woman, and took the place to her left.

'Mona,' she said, sitting; 'how are you?'

The woman sat, keeping her back stiff. 'I am well. I trust you are rested?'

'I had a lovely, long bath. It's a nice place you have here.'

'The Royal Academy is my home, my refuge. Do you remember your time here?'

'A bit. I didn't stay in the keep, though; I had a room in the students' block.'

'I recall it. I have had a hand in the education of the majority of the demigods.'

'Yeah? It's a pity so many of them turned out to be assholes.'

Mona frowned. 'Princess Khora warned me about you.'

'Warned you? Oh. I had a wild thought that Khora actually liked me. Are you telling me I was wrong?'

'No, she liked you, despite that fact that you loathed her.'

'Yeah, "loathed", past tense. I was just warming to her when she was murdered by my brother. Look, before we go any further, I have a problem with you.'

'You do?'

'I do, yes. You can't go raiding other people's minds without permission. It puts you at an unfair advantage. You know everything that's in my head, and I know nothing about you. If you do it again, I'm walking out of here, and you can forget... whatever it is that you want from me.'

'I see. I felt it necessary to ensure that you weren't going to betray me before I invited you here. I needed to know. But, it is done, and I am satisfied with what I found. You have my word that I shall not do it again.'

A servant entered with a bottle of wine. He opened it, then filled two glasses. Mona gave him a slight nod, and he bowed and left. She picked up the wine and took a long sip.

Aila eyed her. 'You were friends with Khora?'

'She was my best friend. We were both born the same year, did you know that? I am only seventy years younger than my brother Marcus, and Khora and I were raised together. We were inseparable for centuries, then her work got in the way and my position at the academy took up more and more of my time. But even to the end, she and I were close. I mourn her death deeply. To me, it feels as if I have lost a limb; part of myself. My fondness for her is the only reason you are here, cousin Aila.'

Aila chuckled. 'It sounds funny, you calling me a cousin. To me you're like one of the God-Children, older and different. I mean, you have a month named after you, for Malik's sake. That must feel pretty good.'

Mona nodded. 'Believe me, the novelty fades after a few centuries.'

'It always annoyed me that Michael's four children got a month each. The eight Gods and God-Children I understand, but four demigods? And why Michael's brats? Why not Isra's? There could have been a month called "Ailan", after me.'

'My father Prince Michael was always the favourite of the God-Queen, and it was she who drew up the revised calendar. You could always go to Tara and ask her.'

'Eh, no. So, what am I doing here, then? I mean, it's nice to chat, dear cousin, but I assume you had a reason for summoning me all the way to Ooste?'

'There is only one reason that matters; the City. The current crisis is worse than anything we have experienced in three hundred years, the worst in a way, because at least during the time of the Civil War, the involvement of the Blades was limited. The so-called Prince of Tara is without doubt, the most stupid and vile person to take over the running of the City, and if something isn't done soon, then I fear it may be too late.'

Aila laughed. 'So you've decided to come out as a rebel?'

'I am not a rebel. All I desire is that we go back to the way we were, before Marcus took over.'

'Do you care about the mortals?'

Mona smiled. 'I know you do.'

'That's a "no", then?'

'Fine. No, I don't particularly care about them, however I don't wish them to burn the City to the ground. If concessions are required to keep them docile, then I am prepared to consider that.'

'What's your plan?'

'Khora informed me that she had made you aware of the true condition of the God-King.'

'She took me to see him.'

'Then you understand how precarious our position is? The only thing restraining Marcus and the God-Queen is their fear that the God-King might emerge to stop their schemes. That is the only reason the God-Queen herself has not left Maeladh Palace. On her own, she could kill almost everyone in the City in a matter of hours. You have met Jade, yes? Her powers are nothing compared to those wielded by the God-Queen. When the greenhides were first annihilated and driven back from the City, who was it that killed them all? The God-King may have led the mortal armies, but it was the God-Queen who slaughtered the eternal enemy. She pushed them back hundreds of miles, allowing the mortals to build the Union Walls. She did the same, centuries later, which allowed the Middle Walls to be constructed. After that, she swore she would never go beyond the walls again, and left the City to her children to look after.'

Mona leaned across the table. 'If her Majesty discovers the truth about the God-King, who knows what she will do? Now, let's talk about your price.'

'What price?'

'I assume you'll want a reward for helping me. If you do as I say, I can assist you with the Quadrant.'

Aila's eyes lit up. 'You know where it is?'

'Which one?'

'There is more than one Quadrant?'

'Our cousin Naxor has one, as I'm sure you already know, but there is another, hidden within Maeladh Palace; the God-Queen took it with her when she left her husband.'

'Do you know what they do?'

Mona raised an eyebrow. 'Of course. Those devices were how the God-King and God-Queen arrived here in the first place.'

'But why did they come here? And why don't they just leave? They could just leave, couldn't they; any time they wanted?'

'They came here fleeing the great war of the gods. Being on the losing side of that war, they needed somewhere to hide. To return would be exceedingly dangerous for them, for the gods that hunted them then, are hunting them still.' She took a sip of wine. 'In fact, it was Malik's brother Nathaniel who created this world.'

Aila blinked. 'Nathaniel?'

'Yes. He created two worlds. This was the first, but something went wrong, which is why half of this world is scorched desert, and the other half dark and covered in ice. So, he created a second world.'

'And what happened to that?'

'I don't know. Whatever passed after Malik and Amalia arrived here is unknown. Naxor probably knows more than anyone else, considering the number of times he has left this world to gather champions for the Great Walls.' She glanced at Aila. 'What do you think? If you help me, then I will help you get the Quadrant hidden in Tara.'

'And what do I have to do to help you?'

'That's easy,' she said; 'marry Marcus.'

Aila nearly choked on her wine. 'What?'

'Only you have the power to placate this beast. He desires you more than anything. Marry him, then wait until your wedding night, then kill him.'

'Could I not, eh... just kill him first? You know, without the wedding bit?'

'You'd never get close enough to him. I have already sent assassins, and each one failed long before they reached Marcus.'

'But, wouldn't the God-Queen destroy me once she'd found out?'

'I didn't say it would be easy.'

'No chance; forget it.'

Mona frowned. 'Khora told me you were brave and resolute. She believed you would do whatever it took to save the City. Was she mistaken?'

'Yes. There are a few things I wouldn't do, and marrying Marcus is pretty much at the top of the list.'

'It might be the only chance to save us all.'

'Tough. Are you going to imprison me, or throw me out now?'

'No. You are welcome to stay; this is not Greylin Palace, but time is running out, Aila. If the Blades aren't recalled to the Bulwark by the time summer begins, then the catastrophe that hits the City might well sweep it away completely. Marcus has only one weakness – you. What would you say to those mortals you care about so much, when the greenhides are ripping them to shreds; that you could have saved them but chose not to because it made you feel uncomfortable?'

'Uncomfortable? You want me to go to bed with that monster; it's a tiny little bit worse than "uncomfortable", thank you very much.'

'It is a sacrifice, I'll grant you, but when you cut the beast's head off and lift it up, imagine the glory you will feel. His power will fall to you, and you, cousin Aila, would be in line to be the next High Guardian of the City.'

'And what about you?'

Mona laughed. 'I have no wish for power; all I want is to live here in peace.'

Aila guarded her thoughts, unsure if Mona was going to read them. She didn't want to refuse again, but there was no way she was going to marry Marcus, especially if she would have to rule the City afterwards. That didn't sound like a reward; more like a punishment.

She sipped her wine. 'I'll think about it.'

CHAPTER 23

NIGHT BLADE

Tara, Auldan, The City – 5th Amalan 3420

Emily sat in a daze. To her left, Daniel was on his feet, pointing at his mother, who was standing a few yards away, her arms folded. They had been arguing for days, at mealtimes, in the evening; in fact, whenever mother and son happened to be in the same room.

'I don't care, mother, I'm not signing that damn piece of paper,' Daniel cried, his eyes lit with rage.

'Stop being so childish, Daniel. This is far too important an issue to decide when you are clearly upset and not thinking straight.' His mother kept her gaze directly ahead, avoiding any glances at her daughter-in-law. 'You have a long, long future ahead of you. Don't throw it away.'

'It's you that is trying to destroy my future,' he yelled. 'It's you that's trying to end my marriage.'

'Your marriage is a sham, son. It took place under false pretences. The Omertias lied to our faces, trying to pass off their daughter as a proper Roser. Utterly shameless.'

'Mother, Emily is sitting right here, and you think you can insult her like that?'

'I'm not insulting her; I'm merely stating a fact – she is not a Roser.'

'So what? Really, who cares?'

'Oh, I'd say about three and a half thousand years of tradition cares. Your forefathers go right back, not only to the last mortal Prince of Tara, but to the first. Do you have any conception what that means?'

'But that will still be true of any children Emily and I have.'

His mother shuddered. 'Please don't bring children into this. Can you imagine the ridicule those poor children would have to bear, once people discovered they were half-Roser, half-... Blessed Amalia, I can hardly bring myself to say it; half-Evader?'

'Mother, I have a revelation for you; guess what? Evaders are people too.'

His mother tutted. 'Why have you descended into rudeness? I know perfectly well that Evaders are people, and I object to any insinuation that I would believe otherwise. However, a Prince of Tara cannot have an Evader wife; the Princess of Tara has to be a Roser.'

Daniel laughed, but without any joy in his voice. 'So that's what this is about; your impossible dream for me? For the one in a million chance that the seas boil over and the sky falls in, and I become Prince of Tara? It's never going to happen, mother. The last mortal prince was nearly two thousand years ago; it's time to let it go.'

His mother's face transformed with anger, her eyes tight. 'How dare you speak to me like that? You shame me with your words. The Aurelians are not only the first family of Tara, they are the first family of the entire City, and every generation has the sacred duty of passing on that birthright to the next. Are you going to be the one that breaks that chain? Your ancestors would curse you if they heard you say such things.' Her face calmed a little. 'I will leave you now. I only came in here to inform you that Lord Nadhew will be arriving shortly, and I need to sit down and breathe slowly for a few minutes before he gets here.'

She turned, and walked from the small sitting room where Emily and Daniel had been sitting.

He sat heavily on the couch. 'I'm sorry. I shouldn't have lost my temper with her.'

Emily tried to smile, but her face seemed frozen, so she took his hand instead. 'It's alright.'

'It's not alright,' he said. 'This is a nightmare.'

'Sorry.'

'Don't apologise,' he snapped. 'What do you have to apologise for? How is this in any way your fault?' He stopped, then lowered his eyes. 'It's me that should apologise, for making you endure the rest of my family. I'm so angry with my mother; I don't know how she can just stand there and say those things, especially with you sitting here.'

'To be honest,' said Emily, 'I'd rather she said it to my face than behind my back. I respect her for that, at least.'

He squeezed her hand and caught her gaze. 'I will never sign that annulment document; never.'

They pulled each other close and embraced, and she felt his arms round her back, holding her. She put her head onto his shoulder, her mind a blur of anxiety and hope. Daniel's response had been the only thing that had kept her going over the previous five days. If he had even shown the slightest sign of giving in to the demands of his parents she might have given up, but he had been bloody-minded in his loyalty to her. From the way his eyes pierced her, she was starting to believe he might love her, though he had never actually said the words to her. But she hadn't said the words either. Did she love him? She didn't know, but she didn't want to leave him.

After a few minutes he broke off the embrace and stood. He went over to a small cabinet and poured himself a gin as Emily watched.

'Do you want one?' he asked.

'No, thanks.'

He came back to the couch, but remained standing. 'We should go out to the villa; get away from Tara for a bit. It'll be quiet up there, at least until the end of the month, then the place'll be inundated with Reapers.' He glanced at her. 'I, uh, didn't mean anything by that.'

'Danny, it's fine. You don't have to watch your words with me. I know the kind of man you are, it was you who said to me before all this happened that you thought the Evaders were the same as everyone else.

I disagreed at the time, but now? What you said means a lot to me, you've no idea how much.'

He nodded. 'What do you think of the villa idea?'

'I don't know. It would be good to get away for a while, just me and you, but who knows what would be happening back here in our absence?'

'They can't do a thing without my signature.'

'Honestly, I wouldn't put it past your mother to forge your signature and file the forms the moment we left the mansion. Then the whole thing would be done, and we'd never know in time to lodge an appeal.'

He stared at the floor for a while. 'You're right. That's exactly what she would do. This is so stupid, I mean you were getting on fine with her before this. She liked you then, she must still like you now.'

'She's cut me off in her mind, as if I'm dead or something. She won't look at me, let alone address me directly. She must know what will happen to me if the annulment goes through. Under Taran law I'd have to go back to my parents' house until I was twenty-one.' She glanced out of the window. 'I'd run away to the Circuit before I did that. I mean it.'

'And I'd be right behind you.' He crouched down by her. 'No one is going to tear us apart, and if I don't sign, there's nothing they can do. If they cut off my inheritance and throw us out onto the street, then we'd work it out. We'd get jobs, and find somewhere to live. I love Pella, the old town, the harbour; imagine living there, or somewhere else if you wanted to, as long as we're together.'

She smiled. 'Pella would do, so long as there was a view of the bay.' She sighed. 'I want to kill Lord Chamberlain, I mean I actually want to watch his face as I push a knife into his heart. I've never wanted to kill anyone before, but now I think I'd happily go to jail for it.'

'Please don't. And besides, you wouldn't go to jail.'

'That's right. If I'd killed him six days ago, I would have got twenty years, but if I kill him today, then, as an Evader, I'd get a noose instead.'

'The City is rotten to the core.'

'Maybe you were right in Pella; maybe the place needs to burn before it can be reborn.' She glanced at him. 'Do you truly not care about being the Prince of Tara?'

He smiled. 'No.'

'You'd make a good prince, certainly a better one than the current occupant of the throne. The God-Queen must be blinded by family loyalty if she can't see what everyone else sees.'

'She might be encouraging him for all we know. What goes on in the royal quarters of the palace is beyond anything we can see. At least with Khora, the government didn't do all of its business in secret.'

'But then we could see all of her mistakes; she must have known that, and yet she chose to remain transparent. And now the Circuit is occupied by rebels, Jade is terrorising the Sanders, Dalrig is besieged, and the Reapers riot every day, all while Marcus hides in Maeladh Palace with his mother. The God-King could end this any day he wanted, so why is he remaining silent?'

'I think he's afraid of his wife. If it came to a fight between them, then she'd win.'

Emily frowned. 'Is it as simple as that? If the God-King allied with Prince Montieth, then he'd have someone as strong as the God-Queen on his side. Or maybe she'd kill them both, I don't know. No one's seen them in such a long time that nobody knows how strong they are any more.'

Talleta tapped on the door and entered. 'Ma'am, sir, Lord Nadhew has arrived and Lady Aurelian wishes you to join them in her study.'

Emily nodded. 'Thanks.'

They got to their feet as the servant left the room.

'I can't see what difference this is going to make,' Daniel said as they set off for his mother's study.

'He's meant to be a good lawyer, so I suppose if there's anything that can be done, he'll find it.'

He glanced at her. 'What would you want to happen? Do you wish you were a Roser?'

'You mean, as if this has all been a mistake? They got the wrong hospital, or the wrong baby? I don't know any more, Danny. What I thought I knew, about myself, about everything, has been turned upside down.'

'You're the same Emily you were six days ago.'

'Not according to Taran law.'

'Then Taran law is stupid.'

They entered the plush study. Oil lamps were burning from the walls, and the grey and wet weather was being hidden by a thick set of dark, velvet curtains that covered the bay window. Lady Aurelian was sitting by a low table in front of her large desk, and the lawyer was seated next her in an armchair.

'Ah, here you are. Sit. Lord Nadhew was telling me that he visited the palace last night.'

He nodded as Daniel and Emily sat side by side on a long couch. 'Yes, indeed, I was at the palace. A most frightful experience getting there in the rain, but I did manage five minutes with Lord Chamberlain in his office.' He frowned. 'He showed me the evidence. It's sound, I'm afraid. The two documents tie Mistress Emily here directly to the hospital in the Circuit where she was born. It seems her grandmother was the owner of the deception, as it is clear to me that Lady Omertia presumed she was getting a Roser baby. I spoke to her about it, and...'

Emily glanced up. 'You spoke to my mother?'

Nadhew nodded to her, and she felt relief that he was at least acknowledging her presence. 'Yes, I spoke to her. Your father wasn't present at the Omertia house when I visited, but I think I learned everything I needed to hear from the kind lady of the household. Obviously she was party to the original deception, however she showed no sign of knowing anything about how or where her own mother had procured the baby.' He glanced back to Lady Aurelian. 'It's clear-cut. From a legal perspective, there's nothing to be done.'

Lady Aurelian took a breath. 'Thank you for your efforts. I had little hope of discovering anything new, but I had to try.' She paused for a second, then raised her eyes to gaze steadily at Emily. 'I want you out of my house immediately. Daniel, you are to remain here. You will sign the annulment papers before Lord Nadhew leaves, so that he can take them directly to the Town Registrars today. It's a dreadful shame, but there we are.'

She stood.

Daniel shook his head. 'When will you believe me? I'm not signing anything.'

Lady Aurelian bit her tongue for a moment then turned back to Emily. 'I told you to leave. Please don't make me call the servants. You have an hour to collect some clothes, and then you will walk out of the side door. The fewer neighbours that see you the better. It's only a twenty minute walk back to your parents' house.'

Emily stayed where she was. 'I'll go if Daniel tells me to.'

'She's going nowhere,' he said. 'You'll have to throw me out too.'

Lady Aurelian paced the floor, her face switching between rage and determination. 'Don't make me do this, Daniel.'

'Throw me out, then. If you can't bear Emily to be here, then I don't want to be here either. Cut me off, cast me out; I'm not leaving her.'

His mother stopped pacing, and gazed at him, shaking her head. 'You foolish, foolish boy. You haven't thought this through, have you? And Emily, I'm surprised at you; I thought you had a legal mind?'

She frowned. 'What do you mean?'

Lady Aurelian smiled at her. 'I haven't paid the fine yet.'

Emily felt her hopes turn to dust. Her eyes began to well, but she forced the tears back as her hand curled into a fist.

'That's right,' Lady Aurelian went on; 'if I throw you both out, it's you who will be liable to pay the fifty thousand gold sovereigns to the Taran treasury. You have twenty-four days left in which to do just that, or Daniel will be going to jail. This is not a choice between staying together and separating; you will be apart whatever you decide to do. With that outcome being the case, would it not be better to spare him years in prison? That is, if you love him, which I seriously doubt.'

Emily stared back at her, her mouth dry.

'You disgust me, mother,' Daniel said. 'You'd rather I went to jail than see us together. Fine, I'd prefer to be in jail than have to live here any longer.' He stood, and reached out his hand for Emily. She took it, without really knowing what she was doing. Her dreams had been obliterated by his mother's words. If they left the mansion together, he would be arrested as soon as the debt became due, and the punishment for not paying debts in Tara was higher than it was for disobeying orders in the militia. Daniel could get five years, she realised as he led her away.

She could feel Lady Aurelian's eyes burning into her back as they went into the hallway. They turned, and went to their rooms on the floor below. Emily sat on the bed as Daniel closed and locked the door. He tucked the key into his pocket and came down to sit beside her. He took her hand, and they sat in silence as the rain hammered off the shutters.

To Emily's surprise, the rest of the afternoon passed peacefully. No one knocked on their door, and it was almost as if nothing had happened. Emily and Daniel had lain on top of the covers of the bed, his arms around her, but they had exchanged few words as the light in the room slowly faded. For hours, Emily listened for sounds outside the door to their rooms, but there was only silence. Then she heard the low noise of Daniel breathing, and she realised he was asleep. She gently lifted his arm and slipped off the bed. She turned and saw his eyes remained closed.

'Danny?'

Nothing. She walked to the dresser and sat, gazing at her reflection. There must be something she could do. She imagined breaking into the palace, finding the office of Lord Chamberlain, and burning the two pieces of evidence that had transformed her into an Evader. She shuddered. She was an Evader, and the destruction of the documents wouldn't change that. An Evader. 'I, Emily Aurelian, am an Evader,' she repeated to herself.

She blinked. She didn't feel any different, but at least her initial revulsion had started to fade. If that was who she truly was, she needed to accept it, and the sooner she did, the better. She turned back to gaze at Daniel. He looked peaceful, despite the troubles she had seen in his eyes. She couldn't let him go to prison. If they left together, they could share twenty-three days side by side, and then she would go to Lady Aurelian and tell her she was leaving for good. She would go down onto her knees and beg her to pay the fine, and then run as far away as she could. The Circuit would do; the place that Roser parents used to frighten their children. *If you're bad they'll come and take you away to the Circuit.*

Her parents had said that to her often, but she recalled that her grandmother had never done so. Her grandmother had always told her she was special; why hadn't she told her the truth? All those lessons she had put her through, the training; it must have been for something. Again, she pushed away the tears that threatened to overwhelm her. She had no one she could depend on apart from Daniel; they were on their own.

She stood and went to the bathroom; the humidity making her want to feel some cool water over her skin. She went in and closed the door, then turned on the cold tap, She placed her hands under the stream of water, letting them cool down, then leant and splashed some onto her face.

She heard a noise from the bedroom, and smiled as she patted her face with a towel. She wanted to speak to Daniel, to tell him that she wouldn't let him go to jail, and to tell him she loved him. She paused. She loved him. She felt joy for the first time in a while as she realised it was true. She smiled and opened the door.

Daniel was lying asleep where she had left him.

Odd, she thought, then a hand went over her mouth. Her arms were grabbed and pulled behind her back as she tried to cry out. Three men, wearing hoods and masks and dressed in black, were inside the room. She struggled in their grasp, and tried to kick out, but they held her firmly, and, without making a sound, they carried her out of the bedchamber. The hallways of the mansion were silent and deserted, but a light was coming from under the door of Lady Aurelian's study as Emily was dragged past it. They came to a small hall by the side entrance and Emily was pushed to the ground, with a knee shoved down onto her back to keep her still. Her wrists were bound with cords, and a thick gag was placed round her mouth, the hand finally coming free from her face. She tried to see what was happening, but her head was being held against the cold floor as more cord went round her ankles. She struggled and writhed, but the three men were too strong.

She tried to breathe, but the gag was making it difficult, and she felt a sheer panic overtake her mind. All rational thought of what was happening fled her, and she retreated into a dark space in her head, her body continuing to struggle, but her mind frozen. She felt a rough blanket cover her, and then she was picked up by two of the men. The third opened the side entrance to the mansion, and they carried Emily outside, where she felt the cold rain hit her face. She blinked, and saw a wagon parked in the driveway. The third man climbed up on to the driver's bench, as the other two lifted Emily up and laid her down on the bottom of the wagon. They jumped up, and squeezed on the seats on either side of her, one placing his boot on her back.

A whip cracked, and the wagon moved over, the sound of the wheels crunching over the driveway lost to the wind and rain. They pulled out onto Princeps Row, and the wagon turned to begin heading down the steep hillside towards the rest of Tara.

The third man turned from where he was holding the reins. 'Good job, lads. Perfect.'

One of the others laughed. 'Craziest job ever, kidnapping a girl from her own house. I was sure that guy was going to wake up, but he didn't. Does that mean we get double, boss?'

'That was the deal; double if he stays sleeping through the whole thing, so I'll be having words with our employer if they try to renege.'

Emily felt the wagon tilt forward as it began to descend the steep slope. Her arms were already aching, and the skin on her wrists felt raw from where the cords were biting. She tried to move her head, but the only result was that the man pushed his boot down more heavily onto her back, pinning her to the floor of the wagon.

'She's trying to squirm free,' he laughed.

'I know how to fix that,' growled the other.

'None of that,' said their boss from the driver's bench. 'We were told not to beat her unless we had to.'

'And who says we don't have to, boss? Maybe she put up a fight?'

'No. I'm not endangering our payday just because you want to punch her. The goods are to remain unmarked if possible, got it?'

The wagon levelled off, and picked up speed, the driver's whip flashing out onto the backs of the ponies. The rain was hammering down on the canvas roof of the wagon, and Emily felt the dampness seep up from the floorboards where she lay.

The men in the back quietened as they passed the bright lights of an open tavern, and Emily caught glimpses of Tarans laughing and drinking through the tall glass windows. A desperate hope that one of them might see her flitted through her mind, but in a moment they had left the tavern behind, and the wagon turned for the harbour.

Where were they going? She peered through the worn slats of the wagon as she saw the masts of the boats tied up along the quayside. Water was streaming down the wide gutters and the wheels were splashing through thick puddles as they slowed and drew to a halt.

The driver jumped down, leaving the other two men in the back.

There was silence for a moment, then she felt rough hands grasp her face and turn it.

'What are you doing?' said the first man.

'Just taking a look at her. I never got a chance in the house. Malik's ass, she's pretty. I can think of better things to do with her than sell her to the Blades.'

'You heard what the boss said.'

Emily looked up at the man who was pawing her, and saw nothing but hatred and contempt for her in his eyes. She was nothing to them, just a victim, or 'goods' as their boss had referred to her. Her mind started looking back on what had happened, for the first time. The men had come into the room she shared with Daniel; they must have known where she would be. She tried to deny it to herself, but there was only one possible explanation. Lady Aurelian.

Daniel would wake up alone, and think she had run away. After that, how long could he hold out on signing the annulment papers? She imagined his mother feigning sympathy and concern, telling him that Emily couldn't have loved him, not if she could run away, and there was only one thing he could do; sign, and end it.

Tears welled in her eyes, and the man laughed, probably thinking that she was crying in reaction to his hand on her face.

'Look at her. I think she's finally realised what's happened. It's all over for you, Evader bitch; no more tricking your way into the houses of your betters.'

Their boss appeared at the back of the wagon. 'It's done,' he said. 'Carry her down to the boat.'

The two men each took an arm, and hauled Emily off the back of the wagon, the rain hitting her as the wind gusted along the harbour front. A large ship was docked by the pier where Duke Marcus had arrived in Balian, and a standard with crossed swords was fluttering from the mast. The cords by Emily's ankles were cut, and she was pushed along, her arms gripped. She was led to a line of others who were standing by the pier. Most had their wrists tied, though some were in chains, and several had been beaten.

A Blade officer was walking up and down the line, while others stood around, their crossbows ready. He waited until Emily had been pushed into place, then nodded. 'Is this the lot?'

A Taran official dressed in the uniform of the palace stepped forward. 'Yes. Twenty fresh criminals for the Bulwark, just as agreed.'

The Blade frowned. 'And not one of them looks like they can fight. Damn greenhide fodder, that's what you're giving me.' He gestured to a group of soldiers. 'Get them on board. We're leaving.'

Blades clustered round the line of prisoners, and Emily was shoved along, her feet stumbling over the coils of ropes lying on the pier. She was pushed towards the gangplank, the prisoner in front of her limping and bleeding from an injury to his leg. She looked for a way to escape, but with her arms tied, even if she managed to jump into the water, she would drown. She turned her head, and caught a last glimpse of the three men who had taken her from the Aurelian mansion. One was smirking, and he waved at her as she was shoved up the gangplank.

The prisoners were led onto the deck, and then down a set of narrow stairs and into the hold. Blades lined them up against both walls, then made them sit, their bows trained upon them. The officer came down and joined them, as the Blades went round, attaching each prisoner to a set of shackles.

'You may not realise it yet,' the officer said, his gaze taking in the twenty prisoners in the darkness of the hold, 'but, as of this moment, you are Blades.'

Emily was sitting at the end of one of the lines, and she felt someone grab her left arm. Her sleeve was ripped off, and a woman in Blade uniform crouched by her. Emily tried to speak to her, but the gag was making it impossible. She watched as the woman began applying ink to her skin, as another Blade held her arm steady.

The woman glanced at the officer. 'Which unit are they joining, sir?'

The officer turned to her. 'The Auxiliary Work Company; for all of them.'

'Yes, sir.' She reached up and pulled the gag from Emily's mouth. 'Can't have you choking to death on the journey.'

Emily gasped, her breath coming quickly. 'Are we going to the Bulwark?'

'We are that, little miss,' the woman said.

Emily felt pain in her upper arm as the woman punctured her skin with the needle, and blood trickled down to her elbow.

'The officer said the Auxiliary Work Company. What's that?'

The woman glanced up at her and grinned. 'That's just the posh name for the Rats.'

'The Rats? Who are they?'

'Oh, you'll see, little miss; you'll see.'

CHAPTER 24

BEYOND THE WALLS

A rrowhead Fort, The Bulwark, The City – 6th Amalan 3420

'Corporal Jackdaw, on your feet!'

Maddie pulled herself up, her raincoat trailing over the mud. 'Yes, sir.'

The officer glanced at the small group of Rats, all of whom were under Maddie's authority. She had kept her rank as corporal, and had found herself as one of the only promoted Blades in the Auxiliary Work Company.

'Is this your work-team, Jackdaw?'

'Yes, sir.'

The officer stared at them with derision and shook his head. 'What a pathetic bunch. Malik save us if we're relying on you lot to protect us from the greenhides.'

'Do you think he will, sir?'

'What?'

'Do you think Malik will come and save us, sir?'

He stared at her. 'And in one moment, I realise why you were sent here.'

'Thank you, sir.'

He shook his head and turned to a soldier. 'Open the gate!'

The door in the outer wall was swung open, and the Rats piled out into the torrential rain. Maddie didn't try to direct them; they had all been in the Rats longer than she had, and most of them ignored any orders she gave. To their left and right, small squads of the Wolfpack were deploying by the moat, the rain hammering off their shields and helmets.

Maddie watched them. At least they were armed, she thought. The Rats had nothing but their tattered uniforms. Several of the Auxiliary Work Company dragged the foldable crane out of the gate with them, and they set it up next to the moat. Maddie jumped up onto the moat wall and gazed out into the distance. The heavy, dark clouds overhead were as thick as they had been for days, and she could see nothing move on the plains in front of the Great Walls. She glanced down. The moat was full, its murky waters a foot below the lip at the top, and the Rats had a bridge in place within minutes. The Wolfpack ran over it, their boots pounding on the wooden boards. Rats followed behind, carrying blocks of stone, and bags of tools. They set them down by the edge of the moat, where a huge chunk of the retaining wall had been destroyed by a falling boulder. Maddie remained by the crane as they got to work, clearing the ruined area, and beginning to fit the replacement blocks. The rain had churned the area within minutes, and Maddie felt her uniform soak through to her skin. It was getting warmer, and sweat mixed with the rain as it trickled down her back.

This was the easy part, she told herself. Greenhides were appearing ever more frequently, but there would be no full scale attack while the rains continued. She glanced back at the solid walls of Arrowhead Fortress. Somewhere in there was Blackrose, walled up and starving. She wished she knew exactly where on the walls to look, as if by knowing she might somehow be able to make it better. At that moment, she might only be fifty yards away from the dragon, but it might as well be a hundred miles.

She helped move the crane out of the way of the bridge, pushing it on its small wooden rollers to the side to allow the traffic to move back and forth quicker. She was getting better at handling the crane, and after watching the others knew how to extend it and fold it away. The other Rats never told the new recruits how to do anything, as if their lives were worth less than those who had been serving in the unit the longest.

She stood back as a member of the Wolfpack jumped down from the bridge.

Maddie wiped the rain from her face. 'Hey!' she shouted to the woman. 'I recognise you.'

The woman turned, her armour and helmet dripping water down her. 'What?'

'Your name's Quill. I'm Maddie Jackdaw; I used to know Corthie.'

The woman frowned at her, then continued on her way. Maddie raised a finger, but Quill, if that was who the soldier had been, had already disappeared into the rain.

'Not very friendly,' Maddie muttered under her breath. She leaned against the moat wall, resigning herself to the rain, the water streaming down her hair and face. She watched the slow progress of the masons as they repaired the edge on the opposite side of the moat. This was her eleventh outing as a Rat in six days. They had all been in daylight, but she knew they would switch to nights as soon as summer began. Her mind drifted as she imagined herself in a warm bath, or curled on her old bed in the lair with a heap of blankets wrapped round her. Nothing about her new life seemed real, and a small part of her would wonder where she was each morning when she awoke, just before the crushing wave of reality struck her.

She wondered if her family knew what had happened to her. Would Kano have bothered to send a letter? She doubted it. Hilde was in hospital, the gate sergeant was stuck in the Circuit, and Corthie was gone; there was no one else who knew what she did, or where she had worked that could tell her family. Some of the staff who looked after Buckler were aware of her, but none knew her background or history. Would Buckler know something was wrong?

She glanced at the other Rats by the crane. Each was tensed, their eyes on the open plains beyond the thin cordon of Wolfpack soldiers.

Maddie tried to copy them, but her attention drifted again, and she watched the rain splashing into the moat.

'Greenhides!' yelled someone, and everyone started moving at once.

Maddie squinted into the distance as the Rats by the moat's edge packed their tools away. The Wolfpack started to retreat, and the first boots thumped off the bridge.

'Get the crane ready,' shouted a Wolfpack officer as he jumped down.

Maddie and the others shoved the crane back over to the bridge, the rollers slipping in the thick mud. With her head down, she heard a scream rise up. She lifted her gaze and saw a mass of greenhides pour across from the right. Claws ripped across the back of a fleeing Rat, and the greenhides charged into the Wolfpack. The bridge filled, with Rats and soldiers all trying to cross at once, as the greenhides cut their way closer to the edge of the moat.

'Lift the bridge!' cried the officer, and Maddie jumped up onto the wooden planks. One of the Rats threw her the end of a rope, and she raced down the side of the bridge, dodging the bodies hurtling the other way. She crouched down, attaching the rope to a metal hoop, and the bridge started to lift. Maddie stared at the remaining Rats and soldiers on the other side. Some were still clambering up onto the bridge as it rose higher, but others behind them were succumbing to the greenhides. A claw swung, and a man's head was sliced off where he stood. The bridge jerked and swung, and it spun around, a dozen Rats and soldiers still holding on as it juddered over the moat. On the far bank, the greenhides were ripping the last survivors to shreds as Maddie and the others watched from the swaying bridge.

'Swing it back!' cried the officer.

'It's too heavy!' yelled one of the Rats. 'There are too many people on it.'

A greenhide leaped up from the side of the moat as the bridge swung over the water. It hit the side of the bridge, its claws tearing through the planks and knocking Rats into the dark waters below. The arm of the crane began to bend under the weight as the others on the bridge panicked. Maddie was shoved aside, and she slipped, her hand gripping onto the edge of the bridge as her legs fell over the side. The greenhide ripped through the others on the bridge, and bodies fell screaming to either side of Maddie, splashing into the moat by her feet. Maddie kept as still as she could as she dangled from the bridge. The greenhide had settled, and was eating one of the Rats it had killed, the blood dripping down between the planks

'Cut the bridge; let it go!' cried the officer from the bank closest to the walls.

'Hey!' Maddie cried, then quietened as she remembered the green-hide sitting a few feet from where her hands were clutching the side of the bridge.

A huge roar of flames erupted along the edge of the moat, and the greenhides screamed and ran as the fire enveloped them. Burnt bodies toppled into the water, and the greenhide on the bridge stood up and shrieked. Maddie glanced up, looking for Buckler as he swooped back down for a second pass. The surviving greenhides fled as another burst of flames blasted the edge of the plain. Crossbow bolts ricocheted off the side of the moat as the Wolfpack began shooting at the lone green-hide balancing on the bridge. Several bolts struck its thick back, and it howled in rage.

Buckler soared down again, heading right for the bridge, his jaws opening to deliver another blast of fire. At the last second he veered up, and one of his rear limbs struck the greenhide, sending it flying into the moat, its arms flailing as it sank. Buckler beat his great wings, hovering over the bridge, then lowered a forelimb, and plucked Maddie from where she was hanging. She cried out in terror as Buckler lifted her clear of the bridge and the crane, then he swept his wings out and carried her away, soaring upwards and away from the moat.

She screamed, though whether if was from fear or exhilaration, she couldn't tell. The wind and rain lashed her as the dragon ascended, the other Rats growing smaller as they left them behind. Buckler flew higher and higher, and then soared down to his eyrie. He hovered above it for a moment, then dropped Maddie. She fell a few feet and landed onto the wooden boards that made up the dragon's high platform. Buckler pulled his wings in and landed next to her.

She stared at him as the rain poured down her face. 'Thanks.'

He tilted his head. 'Dragons do not leave riders to die.'

She nodded as Buckler peered down into the fortress forecourt.

'They'll be wondering where you are,' he said.

'I doubt it; I'm a Rat now. Our lives aren't worth much.'

Buckler turned his gaze to her. 'Tell me what happened; tell me how you came to be a Rat, Maddie Jackdaw. Why has the red gate in my lair been walled up?'

'Blackrose refused to bow before Kano.'

'That obstinate fool. I've given up trying to persuade her to do what's right. I'm guessing you angered Kano, and got yourself thrown into the Rats?'

'You know Kano.'

'Yes, unfortunately.'

'There's more. Kano wanted Blackrose to burn down the Circuit.'

Buckler said nothing for a long moment, his eyes on Maddie. 'He has never asked me to do such a thing.'

'What would you say if he did?'

'I don't know. What has Kano decided to do with Blackrose?'

'Nothing. He's walled her up in her lair; he's leaving her there to starve to death.'

Buckler swung his head away.

'You can save her, Buckler.'

He laughed. 'Me? How? Burn down the lair? Smash through a wall? And why would I endanger my own life for someone who despises me so utterly? For I would be punished, make no mistake about that. Blackrose has been offered so many chances, yet she has spurned them all. No, Maddie Jackdaw, if this is the path she has chosen, then I will not interfere.'

Maddie folded her arms. 'I'm disappointed in you, dragon. Blackrose deserves better.'

'You dare speak to me like this? With one nudge I could push you from the eyrie to your death. Is this how you show gratitude to the one who just saved you?'

'I'm just speaking the truth. If it hurts, that's your problem. Now, get me down from here, please, if you've nothing else to say.'

'You shame me, human, when I have nothing to be ashamed of.'

'I hope it keeps you awake at night, at least until you change your mind.'

'That day will never come.'

Buckler beat his wings and lifted off the eyrie. His forelimbs came down and Maddie was grasped between them and carried upwards. He swooped down to the forecourt, dropped her onto the flagstones, then soared away without a word.

'You!' cried someone.

She got to her feet and turned to see an officer approach.

'Rats are not supposed to be up here.'

She squinted at him. 'Did you not just see that big, red dragon drop me off? Malik's ass, how did you ever become an officer?'

He stared at her, mouth open. 'You can't talk to me like that.'

'I just did. What you going to do; send me to the Rats?'

She walked off before he could reply. As she hurried along, she cast a glance towards the entrance to Blackrose's lair. The door and windows had been sealed up with blocks of stone, cemented into place. You could still tell where the door had been, but over time the contrast would fade, and eventually, no one would know there had ever been an entrance there.

The underground barracks for the Rats was accessible from the Wolfpack Tower, so she headed to the common room. A few soldiers were sitting about drinking, and she saw Quill again, chatting to a few other members of the Wolfpack.

She walked over to the table. 'Hello.'

One of them turned to her. 'What are you doing up here? Rats live downstairs.'

Maddie glanced at him. 'Shut up, you cretin. Hey, Sergeant Quill, you were rude to me outside the walls today; how come?'

Quill frowned. 'I have no idea who you are, and many folk come up to me to ask about Corthie. Honestly, I can't be bothered dealing with them.'

'But I'm not one of those folk who followed him about like a puppy; I actually knew him.'

'Oh yeah? How many times did you speak to him, then?'

'I don't know; lots. My name's Maddie Jackdaw; does that mean anything to you?'

She shook her head.

'So he didn't tell you about me? Interesting. Well, you can be as rude as you like to me in here, but when we're out beyond the walls, I expect a little courtesy.'

One of the other soldiers started to laugh. 'That's you told, Sergeant.'

Quill glared at her. 'Get lost, Rat.'

Maddie put her hands on her hips. 'When Corthie comes back, I'm going to tell him you were awful to me. I just thought you should know.'

She turned on her heels and strode away, heading for the back stairs that led down to the level where the Auxiliary Work Company lived. She opened a door, and started to descend. When she was a few steps down, she heard the door above her open again.

'Wait.'

She glanced up. 'Yes, Sergeant Quill? How can I help you?'

'What did you mean back there, "when he comes back"? Are you delusional? Are you one of those Redemptionists?'

'No and no. And why should I tell you what I mean when you were so rude to me?'

Quill walked down a few steps until she was level with Maddie. 'You don't understand,' she whispered. 'I can't speak about Corthie any more, not in public. Everyone here knows I was close to him, and when they found out he was a traitor I got a hard time, for months. I even got questioned by Kano, which was a nightmare; I thought he was going to kill me at one point.' She lowered her face. 'I'm sorry. I mean, if you actually knew him, then I'm sorry for the way I spoke. Now tell me, please; do you know anything?'

'Alright, are you ready? Corthie didn't kill Princess Khora, it was Kano. And Kano made such a mess of things that someone got Corthie out, alive, and sent him to Tarstation.'

Quill shook her head. 'These are just rumours; I've heard them all before. If that's all you've got...'

'My source was excellent.'

'Yeah? Who?'

'I can't say.'

'Come on. I trusted you just now, when I told you about why I couldn't talk about Corthie in public. If I'm going to see you every day out there beyond the walls, then you're going to need to trust me too.'

Maddie pursed her lip. In truth, although she had seen Quill around Corthie many times, she didn't know how much the ex-champion had trusted her, or even if they really had been close friends.

She made a decision. 'Lady Aila.'

Quill's mouth opened. 'Oh.'

'You knew about her?'

'Her and Corthie? I suspected, let's put it that way. She saved his life in the Circuit, by jumping in front of him and taking three crossbow bolts to her midriff. After, they acted like it was nothing, but I saw the way they looked at each other.' She smiled. 'And she confirmed the rumours as being true?'

'I saw her in Auldan when I was posted there.'

Quill's smiled broadened. 'Thank you. This news makes my heart swell.' She sat on the step, and held her head for a moment. 'Can I ask, how do you know him?'

'I can't tell you, sorry. If Corthie kept it secret, then I think I should too.'

'What? After all that, you're going to keep it from me?'

'I'm, eh.. involved with a dragon, that's all I can say.'

'Wait a minute, were you the Rat who Buckler rescued today?'

'Yes. I've just been speaking to him up on his eyrie. We had a bit of a row, actually.'

Quill laughed. 'Alright, Maddie Jackdaw, I'd better be heading back upstairs.' She stood. 'I'll see you next time we're out.'

Maddie watched her disappear up the stairs, then started descending again, until she reached a long hallway where the Rats had their living quarters. She headed to the room she shared with eleven other Rats. She dreaded opening the door, wondering how many of her room mates were still alive. They usually counted the Rats as they came back in through the outer walls, and in the confusion at the moat, she didn't know what had happened, or who had been killed.

She swung the door open and got a surprise to see every bed occupied apart from her own. Then she squinted, realising that several of the faces were different. She did a quick head-count. Four of the room's occupants were new.

'Hey, Maddie,' called out one of her team. 'Did you enjoy flying?'

Maddie beamed. 'Did you see that? Whoosh! Buckler came swooping in for me, and whee! I was away.'

'I certainly heard you screaming.'

'Well, you know, I was startled. One minute I was clinging onto that damn bridge with my fingernails, and the next I was hundreds of feet up in the air. Had a nice little chat with the dragon after that up on his eyrie. Did I ever tell you I was friends with Buckler?'

Half of the team laughed. She turned to the new group. 'And who's this lot?'

'Reapers,' said the Blade who had spoken before. 'A couple of shipments came in from Auldan this morning.'

Maddie shook her head. 'At this rate, there will be hardly any Blades left in the Rats. Anyway, I'd better go and let the major know I'm alive; I just thought I'd see you guys first.'

She walked back out and headed along to the commander's office, passing the kitchens and the Rats' common room along the way. She knocked on the major's door and waited.

'Enter.'

She walked in. The major's office was one of the few on the lower level that had a window, and the grey light from outside was filtering through. The commander was sitting at a desk, while a young woman was in a chair on Maddie's left, her face bruised.

'Corporal Jackdaw,' said the major; 'you made it back in one piece I see?'

'Yes, sir. Buckler dropped me off in the forecourt, and I walked down.'

The major chuckled. 'Funniest thing I've seen in a while, and at least it's given the others something to smile about. We lost eleven today, the worst tally in a while, and with summer coming up, it's only going to get worse.'

'Yes, sir.'

'One of those lost today was Sergeant Carten. As you're one of the few in the company that came in with a rank, I'm making you sergeant to replace him.'

'You're joking, right?'

'No.'

'But I've only been a corporal for five months, sir, and not a very good one at that.'

'I can only work with what I've got, Sergeant. And the others seem to like you.'

'But they don't do what I tell them, and they know much more about how everything works round here than I do. I mean, sir.'

'Then learn fast.' He paused for a moment. 'There's something else I need from you, Sergeant.'

Maddie groaned. 'There's more, sir?'

'Yes.' He glanced at the young woman sitting silently by the wall. 'This new recruit here, she's going to need watching.'

'Why? Is she trouble?'

'You could say that. She's liable to be lynched, and I don't want that happening. She's already been beaten up twice since she arrived, and I had to call more soldiers down to pull her attackers off. She can swing a fair punch herself, mind you; she went down fighting.'

Maddie glanced at the woman. Despite the bruises on her face, and her cut lip, her eyes shone with defiance.

'Why does everyone want to attack her?'

The major frowned, then turned to the woman. 'Tell the sergeant your name.'

The woman glanced at Maddie. 'My name is Emily Aurelian.'

Maddie winced at her accent. 'Oh dear. Yes. I get it. By Malik's sweaty crotch, what's a Roser aristocrat doing in the Rats? Someone somewhere's made a terrible mistake.'

'Apparently not,' said the major. 'I presumed so at first, and checked the paperwork; it's all in order. What I'm going to tell you now is confidential, Sergeant, so think of it as a test of trustworthiness. Miss Emily here, or Private Emily as we shall call her from now on, is guilty of a deception. Apparently she's an Evader posing as a Roser, who managed to infiltrate one of the top families in Tara.'

'Wow,' said Maddie, nodding. 'Well, I guess if you're going for larceny, you may as well aim for the top.'

The woman glared at her but said nothing.

'She's in your team now, Sergeant,' said the major; 'make sure she doesn't get killed, at least, not by one of us.'

Maddie frowned. 'Thank you, sir.'

Emily stood, and Maddie escorted her out of the office.

'Can you believe that?' Maddie said as they started to walk back down the long hallway. 'Sergeant? What a joke. None of the Rats listen to me; I've only been here six days for Malik's sake!'

Emily glanced at her. 'You've only been here six days?'

'Yup. The worst six of my life. So far. Being in the Rats is just as bad as you've heard it is.'

'I'd never heard of the Rats before coming here.'

'No? Weird. So, if you're a cunning Evader infiltrator of the rich and famous, why don't you lose the accent? It's not going to do you any favours down here.' She shook her head. 'Though it's bad that you got beaten up for it.'

Emily looked her in the eye. 'I threw the first punch.'

Maddie laughed. 'Oh well, in that case... But what about the accent; can you not get rid of it?'

'I don't know; this is the way I've spoken all my life. What the major said in there is lies. I wasn't trying to infiltrate anywhere. Up until a few days ago I was a Roser. I mean, I thought I was. I had no idea I was an Evader.'

'Maybe it's best if you don't say too much, at least when we're with lots of people. I don't care how you sound, but... hang on; you didn't know you were an Evader?'

'I didn't know I was adopted. No one ever told me, and my family kept it a secret.'

'Malik's ass, that's terrible. Must have come as a bit of a shock to you. There are quite a few Evaders in the Rats, but most of them are scum, and I'd steer clear of them, especially if they hear you talk like that. Stay away from the Reapers too, they really hate the Rosers. And the Dalrigians. In fact, stay away from everyone.' She shook her head. 'I'll introduce you to a soldier I know tomorrow when we're out; she'll help watch your back.'

'What do mean "out"? Out where?'

'Beyond the walls. Oh, come on, please don't tell me that no one's told you what the Rats do?'

'No one's told me anything.' She halted in the corridor, not far from the room where Maddie's team stayed. 'We're going out beyond the walls?'

'Yes. That's what we do. Did you not hear the major say we'd lost eleven today?'

'I thought he was talking about losses from sickness or desertion.'

'Nope. All eleven were ripped to shreds and eaten by greenhides. I might have been one of them if the dragon hadn't whisked me away.'

Emily stared at her. 'There's a dragon here?'

'Yes, Buckler. He can be a pain in the ass, but he's alright. Do you know anything about the Bulwark?'

She shook her head. 'I studied history for years, but it was all about Medio and Auldan; the gods and the demigods. The Bulwark was hardly mentioned.'

'Typical,' muttered Maddie. 'For a thousand years we've protected the City, and you lot barely knew we existed.'

Emily shrugged. 'Sorry. I know now.'

'Yeah, now you're a Rat.' She opened the door to their room and strode in, Emily following her. Maddie pointed to one of the new faces. 'Hey, Reaper number three; you're out. Grab your things, and report to the quartermaster. Tell her there's no space in my team for you, and that you need to find another one.'

The man stared at her from the bed.

Maddie strode towards him. 'Go on, out. And, by the way, I'm a damned sergeant now, which means I can dish out punishment duties.'

The recruit got to his feet, picked up a bag, and walked from the room, glaring at Maddie and Emily as he passed.

Maddie pointed to the empty bed, which was next to her own. 'There you go. Do you not have a bag?'

Emily sat on the bed and shook her head.

'Hey,' called out one of the others. 'Are you really a sergeant, or were you just saying that to get him to leave?'

Maddie frowned. 'No, it's true.' She sat on her bed. 'Can you believe it?'

'And who's the new woman?'

Maddie glanced around the room. 'This is Emily Aurelian. If anyone has a problem with her, they'll have to come through me first, understand? If you touch her, I'll smash your teeth in, and then I'll get Buckler to pick you up and throw you to the greenhides.'

One of the younger Hammer recruits raised his hand.

Maddie glared at him. 'What is it?'

'Did you say her name was Aurelian?'

'Yeah, so?'

'As in, Lord and Lady Aurelian, related to the Last Mortal Prince of Tara?'

Maddie frowned. 'What in Malik's name are you talking about?'

'Is she a Roser?' said someone else.

Emily stood. 'I am Emily Aurelian, married to Daniel Aurelian, the heir to the lost throne of Tara. Yes, I sound like a Roser. Yes, I sound like an aristocrat. But I'm a Rat now, like the rest of you.'

The Hammer youth's eyes widened. 'You're married to the heir?'

'Yes, well at least until he signs the annulment papers.' She sat back down on the bed, then stretched her legs down the covers, reclining.

Maddie watched her; she had guts. 'Alright team, introductions are over. Emily might sound like a posh aristocrat, but she's our posh aristocrat, and we're going to look after her. Maybe, if we're lucky, some of her sophistication might even rub off on you savages.' She glanced at her. 'Is there anything you're good at?'

Emily closed her eyes. 'Ask the three guys I knocked out in the common room.'

Maddie laughed. 'You know, I think I'm starting to like you.'

CHAPTER 25

MAKING CONTACT

G rey Isle, Cold Sea – 21st Amalan 3420

Corthie sat on the low bed. His eyes were on the grey light coming through the window shaft, but his thoughts were on Aila. The captain had been keeping him informed of every rumour that reached the Grey Isle, but there were contradictory accounts of where the demigod could be. Some swore she was still inside Greylin Palace, while others claimed she had been seen with a rebel group in the Circuit, which seemed unusual, since the same rebels had publically announced they were opposed to the entire Royal Family, and would execute any that fell into their hands.

Prince Marcus, or the duke, as every Dalrigian still called him, was still hunting her, which meant she had to be alive at least, and that knowledge, though not enough, did help ease Corthie's worries a little. He wondered if she still thought of him. If she believed him to be dead, then maybe she had moved on, after all, they had been apart for a longer period of time than they had known each other, and demigods anyway had a differing set of morals by which they lived. He needed to be prepared, just in case. If he made it back to the City and they were reunited, he had to be ready for disappointment; he had to expect it, otherwise he would be crushed if his dreams were out of touch with reality.

For a while, he had tried to stop thinking about her, but she had been present in his dreams most nights, haunting him. He could be dreaming about anything – the sea, the mountains, or the City, and he would turn and see Aila by his side, and it felt right. Then he would awaken and feel almost bereft again. It was unrealistic to hope that she felt the same. He was nineteen, while she had lived for nearly eight centuries. He frowned. She would still be living, centuries after his death; long after he had grown old and died.

'Are you wanting some breakfast?' said Achan.

'Leave him be,' said Yaizra; 'he's in one of his moods again.'

'I don't get it; he's the happiest guy I know.'

'It must be because he's had to look at your face for so long; that'd bring anyone down.'

Achan brought a bowl over to where Corthie was lying. 'Here,' he said, setting it down next to him. 'Look, mate, we're all feeling helpless. We won't be stuck here forever. Remember that the captain said all those boats arrived in the harbour yesterday? They must be here to take the Blades away, and then we'll be able to move.'

Corthie grunted. He had heard it all before. For over a month the captain had been promising that their departure was only a few days away, and yet they were still trapped in the claustrophobic caverns, idling away the hours as the rain lashed the island day and night.

'Anything I can help you with?' Achan said.

Corthie eyed him. 'Not unless you happen to have a Quadrant hidden in your back pocket.'

'A what?'

'Never mind.'

'He's rambling about his old life again,' said Yaizra. 'All this time that you've been trying to get Corthie to join your revolution, and all he wants to do is go home. Ain't that right, big lump?'

He glanced at her. 'It's one of the things on my list.'

Achan looked a little hurt. 'Is that true? I thought you cared about the folk in the City?'

'It's possible to care about more than one thing at once.'

'So you'll help us, and then go home?'

'I'll help you until I'm able to go home.'

Yaizra laughed. 'See?'

'But what about the Hammers and the Scythes?' Achan said. 'And the Evaders? I thought you felt the same way about slavery as I do.'

Corthie felt his temper rise. 'What do you want me to say, Achan? I was brought to this world against my will; I fought for it, defending the Great Walls, and this is how I'm rewarded? Part of me is tempted to say "Screw the City", let the greenhides ravage it; let it burn to the ground. And even if I could help, we're stuck on this damn island. We're missing the revolution; it's happening right now, without us. Honestly, if given the chance, I would leave today, if it weren't for...' He trailed off, then turned to gaze back out of the window.

'Weren't for what?' said Yaizra.

'Nothing.'

'That wasn't nothing,' she said. 'Come on; if it weren't for what? How much you love being with me and Achan? No, I doubt that. This cavern's been simmering with misery and frustration since we got here; and frankly I'm surprised all three of us are still alive. Is it revenge you're after? You want to kill Marcus?'

He shrugged. 'Aye, I could quite happily kill him.'

'But that's not it, is it?' she said. 'You don't strike me as someone obsessed with revenge. Come on, Holdfast; tell us. Wait, I think I can guess. I remember how interested you were in news about that demigod, the one Prince Montieth was holding hostage. Is that it? Are you in love with Lady Aila?'

Corthie said nothing.

'I knew it!' said Yaizra, clapping her hands together.

'Nah,' said Achan, looking wary. 'Corthie's too smart to fall for one of *them*. The Royal Family are all so cold and arrogant; they hate mortals, despise us. The Evaders are right; the City would be better off without them.'

Yaizra picked up her bowl and came over to where Corthie was lying. 'Have you slept with her?'

'None of your business.'

She grinned. 'But you're not denying that you love her. Wow, so this is what's been driving you crazy all this time? Corthie-big-lump and a demigod. Does she love you, or is it all one-way?'

Corthie glanced at her, seeing the light in her eyes. 'Why do you care?'

She laughed. 'We've been stuck in a cave for a month, and I thought we'd run out of things to talk about ages ago, and now I find out this little nugget of news? I want to hear every last detail, right from the moment you met, until the last time you saw her.'

Achan groaned. 'I don't want to hear about any of this.'

'You don't have to worry,' said Corthie, 'because I'm saying nothing more.'

'Don't be an asshole!' cried Yaizra. 'I'm not going to stop pestering you until you tell me, so you may as well start now.'

There was a noise as Captain Hellis walked into the large cave, and Corthie smiled at Yaizra.

Achan stood. 'Good morning, Captain.'

'Good morning, how are you all?'

'Same as yesterday,' said Yaizra, her grin vanished.

The captain sat on a crate. 'Usual routine. Bad news or good news first?'

'The bad,' said Corthie.

The captain nodded. 'Those boats that arrived yesterday; they weren't to take the Blades away, they actually brought another two hundred of them to the island.'

Yaizra's eyebrows rose. 'But there's only nine days until summer.'

'Yes,' the captain said, nodding; 'they're cutting it fine, indeed. It seems they want to have one final sweep of the island before giving up, but they've also started to arrest half of the town. They believe that some of the locals know where you're being hidden, and they're threatening to drag them off to jail, or send them to the Bulwark as greenhide fodder, unless someone tells them where you are.'

'And is someone likely to tell them?' said Achan.

'Only my husband and I know where you are,' she said, 'but, a few others know that we know.'

'So it's only a matter of time before they get here?'

'Which leads me onto the good news,' she said. 'I've got us a boat. We're leaving tomorrow.'

Corthie sat up, his eyes wide. 'Tomorrow?'

The captain laughed. 'I thought that'd please you. Remember the emergency plan I had bubbling away in the background? Well, I think that the Blades rounding everyone up qualifies as an emergency. Once my name is known to the Blades, it won't be safe for me here, either.'

'So you'll be coming along?'

She nodded. 'Indeed. It might be a while before I can return, depending on how things go. And, between looking after you three, and paying for this new ship, I'm out of money.'

'Sorry,' said Achan, 'and thanks for everything.'

'It's fine, I wasn't blaming you. The time has come to pick a side, and I'll not be bowing before Duke Marcus. This time, the Gloamers are going to fight on the right side of the civil war; no more pandering to the damn Rosers.'

Corthie nodded. 'What are the arrangements?'

'The ship will be leaving before dawn tomorrow. It'll sail out from the harbour, after being thoroughly checked by the Blades first, of course, then it'll tack iceward close to the cliffs. There's a cavern that opens out onto the sea, and I've got rope ladders ready. We climb down into a rowing boat, then get onto the ship, and we'll be away. All I ask is that you are here, and ready to go when I come and collect you.'

'This is great,' said Corthie.

'I would have preferred to wait until the Blades had gone, myself,' she said, 'but under the circumstances, this is the next best deal on offer.'

Corthie got up, restless energy surging through him. One more day. Less than that. By dawn they would be sailing away from the Grey Isle at last.

'I'll be off, then,' said the captain. 'I'll see you all tomorrow. An hour before dawn, alright?'

'Thanks,' said Achan. 'See you then.'

Corthie paced back and forward as she left the cavern, his head buzzing.

'Sit down,' said Yaizra. 'We've got hours to go yet. I mean, packing will take us no more than two minutes. We should try and get some rest.'

'Rest?' he said. 'All we've done is rest.'

A slight smile appeared on the corner of Achan's face. 'There's something else we could do to pass the time.'

Yaizra glared at him. 'No. No way. Get that thought out of your mind, little Hammer boy.'

He shrugged. 'I have a plan worked out. All we need to do is remove the toilet from the cell where the prisoner is being held, then we'll be able to climb up through the hole and rescue her. It'll be simple.'

Yaizra's face contorted into a mask of fury and intense irritation. 'Are you mad? You want to risk everything now that we know a boat's on its way for us?'

'We couldn't have done it before,' he said. 'We had to wait for this moment. That way, we can get the prisoner onto the ship.'

'And what would we tell the captain?'

'Who cares? Once we're all on board, it won't matter.'

She turned to Corthie. 'Tell him, Holdfast; for Malik's sake tell him we're not going to follow his idiotic plan.'

Corthie halted by the window and watched the rain for a moment. 'If we leave without trying to rescue her, then I think we'll always regret it.'

Yaizra cried out in frustration. 'You fools. You're on your own if you do this; I ain't helping you.'

'It'll be easy,' Achan said, 'but we'll need your assistance to lead us through the caverns. Or, you could tell us how your weird symbols work; or even draw us a map if you're absolutely sure you don't want to come along.'

'No,' she said, her face set firm. 'No way.'

'I can't believe I'm doing this,' Yaizra said as she squeezed through the hole in the tunnel floor.

Corthie dropped down after her, then reached up and took the lantern from Achan. He pointed the open shutter ahead of him, and saw the wide pipe continue into the darkness. Behind them, the small circle of sky was almost black, the thick clouds remaining into the evening. Achan lowered himself down, and Corthie passed him the lantern and loosened the mace on his back.

Yaizra glared at the two men. 'At the first sign of trouble, I'm out of here.'

Achan shrugged. 'You're used to leaving people behind.'

'I will punch you in the face, ya little Hammer asshole.'

'Quiet, both of you,' said Corthie. 'Let's just get this done.'

They headed along the pipe, keeping the light from the lantern low against the ground. They followed the bend round to the right, then slowed as they saw the tiny shafts of light seeping through from the floor above.

'It must be around here somewhere,' muttered Achan, as he searched along the edge of the pipe.

Corthie and Yaizra waited. As Achan kept looking, Corthie took a look through the grilles, until he came to the one where he could see the old prisoner. She was lying in the same place as when he had last seen her, writhing and groaning in agony, her shackles and mask still attached to her limbs and face. The blood trickling down her cheeks was fresh, and she was mumbling something over and over. What could she have done to deserve such a punishment? She looked too frail to hurt anyone, but perhaps she had been imprisoned for a terrible crime, committed long before he had set foot in the City.

It didn't matter, he told himself. The torture she was enduring was inhuman and if he could stop it, he would.

'I don't understand,' said Achan, his voice low. 'It should be here.'

'What are you looking for exactly?' said Corthie.

'A way to get under the prisoner's cell. There must be a pipe that connects her cell to this sewage outlet. Once we find it, we can go straight up to get her.'

Corthie turned to Yaizra.

'Why are you looking at me?' she said. 'For all I know, there could be a parallel pipe that runs under the other side of the passageway.'

Achan glared at her. 'But you said you'd explored all of these caverns and pipes.'

'And I've never claimed to have found one that goes under her cell.'

'Why didn't you tell us this before we left?'

'I tried to, but neither of you were listening, you were both so set on your little plan. In the end, I reckoned you would have to see for yourself before you'd believe me. There's no way to get her out, so we should take one last look to wish her all the best, and then get our asses out of here.'

'Forget it,' said Corthie. 'We're not leaving without her.'

'But there's nothing we can do, big lump.'

Corthie walked over to one of the shafts that led down from an empty cell above their heads. He reached up with his hands, and pressed them against the cut stone blocks that surrounded the shaft.

Yaizra frowned. 'Um, what are you doing?'

He glanced at her. 'Pass me your knife.'

'Why?'

'Why do you think? If I can loosen this mortar, I might be able the lift the slab.'

'Or it'll fall onto your head.'

He held out his hand. She sighed, and pulled her knife from her belt.

'Thanks,' he said, taking it. He rammed it up into the crack that ran between two blocks, powering his battle-vision as he did so. He pulled the blade through the ancient mortar, sending splinters and fragments of it spilling over his face and hair. He finished one side of a block, then began on the next.

'I'd stand back if I were you,' Yaizra said to Achan. 'Big lump's going to bring the whole damn ceiling down on us.'

Corthie gouged out another thick chuck of mortar, some of the stone coming away at the same time, sending dust down as well as the fragments. The rock over his head groaned, and he put his free hand up to support it, bracing his feet against the ground.

'Amalia's ass,' he heard Yaizra whisper. 'This is not going to be quiet.'

'Aye,' he said. 'We'll need to be quick. Get ready.'

The first stone block loosened and Corthie shoved the knife into his belt and used both hands to lower it, straining under the weight. He manoeuvred it as far as the top of his head, then threw it down in front of him, It landed with a great thud, cracking the bottom of the pipe and splintering into huge pieces. Corthie gazed up. He could see through to the empty cell above him, but the gap was still too narrow.

'One more, I think,' he said, taking the knife into his hand again.

He pushed the blade into the mortar of the next block along. A loud crack rang out, and he threw himself to the side as a dozen huge blocks all fell at once, making a thundering roar and clatter as they dropped six feet onto the ground. The echo resounded through the pipe for several seconds as Yaizra and Achan stared open-mouthed.

Corthie pulled himself to his feet. 'Oops.'

He looked up. Half of the floor of the cell above had collapsed into the pipe, the toilet included. He clambered up onto the pile the rock fall had created, and pulled himself into the cell.

'Be quick!' cried Yaizra. 'That noise will have woken the entire fortress.'

Corthie clambered to his feet, and edged round the great hole in the floor of the cell. He reached the door and pushed. It opened, and he puffed his cheeks in relief. He took a quick glance to either side, then stepped out into the passageway. He hurried to the cell opposite where the old prisoner lay mumbling, and pulled on the gate.

It was locked. 'Damn it.'

He gripped the bars with both hands and pulled with all his strength, but they were too strong. He took his mace from his back and held it up, trying to judge the angle he would need to strike the lock. A hand touched his leg and he looked down. The prisoner had stretched her arm out through the bars, and her fingers were brushing his boot. He lowered the mace and crouched next to her.

'Can you hear me?' he said.

Her mumbling stopped.

'We're going to rescue you; we're just trying to work out how.'

Her hand reached up and he glanced at it. She might have death powers for all he knew; maybe that was why she was being kept alone. He was immune to all mage powers that were sent through the air, but what would a physical touch do to him? But maybe she was just an old woman, desperate for any sign of kindness. He took his hand off the mace and pressed his fingers into hers. She gripped his hand, but he felt no powers from her.

The sound of approaching footsteps reached his ears and he cursed.

'I have to go; I'll be back soon,' he said, pulling his hand from the woman's grasp. He hurried up the passageway and went into the next cell along, keeping to the shadows behind the wall.

He heard a door open.

'Seems quiet,' said a voice with a Blade accent.

'That noise came from in here, I'm sure of it.'

Footsteps came up the passageway. 'The prisoner's still here.'

'Malik's ass!' cried the other voice. 'Look in here.'

'What?'

'The entire floor of this cell's collapsed. I knew this building wasn't safe; it's like two thousand years old or something. If we don't get off this miserable island soon I reckon the whole fortress will fall into the sea.'

'Yeah. I guess we'd better go and report it.'

'Should we move the prisoner?'

'Why?'

'In case the rest of the floor falls in.'

'Nah. Leave her. No one round here seems to know who she is anyway. There's no record of her in the books, and I don't want all the hassle that'll go with trying to explain to the commander that we've got a prisoner we know nothing about. Let's just forget what we saw. I mean, we'll be off this rock soon, whether we find the ex-champion or not.'

The footsteps faded away, and Corthie heard the door close again. He peered round the edge of the cell, and down the corridor. So the Blades didn't know who the prisoner was, he thought. It didn't mean much, considering that they had only been on the island for a few months, but it was strange that there were no records in the fortress about her. He glanced down at her again, then turned to the cell he had climbed up through and leaned over the edge.

'Hey,' he called out in a low voice.

Yaizra's face appeared through the broken floor.

'The soldiers have gone. I need a knife, or something that will get through a lock.'

'You snapped my knife breaking the ceiling,' she said.

'I thought you were supposed to be a thief? Can you not pick it?'

'I haven't brought all of my tools.'

Corthie suppressed a frown. 'Can you come up here and try?'

He stretched his arm down through the hole as she reached up, and he pulled her into the cell. She scrambled to her feet, then went to look at the lock on the cell door where the prisoner lay.

'It's completely rusted up,' she said. 'Even if we had the key it probably wouldn't open.'

Corthie swore, his impatience rising. 'I'm going to have to smash the door in.'

'No,' Yaizra hissed. 'Even if you manage it, she's still chained to the wall, in three places. I can probably get the shackles off; they look fairly simple compared to the door, but it'll still take me twenty minutes, at least. It might be time to give up.'

'No. There has to be a way. You need twenty minutes, aye?'

She shrugged. 'Half an hour to be on the safe side.'

'Right. I know what to do. I'll smash in the door, and you get to work. As soon as you've freed her, carry her down to the outlet pipe, and I'll follow later.'

'What do you mean "later"? Where will you be?'

'The noise will bring more guards; I'll hold them off.'

She stood to face him. 'No, Corthie, you can't do this. Our escape from Tarstation, then getting away from the western bank, it will have been for nothing if you get yourself caught now. Sometimes you just can't get what you want. Sometimes giving up is the only way.'

'I can't accept that. I told her I would get her out of here, and I will.'

'You told her? Corthie, she's demented with pain; look at her. She won't have understood a word of what you were saying.'

'I believe she did.'

'You believe? Right. You're an idiot, big lump. She could be a murderous criminal for all we know, and you're going to throw your life away for her?'

'I won't be throwing it away if we save her, and besides, I'm not going to get caught.' He picked up his mace from where he had put it down. 'Stand back.'

Yaizra shook her head and edged away.

Corthie crouched by the old prisoner and took her hand. 'There's going to be a loud noise; that'll be me smashing the door in, and then my friend is going to remove the chains and carry you out. Alright?'

The old woman squeezed his hand for a second, but it was so slight that he wondered if he had imagined it. He stood, and hefted the mace in both hands, feeling his battle-vision power thrumming through him, and filling him with strength. He glanced at the lock, then at the heavy end of the mace, and brought the weapon down as hard as he could. A clang of metal striking metal roared through the air as the end of the mace connected with the lock. The mace head shattered into pieces, but the lock remained. Corthie dropped the long handle, cursing. Yaizra stepped forward and pulled at the door. It moved, slightly.

'It's loose,' she said. 'Kick it, big lump; give it all you've got.'

Corthie raised a boot and slammed it into the lock. It gave way, the door grinding and squealing on its hinges. Yaizra yanked the bars, and the door swung free. She grinned at him, then frowned as the noise of voices and footsteps approached.

'And now you've got no mace,' she said.

He picked up the handle. 'No, but I have a big stick. Just get her free; I'll deal with the rest.'

Yaizra rushed into the cell and Corthie turned to face the end of the corridor. He hurried along it, reached the door and pulled it open. Outside was a stone hallway, with other doors, and a series of oil lamps were burning against the wall. At the end of the hallway a set of stairs climbed upwards. Corthie closed the door behind him, and stepped forward. Ahead of him, the first Blades were coming down the steps.

Corthie took a breath. Half an hour, he thought, then he gripped the handle in both hands and charged.

CHAPTER 26

INTO THE SNARE

O oste, Auldan, The City – 21st Amalan 3420

Aila glanced up from the book she was reading as Mona walked into the quiet study. She walked over to the dark windows and closed the shutters to the night sky, then glanced at Aila.

'It's done.'

Aila felt her heart start to race. 'It is?'

'Yes. I have sent the vision message to Prince Marcus; he's boarding a ship as we speak.'

'Was he... pleased?'

Mona frowned. 'He was surprised, at first. I told him everything that we had agreed upon, that you had changed your mind after being treated so badly by Prince Montieth, and by the rebels in the Circuit, and that you had realised your error. He asked if you loved him.'

Aila cringed. 'And what did you say?'

Mona sat down next to her. 'I told him it might be unrealistic to expect love so soon, but that you were open-minded about it. He replied that three hundred years was a long enough time, and got angry. He calmed when I told you were waiting here for him to collect you; he ceased the name-calling at once. He asked me to ensure you didn't leave the academy grounds, and then he informed me that he was on his way.'

Aila rubbed her face. 'Malik's ass, this is a terrible mistake.'

'You're doing a very brave thing, cousin. You may very well have saved the City single-handed. Every Blade involved in the siege of Dalrig, and all the soldiers out hunting for you, can now be reassigned back to their positions on the Great Wall in time for summer.' She took Aila's hand. 'And then, once you are alone with him in the wedding chamber, you can end the tyrant's misrule.'

'This is the part that worries me more than anything else,' she said. 'How will I find the courage to kill him? He's strong, almost as strong as Corthie, and he'll be suspicious. Even if he's blinded by what he thinks is love for me, someone will have warned him to be careful. The God-Queen will suspect me, surely.'

'The God-Queen can't read minds, and besides, she won't be coming here.'

'No, but what if Marcus drags me straight back to Tara? She'll be there, in Maeladh Palace.'

'Remember, I will help. I've put a link into your mind that will allow me to locate you easily; just as I have done with my son. All you need to do is focus your mind on me, and I will enter your thoughts. If Marcus is in the same room as you, I will then transfer my mind to his. I have the power to send him into a deep sleep, and you will have your opportunity. Take my brother's head from his shoulders, just to be sure, and then run.'

Aila put her elbows on the table and held her head in her hands. 'I can't do it.'

'It's too late,' said Mona; 'the game has begun.'

'We don't even know when I'll be alone with him. What if he wants a long engagement?'

Mona smiled. 'If you aren't married by the end of today, I will be very surprised, dear cousin. Marcus has desired you for so long, he'll not want to waste a single moment.' She tilted her head a little. 'I wonder what it is about you that has so bewitched him. You're pretty, and younger-looking than I remember, but you've never, ah, made much of an effort with your appearance.'

'It's nothing to do with how I look,' said Aila. 'It's because I'm the only one who's ever rejected him. His ego can't handle it. He wants me because I said no. I honestly believe that, if I gave myself to him, he'd lose interest in me the moment it was over.'

'You may be right. As his sister, I can only apologise to you for his behaviour. He was always a brute; always a bully, and my father indulged him.'

'What was it like having Prince Michael as your father?'

Mona frowned. 'It was different for me, because I was the only child out of my siblings who didn't have battle-vision or death powers. To my father, I was the useless child, the one he didn't need, and he barely spoke to me once I had been packed off to the Royal Academy, which was a blessing, to be honest. It was the only way I managed to stay out of the first Civil War. When my two sisters were slain by Princess Yendra I realised how lucky I was.'

'I watched your father die.'

'Yes, I know. It was a day of mixed emotions for me. I mourned him, but at the same time I knew that Yendra had done the right thing. And I mourned her death too, secretly, as did Khora.'

Aila snorted. 'Khora betrayed Yendra, right at the end of the war. How it ended was her fault; she tricked Yendra.'

Mona smiled. 'No.'

'What do you mean, "no"? I was there. I heard the reports that Khora was sending Yendra. Did you know that she was pretending to help the rebels?'

'She wasn't pretending.'

'Then why did she send a deliberately false report? She tricked us, right at the end.'

'Khora was too proud to tell you the truth, Aila. She didn't trick Yendra, it was my father. He had discovered that Khora was leaking secrets to Yendra, and so it was he who gave Khora the false information, knowing that she would pass it on to the rebels.'

Aila stared at her, and she felt her eyes start to well. 'No, but... why didn't she ever tell me that? You mean I hated her for centuries for nothing?'

'Khora never liked to look back; she had no place in her heart for regret. All that mattered to her was keeping the City together and trying to steer it safely into the future. At the end of the war, both Michael and Yendra were dead, and she had to rebuild. I advised her to tell you, but her pride got in the way. It was the same with the death of her twin sister, Princess Niomi. That wasn't Khora's fault either, but she took the criticism and the hatred that were flung her way, and kept silent, rather than put the blame where it was due, on Niomi. Her sister invited her to Icehaven for secret talks, and then betrayed her, and Khora barely escaped with her life.'

Aila wept, her head in her hands.

'Khora had no concern about how others perceived her,' Mona went on. 'A fine attribute, in certain situations, but one that left her almost friendless and alone at the end. She contacted me the evening before she died.'

'Did she?'

'Yes. I want you to know how happy she was.'

'Happy?'

'You had gone to her, of your own accord, and you had listened to what she had said. She loved you, cousin.'

Aila thought of every insult she had thrown at Khora. She had mocked her son's death, by joking about the Fog of Balian. She remembered Balian, and how she and a mortal warrior had killed him in front of his mother's eyes, only minutes before Yendra had slain Michael. Aila had been cruel and spiteful in her dealings with Khora for hundreds of years, and the woman had loved her?

Mona squeezed her hand. 'You are proving today that Khora was right about you. The task you are undertaking; she would be very proud, Aila; I wish she were here to see it.'

'Is that why you waited until now to tell me this? To steel me?'

'Partly. You needed to know, and now seemed like a good time.'

Mona got up and walked to a cabinet. She opened a bottle of brandy and filled a glass, then brought it back to the table where Aila was sitting.

'Drink this,' she said. 'I have a feeling you may need to be a little fortified today.'

'How long have we got before he gets here?'

'An hour, perhaps, depending on the winds in the bay, and if a boat was ready for him at this time of night.'

The door to the study burst open, and a man ran in.

'Mona,' he cried, 'I need to hide. I...' He stopped as his eyes fell on Aila.

'Naxor?' Aila yelled. 'What in Malik's name are you doing here?'

'Cousin Aila, I could ask you the same thing. And why are you looking so young?'

'Sit down, Naxor,' said Mona, 'and tell me your troubles.'

The demigod continued to stare at Aila. He seemed agitated, and sweat had formed on his brow. Instead of sitting, he strode to the cabinet and poured himself a brandy.

'Why are you here?' said Aila. 'I thought you were...?'

'On Lostwell?' he said. 'Don't worry, Mona knows about it. Mona knows most stuff. She was a good friend to my mother.'

'I have been acquainting Aila with the truth as regards that,' Mona said. 'Now, please answer her question, as I too was not expecting to see you again for some time. The last occasion you visited, you seemed to make it clear to me that you would not be returning any time soon.'

He sat, and downed half of the brandy in one gulp. 'I'm on the run.'

Mona frowned. 'From Lostwell?'

'Yes, unfortunately. Imagine, I'm a fugitive on both of the damn worlds I can travel to. If I knew how to work that damned device properly, I guess I could go anywhere, but I only know how to travel between there and here.'

'And who is pursuing you on Lostwell?'

He glanced up, and stared at Aila. 'The Holdfasts.'

'What?' said Aila. 'Corthie's sister?'

'His sister, his aunt, and one other. Three women, all with more powers than I possess. Two of them have battle-vision; the full range of vision powers to be honest, and the other one is even more dangerous. She can't fight, but she doesn't need to. Her powers can control anyone she wants; she can make them do things against their will, and she's immune to every god-power.' He took another gulp of brandy. 'They found Gadena, and traced Corthie's sale to Lord Irno, and went to his castle next.'

'Is my brother alright?' said Aila. 'And Vana?'

'The Holdfasts were interrogating them when I left. I'm sorry, I had no choice but to flee; they were too powerful for me.'

Mona nodded. 'And do they have a Quadrant of their own?'

'I didn't see it, but they must have, otherwise how could they have travelled from their own world to Lostwell?'

'Then, they will be coming here.'

'Yes. This is another reason I'm back; to warn you.'

'They're coming for Corthie?'

'Yes.'

Aila shook her head, trying to take it in. 'Why has it taken them so long to find him?'

'You know, dear cousin,' Naxor said, 'I didn't stay around to ask them. I saw the way they tore through Irno's guards, and decided that they weren't in a particularly talkative mood. Listen, we have one thing in our favour; no one knows exactly how to find this world; I've always been careful to keep its location a secret. Neither Irno, nor Vana, know how to find it, so the Holdfasts won't be able to take the information out of their heads. The bad news is that Vana met Corthie once, here in Ooste at the Royal Palace, so they will know he's on this world.'

'Let's deal with one thing at a time,' said Mona; 'for, in truth, we do not know if or when any of these Holdfasts will arrive here.'

Alia frowned. 'And if they do?'

'Then I suggest, for all our sakes, that we help them find Corthie. They do not sound like the type of beings we would wish to be enemies.'

'And what about me?' cried Naxor. 'I'm the guy who bought him! Do you think they'll just forgive me?'

'Calm yourself, cousin. We are not powerless. Irno and Vana, for all their attributes, possess no vision powers. I'm sure the mightiest among us shall be able to resist.'

Naxor shook his head. 'Forget it. Corthie's sister, the one who can't fight, her powers outstrip us all; weren't you listening? She could destroy the God-Queen in a second.'

'Dear Naxor, could it be, that in your fear and confusion, you are exaggerating a little? It is not possible for mortals to possess the powers you are talking about.'

'Dear Mona,' he replied, 'I saw what I saw.' He glanced at Aila. 'So, why are you here? I thought you'd be battling alongside the rebels in your beloved Circuit.'

She put on a smile. 'I'm getting married to Marcus; he'll be here any minute.'

The look on his face almost made up for the knot of anxiety that was twisting in her guts. Almost, but not quite.

Aila watched from a high window as a long row of carriages pulled up in front of Mona's keep. Blades were marching alongside them in large numbers, and they fanned out through the dark lanes to surround the tall building, sealing off any possible route to escape. Naxor had taken himself down to the basement, and was skulking in a small cellar. He had tried to dissuade her from following through on Mona's plan, but Aila knew it was too late to change her mind. She had given him the small bag containing her possessions to hide with him, but had omitted to mention anything about the vial she had buried under her clothes.

The lead carriage halted, and a Blade swung the side door open. A huge figure emerged into the torrential rain, the water rolling down his steel chestplate. Another Blade knelt before him and offered the prince the great sword that had belonged to his father Michael, and Aila shuddered as she saw it. Marcus lifted the enormous sword in one hand, and slid it into the long scabbard strapped to his back. He gazed around for a moment, then ascended the stairs to the entrance.

Aila turned away from the dark window and glanced at her reflection in a tall mirror. She felt sick. Her red dress flowed from her neckline to her ankles, and one of Mona's servants had spent time on her hair, lifting it above her shoulders into a style favoured by rich Taran women. She even had make up on, more than she normally used, and she hated it. It made her face look even younger, and she wished she hadn't opened the salve.

She walked to the door and pushed it open. Voices were filtering up from downstairs, and her chest tensed as she heard Marcus speaking to Mona. She couldn't make out the words, but his voice was unmistakable. She approached the top of the wide staircase just as he reached the bottom step, and their eyes met.

A shiver of fear ran down Aila's back as Marcus stared at her. He was enormous, as tall and broad as his father had been, and only an inch shorter than Corthie, whose form he seemed to mock. She longed for Corthie at that moment, her wildest dreams imagining him suddenly appearing and striking her cousin down, and then he would smile and take her into his arms.

'You are even more beautiful than I remember, Lady Aila,' said Marcus, his low voice calling to her from the bottom of the stairs. 'Why don't you come down?'

She froze for a moment, aware of the many eyes watching her. Mona was there, and her son, along with at least twenty soldiers in Blade uniforms, and a host of courtiers and servants; and every one of them was staring at her. She swallowed, and began to walk down the stairs, hitching up the hem of her skirt to avoid tripping.

Marcus turned to Mona. 'My thanks, sister, for your part in this; it shall not be forgotten.'

Mona bowed low. 'I do what I can, brother.'

Aila reached the bottom of the stairs and faced Marcus, her eyes level with his broad chest. He looked down at her, his eyes roving over her body, and she kept her face steady. She hated herself for what she was doing, and all her instincts told her to run, but it was too late. Soldiers were everywhere, and escape was impossible.

'I wish to speak to Lady Aila for a moment,' Prince Marcus said, his tone light. 'Everyone else remain here. Sister, is there a room nearby where I may be alone with her?'

Mona said nothing for a moment, then nodded. 'The door to the reception room is right behind you, brother.'

'My thanks.' He gestured to Aila, then accompanied her to the door. He opened it, then Aila heard him follow her into the large chamber, its white walls reflecting the shadow of the rain against the tall, dark windows.

Marcus closed the door as Aila turned.

She bit her lip. 'What do you want to speak about, Marcus?'

He smiled, then struck her across the face, a heavy blow from his gloved right hand. She fell to the floor, her arms splaying as she hit the marble tiles. He stepped forward and stood over her, his face transformed into a mask of rage.

'That's for making me wait. Look at you, dressed up like a little whore, but I know the spite that dwells in your heart. You submit to me now, at last, only because you have nowhere else to run. I will break you, Aila, break you into a thousand pieces and then put you back together again; turn you into a woman fit to be my wife.' He eyes travelled down from her face. 'Scream all you like; no one will come to help you, do you understand? You're mine now.'

Aila lay frozen on the cold marble, her mouth dry, her hands shaking.

Mona, help me.

Nothing.

'Get up,' Marcus said, his eyes never leaving her.

'Brother?' came a voice from the door.

He turned, scowling. 'What?'

'Our grandmother is here.'

Marcus's face fell. He glanced at Aila. 'This will have to wait.' He strode to the door, then turned back. 'I told you to get up.'

Aila tried to control her breathing. She got to one knee, then stood, her legs unsteady. She suppressed the tears of rage and desperation that threatened to overwhelm her. She was going to kill him. She had to keep her nerve. She had been worried that she might not be able to go through with it, but she knew then for a certainty that she would enjoy cutting his head off.

'And,' Marcus said, 'make sure you smile for the God-Queen.'

She frowned. What? Mona's words about their grandmother came back to her. She walked to the door, and Marcus opened it. Outside in the hallway, the Blades and courtiers were all prostrated on the floor, their faces lowered, while Mona was on her knees.

To their right strode the God-Queen, tall and beautiful; her robes flowing with gold and silver thread. A large diamond sat in the centre of a gold band on her brow, and she gazed over the people in the hallway. Behind were soldiers of her personal guard, and a few mortal courtiers and ministers.

'Stand,' she said to Mona.

'Your Divine Majesty,' Mona said as she rose to her feet. 'The Royal Academy is honoured that you have blessed us with your presence.'

The God-Queen smiled. 'As my grandson was coming here anyway, I felt it was the right time to return to Ooste.'

Marcus frowned. 'I thought you were going to remain in your carriage outside, grandmother.'

'You were taking so long I was starting to wonder if you had got lost, Marcus.' She turned her attention to Aila, who was standing next to Marcus, her head bowed. 'So here is the little bride. Frankly, I don't see what the fuss is about; Aila has always been weak, one of several disappointing grandchildren who lack the nerve to do what has to be done. Personally, I think you'll tire of her soon, Marcus; I believe it all was about the chase for you.'

'I intend to marry her as soon as we return to Tara, grandmother.'

She raised an eyebrow. 'That won't be tonight.'

'Are you staying in Ooste, your Majesty?' said Mona.

'Yes, for a short while at least.'

'But, grandmother,' said Marcus. 'You know my plans. We should return to Tara. I have waited three hundred years to claim Aila as my wife, and I do not wish to wait another night.'

The God-Queen sighed. 'Very well.'

'Shall we return to the boat, then, grandmother?' said Marcus, smiling.

'That's not what I meant,' she said, raising a hand. 'I am the God-Queen of the City, and my word is law. With this authority, I hereby join you, Prince Marcus of Tara, with you, Lady Aila of Pella, in holy and unbreakable matrimony. I decree that you are now husband and wife, in law and in fact, from this moment, until you are separated by death.'

Aila's mouth opened.

'This is not how I wanted it,' cried Marcus.

Queen Amalia frowned at him. 'You said you were impatient to be wed, and, as I do not intend to return to Tara this evening, I thought this would please you. Kiss your wife, Marcus.'

'But I had a whole wedding planned for Maeladh Palace,' he went on, 'the entire town would witness us being joined together. Music, flowers, a parade of the entire Roser militia, and a feast for every Taran citizen. This was going to be my way to please the people, and you've stolen it from me.'

'You're making a fool of yourself, Marcus,' she said. 'There is nothing to prevent you from doing all of that when we decide to return to Tara. Only now, you can enjoy your new bride before then.'

Marcus glared at the God-Queen, then stormed away, leaving Aila standing by the doorway alone.

The God-Queen glanced at her, a smile on her lips. 'Congratulations on your wedding, Lady Aila; does it make you happy? No need to answer; I can see the joy radiate from your eyes.'

Aila stared at the God-Queen, a hundred angry responses ready on her lips.

'If I may, your Majesty?' said Mona.

The God-Queen raised an eyebrow. 'Yes?'

'I was wondering, your Majesty, if your royal party intends to stay within the academy this evening? I can have the best rooms made ready immediately for your comfort.'

'Don't be ridiculous, Mona. I seem to recall that there's a perfectly good palace in Ooste.'

'The Royal Palace, your Majesty?' said Mona, her voice straining a little.

The God-Queen arched an eyebrow at her. 'Is there another? Yes, of course the Royal Palace. I assume my husband is within its walls?'

'I assume so, your Majesty.'

The God-Queen nodded. 'I think it's time to pay him a visit. His silence in recent days has troubled me somewhat, and yet at the same time it has given me hope. His lack of opposition to my actions may herald a welcome change of mind on his part, and I wish to see if that is true. Is there anyone else in the palace currently?'

'Only Lady Doria, your Majesty,' said Mona. 'She resides there as his personal assistant.'

Aila glanced at her as she spoke. Mona seemed calm on the surface, but faint lines by her eyes betrayed her anxiety and fear.

'Perhaps, your Majesty,' she said, 'it would be wise to send a message to the blessed God-King prior to any meeting. His Majesty might not welcome an unexpected visit.'

'How dare you?' the God-Queen cried, and Mona cowered back a step. 'Are you trying to tell me how to act towards my husband? I should strip the flesh from your bones for such impertinence.'

'I'm sorry, your Majesty,' Mona said, bowing low; 'forgive me.'

The God-Queen gave her a look of utter contempt. 'Pathetic.' She turned to Aila. 'Bride, accompany me to my carriage. You shall be staying in the Royal Palace tonight also, so you can share a bed with your new husband, wherever he is.' She glanced at her courtiers. 'Someone find the prince, and tell him we're going.'

Aila lowered her head and began to follow the God-Queen as she strode down the hallway.

You're doing great, she heard in her head.

But, Mona, I'm terrified, I can't deal with Marcus; I can't do this.

You can. You must. The plan remains the same, only you'll be in the Royal Palace instead of Tara. Call for me, and I'll be there.

But what about the God-King, Mona; what should I do?

Act. You know nothing; you're just as shocked as they are. We can get through this, Aila. I trust you; I believe in you.

Mona's voice fell silent as they approached the front doors. Guards pulled them open, revealing the dark rainswept courtyard in front of the keep. The sky was lightening a little towards sunward, Aila noticed.

Marcus joined them on the steps. He didn't glance at Aila as they descended the stairs, his face a mask of sullen anger. Courtiers held umbrellas out as they crossed the courtyard, and Aila cast a last look back at Mona standing by the entrance doors of the keep before being helped up into a carriage. She sat down next to Marcus, with the God-Queen opposite her, and the door was closed.

The carriage moved off, and Aila's spirits dwindled.

The God-Queen laughed. 'Such a happy couple! Now, Aila's expression I was expecting, but I thought you'd be pleased at last, grandson? Isn't this what you've wanted for a long time? Isn't this what you wasted our forces for? All the lives of the Blades you have thrown away in pursuit of your bride; were they worth it?'

He glanced up at her, his brows heavy. 'Yes.'

'Really? Do you trust her?'

'No.'

'Well, at least you're not that stupid.' She raised her hand, and Aila felt a power grip her throat, making it impossible to breathe. 'So, little Aila, what are you planning? Do you expect me to believe this charade?'

Aila gasped, feeling light-headed, as her hands clutched at her throat.

'Stop it, grandmother,' Marcus said. 'If anyone's going to kill her, it'll be me.'

The God-Queen lowered her hand and Aila took a ragged breath, her throat and lungs burning in pain.

'Must we visit the God-King?' said Marcus. 'If he doesn't want to get involved, we should leave him alone. If we arrive at the palace and anger him, he may decide to help our enemies.'

'You worry too much, grandson. If I suspect that to be the case, then I shall strike him down. I would rather reconcile, but there is no middle ground; not any more.'

The carriage pulled through the empty streets and into the fore-court of the great palace, its white façade shining in the pale moonlight.

Aila blinked. The rain had stopped.

Marcus noticed it at the same time, his mouth opening. 'Stop the carriage!'

He swung the door open as the carriage was still moving and leapt to the flagstones. He called on the closest Blades and the line of carriages shuddered to a halt.

'Get the orders to every unit of Blades in the City!' he shouted, his eyes wide. 'All must return to the Bulwark immediately. Now!' The Blades scattered, most running back down towards the harbour of Ooste. Marcus stared up at the sky as Aila stepped down from carriage. The clouds were clearing in a wind gusting from sunward, and the stars were visible for the first time in two months.

She walked up to Marcus. 'Summer come a little early this year, has it?'

He glared at her. 'If you weren't my wife, I'd kill you for saying that.'

The God-Queen joined them. 'Pay no heed to the weather. The Great Wall has a dragon to defend it while the Blades hurry back to their posts. For now, we have a more urgent matter to attend to.' She strode off towards the entrance to the Royal Palace, as guards and courtiers formed up to flank her.

She turned back to see Aila and Marcus still standing by the carriage. 'Come, you two; it's time to see your grandfather.'

CHAPTER 27

THE RAT AND THE WOLF

A rrowhead Fort, The Bulwark, The City – 21st Amalan 3420
Emily squeezed through the half-open gates into the dimly lit hallway, her uniform soaked and covered in thick, dark mud. The days and nights were blurring into one for her, and she slumped down by a wall with the other Rats in her team. Water was passed along the line, and she took a drink, then splashed her face to waken herself.

'You alright there, Emily-Wemily?' said Maddie, crouching down next to her.

'Yes, Sergeant.'

'Yeah? Let me see your hands.'

She held them out.

'Still steady? Excellent. Budge up a bit.' Maddie sat down next to her. 'We made it through another job, and this night work's getting us used to what it'll be like in summer. That's when we'll start to attract an audience; you know, from the walls.'

Emily glanced at her. 'People watch the Rats?'

'Oh yeah, it's practically like a spectator sport. All the nearby Blades go up to the battlements. They place bets on how many will survive each night, and how many greenhides get killed. Corthie skewed all the stats last summer, he was killing fifty every shift at one point. Malik's ass, I wish I'd been a Rat back then instead of now.'

'They place bets on us? How vile.'

'They need something to do, I suppose. The Rats and the Wolfpack are the only Blades who actually ever come face to face with the green-hides; everybody else just shoots them from the safety of the walls. And considering it's usually only criminals and rejects who end up in the Rats, not many Blades have much sympathy for us.'

Emily shook her head. 'So the rest of the City doesn't care about the Bulwark, and the Blades don't care about the Rats, when we're the ones in the most danger? I have been blind all these years not to realise this, and now that I have realised it, it's too late. Every one of us sitting here will probably be dead within a month.'

Maddie gave her a look. 'Speak for yourself, little miss I'm-not-a-Roser-honestly. When the Blades get back from the rest of the City, the Wolfpack will be reinforced; it'll be triple the size it is now. Most of them are as dumb as a donkey's behind, but as long as they're between us and the greenhides, we've always got a chance.'

'I haven't seen a single one of them kill a greenhide yet,' Emily said. 'They just run away at the first sign of them. Their presence doesn't fill me with any great sense of security out there. You know, I'm much better with a sword than I am at moving cranes about and building bridges. Is there any way to transfer from the Rats to the Wolfpack?'

'I doubt it,' Maddie said. 'Well, I've never seen it happen. Maybe if you killed a greenhide, they'd let you in, who knows? Anyway, I'd better go and find an idiot officer, and ask them why we're still sitting here.' She got to her feet. 'See you later, princess.'

Emily nodded, and watched as Maddie walked away down the long line of Rats. She had stayed close to the sergeant throughout her fifteen days in the Auxiliary Work Company, learning from her and trying to keep on her right side. Four of the recruits who had joined the same day as Emily were already dead, and Maddie's help was probably the main reason she was still alive.

She gazed at her hands. They were steady, but they were also covered in cuts and abrasions, and a blister on her left palm was still healing. Her nails were cracked and broken, and she frowned; would they ever have a chance to grow again? And that was just her hands. Her body was exhausted, and she had aches and pains from muscles and joints that were worse than anything she had experienced while training in her grandmother's house. From the way the other Rats talked, summer consisted of a four-month-long nightmare, and she had to resign herself to the fact that she probably wouldn't survive it. Every time she went out beyond the walls could be her last. In her old life, she had always planned for the future; she had pictured living with Daniel and their children, and then their children growing up as she lived into a long old age with her husband by her side. In the Rats, every day of survival counted as a blessing, and no one thought beyond getting through each shift.

A man to her left leaned over. 'The sergeant can't watch your back forever, you piece of Roser scum.'

'She doesn't need to,' Emily said; 'I can look after myself.'

'Yeah? Maybe we should put that to the test.'

'Hey,' called over a Rat sitting along the wall opposite. 'Leave her.'

'Why?' the man sneered. 'What's she to you?'

'She's Lady Aurelian, and you should show her some respect.'

'Kiss my ass. Are you one of those stupid Hammers?'

'I am, and I'm not alone.' He glanced at Emily. 'There are plenty of Hammers in the Rats these days, and we all know who you are, ma'am.'

She frowned. 'You do?'

'There's a Hammer in your team, and he told the rest of us. You're married to the heir, aren't you?'

She paused for a second. She hadn't received any official notification that her marriage had been annulled, but that didn't mean it hadn't happened. 'I am, yes.'

The Hammer smiled. 'I always mocked that legend at school. It's amazing to think it's actually true.'

The man to Emily's left snorted. 'You Hammers are delusional. You're more gullible than the damn Redemptionists. And besides, did you not hear; she's a fraud. She lied her way into that Aurelian family you keep going on about, that's why she's here – she got caught.'

'That's a lie,' said Emily. 'I was adopted, and didn't know. I never tried to trick anyone.'

'Then why are you here?' said the Hammer.

'I was abducted from my home in the middle of the night, bound, and placed onto a boat.'

'By who?'

'I don't want to say, because I have no proof and I might be mistaken. Someone who didn't want me around any more.'

The man to her left sniggered. 'It was probably her husband.'

'You'd better watch yourself,' said the Hammer, glaring at the man, 'or you might end up regretting those words. You probably don't realise it but, right at this moment, there are four other Hammers sitting close by, all listening. If you don't get up and walk away, all I have to do is call on them, and you won't be going back outside for a while because you'll be in the hospital.'

The man shrugged at first, then glanced around at the Rats sitting along the walls of the hallway. He swore under his breath, then stood and shuffled away down the line.

'Thank you for your support,' said Emily. 'What's your name?'

'Torphin, ma'am,' said the Hammer.

'Were you joking about the other Hammers in the line?'

Torphin laughed. 'No.' He looked down the hallway. 'Show her.'

At least eight other Rats raised their arms.

Emily bit her lip. 'And how long have you been... watching me?'

'Since you got here. Fifteen days ago, wasn't it, ma'am? And there are more Hammers in the other Rat companies, not just in this one. What we all want to know is, what's your plan?'

Emily swallowed. Plan? What was it they wanted from her? She remembered the reaction of the young Hammer in the quarters where her team slept; did they somehow believe the Aurelians were going to save the City? Torphin had called it a 'legend'.

She could feel the eyes of the other Rats in the hallway on her; not just the Hammers, but everyone was now listening.

'Being abducted wasn't part of my plan.'

'You're here for a reason,' Torphin said. 'The oppressed of this City have been waiting a long time for a mortal to unite them.'

One of the other Rats laughed. 'She's a Roser. A Roser will never unite the people.'

'I'm not a Roser,' she said. 'My husband is a Roser; I'm an Evader.'

'Yeah? And where is your husband?'

Sergeant Maddie walked back into the hallway before Emily could respond. 'Bad news, everyone,' she yelled at the Rats. 'We're going back out. Apparently a big chunk of the moat wall has collapsed with all the rain, and we have to fix it, tonight.'

Groans and curses rose through the air.

'Don't shout at me about it,' Maddie cried. 'Get up off your asses and start moving. The breach is a mile and a half iceward of here.'

The Rats slowly got to their feet. Torphin gave Emily a quick nod, then headed down the line as a gate in the hallway opened. They filed outside, into the clear channel between the outer and inner walls, and were soaked by the rain within seconds. Emily caught up with Maddie as they marched along, their heads bowed.

'Can I ask you something, Sergeant?'

'Course you can, princess.'

'Did you know that there's a group of Hammers keeping an eye on me?'

'Yup. Crazy fools. Reminds me of the folk who followed Corthie last year, except you haven't got quite as many as him. The novelty will wear off, once they realise you're not here to save them all.'

Emily smiled. 'Maybe I am.'

'I hope you're joking.' She looked up and glanced around. 'It's so weird seeing the walls deserted like this. Normally these battlements would have Blades all the way along them if a Rat job this important was happening, and we'd have support from artillery and whatnot.

Throwing-machine-things.' She looked up as the rain rolled down her face. 'Buckler had better still be awake, lazy lizard that he is.'

'Do the Blades have legends about the Aurelians?'

'Are you still on about that? No, is the simple answer. I hadn't even heard about it until you arrived. What is the legend, exactly?'

'I was hoping you'd know.'

'Why don't you just ask one of the Hammers?'

'Because then they'd find out that I knew nothing about it either.'

'So? Oh, wait a minute; I get it. You're thinking of how you could use this little legend to your own advantage. I'd be careful with that approach; the Hammers might get quite upset if they find out you're toying with them.'

'It's not that; I just don't want to offend them. It'd look rude if an Aurelian doesn't know anything about a legend that involves them. You could ask them, Sergeant, and then you could tell me. Please?'

'I'll think about it. Are you still actually married anyway?'

'Yes. I think so.'

Maddie laughed. 'You're almost as crazy as I am.'

They walked on for another twenty minutes, then stopped by a postern gate in the outer wall. A squad of Wolfpack soldiers was waiting for them, streams of water falling down their helmets and armour. Maddie walked off to join a small group of sergeants and officers by a huge pile of freshly-cut blocks of stone. Emily noticed Maddie's friend Sergeant Quill among the members of the Wolfpack, but many of the others looked new, and from the way they were glancing at the Rats, she suspected that several had never been beyond the walls before. Emily smiled. Compared to them, she was a seasoned veteran of going 'outside'. She wiped the rain from her face. It was warm, she noticed, warmer than it had been in days, and she wondered how many hours it would be before she would be dry again.

She saw a soldier speaking to some Rats ahead of her, his voice lost in the thundering rain. He was slowly moving down the line. His face was lost in the shadows, but something about his poise and stature reminded her of Daniel. She frowned. Daniel would be tucked up warm in his bed, or passed out from drinking too much gin.

His voice drifted down the line as he got closer, and she felt a nudge in her back.

'Hey,' said Torphin. 'Is that guy looking for you?'

'I seriously doubt it.'

Torphin tilted his head to listen, and Emily did the same.

'I'm looking for an Emily. Have you seen an Emily?'

Her heart seemed to stop for a second, then she ran. She shoved her way through the lines of Rats, and saw the man turn to see what was causing the noise. He squinted through the crowd.

'Daniel!' she cried.

His face changed; his eyes widening. He ran to her and she pulled him close, her arms gripping him as she buried her face into his neck. He put his own arms round her shoulder and held her. She started to cry, ignoring the dozens of watching faces, oblivious to the rain.

'I'm here,' he said. 'Thank Malik you're alive.'

'Are we still married?'

He laughed, pushing her back a little to look at her. 'Of course we are. I told you I'd never sign that form.'

She raised her fingers to his face. 'What are you doing here?'

'I came to find you. I'm a Blade now; I volunteered.'

'You threw away everything for me?'

'Everything? Emily, you are everything to me.'

She tried to answer, but her tears wouldn't stop.

'Do you think I wanted to live in that house without you?' he said. 'Don't cry.'

'But how did you find me?'

'I never believed my mother's story that you'd run away, but to be honest, I had no idea where to start looking. Then, I got a letter, telling me you were a Blade in Arrowhead Fortress, and I left right away.'

'A letter? I don't understand.'

She heard a cough, and they turned.

'That was us,' said Torphin. 'Sorry to interrupt, but are you Lord Aurelian?'

Daniel frowned. 'No; my father is.'

'Then you're the heir?'

'I guess so.'

Torphin turned, and raised his fist into the air. 'It's him. The heir is here!'

A cheer erupted from the Hammers among the crowd, and Daniel glanced at Emily.

'I'll tell you later,' she whispered. 'Just acknowledge them for now.'

He nodded, and lifted a hand, making the Hammers cheer again.

'What in the name of Amalia's chastity belt is going on here?' yelled Maddie as she returned from the huddle of officers. She pointed at Daniel. 'Who's this joker?'

Emily smiled, her arms still wrapped round his waist as they stood in the pouring rain. 'My husband appears to have joined the Wolfpack, Sergeant.'

'Oh.' She prodded Daniel with a finger. 'So you are real? What happened to the annulment?'

He smiled. 'I didn't sign.'

'Well, this is weird. I don't think I've ever heard of a Wolfpack soldier being married to a Rat before.'

Quill approached. 'Private, get your hands off that Rat. Where do you think we are right now?'

Maddie glanced at her. 'He's, uh, her husband.'

'What? Doesn't matter, we've got a job to do. Fall in, Private; come with me. We're going out first.'

Emily leaned up to kiss him before he pulled his arms from her.

'Take care,' she said.

'You too.'

'Don't worry about me; this will be my twenty-fifth time outside since I got here. Stay with Sergeant Quill; she knows what she's doing.'

He nodded, then turned and followed the rest of the Wolfpack as they went through the postern gate.

'You don't look very happy,' said Maddie.

'Oh, I am, believe me. Well, I was until I watched him walk out of the gate, and now I'm worried for him.'

'Has he got any military experience?'

'Yes, lots.'

'Then he's got a better chance than most. Now, how are we going to figure out your sleeping arrangements?'

'What?'

'Cause he sure ain't sleeping in the team's quarters with the rest of us. I'm not having that going on when I'm trying to sleep.'

'Right now, there are a million other things on my mind.'

'Yeah, right; I saw the way you were clinging onto him, and the way he was looking at you.'

They watched as the last of the Wolfpack went through the gate, then Maddie turned to the rest of her team. 'Right, we're next. This'll be a long job, and if we don't finish it tonight, then we'll be back out again tomorrow. Let's go.'

Maddie led the way, and the Rats hurried through the gate. Emily glanced around. A section of the moat retaining wall four yards long had collapsed, its stone blocks gone.

'This'll take days to fix,' she said.

'Yeah, maybe,' said Maddie, 'but we'll have to get it done; we can't leave a hole this big for summer.'

Emily nodded and got to work, dragging the blocks from the channel between the walls out to the side of the moat. Each time she dropped one off, she glanced around to see if she could locate Daniel, but the Wolfpack had fanned out in a wide arc with their backs to the Rats, and she wasn't sure which of the soldiers was him. The Rats settled down to their tasks, the crane lifting the blocks brought by Emily and the others onto the bridge as quickly as they could handle them, and others dragging them across to the far side of the moat where the stonemasons were busy.

A howl echoed through the air, and the Rats all glanced up. It seemed far away though, and they were back to work after a few seconds. A Rat cried out as a block dropped from the bridge onto his foot. The stonemasons called for a replacement Rat, and Emily sprinted over the bridge as the injured man was carried away. There was no crane on the far side of the bridge, and it took four Rats to lift each block down to the ground next to the breach. Sweat appeared on her brow as she helped carry the huge blocks.

'Faster,' called the chief stonemason, waving his arm. His frown vanished as he glanced into the distance, then his eyes widened. 'Greenhides!'

'Over the bridge!' cried the officer from the side closest to the walls. 'All Rats, get back here!'

The four workers dropped the stone block, and Emily turned to squint through the gloom. She knew the bridge would remain in place so the Wolfpack could cross, and her eyes scanned for Daniel. She saw the greenhides approach through the rain, racing at an angle from the sunward direction. She stared, not at the greenhides, but at the patch of clear sky developing along the horizon above them. One by one, the stars were reappearing.

The soldiers of the Wolfpack were retreating, and she checked the faces of each as they came closer. Another roar ripped through the air, from iceward, and Emily turned. A large group of greenhides were also approaching from that direction, and they were much closer than the others. They crashed into the thin line of soldiers, their claws flashing as they ripped through two Wolves. The rest of the soldiers fled, rushing towards the bridge, their cohesion lost in the panic. One soldier fell, his sword flying from his hand. He jumped to his feet and leapt for the bridge, and Emily picked up the sword from the mud. It felt light in her hand after so many years of practising with a heavier wooden weapon, and she swung it as the last soldiers raced back to the bridge. She caught sight of Daniel, at last, on the right, a pair of greenhides ten yards behind him as he ran towards the bridge.

She waited. Soldiers piled past her, jumping up onto the wooden planks and racing over the moat, none even glancing in her direction as they fled. She backed up onto the bridge, her legs tensing. The lead greenhide chasing Daniel was only feet away from him, and Emily held still until his hands reached for the planks then she sprang through the air, the sword pointing downwards, the hilt gripped in both hands. The blade slammed down into the greenhide's face, entering through its left eye. Emily let go of the sword as the beast fell to the ground, shrieking. She rolled away through the mud, then felt hands reach down for her. She was hauled up onto the bridge as it lifted into the air, the crane pulling it away from the swarm of greenhides. Emily stared down at the beasts, their claws slashing through the empty air as the bridge was swung to safety. She glanced up. Daniel, Torphin, and two other Rats were on the bridge with her.

'You got it,' Daniel said, his eyes on the far bank; 'you killed it.'

She smiled. 'One down, as the Rats would say, only six billion to go.'

He turned to her. 'You saved my life. I'm a Wolf and you're a Rat; isn't it supposed to be the other way around?'

'I'll let you off,' she said; 'it's your first day.'

Torphin laughed. 'It was beautiful to watch. You saved the heir; you are destined for each other.'

'These guys helped pull you up,' said Daniel.

'They're Hammers,' Emily said.

'Am I supposed to understand what that means?'

'Hey, guys,' said Torphin. 'The rain's stopped.'

The bridge was swung round to the near bank, and they clambered off. Around them, every Rat, and every soldier of the Wolfpack, was staring at the sky.

Maddie approached, her eyes on the horizon. 'Summer.'

Emily nodded. 'This is bad, isn't it?'

'It could be. Some years it takes the main horde a few days to get here, other years, it's like they're waiting.' She squinted into the distance.

A Blade up on the battlements of the outer wall behind them began shouting. 'They're coming; all of them!'

Emily stared. The clouds were breaking up as a wind gusted from sunward, and the two moons appeared in the sky, their silver light illuminating the plains in front of the walls. From end to end, the ground seemed to be moving, as if a tide was rolling towards them.

'Take a good look, Rats,' Maddie called out to her team. 'For those of you who have joined us from the other eight tribes, this is what we get to see every year.' A few began to edge back towards the postern gate. 'Stay where you are,' she went on. 'The moat'll stop 'em. I want you all to see this.'

The Rats and the Wolfpack stood by the edge of the moat, behind the low wall at its lip, every eye on the sea of greenhides. The first groups reached the far bank, and stood shrieking across the water, their claws clacking. Emily moved closer to Daniel, and she felt his hand take hers as they watched.

Maddie stepped up onto the frame of the crane and pointed at the eternal enemy. 'In a few days, the water level in the moat will start to go down, and for most of the summer this stretch will be dry. Around four miles of moat dries up every year, and that's when things can get rough. Welcome to summer.'

There was a whoosh from the dark sky overhead as she said the words, and Emily glanced up to see Buckler soar past.

'What was that?' cried Daniel, staring.

'It's our dragon,' Emily said.

Maddie raised her fists in the air. 'Go get them, Buckler!'

'Is this really happening?' said Daniel.

'I'm afraid so, Danny. Does your mother know you're here?'

'I'm not sure. She'll probably track me down sooner or later, but I don't know what she'll do when that happens. We didn't part on good terms. By the way, where did you learn to use a sword?'

'My grandmother made me take lessons.'

'Listen, there's something I need to say to you, something I should have said before.'

Buckler swooped low, sending a stream of flames ripping through the mass of greenhides. Dozens were consumed by the fire as it rained down on them, and the howls and shrieking rose into a cacophony.

'Amalia's breath,' Daniel muttered, his eyes glowing with the reflection of the flames.

'Right,' said Maddie; 'get the crane and the bridge packed away and back behind the wall. Gather up the tools first; don't leave them to rust in the mud, the last thing I need in my life is a rusty spanner. And let's have a little cheer for our own princess, who bagged her first greenhide tonight!'

The Rats cheered.

'I'd never thought I'd see a Rat protect a Wolf,' Maddie went on, laughing. 'Just goes to show that we're not all useless!'

Behind her, Buckler swooped down for another low pass, and Emily's eyes followed him as he descended. She frowned. He was too low to use his flames without burning himself, and his rear limbs were extended, the claws out.

'What's he doing?'

Maddie turned, and shook her head. 'Idiot lizard's just showing off now.'

Buckler grasped into the mass of greenhides, lifting one in each rear limb, but a third greenhide clung on as he started to ascend. It scrambled up onto the dragon's left wing, then fell back, its claws lashing out. They connected with the wing, each claw piercing it and ripping downwards as the greenhide fell. Buckler cried out in agony, his wing drooping, and another greenhide leapt up, its claws grasping round the dragon's neck. The weight was slowing the dragon, and his left wing had been ripped to ribbons. More greenhides jumped, and they pulled the dragon lower.

Buckler let out a blast of fire, incinerating every greenhide in front of him as the Rats and Wolves watched from the other side of the moat.

'Swing the bridge over!' Maddie yelled.

The officer stepped forward. 'No! We do that, there will be a thousand of those monsters over here within seconds.'

'But we can't leave him!' Maddie screamed. 'No, Buckler!'

The dragon lashed out with his forelimbs, and unleashed another stream of flames, but greenhides were swarming all over his back and wings, carving him up with their claws. He beat his ripped and ragged wings, sending a dozen greenhides flying, and managed to get a few feet into the air, but he was dragged back down again by the horde, and his head disappeared into the mass. He cried out, a great howl of agony and fear, and Emily could feel the air shake with its strength. Then, slowly, his body began to slip down, and he fell to the side, crashing into the moat, his bulk sending a wave of water over the side. On the near bank, no one moved for a second as everyone stared, then the panic began. Buckler's body was blocking the moat, and greenhides began scuttling across it, using it as a bridge. There was only a short gap of water between the dragon's body and the wall, and the first greenhides were scaling it in seconds.

The Rats and Wolves raced for the postern gate, shoving and pushing each other in their haste to escape the approaching tide of beasts.

Emily found Maddie to her left and Daniel to her right in the thick press of bodies as they squeezed their way closer to the open gate. Behind them, the greenhides began tearing into the back of the escaping crowd, and the cries of the dying rose up to fill her ears. Emily kept her gaze on the gate, resisting a base urge to look back.

Daniel grabbed her arm as he shoved through the crowd with his shoulder. 'If this is it, Emily,' he said, his voice almost lost amid the shrieks and screams; 'I love you.'

She held onto his hand as the greenhides got closer. 'I love you too, Danny.'

CHAPTER 28

ANOTHER NAME

A rrowhead Fort, The Bulwark, The City – 21st Amalan 3420

Maddie was shoved forward in the tight press. She was aware of Emily on her right, but her mind seemed frozen in shock. She was pushing towards the postern gate with the other Rats and Wolves as the greenhides cut their way through the crowd behind her, yet her thoughts held only one thing.

Buckler.

The red dragon was dead.

One stupid mistake, one simple misjudgement, and the Champion of the Bulwark had fallen.

The screams grew louder. Maddie reached the doorway of the gate and almost fell through, the crowd fragmenting and running as soon as they had passed the threshold.

'Sergeant!' cried one of her team. 'What do we do?'

Maddie stared at him, her mind foggy.

'Sergeant!'

She glanced back at the gate. The last remaining Rats were still entering, the greenhides only feet behind them.

'Close the gate!' she screamed.

A group of Rats hurled themselves at the back of the stout, iron-framed door, but bodies were blocking the entrance, and it barely moved.

'We have to go!' cried Quill, standing close by with what was left of her squad. 'We have to warn Arrowhead.'

The gate burst open as a greenhide barged through, its teeth and claws bloody.

'Run!' yelled Maddie. 'To Arrowhead!'

She saw Emily standing staring at the greenhides and grabbed her arm. 'Move, princess.'

The Rats and Wolves fled, running as fast as they could as more greenhides charged through the postern gate. Maddie glanced up as they ran, but no one was on the battlements. The gates of the fortress that led to the outer walls would be open, and if the greenhides got in there as well, then the inner wall would also be breached and the enemy would be inside the Bulwark.

She risked a glance over her shoulder. Greenhides were crouching by the postern gate, stooping down to eat the Rats they had killed there, but others were trying to push past them to enter the channel between the outer and inner walls.

'Sergeant,' Emily called out as they ran; 'What do we do?'

Maddie frowned. Why was everyone expecting her to know what to do? The outer wall of the Bulwark had never been breached in a thousand years.

'We need to get to Arrowhead, and close all the gates,' she said, loud enough for the others to hear. 'If we do that, we can keep the greenhides trapped between the walls.'

'But, Sergeant,' cried another Rat, 'what about Stormshield and the other fortresses?'

Maddie almost screamed in frustration. 'We've got to hope that someone's up on the battlements, and they see what's happened.'

'And if there ain't?'

'What do you expect me to say? Do you think I can perform miracles? Just keep running.'

'They're coming!' cried another Rat.

Maddie kept her legs moving, her heart pounding as they approached the fortress of Arrowhead. Not a single Blade could be seen up on the battlements; the few soldiers that were still inside were probably all asleep. In fact, she thought, most of the Bulwark would be sleeping, completely unaware of the disaster that had just occurred. All it would take was for there to be one unlocked gate in the inner wall, and the Bulwark would be plunged into a nightmare. With the great majority of the Blades on duty in other parts of the City, and their dragon-champion dead, there was nothing that could stem the tide of greenhides.

Not quite nothing, she thought.

She scanned around for Quill. 'I have an idea.'

Quill nodded as she ran.

'I'll need every Rat I can get my hands on once we're inside Arrowhead and the gates are closed.'

'Will it work?'

'I don't know, Quill. If it doesn't, then we're all screwed.'

They reached the first gate in the walls of the fortress, the same one that they had left from when they had started the job. The Rats and Wolves halted for a second, panting, and spluttering.

'You take this gate,' said Quill to Maddie; 'I'll take the Wolfpack and we'll go round to the next one.'

Maddie nodded. 'Where's the officer?'

'Got his head ripped off by the moat.'

She glanced back and saw the flood of greenhides running between the two walls towards them. 'Good luck, Quill.'

The sergeant ran off, and Maddie ushered her Rats through the gate. The second they were inside, they swung it shut and barred it. A moment later, the greenhides hit it, their claws scraping and battering off the door.

'Don't stand there staring,' Maddie yelled. 'Come on.'

Emily turned to her, panting. 'Will it hold?'

'If it doesn't, then let's not be here when it happens.' Her eyes caught sight of her husband. 'Hey, you! You're supposed to be with the Wolfpack.'

'I'm not leaving Emily,' he said. 'You can court martial me as soon as this is over, Sergeant.'

'Malik's ass,' she muttered, as the rest of the Rats stared at her. Her mind felt like it was going to explode. Every worst nightmare was coming true, and the decisions she made could save, or kill, thousands. She tried to control her breathing, but it was coming in ragged gasps.

'I heard you had a plan,' said Emily.

'What?'

'A plan?'

Maddie nodded. 'Yes. Follow me.'

She raced off down the hallway, and descended a flight of stairs to the Rats' quarters.

'Gather tools,' she cried. 'Pickaxes, sledgehammers, bolt-cutters, saws.'

She noticed some of the Rats hang back while the others ran off to do as she had ordered. The remaining Rats were standing next to Emily and her husband. All were Hammers.

'Get to work,' Maddie said.

'We're only here to protect the Aurelians,' said one. 'We don't take orders from the Rats any more. It's over.'

Maddie stormed over, her fists clenched.

'Do as she says,' said Emily. 'By helping her, you're helping us.'

The Hammers nodded. 'For you, ma'am, we'll do it.'

They ran off to join the others as Maddie glared at Emily.

'What in Amalia's name are you doing, princess? Have you forgotten you're a Rat?'

'I haven't forgotten anything,' said Emily. 'I'm just trying to survive.'

'I don't understand,' said Daniel. 'Why are those Rats following us?'

'I've told you; they're Hammers,' said Emily. 'They have a legend about us.'

'A what?'

'They think we're going to reunite the City and save it.'

'They're idiots,' said Maddie; 'the Bulwark's full of gullible fools that cling on to any mad hope they find. It was supposed to be Buckler; then it was supposed to be Corthie; and now it's you two dumplings.'

'We're ready, boss,' cried a Rat.

Maddie turned, still not used to being referred to as 'boss'. The Rats were all holding the tools she had asked for.

'Right,' she said; 'we're going up to the forecourt and entering Buckler's lair. There's a wall we need to smash down.'

'Why?' said one of the Hammers.

'Stop questioning my damn orders!' she yelled. 'Just do as you're told.'

She raced off towards the stairs, and heard the boots of the others follow her. She climbed up and emerged into the huge courtyard of the fortress. Screams were echoing up from beyond the high curtain wall, but no greenhides were in sight. Maddie led the Rats over to the entrance to Buckler's lair, where two guards were posted.

'What's going on outside?' one cried as Maddie approached.

'Buckler's fallen,' she said. 'He's dead.'

The two Blades stared at her.

'The greenhides have breached the outer wall,' Maddie went on, as another scream split the air, following by shrieking and howls.

'What do we do?' said one of the guards.

'Why in Malik's name is everybody asking me that?' Maddie cried. 'I don't care, just get out of the way.'

'Why? Are you Rats going to loot the place?'

'I'm losing my patience,' Maddie yelled. 'If you don't scram, we're going to charge right over the top of you.'

The two guards glanced at each other, then at the mob of Rats with hammers and pick axes. They ran, hurrying away towards the entrance gates of the fortress.

Daniel frowned. 'Shouldn't we be running in the same direction?'

'Shut up,' Maddie said. 'Heir or no heir, you're getting right on my nerves. Everyone, follow me.'

She sprinted through the entrance and they descended the long ramp into the lair. A few of Buckler's staff were around, working as if nothing was wrong, and they all glanced up as Maddie and the Rats appeared.

'Ignore them,' Maddie shouted; 'this way.'

She veered to the left down a large tunnel, then saw the new wall ahead of her, a solid barrier of brick and stonework.

She pointed to it, then turned to the Rats. 'Bring it down!'

'The wall?' said one.

'Yes, the damn wall.'

'All of it?'

She fought back tears of frustration. 'Yes. Bring all of it down.'

The Hammers glanced at Emily and Daniel.

'Do whatever she says,' cried Emily, grabbing an axe.

The Rats got to work. Some leaned ladders against the wall and began hacking away at its upper levels, while others starting removing bricks and stones from the bottom, swinging their hammers and pick axes as Maddie watched.

'What is going on?' shouted a soldier on Buckler's staff. 'You can't come in here and do this. That wall was built on the express orders of Commander Kano.'

Maddie punched him in the face, her pent-up frustration bubbling over. Other soldiers ran over to help their colleague, and the Rats joined in. A soldier raised a crossbow, and a Rat battered him across the chest with a sledgehammer as a huge brawl developed in the tunnel. Emily hurried to Maddie's side, and clubbed a soldier on the back of his head with the handle of her axe.

'Look out!' someone shouted. 'The wall's coming down!'

There was a great crack, then a thunderous roar as the stone blocks and bricks collapsed. The Rats and soldiers were sent flying to the ground as dust and rubble filled the air. Maddie scrambled to her feet, seeing the red gate at the end of the tunnel.

She grabbed Emily's arm. 'Find some bolt-cutters and follow me.' She turned to the others. 'Everyone else, stay outside.'

Maddie raced ahead, sprinting for the door-hatch cut into the gate, ignoring the confusion in the tunnel. She tried to open the door, but it was locked. She turned, and saw Daniel approach, a large axe in his hands.

She pointed at the door, and Daniel swung the axe at the lock, splintering the wood and hacking through it. The door swung free and Maddie jumped through.

'It's me!' she cried into the darkness. 'Don't burn me.'

'Maddie?'

'Yes, we've come to get you out of here.'

'Who are you speaking to?' said Emily, squinting into the cavern.

'An old friend.' With no lamps lit, the lair was filled with shadows. Maddie stepped forward, then Blackrose swung her head down, stretching it as far as her shackles would allow.

Emily screamed.

'I don't have time to explain,' said Maddie, 'but yes, there's another dragon.'

'Another one?' said Daniel. 'An hour ago, I didn't know there were any.'

'I told you to wait outside,' Maddie said. 'Damn it; it doesn't matter. Bring that axe.'

Maddie strode forwards as Blackrose gazed at Emily and Daniel.

'New companions, Maddie? Tell me, what is happening? I heard Buckler call out in distress.'

'The greenhides got him,' said Maddie, feeling her eyes well again. 'I'm sorry.'

Blackrose lifted her head, her eyes burning. 'The young dragon is dead?'

Maddie wiped her eyes and nodded.

'And you are here to rescue me?'

'Yes.'

'You smashed down the wall beyond the red gate? What a pity you couldn't have done it before my kin was allowed to be slaughtered; then I might have been able to prevent it. Did he die alone?'

'He was on the other side of the moat from us, Blackrose, and now the greenhides are through the outer wall. If we don't stop them, they'll overwhelm the Bulwark.'

'So? Am I supposed to feel sorry for the humans that have imprisoned me now that they are finally going to learn the true meaning of despair? I expected better of you, Maddie.'

'I don't have time for this, Blackrose. Help us or not, we're getting you out of those shackles.' She gestured to Emily and Daniel, who were still staring up at the black dragon. 'Don't just stand there, come on.'

'Yes,' said Blackrose, 'if I was going to eat you, I would have already done so.'

'Damn it, of course; you're hungry,' said Maddie. 'You can eat your fill in Buckler's lair once we've freed you.'

They went into the main lair, and Maddie lit a few lanterns, noticing that Blackrose was still wearing the rider's harness.

'She's enormous,' said Emily, her mouth hanging open.

'It's definitely a "she", is it?' said Daniel.

Blackrose growled and lowered her head directly before Daniel. 'If I hear you speak again, it shall be the last words you say, insect.'

Maddie pulled Daniel away by his sleeve, then shepherded him and Emily up beside the dragon's right flank, where the thick chain connected her to the wall.

'Get to work,' she said. 'Daniel, start hacking away the stonework where the chain meets the wall. Emily, bring those bolt-cutters up here.'

Emily and Maddie lifted the huge set of cutters up to the chain, but the links were thicker than the tool's reach, and Maddie threw them to the cavern floor in frustration.

Emily crouched by the chain. 'We need a steel pin and a hammer, Sergeant. I'll get them.'

She raced off into the cavern.

Blackrose glanced at Maddie. 'You are hurting, little one, as am I. Buckler had another four hundred years of life before him, and my heart cries out in grief. I sense you wish to give up and lie down, but you must be strong, Maddie. If you free me, then I will fly again, and you will fly with me.'

Maddie glanced up at her. 'Do you mean that?'

'Do I ever lie?'

Daniel raised his hand. 'What do you want me to do?'

'Wait for Emily.' Maddie sat on the ground, and rested her head in her hands. 'This can't be happening.'

'I don't understand,' said Blackrose. 'If the greenhides have breached the outer wall, then why can't I hear the sound of soldiers? Is no one fighting back?'

'There's no one here, Blackrose. Marcus stripped the garrisons bare and sent all the Blades into the rest of the City. And then the rain stopped early.'

'So Buckler's death is the fault of Marcus?'

'In a few hours there will be a lot more than just Buckler to mourn. My family's in Sector Six, just a couple of miles from Stormshield. If the greenhides break through there…'

'That won't happen, will it?' said Daniel.

'There's a plan of what to do in every situation,' Maddie said; 'involving sealing the gates of the fortresses and inner wall. In theory, the greenhides shouldn't be able to get any further, but you saw the gate at Arrowhead. It was wide open, because no one really believed that the greenhides could ever penetrate the outer wall. It's held for a thousand years.'

'Nothing lasts forever,' said Blackrose. 'Complacency and arrogance always earn their reward in due course.'

In the distance, the peal of a bell sounded.

'That's the alarm,' said Maddie. 'Everyone who hears it will know what's happened. The children and old folk will start withdrawing to the Middle Walls, while everyone of fighting age will be hurrying to the defend the Bulwark. Well, they would be, if there were any around.'

'And what will we do?' said Daniel. 'Run, or fight?'

'We fight,' said Maddie. 'We're Blades. The greenhides will kill us all, but if we can slow down their advance, then the others will be able to make it to safety behind the Middle Walls. This is our destiny; it's the perfect meaning of what the Blades are for.'

'Expendable,' he said.

'Yes.'

'Marcus has to die for this.'

Blackrose tilted her head. 'And are you going to kill him, little insect?'

'I hope so, but as long as someone does it, I don't care.'

'You don't sound like a man from the Bulwark, and neither does the girl you are with.'

Maddie snorted. 'Somehow I've ended up with a Roser aristocrat in my team, and this is her crazy husband, who left his life to join her.'

'True love,' said Blackrose; 'it still exists, then?'

Emily ran back into the lair, with several Rats following her; all Hammers, Maddie noticed. They skidded to a halt a few yards from Blackrose, their eyes widening.

Emily gestured to two of the group, and they rushed forward. One had a long steel pin, and she knelt by the shackles next to the dragon's rear limb where the chain began. The other followed, wielding a hammer. The woman raised the pin, and the man swung down, driving the pin into the joint where the chains met.

'One more!' she yelled, and the man swung again.

The pin drove the connector free, and the chain dropped to the ground with a clang. The two Rats retreated back to where the others were gathering as the dragon stretched its rear limb.

'Clear a path for Blackrose,' Maddie yelled. 'Run ahead, and make sure there's plenty of food for her.'

Again, the Hammers looked to Emily and Daniel for confirmation. Emily urged them away, and they sprinted from the cavern.

She glanced at Maddie as they walked after them. 'Sorry. I keep telling them to do what you say.'

'I know you do, princess. I have even less authority as a sergeant than I had as a damn corporal. And can you two stop holding hands? It's driving me crazy.'

She looked back, and saw that Blackrose was following. The black gate was still wide open, and she passed through, glancing back as she did so.

'I shall not be returning here,' she said, 'no matter what occurs.'

'Can you fly?' said Daniel.

'Why don't you ask my rider?'

'Your rider?'

'That's me,' said Maddie. 'This is where I worked before I got thrown into the Rats.'

'Why was the cavern walled up?' said Emily.

'Because she was a bad dragon,' Maddie said. 'She refused to bow before Kano so he decided she should starve to death as a punishment. Damn demigods; they're supposed to protect the City, and they've completely screwed it.'

'I did also try to burn him to death,' said Blackrose, 'though with good reason.'

They came to the red gate, and Maddie swung it open on its greased rollers. Beyond was the heap of rubble from the collapsed wall, and a large crowd had gathered. Most were Rats, but there were some of Buckler's staff, and a few from the Wolfpack mixed in. They stared in silence as Blackrose strode up the tunnel, stepping over the piles of debris.

'This is Blackrose,' Maddie said, standing in front of the dragon.

Quill walked through the crowd, shaking her head. 'And to think I doubted your plan, Maddie. You've found us another dragon?'

Maddie glanced at her. 'Is Arrowhead safe? Are the gates closed?'

'Yes. Every gate that opens between the outer and inner walls has been locked and barred, but the greenhides are spreading iceward and sunward, and I don't know about the neighbouring forts.'

'Thank Malik for that. At least we're safe in here for a while.'

'Do you need help? What can we do?'

'Find Buckler's food stores and open then up. Bring as much as you can here.'

Quill turned. 'You heard her; come on. The black dragon will save us.'

Many in the crowd began moving at her words, and Maddie gazed up at Blackrose.

'Don't say anything,' she said to the dragon.

'I haven't promised to save anyone.'

'I know that; but please don't say it to them. You've given them hope.'

'That wasn't my intention.'

Emily frowned. 'What are you going to do, Blackrose?'

'That depends. Where is Corthie Holdfast?'

'Who?' said Daniel.

Blackrose gave him a cold stare.

'He was a champion, remember?' said Maddie. 'He used to kill fifty greenhides a day.'

'Oh, him. Wasn't he executed?'

'He's alive, and Blackrose and I are quite fond of him.' She turned to the dragon. 'I've been in the Rats ever since they dragged me out of here. I've heard nothing.'

The first baskets of food began to appear in the tunnel, carried by soldiers and Rats.

'Give the dragon peace to eat,' Maddie cried, waving her arms at any remaining in the tunnel. 'Everybody out.'

She waited until she was alone with Blackrose, then crouched down by the dragon as she began to eat. Maddie leaned into the thick, black scales, a hand over her eyes.

'It's coming true, isn't it?' she said. 'My worst nightmare.'

Blackrose glanced at her. 'I thought it was your deepest desire?'

'I was wrong. Emily's exactly the type of person I meant; rich, entitled, and clueless about the Bulwark. She's never given a thought to what goes on here for a moment of her life; never wondered what it takes to defend the City for a thousand years. And yet, I like her. It's not her fault she's ignorant. She's realised her mistake, so what good would her death do?'

'You talk as if the greenhides are already in Tara. Your Middle Walls will hold them, it is your people, your kin, who are in danger. The

Blades, the Hammers and the Scythes, they will fulfil their purpose at last; dying so the rich and entitled can live.'

'The Middle Walls are two thousand years old; they're crumbling and falling apart. They might hold for a while, but not indefinitely.'

'Nothing lasts indefinitely.'

'So you keep saying.'

'Maddie, did you think this City would last forever?'

'No, but I didn't think it would fall in my lifetime. I'm so tired.'

They fell into silence, the only sound coming from Blackrose eating, and the distant peal of the bells. Maddie closed her eyes, but her head filled with images of the greenhides tearing their way through the Rats and Wolves by the moat. If only she had acted quicker, maybe they could have got the postern gate closed before the greenhides had forced their way through.

'Maddie?'

She glanced up to see Quill standing a few yards away, as if she were wary about getting too close to the dragon.

'Yeah?'

'Can you come here for a minute?'

She got to her feet and walked up the tunnel.

'There's bad news,' Quill said. 'The greenhides have broken down one of the gates leading into Arrowhead. They're inside the fortress.'

Maddie nodded, though she barely took in the words.

'We're going to hold them off for you, Maddie,' Quill said. 'We'll give you a chance to get the dragon into the air. Do you... I mean, will you be, ah, riding on her?'

'Yes.'

'Alright. The Rats are building a barricade at the entrance to the lair, but we haven't got long. You hold all our lives in your hands, Maddie. Good luck.'

Maddie stared at her as she ran away towards the sloping entrance to Buckler's lair.

'I'm ready,' said Blackrose behind her.

They walked to the Dragon Port, Maddie in the lead, as they

climbed the angled tunnel. She saw the small rectangle of sky ahead, where dozens of stars were shining in the clear sky. She reached the top, and stared out. Below the walls was a sea of greenhides, shimmering in the silver light of the two moons, and stretching into the dark horizon. Down to her left, in the distance she saw a thick line of greenhides crossing the moat, like ants on the branch of a tree.

Blackrose joined her at the top and gazed around. 'I see my slain kin. It mars what would otherwise be a beautiful night. I have longed to gaze upon the stars for ten years, and now I will remember Buckler whenever I see them. His death heralded my freedom and I will honour him for that.' She glanced at Maddie. 'Climb up, rider.'

Maddie gripped the ropes that were fastened to the straps of the harness, and scrambled up onto Blackrose's back. She tucked her feet into the grips, and clutched the bar at the front.

'Damn it,' she said. 'I forgot to bring a blanket.'

'Kaula,' said Blackrose.

'What?'

'That's the second of my names; given by my father when I was two years old.'

'Mela-Kaula?'

'Yes. There is more, but that will do for now.'

Blackrose launched herself off the platform, and unfurled her wings to their widest extent. She soared down over the greenhides, then banked to the left as Maddie clung on. They flew back over Arrowhead fortress, then turned right, and Maddie could see the gate in the outer walls that had been breached. Thousands of greenhides had penetrated the channel between the two walls, and more were swarming in with every second that passed. They raced iceward, and the fortress of Stormshield came into view. Like Arrowhead, there were no Blades up on the battlements, and none on the high artillery platforms. As they got closer, Maddie saw the interior of the fortress. Greenhides were everywhere. Some were breaking through the side gates of Stormshield, and were pouring into the Bulwark. Screams and shrieks rose up to them as she watched Blade civilians fleeing in panic from the greenhides, then she looked away as one group was overtaken.

'It is done,' said Blackrose. 'The eternal enemy of the City has breached the Great Walls. It is over.'

'It's not over,' cried Maddie. 'You can stop them, Blackrose; you can close the breach, and then burn every one of those monsters that got inside.'

'Which monsters do you mean, rider? The ones who imprisoned me for ten years? The ones who shackled me, starved me, and walled me up? Are those the monsters you're referring to?'

'Please, Mela, you know what I mean. My family's down there somewhere. They had nothing to do with locking you up.'

'Guide me to their house.'

Maddie blinked. 'Alright. Left, then down.'

Blackrose banked at a steep angle and Maddie grasped the handle and kept herself low as she scanned the rooftops. She saw the circular plaza of Sector Six.

'Right a little bit.'

The dragon soared down, the wind rushing past Maddie's face. On the flat roof of a house, she saw someone operating a machine. It was shooting long, steel bolts down into a mass of greenhides in the street below.

'That's my sister!' she screamed at Blackrose. 'The one shooting from the roof. Drop me off next to her.'

Blackrose rushed down, then hovered over the roof of the house. Maddie pushed herself free of the harness and leaped down.

Her sister stared at her, tears shining on her cheeks.

'It's me, Rosie,' Maddie yelled. 'Where's mum and dad?'

Rosie ran into Maddie's arms, weeping. 'The greenhides got them.'

Maddie cried out, a howl of anguish and pain as she wept into her sister's shoulder. A burst of flames surrounded them, ringing the house in a circle of fire.

'We have to leave,' said Maddie.

'But there's nowhere to go.'

Maddie pointed up.

Rosie staggered back a step, her eyes wild.

'Climb up with me,' Maddie said.

She extended her hand and Rosie took it, then started to pull herself up the ropes. Maddie clambered up after her sister, and pushed her down into the harness, sitting right behind her, with an arm round her waist.

'Go, Blackrose; we're on!'

The dragon beat its wings and soared back up into the sky. She banked again, then turned iceward.

'Where are you going?' cried Maddie. 'We have to seal the breach.'

The dragon increased her speed, but said nothing.

'Blackrose!' Maddie screamed. 'You have to save the City!'

'Save those who tried to kill me?' the dragon said. 'No, I think not.'

Maddie put her head down by her sister's as the wind rushed past. The Bulwark passed by underneath, followed by the ice walls, and then they were out, the City dwindling into the distance behind them.

CHAPTER 29

THE MASK SLIPS

G rey Isle, Cold Sea – 21st Amalan 3420
Corthie charged at the Blades coming down the stairs. He swung the heavy mace handle, catching a soldier on the side of his helmet and sending him toppling to the ground. Corthie held back on his battle-vision, not happy with the idea of killing too many Blades that might be needed at the Great Walls once summer began. He ducked a sword swing, and rammed the end of the handle into the man's guts. Even though they had the advantage of the stairs, Corthie's height and reach still out-matched them, and he felled another two with a powerful sweep that knocked their legs away.

The others fled up the stairs, and disappeared round a corner. Corthie decided against chasing them. Once they were alerted to his presence, the next soldiers would have their crossbows ready, and he had no intention of going down like he had at Cuidrach Palace. He quickly stripped the largest Blade of his armour and strapped it on, then unfastened another chestplate to use as a shield. No helmet would fit him, but he bent a greave into a ring round his neck to protect his throat. When he had covered himself with as much metal as would fit, he picked up the long handle and began to ascend the stairs, keeping his head low.

Voices began to drift down to him.

'I don't care how big he is,' snapped a voice; 'was it the ex-champion?'

'I didn't get a good look at his face, sir.'

'It must be him,' said another voice; 'there can't be two warriors of his size on the island.'

'Summon the garrison, Captain,' said the first voice. 'I want him cornered here. For now, shoot anything that comes up those steps until they arrive.'

'Do we know how he got in, sir?'

'Someone reported hearing noises coming from the old dungeons.'

Corthie blocked the voices out and got ready. If the whole garrison was coming, then he would have to retreat into the cells to escape, and they would follow him into the tunnels, even if Yaizra had managed to free the old prisoner in that time. He powered his battle-vision, feeling it heighten his senses and fill him with energy. He pulled the chestplate in front of him and ran up the stairs. Ahead was a line of kneeling guards, all holding their crossbows level. The first bolt whistled a yard to Corthie's right, the second glanced off his makeshift shield, and then he was among them, swinging the handle and battering the guards. He saw a group of others close by in the stone hallway, including two officers. He downed the last guard in the line with a blow to the back of his head and charged at them. One officer drew a sword, and Corthie struck his wrist, then rammed the other end of the handle into his nose, sending a gush of blood spraying out as he fell to the ground. He knocked out the other officer, then saw a man cowering behind them, his hand raised.

'Don't! Corthie, it's me; Tanner!'

Corthie stayed his hand.

'So, lad, eh... how have you been?'

Corthie laughed. 'What are you doing here?'

'Same as every other Blade on this damn island; searching for you.'

'What happened to the Wolfpack?'

'They're still there; but officers came and took about half of us away;

said we would be back for summer. I spent a bit of time on the border with Dalrig, and then I was put on a ship and brought to the island. I volunteered to stay back here in the fortress, as I didn't want to run into you somewhere in the hills. I guess that didn't work out as I'd planned.'

'Is Quill here too?'

'Nah, she's still in Arrowhead as far as I know.'

Corthie glanced at his old friend. 'How many Blades are in the fortress right now?'

'Hardly any, and I think you've knocked them all out. Everyone's searching the hills and caves for you; either that or they're checking the boats that leave the harbour. You've given us a right chase this last month.'

'Did they manage to send a message to the rest of the garrison before I came up the stairs?'

'No, no. I don't think so.'

'So I'm in the clear? As long as you're not thinking of turning me in. You wouldn't do that to an old friend, would you?'

'Of course not!' Tanner said, raising his palms.

'Then why are you acting so terrified?'

'You clubbed a dozen folk half to death with that thing you're carrying, and I, uh... well, you murdered Khora. I didn't see that coming, lad, and I didn't believe it until I spoke to a few Blades who'd been there, at Cuidrach Palace. That was rough, lad, what you did.'

'They were lying to you. I didn't kill her.'

'So you say. And then an entire company of Blades was slaughtered on the western bank, at that ruined town. I suppose you're going to say that you didn't kill them either?'

'I didn't; it was greenhides.'

'Right. Sure.'

'You don't believe me.'

'I'm a criminal myself, lad, and I've heard every excuse uttered by every murderer. You lie to yourself so often, eventually it becomes the truth in your mind. Listen, if you say there's no quarrel between us, then I'll believe that.'

'I'm angry that you think I'm lying, but I'm not going to hurt you. You arrived in this world on the same day as me, and I learned a lot from you last summer. We were friends, weren't we?'

'Yes, lad; we were. We had plenty of good times in the Wolfpack common room, and then when we lived in that fancy apartment at the top of the tower.' He laughed, but it sounded forced. 'Boy, you could put away the booze. You have my word, son; I'll make no move on you if you do the same by me.'

Corthie nodded.

One of the Blades on the ground groaned and lifted his head. Corthie glanced down and thumped him on the back of the helmet with the butt of the mace handle. His eyes were only off Tanner for a moment, but it was enough. His arm flashed out with a dagger, striking Corthie in the side between the plates of borrowed armour. Tanner's hand let go of the knife, and he swung his fist into Corthie's chin, and the champion fell backwards clutching his side, as blood seeped between his fingers.

'Nothing personal, eh?' Tanner said, then he took off down the hall-way, sprinting for the doorway at the end. Corthie glanced up, and drew upon all of his battle-vision as he pulled the blade from his side and threw it at Tanner. Exhaustion hit him like a wave, and his eyes were closed before he saw where the flight of the knife had ended.

A warm breeze woke him, and he opened his eyes. Blood had pooled under his body, and he felt the searing pain from the wound in his side. The blade had been short, but he was weakened by the blood loss. He glanced up. No one in the hallway was moving, and he guessed he hadn't been unconscious long, judging by the exhaustion he felt. If he was going to be able to move, he would have to power up his battle-vision again. He had a low-level burst of about an hour left in him, he guessed, and then he would be spent.

He drew on his powers, feeling the pain fade into the background, and his strength return. He got to his feet and walked along the hallway. Tanner's body was sprawled across the flagstones, the knife protruding from the back of his neck.

'Sorry,' Corthie muttered.

One of the Blades started crawling across the ground, his face a bloody mess, and Corthie stepped over him as he walked back to the stairs. He passed a narrow window and paused.

Something was different.

The rain; it had stopped. Did that mean summer had arrived early? He wasn't sure, but from what he remembered Achan and Yaizra saying, once that rains had ended, then that was it for four months. His thoughts went straight to the Great Wall. If things had got so bad that they had pulled members of the Wolfpack out of the Bulwark, then who was left to defend the walls? At least they had Buckler. The Blades would be leaving the Grey Isle immediately, he realised, so they could hasten back to their summer positions. That would mean they would be returning to the fortress, he thought, just as he heard a noise echoing down through the ceiling above him.

Damn it. They were back.

He ignored the throbbing pain, his powers helping him to suppress the worst edges of it, and took a moment to examine the injury in his right side. He ripped a strip of cloth from his cloak and folded it against the wound, pressing it in to staunch the flow of blood. A surge of dizziness made his head feel light, and he knew he was on borrowed time. He leaned down and picked up the mace handle, then, using it as a walking stick to support his weight, he began moving towards the stairs.

He was halfway down when the first Blades reached the hallway and saw the bodies.

At first there was nothing but confused shouting, then someone pointed. 'There he is!'

Corthie pushed himself on, reaching the bottom of the stairs. There were several doorways leading off from the dark hallway, and he went straight through the one that went to the cells. He checked the door for a bolt as soon as he had closed it, but the lock required a key. He took the long mace handle, and wedged it against the door.

He staggered back a few paces, hearing the Blades enter the hallway. His eyes went to the cell where the old woman had been shackled. It was empty, the chains lying coiled on the filthy floor. He smiled, sending a thanks to Yaizra in his mind. He crept across to the cell opposite, and entered through the open door. Below him stretched the hole he had made in the floor. Water from an old pipe was leaking down through the gap, dripping in a small waterfall over the edge. He glanced back at the door at the end of the corridor. It was being shaken, but wasn't opening, and he hoped the soldiers would search the other doorways first. He lowered his legs into the hole, and tried to drop himself down gently, but his fingers slipped in the stream of water, and he fell backwards, landing onto the high pile of rubble created by the breach. He rolled off it, clenching his teeth in agony, and clutching his side.

A light attracted his eyes and he glanced up. He struggled to his feet, and stumbled down the outlet pipe towards the low glow. It was the approaching dawn, he realised as he walked along the gradual bend in the pipe; it was the growing light in the sky towards sunward that he had noticed. He stared at the patch of sky at the end of the pipe, the reds and pinks already spreading across the horizon.

He must have been unconscious for longer than he had thought. Would the ship wait for him? There was no sign of Yaizra or Achan, or the prisoner, so they must have returned to the cavern where they had been hiding. At that moment, they were probably boarding the ship that the captain had arranged, while he was still underneath the fortress. He stared at the light for another moment, trying to summon the energy and will it would take to get through the labyrinth of tunnels and caverns. The sky was beautiful, and the air was already warmer than it had been the day before. It seemed as though the world was waking up after its long Freshmist slumber.

He turned, and made for the hole in the ceiling of the pipe. As he was reaching up with his arms, the sound of a door being battered in rang down the outlet pipe from the direction of the cells, and within seconds he could hear voices echoing towards him. He pulled himself up into the narrow tunnel, his legs dangling for a few seconds as his side rubbed against the ragged edge of the gap, leaving a trail of blood behind. He rolled his legs up and lay down for a moment, panting as the footsteps and cries of the Blades grew closer.

His mind went to Tanner as his body refused to move. It had been stupid of him to take his eyes off him for even a second, but it was the fact that his old friend hadn't believed him that hurt more than the betrayal. Maybe all of the Blades felt that way; maybe they had taken the official story as the truth. He could imagine that Blades who had never met him might believe it, but Tanner knew him as well as anyone. The old veteran had just wanted to serve out his time and return home, Corthie thought, he had never really been a friend. He trusted people too easily, that was his problem.

He grunted and got to his feet, anger now helping him as he vowed never to be taken in so easily again. People were weak; they might pretend to be your friend, but when things got rough, they would abandon you, just as Yaizra had left Achan to die. And now he would die, lost in the maze of tunnels, alone.

His eyes caught something on the bottom of the tunnel, and he frowned. He took a closer look. Someone had scrawled a tiny arrow in chalk onto the stones of the ground. He was positive that it hadn't been there before, he had been sitting by that spot before they had entered the outlet pipe. Yaizra or Achan must have done it, and he smiled.

Voices drifted up from below.

'Look, sir; blood.'

'He's gone up there,' came another voice. 'Get after him. If he gets away before we have to board those ships, then Commander Kano will flay every one of us.'

Corthie got moving, staggering along the tunnel as quickly as he could. He knew that the pursuing Blades would also see the arrows, but that didn't matter as he was dripping blood all over the tunnel anyway. He squeezed through a small opening, his fingers leaving bloody marks on the wall, as his eyes scanned for the next arrow. He saw it, and turned left at a junction, his legs swaying but still going. He halted, the light too dim to see any more.

Behind him, he heard the clatter and noise of soldiers climbing up into the tunnels. They had lanterns with them, and he forced himself to wait until they began catching him up, so he could use their light to keep going. He leaned against a wall in the darkness, hiding behind a lip of rock as the soldiers got closer.

'More blood, up there,' said one.

'He could be anywhere in here. Shine that lamp up ahead.'

Corthie felt his eyes try to close as he slumped against the wall. If they found him in that state, they would kill him, or worse, they would haul him away in chains for Kano to deal with. He focussed on the reasons for staying alive, trying to find something that would make him carry on. His family were out there somewhere, he had to remember that. His sister would never give up searching for him; and if his mother had been with him, she would chide him for even harbouring thoughts about giving up. He was a Holdfast, a member of the only mortal family that the gods feared.

It didn't work. The soldiers were getting closer, and he remained against the wall, weakening with every second that passed.

Aila. If he died or was captured, he would never see Aila again. Something stirred within him. He loved her, and despite the doubts he held about whether she felt the same way, if he died, he would never know. He clenched his fists.

The first soldier peered round the edge of the lip of the tunnel, and Corthie smashed him in the face with his right fist, breaking his jaw. He yanked the lantern from his hand as the soldier fell, then turned and ran, dredging up the last of his powers to move his legs. A crossbow bolt skittered off the side of the tunnel wall next to him, then he dived into a branch that led off to the right, seeing the tiny arrow scrawled onto the middle of the ground.

The next few minutes were a blur as he raced along. The shouts and cries of the chasing soldiers were a constant companion as he ran through the twisting lanes and tunnels. Before he knew where he was, he burst out into the cavern where they had been living for over two months.

'You took your time, big lump.'

He staggered forward and fell onto the ground.

Yaizra ran over. 'Malik's crotch, what's wrong?'

He glanced up at her. 'Behind me. Blades are coming.'

'Did you get stabbed? Amalia's breath, look at all the blood.'

She grabbed his arm and tried to haul him up, and he pushed himself back to his feet.

'Blades,' he gasped.

'Yeah, I heard you the first time,' she said, putting her arm round his waist and taking some of his weight. 'You're a heavy bugger and no mistake. Come on.'

They staggered together along another tunnel, which was low and headed downwards at a steep angle. Corthie put a hand on the wall to his right to steady himself, as Yaizra urged him on.

'Where's Achan?' he said.

'That little scamp's already gone to the boat with the prisoner we freed. Hopefully they'll wait for us two.'

'You stayed?'

'Of course I stayed. All I've thought about for two months is leaving Achan behind. Did you think I would ever do that again? You're a pain in the ass, Holdfast, but you're my pain in the ass.'

'Down here!' cried a voice behind them from the top of the tunnel.

'I hope you can go a bit faster,' Yaizra said, as she picked up her pace.

Corthie pushed himself on as they turned right at a tunnel junction. Ahead, there was a much lighter section of tunnel, where the dawn light was reaching. They turned again, and he felt the wind on his face. The tunnel came to an abrupt end, and he held onto the side wall as he looked down. The Cold Sea spread out before them, glistening in shades of red and peach as the sky lightened. Sitting on the waves was a tall ship, with two high masts, anchored fifty yards from the sheer wall of cliffs. Bobbing between the ship and the cliff was a rowing boat.

'Here's the rope ladder,' said Yaizra, pointing at the edge of the tunnel.

A crossbow bolt ricocheted off the floor by their feet.

'No time for that,' he said, grabbing her arm.

He sprang from the edge of the rockface, pulling Yaizra with him as she screamed. They fell through the air for thirty feet, then crashed into the freezing waters of the Cold Sea, plunging down below the surface. Corthie kept a grip of Yaizra's arm as he kicked with his legs, and they burst back up onto the surface.

'You crazy asshole,' yelled Yaizra; 'I can't swim!'

Crossbow bolts hit the water around them, as Corthie pulled Yaizra towards the rowing boat. Three sailors were on board, and they were moving the small craft closer to them. They reached down, and hauled Yaizra into the boat, then Corthie lifted his arms and clambered in, nearly capsizing the vessel as water tumbled in after him. He collapsed onto the bottom of the boat as the sailors gripped the oars.

From the bottom of the vessel, Corthie glanced up at the massive cliff face. A small group of Blades were standing at the tunnel entrance where they had jumped from.

'Ha! Look at them,' Yaizra yelled as she made a rude gesture in their direction. 'Screw you, assholes!'

Corthie laughed, then passed out.

He awoke on a bed, and immediately became aware of the ship's motion beneath him. He opened his eyes, to see a small cabin. The shutters had been opened and the red light of a summer's morning was filling the room. He clutched his side, and saw that his wound had been bandaged.

'Hey, big lump; try not to wriggle about too much.'

He turned, and saw Yaizra sitting next to him. Behind her was another bed, upon which the old prisoner was lying. Her iron face mask was still on, and there was blood on the side of her pillow.

'Yup,' said Yaizra; 'there she is. I hope she was worth getting a knife in your guts for.'

'Why does she still have the mask on?'

'Achan's worried about removing it when we're at sea, with no doctors around.'

'It's a reasonable concern,' Achan said from the corner of the cabin. 'I have a suspicion about what that mask really is.'

'What do you mean?' said Corthie. 'It's causing her pain; we should remove it.'

'If it is what I suspect it is, then she should already be dead. Another day of wearing it won't do any more harm.'

'Another day? Where are we going?'

'Icehaven,' Achan said, frowning. 'Yes, Yaizra won the argument. Only, to avoid the Blade patrols, the captain's insisting we first head iceward for the entire day, and then sweep back round in a big loop. It'll be morning tomorrow before we arrive.'

Corthie nodded. 'Then we should take the mask off her.'

Achan got up and walked over to where the old woman lay. 'I don't know.'

'What is it that you're suspecting?'

'It's just a theory. If you look at the mask closely, where's the blood coming from? With that kind of blood loss, this old woman should have died a long time ago.'

'Yaizra?' said Corthie. 'We have one vote apiece. What do you think? Off or on?'

She frowned at the old woman. 'Off.'

'Fine,' said Achan. 'Brace yourselves, this might not be pleasant.'

He reached forward, and tilted the woman's head to the side. His fingers went to the thick, leather straps that bound the mask to the prisoner's head, and he struggled with the buckle.

'It's rusted into place,' he said.

Yaizra handed him a knife. He frowned, then cut through the leather strap. With both hands, he started to lift the mask from the old woman's face. Built into the inside of the mask were two long nails, each two inches in length, that had been driven into the woman's eyes. She convulsed as the mask was ripped free, the two nails dripping blood down her face and onto the sheets.

Yaizra put a hand to her mouth. 'I think I'm going to be sick.'

Corthie stared at the old woman. The two nails had gouged out holes into the woman's head, her eyes almost completely gone, and the two holes filled with blood. The woman writhed on the bed, her hands going up to her face as Achan wound a bandage over her eyes.

He held up the mask, then threw it to Corthie. 'Happy now?'

Corthie stared at the mask. The inside was filled with pus and blood, the two nails gleaming in the sunlight. 'How could she have survived this?'

'It's a god-restrainer,' Achan said. 'I've read about them. The nails are to stop their vision powers, and also to tax their self-healing. With the constant pain, their healing is slowly overloaded, and they start to age, unable to deal with the injury. She could have been in that prison for a very long time.'

Yaizra stared at the old woman as she started mumbling again. 'She's a god? What's she saying?'

Achan leaned close to the old woman's face. 'Kahlia, I think.'

'Kahlia?' said Corthie. 'I've heard that name before, but I can't remember where.'

'She was a demigod,' said Achan, sitting on the bed. He rubbed his head. 'She was killed in the Civil War.

'This can't be her, then? This isn't Kahlia?'

'No. A demigods powers aren't sufficient to endure three centuries of this torture. Only a true god could have survived this.' He shook his head. 'There's only one person this can be, but I can barely believe it.'

'Who?' said Corthie.

Achan glanced up at them. 'It's Kahlia's mother. It's Princess Yendra.'

CHAPTER 30

KING-IN-WAITING

O oste, Auldan, The City – 21st Amalan 3420

Soldiers swung open the tall doors of the Royal Palace and bowed as the God-Queen swept through. Below her on the stairs, Marcus and Aila followed, as more Blades escorted them. The new prince's face was contorted with fury, and he avoided looking anywhere near Aila as she walked by his side into the palace.

'Your gamble failed,' she said quietly. 'You risked the entire City hoping that summer would arrive on time, and you lost.'

He turned to her in the vast, marble-lined entrance hall. 'One more word, wife, and I'll throttle the life out of you,' he said raising his hands towards her throat as the soldiers stood by.

Aila didn't flinch. 'Are you going to hit me again?'

Marcus sneered at her, then laughed. 'Just wait until we get to our wedding chamber, and it's just me and you. I'm going to make you choke on those words.'

'Marcus, darling,' called the God-Queen, her voice echoing across the huge hall; 'come along.'

He strode away to join her, and Aila walked behind. She glanced back, but Blades were all around her to make sure she didn't escape. If she could get out of sight of them for a second, then she could switch her appearance and make a run for it. She frowned. What about Mona's plan? If she ran, then Marcus would still be alive in the morning, and legally, she would still be his wife.

The guards eyed her as they walked, and she wondered if they had been told about her powers.

'Should you guys not be back at the Great Wall?' she said in a low voice.

None answered her.

'Come on, I'm married to the prince, surely you can talk to me. What's happening in the Bulwark? Are there enough soldiers to defend the City?'

'With all due respect, ma'am,' said an officer, 'if you had given your-self up earlier, then the Blades could have been redeployed days ago, and this situation could have been avoided.'

'So you're blaming me for this? Malik's ass. And I guess if Corthie hadn't escaped, and if Prince Montieth hadn't rebelled, everything would be roses and sunshine? It's everybody else's fault, yeah? How safe do you feel with my brother in charge of the Bulwark? You all know Kano; do you really think he's capable of protecting the City with no soldiers? Marcus has screwed everything up, and you're still defending him.'

They reached a set of doors at the end of the hall and entered a reception room. The God-Queen and Marcus were waiting in the centre of the chamber as Lady Doria approached, her head bowed.

'Your Majesty,' she said, getting down onto her knees before Queen Amalia.

'Where is my husband?'

Doria lifted her head a fraction, her eyes scanning the room. She saw Aila there, but her expression remained serene. 'The God-King is sleeping in his private chambers, your Majesty. Would you like me to awaken him and inform his Majesty that you are here?'

'At last; someone with some sense,' the God-Queen said. 'Yes, girl, do so immediately.'

Lady Doria bowed low, then rose and backed away from the chamber.

Queen Amalia turned, glancing round the room. 'I can't say the place has changed much in three hundred years. A little worn and threadbare, perhaps.'

'I much prefer Maeladh Palace,' said Marcus.

'I find there to be more air and light in this palace compared to Maeladh, grandson,' she said, as servants entered through the doors.

'Your Divine Majesty,' one said as they all bowed; 'Lady Doria has informed us of your presence and has sent us to make your visit here as pleasant as possible. Would you care for some refreshments?'

The God-Queen nodded. 'Red wine.'

'At once, your Majesty,' said the chief servant. He clicked his fingers and another ran off.

'And tell me,' the God-Queen went on, 'what is the state of the chambers in the sunward wing? Are they suitable to move into immediately?'

The chief servant blinked. 'Am I to understand, your Majesty, that some of your party wish to remain in the palace for some time?'

'Yes. I shall require my old rooms, and Marcus and his charming bride can have the floor directly below mine.'

'I shall personally make sure of it, your Majesty,' the man said, bowing again, then hurrying away.

Queen Amalia turned to Marcus. 'I'm going to let you in on a little secret while we wait for my husband to join us. You may have wondered in the past; how is it that I was able to live for so long with someone with such powerful vision skills? Being married to a person that can read your mind can be taxing, especially after a few millennia, so the old gods came up with a solution.'

'A solution, grandmother? You mean there's a way to stop them from reading your mind?'

'Indeed. A temporary measure only, but one I feel it might be wise for us to take now.' She slipped her hand into her robes and withdrew a small metal box. She opened it, and Marcus peered in.

'What are they?' he said.

'Eye-shields. Thin membranes that one places over the eyes. They are annoying, and shouldn't be worn for too long, but they effectively block vision powers from entering your mind through your eyes.'

Aila watched as the God-Queen placed her little finger into the box. She lifted it out, and a small, transparent disk glinted in the light on the end of her finger. She pulled her eyelid up, and carefully slid the disk over her right eye, then repeated the motion with her left eye. She blinked.

'Now you do it,' she said, passing the box to Marcus.

Aila cursed. How would Mona send him to sleep if she couldn't access his eyes?

The prince struggled with the disks for a few moments, then got them onto his eyes. 'They rub against my eyelids,' he said; 'most uncomfortable.'

The God-Queen nodded. 'They're worth the irritation. The last thing we want is for my husband to get into our heads.'

Marcus glanced at Aila. 'What about her?'

'She has nothing in her head that need worry us, and besides, I only have two pairs. They are exceedingly hard to make, so don't lose or break them.'

Servants entered with trays of wine and small, delicate snacks. They went first to the God-Queen and Marcus, and then to Aila, who took a glass of red wine.

Aila took a sip, and wondered what Lady Doria was doing. She should be running away as fast as she could, if she had the slightest amount of intelligence, she thought. She stepped forwards, tired of being in the background.

'What's your plan for the City?'

The God-Queen and Marcus turned to her.

'Say the Bulwark is safe,' Aila went on, 'and the Blades make it back in time to defend the walls? What then?'

'Then we deal with the Circuit,' said Marcus; 'bring it to its knees. Give the Evaders a choice – submit or die. After that, we blockade the harbour of Dalrig until the Gloamers are faced with the same choice. This City will be united, under my rule.'

Aila nodded, restraining herself from saying what she wanted to say. 'Alright. What is my part in this?'

'To provide sons and daughters, of course,' said the God-Queen; 'a new generation to run the City. As will Kano and Lydia, and the other demigods.'

'But our children shall be the heirs to the City,' Marcus said. 'That was always the original plan, for power to descend down the line of the firstborn. My father was the eldest of the God-Children, and I am his eldest child. Khora was nothing but a usurper, a thief.'

'Is that why you had her murdered? I was there, remember? I saw what my brother did.'

Marcus's face reddened. 'I was close to executing your brother for his incompetence in that affair. Letting you leave was bad enough, but to have allowed that mortal to have survived was almost unforgivable.'

'By "mortal", you mean Corthie Holdfast?'

'I do.'

'Are you not worried he'll return?'

'He won't return. My forces have driven him to the Grey Isle, and he won't escape again. I have surrounded him in a ring of steel.'

'Let him return,' said the God-Queen. 'If this mortal were to come here, I would kill him in a second.'

Aila nodded. She doesn't know about his immunity, she thought; either that, or she thinks she's too powerful for him to withstand.

The God-Queen frowned, and glanced at the door. 'Where is Lady Doria?'

'Should I go and look for her?' said Aila.

'You?' the God-Queen said. 'I don't think that's a good idea. If my husband caught you wandering around the palace who knows what he'd do.' She turned to one of her mortal courtiers. 'Lord Chamberlain, would you please locate Lady Doria?'

The mortal bowed, then strode towards the door. A couple of palace servants glanced at each other and got out of his way, and he opened the door and went through.

The God-Queen smiled. 'Did you see that bruise under Chamberlain's eye?'

Marcus shrugged. 'I wasn't looking.'

'Lady Aurelian gave him that yesterday when he taunted her about her son.'

'Did you see this?'

'Of course not, have you ever seen me mingle with Taran aristocracy? No, Chamberlain told me. He was more angry than I'd ever seen him; it amused me.'

'What happened to her son?' said Aila.

The God-Queen raised an eyebrow. 'I hardly thought such gossip about Taran society would interest you.'

'If you're talking about Daniel Aurelian, then I met him once. He carried out an atrocity in the Circuit.'

'He has been expelled from the militia,' said Marcus, 'for disobeying orders and punching an officer. I had to sign the form discharging him from service. And now he's run off to join the Blades, apparently.'

'At least someone will be at the wall.'

Marcus's smile dropped away, and he narrowed his eyes.

The God-Queen sighed. 'I've had enough of this. My husband is clearly delaying for some reason, and my patience is wearing thin. Come, it is time to dispense with etiquette.'

She walked across the hall, gesturing to the servants to open the doors. They did so, and the God-Queen walked through. Aila and Marcus followed along with the escort of Blades, and they went to the left, where a series of high chambers were laid out. Each was empty, or had a small collection of furniture, all covered in dust-sheets. The paintings and tapestries were also covered.

'What is all this?' said the God-Queen. 'The palace looks hardly lived in.'

They went deeper into the palace, and Aila's anxiety rose with every step. She tried to prepare herself for the moment the God-Queen discovered the truth. She had to look surprised, or she would probably be dead in a second. They passed the last windows, and entered the part of the palace dug into the side of the cliff face. The God-Queen entered a suite of private rooms, all of them empty and deserted.

She frowned and turned to Marcus. 'Before Lady Vana vanished,' she said, 'she was absolutely certain my husband was here?'

'Yes. I asked her many times, and ordered her to let me know at once if he set foot outside the palace. He was here the entire time.'

'But these rooms haven't been lived in for years. Where is he?'

'Perhaps he retired to a smaller suite? He was on his own for a long time.'

There was a cough from behind them, and Lord Chamberlain raised his hand. 'Your Majesty, if I may? I have just returned from searching the rooms close to here, and I think I may have found where his Majesty might have been living.'

The God-Queen frowned. 'Show me.'

The mortal led them through the rooms, and they went deeper into the cliff face. He opened a door, and they entered the cavern with the pool that Aila remembered from her last visit. The stalactites were glistening in the light of a dozen high lamps, and the waters of the pool were reflecting their radiance. Lord Chamberlain gestured to an alcove in the wall of the cavern, where a bed lay. The God-Queen walked up to it, and the others followed.

The alcove was a mess, with food and empty bottles, and evidence of opium use scattered about.

Queen Amalia eyed Lord Chamberlain. 'Are you suggesting that the God-King of the City sleeps in this sordid cave?'

'It is the only place where I have seen evidence of anyone sleeping, your Majesty, excepting the quarters of Lady Doria, which I have also searched. She is not there, but there is nothing to suggest that his Majesty was using those rooms.'

'And what about his harem?' said the God-Queen. 'I know he had one after our separation.'

'It no longer exists, your Majesty; the rooms are all empty.'

'There's a tunnel at the back of the cavern,' said Marcus. 'Did you go up there?'

'No, your Grace,' he said, bowing. 'I went to find your royal presences after I discovered this cavern.'

'It's the oldest part of the Ooste salve mine,' said the God-Queen. 'It's completely exhausted, as you can see. There were small threads of salve throughout the rock here, and I remember when we first found it. The mine continues on through that tunnel to reach the ore within the heart of the hills.'

Marcus glanced at the Blades. 'Send half of the squad in, Captain. If there's anyone in there, bring them out alive.'

'Yes, sir,' the man said. He gestured to a sergeant, who selected six of their Blade escort. The soldiers lit a lantern, and they filed through the entrance into the tunnel.

Aila looked around for somewhere to sit. She walked to the back wall, and sat on a low chair.

Stay exactly where you are for the next few seconds.

Naxor?

Yes. Listen, don't move; you're in the perfect position for what I'm about to do.

Wait, no! They have something in their eyes...

Too late. Naxor had left her head before he had listened to her words. Her heart pounded as she glanced around. Naxor burst through the door into the cavern, a sword in his hand. He rushed into the group of courtiers and guards, and raised his fingers. They fell around him, the weapons of the Blades clattering to the floor of the cavern, and the courtiers dropping like cut wheat.

Naxor stared at the God-Queen and Marcus, who were the only ones who had remained on their feet.

'Why, Lord Naxor, how lovely to see you,' said the God-Queen.

A look of terror swept over Naxor's face. 'But how? You should be sleeping.'

Marcus swung his sword from across his back. 'Let me, grand-mother. I've waited a long time for this.'

'Do not kill him, Marcus, darling. I need him for something.'

Marcus scowled.

The God-Queen frowned at him. 'I didn't say you couldn't hurt him. Feel free to inflict as much pain as you like.'

Naxor seemed frozen as Marcus approached, gripping the Just. At the last moment, Naxor raised his sword, but a single sweep from Marcus knocked it from his hand and sent it flying across the floor. Marcus raised his sword and plunged it down, striking the centre of Naxor's chest. The blade passed through, thrusting out of his back. Marcus kept pushing, until the tip of the sword touched the ground, leaving Naxor suspended on the blade for a second, then he slid down it, a streak of blood remaining against the sharp edge.

Marcus knelt by him as Aila jumped to her feet.

'Leave him alone,' she cried.

The God-Queen raised a finger, and Aila felt her neck constrict. She flung her hands to her throat, and sank to her knees. Marcus turned back to Naxor. He drew a knife, then slammed it down through Naxor's neck, driving the blade inches into the rock of the cavern floor. He then punched him in the face three times, smashing his nose and chin. He stood, and nodded to his grandmother.

The God-Queen lowered her finger, and Aila could breathe again. She gasped in a lungful of air, her throat burning as her self-healing soothed the pain. She rushed to Naxor's side. Blood was coming from his guts, his neck and his face, which had healed a little, but his body was shuddering, and his eyes were closed.

'Don't touch him,' said Marcus. 'If you do, he loses a thumb.' He glanced around at the sleeping bodies of the courtiers and guards. 'Handy things, those eye-pieces.'

'Indeed,' said the God-Queen. 'When the God-King finally gets here I shall ask him to awaken our mortals for us.'

A sound came from the entrance to the tunnel beyond the pool, and moments later the Blades reappeared. One held the arms of Lady Doria.

'No sign of the God-King, your Majesty,' he said; 'but we found Lady Doria, and a boy.'

'A boy?' said the God-Queen.

A youth of about fifteen was dragged forward by two Blades. He was kicking and screaming, and trying to bite the arms of the soldiers gripping onto him.

The God-Queen narrowed her eyes. 'Bring Lady Doria here. I wish to ask her a few questions.'

The lead soldier hauled the demigod round the edge of the pool and brought her before the God-Queen and Prince Marcus. Doria glanced down at the bodies littering the floor, her eyes catching on Naxor.

'Beloved granddaughter,' said the God-Queen, 'would you care to explain the whereabouts of the God-King?'

Doria fell to her knees. 'I couldn't find him, your Majesty.'

'So you thought you'd hide in a tunnel with this unruly boy?' She glanced at the youth again, and her expression slowly began to change. She bared her teeth and raised a hand, and Doria fell to the ground, grasping her throat as she choked. 'I will cause your flesh to rot and fall from your face, Doria. I will not kill you, but you will suffer. Now, answer me – where is my husband?'

Doria let out a loud gasp as she took in air. The skin on her face began to mottle, and patches with a greenish-grey tinge appeared on her cheeks. Her hair began to fall out and she screamed. Blood trickled down from her eyes and she writhed on the floor, her fingers covering her face.

'I can make it stop,' said the God-Queen; 'answer me.'

Doria raised an arm and pointed to the youth. 'There is your husband; there!'

The God-Queen lowered her hand and Doria collapsed onto the floor, her face slowly starting to heal as she sobbed.

Marcus stared at her. 'Explain.'

'It was the salve,' Doria said; 'he had too much salve, and it changed him into... into what you can see with your own eyes.'

A tear rolled down the God-Queen's face, though her features remained calm. 'When did this happen?'

'About eighty years ago.'

'Did Khora know?'

'Yes.'

The God-Queen's face twisted with fury. 'Who else?

'Just me and my mother. And Naxor, he knew too. That was all.'

'So Khora and her children were engaged in a vile conspiracy?' said Marcus. 'They kept this from the rest of the City? What about your mother's other children?'

'No, none of them knew; I swear on my life.'

Queen Amalia walked forward to where the two soldiers were holding the youth. The God-King's eyes were wild, and he was still struggling.

'Do you know who I am, husband?'

The youth tried to kick out at her, his face twisted with a feral rage, his eyes bloodshot and wide.

'Oh Malik, how you have fallen. Even though we parted three centuries ago, a small part of me retained the hope that one day you and I would be safe to leave this world, this world that we have saved and cursed at the same time. Once you were one of the mightiest vision gods of the ages, and now you are reduced to this. Destroyed by the very thing that secured our lives here. When I return alone at the end of days, I will tell the other gods that you died a noble and heroic death, so that none shall know of your shame.'

She turned to Marcus. 'Grandson, take his head; make it quick.'

The two soldiers pushed the God-King to his knees, and shoved his head forwards as the Prince of Tara gripped the Just in both hands. Doria scrambled out of the way, and ran to where Aila was crouching two yards from Naxor's body. Marcus took a step forwards, and raised his father's sword.

He glanced at the God-Queen, and she nodded, then looked away. Marcus swung the sword down, cleaving the neck of the God-King in a single blow. The head fell to the floor, then rolled down the slope into the pool, a stream of blood flowing after it. The soldiers let go of the body and it slumped to the ground.

The God-Queen opened her mouth and let out a scream of rage and pain that echoed off the walls of the cavern. With her eyes burning, she raised a hand to the seven Blades who had returned from the tunnel, and their bodies burst apart in an explosion of flesh, bone and blood, spattering the walls and the floor. She bowed her head, weeping, as Marcus sheathed the Just and took a step back.

Doria clutched Aila's hand. The skin on her face had healed, and fresh hair was already growing in to fill the patches that had been lost.

No one spoke as the God-Queen wept in front of them. She knelt and placed a hand on the headless corpse, and it withered away into dust, melting before their eyes. She glanced at the head in the pool, then rose to her feet and wiped her eyes.

'No mortal must ever learn of this, grandson. We shall make it known that the God-King and I have reconciled, and that I am now living with him in the Royal Palace here in Ooste. All but yourself will be forbidden from entering the inner quarters. Aila and Doria, drag the bodies of those sleeping out of here, and take them to the reception hall by the stairs. I shall speak to them when they awaken.'

Marcus nodded. 'What about Naxor?'

'Keep him restrained for now while I deal with this mess. Hide him close by, so that I can talk with him later. Lady Doria will also live here, to serve me, and Aila will stay, of course, as your bride.'

Doria glanced at Aila, her eyes wide.

The two demigods got to their feet. They each took an arm of a large Blade, and began dragging him from the room, while Marcus slung a courtier over his shoulder.

'You are now the king-in-waiting, Marcus,' Queen Amalia said. 'You have much to live up to.' She crouched down and picked up the head of Malik from the pool as Aila and Doria dragged the first body from the cavern. Marcus walked by them as they followed the hallway towards the top of the stairs.

Mona, if you can hear me, the God-King is dead. You can't help me.

Marcus has something in his eyes; he blocked Naxor, and captured him. It's over, Mona; we lost.

She closed her eyes, but heard nothing in response. They reached the top of the stairs; at the bottom, a Blade was running across the marble floor.

'Hey!' cried Marcus. 'You shouldn't be in this part of the palace.'

The soldier skidded to a halt. 'Sorry, sir,' he panted, 'but thank Malik I've found you.'

Marcus dropped the courtier to the floor and bounded down the stairs as the soldier got to his knees before him.

The prince glared at him. 'Well?'

The man began to sweat, his hands shaking. 'Buckler is dead, sir.'

Marcus staggered. 'How? No.'

'And the greenhides, sir, they've broken through the wall.'

'The outer wall?'

'The Great Walls, sir; they're loose in the Bulwark, thousands of them. I've come all the way from the Middle Walls to tell you, sir, and I saw them with my own eyes approaching as I left.'

Aila watched as Marcus lowered his head. He said nothing then, without a glance backwards, he strode from the hallway, heading towards the main entrance.

Aila glanced at Doria. 'Now's our chance,' she whispered.

'Stay where you are, girls,' said the God-Queen behind them. 'You will not be leaving this palace; if either of you attempt to do so, I will kill you both.'

Aila took a step back. 'Didn't you hear? The greenhides; the walls...'

'I heard,' Queen Amalia said. 'It means nothing. The Middle Walls will hold them, and then, if they fail, the Union Walls will, but what does it matter in the end; even if they reach the walls of this palace I will not fear them.'

'But you could go to the Bulwark,' Aila said, 'you could kill them.'

'I have killed millions of greenhides for this City. It never makes any difference; they always come back. No, if they come here I will deal with them, but I'm not risking myself for this City again.'

Aila stared at the God-Queen. 'But what about all of the people who will die?'

The God-Queen laughed. 'Dear Aila, don't you know? Mortals die every day.'

The Mortal Blade - The Royal Family

The Gods	Title	Powers
Malik	God-King of the City - Ooste	Vision
Amalia	God-Queen of the City - Tara	Death

The Children of the Gods		
Michael (deceased)	ex-Prince of Tara, 1600-3096	Death, Battle
Montieth	Prince of Dalrig, b. 1932	Death
Isra (deceased)	ex-Prince of Pella, 2001-3078	Battle
Khora (deceased)	ex-Princess of Pella 2014-3419	Vision
Niomi (deceased)	ex-Princess of Icehaven, 2014-3089	Healer
Yendra (deceased)	ex-Princess of the Circuit, 2133-3096	Vision

Children of Prince Michael		
Marcus	Duke, Bulwark, b. 1944	Battle
Mona	Chancellor, Ooste, b. 2014	Vision
Dania (deceased)	Lady of Tara, 2099-3096	Battle
Yordi (deceased)	Lady of Tara, 2153-3096	Death

Children of Prince Montieth		
Amber	Lady of Dalrig, b. 2035	Death
Jade	Lady of Dalrig, b. 2511	Death

Children of Prince Isra		
Irno (deceased)	Eldest son of Isra, 2017-3078	Battle
Berno (deceased)	'The Mortal', 2018-2097	None
Garno (deceased)	Warrior, 2241-3078	Battle
Lerno (deceased)	Warrior, 2247-3078	Battle

Vana	Adjutant of Pella, b. 2319	Location
Marno (deceased)	Warrior, 2321-3063	Battle
Collo	Khora's Secretary, b. 2328	None
Bonna (deceased)	Warrior, 2598-3078	Shape-Shifter
Aila	Adjutant of the Circuit, b. 2652	Shape-Shifter
Kano	Adj. of the Bulwark, b. 2788	Battle
Teno (deceased)	Warrior, 2870-3078	Battle

Children of Princess Khora

Salvor	Governor of Pella, b. 2201	Vision
Balian (deceased)	Warrior, 2299-3096	Battle
Lydia	Gov. of Port Sanders, b. 2304	Healer
Naxor	Royal Emissary, b. 2401	Vision
Ikara	Governor of the Circuit, b. 2499	Battle
Doria	Royal Courtier, b. 2600	None

Children of Princess Niomi

Rand (deceased)	Warrior, 2123-3089	Battle
Yvona	Governor of Icehaven, b. 2175	Healer
Samara (deceased)	Lady of Icehaven, 2239-3089	Battle
Daran (deceased)	Lord of Icehaven, 2261-3063	Battle

Children of Princess Yendra

Kahlia (deceased)	Warrior, 2599-3096	Vision
Neara (deceased)	Warrior, 2601-3089	Battle
Yearna (deceased)	Lady of the Circuit, 2604-3096	Healer

THE NINE TRIBES OF THE CITY

There are nine distinct tribes inhabiting the City. Three were in the area from the beginning, and the other six were created in two waves of expansion.

The Original Three Tribes – Auldan (pop. 300 000) Auldan is the oldest part of the City. United by the Union Walls (completed in 1040), it combined the three original tribes and their towns, along with the shared town of **Ooste**, which houses the Royal Palace, where **King Malik** lives.

1. **The Rosers** – (their town is **Tara**, est. Yr. 1.) The first tribe to reach the peninsula where the City is located. Began farming there in the sunward regions, until attacks from the Reapers forced them into building the first walled town. **Prince Michael** ruled until his death in 3096. **Queen Amalia** governs the Rosers from Maeladh Palace in Tara.

2. **The Gloamers** – (their town is **Dalrig**, est. Yr. 40.) Arrived shortly after the Rosers, farming the iceward side of the peninsula. Like them, they fought with the Reapers, and built a walled town to stop their attacks. **Prince Montieth** rules from Greylin Palace in Dalrig.

3. **The Reapers** – (their town is **Pella**, est. Yr. 70.) Hunter/Gatherer tribe that arrived after the more sedentary Rosers and Gloamers. Settled in the plains between the other two tribes. More numerous than either the Rosers or the Gloamers, but are looked down on as more rustic. **Prince Isra** ruled until his death in 3078. **Princess Khora** now rules in his stead, but delegates to her son, **Lord Salvor**, who governs from Cuidrach Palace in Pella.

The Next Three Tribes – Medio (pop. 400 000) Originally called 'New Town', this part of the City was its first major expansion; and was settled from the completion of the Middle Walls (finished in 1697 and originally known as the Royal Walls). The name 'Medio' derives from the old Evader word for 'Middle'.

1. **The Icewarders** – (their town is **Icehaven**, est. 1657.) Settlers from Dalrig originally founded a new colony at Icehaven to assist in the building of the Middle Walls, as the location was too cold and dark for the greenhides. After the wall's completion, many settlers stayed, and a new tribe was founded. Separated from Icehaven by mountains, a large number of Icewarders also inhabit the central lowlands bordering the Circuit. **Princess Niomi** ruled until her death in 3089. Her daughter, **Lady Yvona**, now governs from Alkirk Palace in Icehaven.

2. **The Sanders** – (their town is **Port Sanders**, est. 1702.) When the Middle Walls were completed, a surplus population of Rosers and Reapers moved into the new area, and the tribe of the Sanders was founded, based around the port town on the Warm Sea. Related closely to the Rosers in terms of allegiance and culture. **Princess Khora** rules, but delegates to her daughter, **Lady Lydia**, who governs from the Tonetti Palace in Port Sanders.

3. **The Evaders** – (their town is the **Circuit**, est. 2133.) The only tribe ethnically unrelated to the others, the Evaders started out as refugees fleeing the greenhides, and they began arriving at the City c.1500. They were taken in, and then used to help build the Middle Walls. The largest tribe by population among the first six, though the other tribes of Auldan and Medio look down on them as illiterate savages. **Princess Yendra** ruled until her death in 3096. **Lady Ikara** rules from Redmarket Palace in the town's centre.

The Final Three Tribes – The Bulwark (pop. 600 000) The Bulwark is the defensive buffer that protects the entire City from greenhide attack.

Work commenced on the enormous Great Walls after the decisive Battle of the Children of the Gods in 2247, when the greenhides were annihilated and pushed back hundreds of miles. They were completed c.2300, and the new area of the City was settled.

1. **The Blades** – (est. 2300.) The military tribe of the City. The role of the Blades is to defend the Great Walls from the unceasing attacks by the Greenhides. Their service is hereditary, and the role of soldier passes from parent to child. Officials from the Blades also police and govern the other two tribes of the Bulwark. Their headquarters is the **Fortress of the Lifegiver,** the largest bastion on the Great Walls, where **Duke Marcus** is the commander.

2. **The Hammers** – (est. 2300.) The industrial proletariat of the Bulwark, the Hammers are effectively slaves, though that word is not used. They are forbidden to leave their tribal area, which produces much of the finished goods for the rest of the City.

3. **The Scythes** – (est. 2300.) The agricultural workers of the Bulwark, who produce all that the region requires. Slaves in all but name.

NOTE ON THE CALENDAR

In this world there are two moons, a larger and a smaller (fragments of the same moon). The larger orbits in a way similar to Earth's moon, and the year is divided into seasons and months.

Due to the tidally-locked orbit around the sun, there are no solstices or equinoxes, but summer and winter exist due to the orbit being highly elliptical. There are two summers and two winters in the course of each solar revolution, so one 'year' (365 days) equates to half the time it takes for the planet to go round the sun (730 days). No Leap Days required.

New Year starts at with the arrival of the Spring (Freshmist) storms, on Thanalion Day

New Year's Day – **Thanalion Day** (approx. 1st March)
    -- **Freshmist** (snow storms, freezing fog, ice blizzards, high winds from iceward)
    - Malikon (March)
    - Amalan (April)
    -- **Summer** (hot, dry)
    - Mikalis (May)
    - Montalis (June)
    - Izran (July)
    - Koralis (August)
    -- **Sweetmist** (humid, stormy, high winds from sunward, very wet)
    - Namen (September)
    - Balian (October)
    -- **Winter** (cold, dry)
    - Marcalis (November)
    - Monan (December)

- Darian (January)
- Yordian (February)

Note – the old month of Yendran was renamed in honour of Princess Khora's slain son Lord Balian, following the execution of the traitor Princess Yendra.

AUTHOR'S NOTES

SEPTEMBER 2020

Thank you for reading *The Dragon's Blade*! The release of this book marks the beginning of a new stage of my writing career, as it is the first one to come out since I moved to becoming a full time author. The support and encouragement I have received from readers, friends, family and colleagues has been more than I could have asked for.

Being full time will hopefully mean even more books coming in the future!

RECEIVE A FREE MAGELANDS ETERNAL SIEGE BOOK

Building a relationship with my readers is very important to me.

Join my newsletter for information on new books and deals and you will also receive a Magelands Eternal Siege prequel novella that is currently EXCLUSIVE to my Reader's Group for FREE.

www.ChristopherMitchellBooks.com/join

ABOUT THE AUTHOR

Christopher Mitchell is the author of the Magelands epic fantasy series.

For more information:
www.christophermitchellbooks.com
info@christophermitchellbooks.com

Printed in Great Britain
by Amazon

64346784R00254